TAKEN

"I have to catch my bus," Jon said, gesturing down the road. The man's smile was making him uncomfortable.

"I don't think so, Jon," the man said, quickly pushing back his coat and pulling something from his waistband.

A gun . . . pointed right at Jon.

Jon's throat went dry. "How do you know my name?"

The man nodded toward the back of the van. "Get in. We'll have time to talk inside. Plenty of time."

Quickly, Jon weighed his options. He was a fast runner. If he made a break for it, he could be down the road in seconds, darting off the roadside to hide behind trees or bushes. He was fast . . . but a bullet was faster, and the ditch at the roadside was too steep to cross. He'd be trapped down there, a clear target.

But he had to get away from this man, because everything in his gut told him this guy was the one chasing him in his nightmares.

The killer.

Oh, God.

This was the man . . . the gun . . .

His heart pounded, his pulse thrumming at the realization that this was the man who wanted to end his life . . .

Books by Lisa Jackson

SEE HOW SHE DIES
FINAL SCREAM
RUNNING SCARED
WHISPERS
TWICE KISSED
UNSPOKEN
IF SHE ONLY KNEW
HOT BLOODED
COLD BLOODED
THE NIGHT BEFORE
THE MORNING AFTER
DEEP FREEZE
FATAL BURN
SHIVER
MOST LIKELY TO DIE
ABSOLUTE FEAR
ALMOST DEAD
LOST SOULS
LEFT TO DIE
WICKED GAME
MALICE
CHOSEN TO DIE
WITHOUT MERCY

Published by Zebra Books

RUNNING SCARED

LISA JACKSON

ZEBRA BOOKS
KENSINGTON PUBLISHING CORP.
http://www.kensingtonbooks.com

ZEBRA BOOKS are published by

Kensington Publishing Corp.
119 West 40th Street
New York, NY 10018

All Kensington titles, imprints, and distributed lines are
available at special quantity discounts for bulk purchases
for sales promotion, premiums, fund-raising, educational,
or institutional use.

Special book excerpts or customized printings can also be
created to fit specific needs. For details, write or phone the
office of the Kensington Special Sales Manager: Attn.: Special Sales Department. Kensington Publishing Corp., 119 West
40th Street, New York, NY 10018. Phone: 1-800-221-2647.

ISBN-13: 978-1-4201-0182-9
ISBN-10: 1-4201-0182-X

First Printing: August 2010

Previously published in an unrevised edition under the
title *Wishes*.

10 9 8 7 6 5 4 3 2 1

Printed in the United States of America

*Special thanks to Beth Corey and
Nancy Bush for all their help.*

Dear Reader,

Here's the deal: I love this book. So when I was asked to rewrite it, to ramp up the suspense, I jumped at the chance! Originally titled WISHES, the book with its new, more intense scenes is now RUNNING SCARED. Yes, the characters are the same and the story, too, is much like the original, but this version has been retooled; scenes added and deleted, the suspense notched up, and a deeper insight into the characters added.

Don't get me wrong. I loved the original version, enough so that I was thrilled the book would be reissued, with a new emphasis on suspense. How fun is that?

Few authors get the privilege to go back and rewrite one of their favorite works, so I feel extremely lucky that I was offered the chance to hang out with these characters again and tweak their story. It was a fun ride! I hope you agree.

Enjoy!
Lisa Jackson

Prologue

Boston, Massachusetts

1980

Free!

Kate Summers pulled the last page from her word processor and dropped it with the others in her OUT basket. Now for the hard part—saying good-bye and making a quick exit. She glanced at the pebbled-glass door to Tyrell Clark's office. His desk lamp shined through the opaque barrier.

Get a grip, Kate. You can do this.

She'd agreed to work late, hoping that he wouldn't return, but she hadn't been so lucky. She'd heard his heavy tread on the back stairs just forty minutes before, and though he hadn't paused at her desk, hadn't so much as glanced in her direction as he'd beelined to his office, she knew she couldn't leave without collecting her last paycheck and a letter of recommendation.

The rest of the building was quiet. Only the soft rumble of the structure's tired furnace and the muted sounds of traffic outside disturbed the silence in the once-hallowed halls of Clark & Clark. The elder Clark, Tyrell Senior, had died just two years before and now there was only his son to carry on the tradition. In the meantime business was shrinking. The staff that had once filled eight offices now occupied just two. Tyrell, a brilliant lawyer, also loved women, drink, and a friendly, if fatal, wager at the race track. And he had not only the

IRS after him but other, more sinister adversaries—loan sharks and bookies and the like.

In two days Kate planned to leave Boston—and the nightmare she'd been living—behind. She'd never have to set foot in the offices of Clark & Clark again. All she had to do was ship her meager belongings to Seattle and hand her keys over to the landlord of her small apartment—four tiny rooms that had been her home for the past three years. A lump filled her throat, but she ignored it.

No more memories. No more pretending. A new start. That's what she needed.

"Kate?"

She sucked in her breath.

From the adjoining office, Tyrell Clark's voice, smooth as well-oiled machinery, caused a chill to creep up her spine. She hated that well-modulated, nearly patronizing tone.

"No more," she whispered under her breath, and one of her hands curled into a tight fist. She didn't have to put up with his advances—gentle touches and suggestive innuendos—a second longer. She found her coffee cup, favorite pen, address book, and dropped them all into her oversized bag.

"Before you leave, I've got something I want to discuss with you."

The light in his adjoining office snapped off. Her stomach knotted in apprehension.

Now what? Bracing herself, she glanced at the clock. Nearly seven. And she was alone with him. The building was probably empty. Nervously she looked out the single window in the reception area, through the trails of rain that drizzled down the glass. Outside it was dark except for the illumination from streetlamps and the flash of headlights from cars as they passed. She'd been a fool to stick around after Rinda had gone home for the day, but she'd needed the money the overtime would bring, had naively thought that Tyrell wouldn't return from his late afternoon meeting with a client. She'd been wrong. *Stupid, stupid girl.*

He scraped back his chair and it squeaked as he stood. His familiar tread followed.

Just a few more minutes. You can handle it, Kate. Whatever you do, don't blow it; you need his letter of recommendation so you can get another job in Seattle.

She managed a thin, watery smile as he approached her L-shaped desk. *Fake it,* she told herself, though her palms began to sweat. *Be friendly, but firm.* She resisted the urge to wipe her suddenly moist hands on her skirt. *A few more minutes, then you'll never have to see him or put up with his harassment again. Just hang in there.*

Tyrell was an imposing man and a cliché of the highest order. Tall, dark, and handsome, he'd been compared to Clark Gable's Rhett Butler time and time again. He made it a point to see that his tie was never askew, his dark hair always in place, his three-piece suits without so much as a thread of lint or wrinkle to detract from his polished image.

Except lately. He'd been slipping. His shoes weren't always shined to a high gloss, a few gray hairs had dared invade his temples, and lines of worry had collected near the corners of his mouth. But it was his eyes that had changed dramatically. Usually full of a mischievous light, they'd dimmed with worry and he was forever playing with the wristband of his watch, as if he were running out of time. She knew why. The continuous correspondence from the IRS explained it all.

"So this is good-bye," he said.

"Yes." She reached for her purse. "I was just getting ready to call it a day." Her mind was spinning ahead, creating an excuse to flee the building.

"I thought we might have one last drink together."

"Sorry." Not really. "I told Laura I'd stop by. I'm already late."

"Your sister will understand." He picked up her favorite paperweight—a crystal porcupine—and tossed it lightly, as if testing its weight. "This is important." He offered her an infectious smile that had worked its magic on dozens of women with weaker hearts and landed them in his bed. The sorcery hadn't affected Kate. She wasn't interested in a man, any man, and especially not one as well worn as Tyrell. And now his grin seemed forced, his usually tanned skin, paler, as if the life were being sucked out of him.

"What?" Her damned curiosity always got the better of her.

"I thought you might like to be a mother again."

She felt as if the floor had just dropped out from under her feet. "A mother?" she repeated, her voice a whisper. Her head began to pound. She'd never known him to be so outwardly cruel. "If this is some kind of joke—"

"It's not."

She could barely breathe, hardly hear above the dull roar in her ears.

"I'm offering you a son. No strings attached. Well, not many." Easing his hip onto the edge of her desk, he clasped his hands around one knee and stared at her with dark knowing eyes. The tic beneath his eye kept up its steady rhythm.

"I don't understand," she replied, trying to calm down.

"It's a long story and one I'm not privileged to discuss in too many details, but I have a client, an important, socially prominent client, whose daughter just had a baby—a little boy—out of wedlock. He was born this afternoon."

"You—you want me to adopt him?"

He hesitated, his eyebrows drawing together. "Not just adopt him, Kate. I want you to take him with you to Seattle and pretend that he's yours. The child's white, his hair dark and he could certainly pass as yours."

"What? Wait a minute—"

"Just hear me out, Kate," he insisted and the roar in her ears became louder. He reached into the inside pocket of his suit jacket and withdrew an envelope. From within, he found a Polaroid snapshot, which he handed to her. The picture was of a newborn infant, still red, eyes out of focus as the camera had flashed. Little fists were coiled and his expression was one of shock at being brought into the harsh lights of the real world.

"Oh, God," she whispered.

"I thought you wanted another child."

"I do, but . . ." There was nothing—*nothing*—she'd love more than a child. But the idea was impossible. A pipe dream. *You had your chance,* she reminded herself grimly before the tears could come again.

"Are you serious?" she asked.

"Absolutely."

A small drop of hope slid into her heart.

"I don't understand." This conversation was moving too fast. Way too fast. "You want *me* to adopt him?" She felt as if she had cobwebs in her mind that were slowing down her comprehension, as if she couldn't quite keep up with the discussion. "What's the catch?"

"The catch," he repeated under his breath and bit his lower lip. "Unfortunately, there is one."

"Always is." Trepidation chased away that little bit of hope.

"I prefer to think of it as a condition that comes with this kind of instant motherhood."

Motherhood. The sound of the word brought back images of her own mother and a small farm in Iowa. Spring flowers, the scent of mown hay, and cinnamon lacing the air from Anna Rudisill's prize-winning apple pies. Her mother's kind smile or razor-sharp tongue when one of her daughters dared take the name of the Lord in vain whispered through Kate's mind. Summers had been full of hard work and long days, nights staring up at a wide dark sky sprinkled with millions of stars. The winters had been fierce, frigid, and brutal as well as gorgeous with the thick blanket of snow that crunched under Kate's boots as she trudged through the drifts to the barn holding on to her mother's hand. Icicles had hung from the eaves of the barn, and even the moisture collecting on the flat snouts of the cattle had sparkled in the pale winter sunlight.

From those few glorious years, Kate's mind spun ahead as it always did, past the unhappy and horrifying part of her childhood to her short-lived marriage and her own darling baby girl. *Erin. Sweet, sweet baby.* If only her precious daughter had lived! Guilt squeezed Kate's heart in its cruel, unforgiving fist. She blinked and found Tyrell still balanced on the desk's corner, that pulse beneath his eye jumping.

"Why?" she finally asked. "Whose baby is this?"

"I can't say, but the mother doesn't want him—she's broken up with the father and the family just wants to get the whole unhappy incident behind them. They don't want any publicity, any hint of a scandal, and so far they've managed to keep the pregnancy a secret. Now, all they have to do is make sure the baby is brought up by someone who will keep their secret and love the little boy as her own."

"But I'm single . . . I don't have a lot of money and there are hundreds of couples anxious to . . ." Something was wrong here. Very wrong. She glanced at the picture again and already this precious child, this *un-wanted* and unloved baby, was starting to attach himself to her. "What about the father?"

"Bad news."

"He doesn't know?"

Tyrell shook his head. "The family doesn't want him to ever find out."

"But he has rights—"

"He's in prison."

"Oh, God."

Tyrell's lips flattened together and he set the paper-weight back on the desk. "The guy's bad news—some-one my client's daughter hung around with just to rebel against her folks. He's into drugs, leather, chains, mo-torcycles, and crime; everything my client abhors. The guy also has a history of violence—serious, domestic vio-lence. There's a rumor floating around that he already had a son who died suspiciously as an infant. The police couldn't prove that he was the reason the kid quit breathing, but they suspect him. My client doesn't want anything like that to happen to his grandchild. Right now the kid's safe as the father is locked up for assault, so he's out of the picture. Won't be paroled for a few years. Believe it or not, the family wants what's best for the baby."

"As long as he doesn't inconvenience them."

"If you don't want to do this, Kate—"

"No!" she said so vehemently she surprised herself. *It's not the baby's fault that he isn't wanted, is considered nothing more than a nuisance.*

Kate felt sick inside but the first little glimmer of what he was suggesting tugged at her heart. Could she? Could she take this child and pretend that he was hers?

A baby. A newborn. Her own child. A mother again.

Tyrell tugged on his tie.

"You know, Tyrell, this just sounds like trouble. Big trouble." *But there's a baby involved, a baby who needs a mother, a child whom you need to care for.* "The girl should tell her folks to take their Machiavellian opinions about children being born out of wedlock and shove them. That child belongs with his mother!"

"It's not that simple," Tyrell said, the patience in his voice belied by the lines of tension near the corners of his mouth. "The baby's mother . . . she's not well either, or at the least stable. She's been in and out of mental hospitals for depression; always on some kind of medication, though the doctors have assured everyone that the baby's healthy. The girl's been monitored ever since she found out about the pregnancy. It's been decided that the best thing would be for the baby to be adopted privately to someone who lives out of state. You're moving to the West Coast, and since you lost your own family, I thought it would only make sense . . ." He let the thought trail off, leaving it to be finished by her own imagination, attempting to persuade her that he was only trying to help. She didn't buy it.

"As I said, the deal would be that you would claim the baby was yours—we'd even manage to make the birth certificate say as much."

"How?"

"When you have money, anything's possible. My client has money, lots of it. And influence. It's not that difficult to get a phony birth certificate and you'll be moving so far away that no one will ever guess the truth." He glanced pointedly down at the pictures resting on the corner of Kate's desk, then picked up a framed photograph of Kate holding Erin as an infant. Her husband, Jim, was standing beside them, ever the proud father. Jim was smiling widely, his arm around Kate's shoulders, her own eyes shining with pride and happiness. The perfect family. How long ago it seemed.

Kate's heart tugged and tears clogged her throat, tears she needed to hide. Oh, God, could she go through with this? Could she not? She knew she should leave, right now, before he reeled her in and she became a part of something corrupt, something darker than it appeared on the surface. Something she wanted. Standing, she slung the strap of her purse over her shoulder. "I think I'd better go. Laura's waiting for me—"

Setting the picture back in its resting place on the desk, Tyrell straightened, then walked slowly around the desk to stand behind her. Gently, he placed his hands on her shoulders.

She shifted away, turned, and glared at him. "Don't."

"I know how hard it was for you to lose Jim and Erin," Tyrell said kindly. "You . . . well, you've never been the same. I thought that this might be a godsend to you, to give you new purpose, a child. But if you'd rather pass—"

"No!" she blurted out, though her rational mind told her to walk out the door, to stay as far as possible from Tyrell and his unethical scheme. This was crazy. Ludicrous! Impossible! *Illegal, for crying out loud!* And yet despite all her well-laid arguments, she couldn't let this opportunity slip through her empty fingers. *A baby! Her baby!* "I—I don't know what to say, I mean, I'd have to know more. How do I know this baby isn't kidnapped?"

His face muscles relaxed. He knew he had her and she felt incredibly weak and manipulated. "Trust me, Kate. We're talking about a newborn who isn't wanted, who needs a mother, who deserves to be loved. He'll have to be hidden far away so that his psycho of a father never finds him. This is an opportunity for you to be a mother again—an opportunity that may never happen otherwise."

She blinked against a sudden wash of hot tears. For the past two years she'd felt an overwhelming sense of guilt and remorse for the deaths of the two people closest to her. Maybe this was a chance to make it up; or maybe it was God's way of giving her a reason to live.

"Okay, so it's decision time. What'll it be? Have we got a deal?"

"I need time to think."

"There is no time." He sighed heavily. "You know, Katie, I thought this would make you happy."

"It . . . it would."

"So you'll do it?"

She hesitated only a second. Inside she was shaking. "Yes."

"Good." He hesitated, tugging at his lower lip. "There is one other thing, Kate."

She braced herself. "What's that?"

"You know how much I think of you, how . . . well, how I've tried to get close to you."

She closed her eyes for an instant. "I don't want to hear this."

"Even before Jim was killed."

"I know, Tyrell." She stepped away from him, the backs of her calves brushing up against the seat of her secretarial chair.

"And I wasn't as much of a gentleman as I should have been." He ran a hand through his hair, as if he were embarrassed. "I feel badly about it, really. I'd like to make it up to you."

"By what? Allowing me this adoption?"

"Not adoption. Remember that. This child is your own flesh and blood." He stared at her long and hard, as if silently assessing her mettle, determining if she was up to the role she'd have to play. "God, you're beautiful."

She swallowed hard.

"You know, I think I'm half in love with you. Can you imagine that? Me—the confirmed bachelor. Anyway, I would have done anything for you, Kate. *Any*thing. After Jim died, I thought I could help you get over him, that we could get together."

"It . . . it could never happen," she said firmly.

He stared at her for a long minute, and as if he finally understood that she wouldn't change her mind, he let out a sigh. "Yes, well, I figured as much, but I thought it was worth at least saying aloud." Clearing his throat, he walked to the window and stared outside. The reflection from a stoplight flashed red against his skin. "Well, now that I've thoroughly embarrassed myself, I suppose we should get down to business."

She waited, watching the play of emotions cross his face. He looked cornered and defeated, but she had to remind herself that Tyrell Clark was like a cat with his proverbial nine lives. No matter what, he always landed on his feet. She'd seen it time and time again.

"I'll get the necessary paperwork together and then you'll leave town with your newborn son." His face clouded a bit. "I wish . . ." Shaking his head, he chuckled without a trace of mirth. "Oh, well, you know what they say about wishes and beggars. As part of the deal, I'm giving you ten thousand dollars."

"Oh, no—"

"For the child. It will be expensive at first." He saw the questions in her eyes. "It's not from me. The maternal grandfather wants to be sure that the baby is cared for properly. If you don't need the cash now, you can always buy bonds—think about the future, college or a house or whatever." He waved off her concerns but she felt sick inside. Adding money into the deal gave it a darker, more corrupt hue.

"So the grandfather is financing all this?"

"You might not approve of it, Kate, but you should look at it as a gift. No one's twisting your arm," he reminded her. "What would you like to call him?"

"What?"

"He'll need a name."

"Oh, Lord. I don't know. How about Jon? Jonathan Rudisill Summers."

"Clever girl," he commented. "Your maiden name and Jim's." He smiled to himself.

"How will I know that no one will ever contact me? Want the boy back?"

"You have my word."

He slid the envelope that had held the photograph in it across the desk. "Here's the cash."

"I don't want the money."

"Take it, Kate. Look, you're going into this with your eyes open, but you've got to promise to practically fall off the face of the earth and, no matter what, pretend that the baby is yours."

She swallowed back her last, lingering doubts and picked up the bulky manila envelope. "I will," she vowed because somewhere in this city an innocent newborn boy lay in a bed alone and frightened. He needed her.

And God only knew how much she needed him.

BOOK ONE

JON

1995

Chapter 1

Run, run, run!

Jon raced through the dark city, his sneakers slapping against the wet pavement, his heart pounding so hard he thought it would explode. Piles of dirty slush lined the unfamiliar streets, snow fell from the sky, dancing in the pools of light cast by the streetlamps. Far away he heard the sound of a siren and over it all the muted strains of a Christmas carol.

"God rest ye merry gentlemen, let nothing you dismay . . ."

Where the hell was he?

And who was chasing him?

Killer.

The word rang through his brain.

What?

The one who wants you dead.

As in dead and buried. Six feet underground, covered in ripe soil . . .

No!

Breathless, he glanced over his shoulder and saw a

looming shadow, dark and swift, a weapon in one gloved hand as it swept the poorly lit streets.

God help me.

Jon turned sharply, slipping and catching himself with one hand, to sprint forward, into a narrow alley, where the cheery Christmas lights no longer blinked, where only dark oblivion awaited him.

Please don't let this be a dead end, he silently prayed as the sounds of the carol oozed through the night.

". . . to save us all from Satan's power when we have gone astray . . ."

He nearly ran into the brick wall.

Oh, God, a blind alley!

He heard the sounds of his pursuer so close behind, felt his skin crawl, and his soul go numb as he turned and knew that there was no way out . . .

Jon Summers opened his mouth to scream . . .

And woke up with a jolt. He was shaking, the sheets of his twin bed wet with sweat, his heart tattooing in his eardrums as the recurring dream . . . the nightmare he knew to be a premonition, faded into the gray light of dawn.

He let out his breath and hoped to God that he hadn't screamed aloud and woken his mother. Fingers twisting in the bed sheets, he slowly let out his breath and knew, deep in his heart, that his dream was a foreshadowing of events to come. They might not play out exactly as he'd envisioned, but they sure as hell were going to play out.

Oh, God, why me? he wondered as he always did whenever a vision passed behind his eyes. The ones at night scared the hell out of him and the ones during the day . . . well, he just had to hide those or else all the other kids would think he was a freak—not that they didn't already.

Kicking off the tangled sheet, he ran a hand around

his jaw and felt a little bit of stubble on his chin. He needed a smoke and knew his mother wouldn't approve. She didn't approve of much he did these days, but she'd really flip out if she knew about this latest vision. Swiping the sweat from his forehead, he pushed Houndog out of the way, climbed out of bed, and plowed through the towels and clothes on the floor of his closet. Without turning on a light, he kneeled down, his fingers skimming the baseboard until he found the spot where he'd rolled up the carpet and cut a hole in the floorboards this past summer. Inside was his stash of all things his mother considered contraband.

Slowly he lifted the board and reached into the dark hole. His fingers moved deftly over an old copy of *Penthouse* he'd found in the recycling bins just outside of town, a jackknife he'd purchased with his own money, a box of condoms Billy Eagle had swiped from an older kid, all the cash he had in the world—about seventy-eight bucks—and a framed picture of Jennifer Caruso. Finally, the tips of his fingers brushed against his pack of cigarettes and lighter.

Not making a sound, he padded barefoot, wearing only his flannel boxers, to the window. Houndog let out a muffled bark as Jon unlocked the latch and shoved the glass open, but the half-grown pup didn't move from his spot on the bed. Jon propped the window up with a stick, then climbed outside to the roof, where he sat on the old asphalt shingles. It was cool outside, the air brisk. Winter was coming, the night air frosty. Thousands of stars glittered in the sky and a solitary cloud passed in front of a lazy half-moon, just as it had in his vision.

Shit. His heart was beating about a million times a minute. Hands trembling, he lit up and felt the warmth of smoke roll down into his lungs. *What's wrong with me? Why can't I be normal?* The same old questions he'd been asking himself for years rambled through his head, but tonight they seemed even more critical than ever. Jennifer Caruso wouldn't go out with a weirdo like him, someone who could touch her and look into the future, not when she could have other, normal boys who played football like Dennis Flanders.

He drew hard on his Marlboro again and peered through the boughs of the pine trees surrounding this old place his mother rented. Five miles outside of town, the scrap of land was isolated except for the neighboring spread, the McIntyre ranch, which had stood empty for a few weeks, ever since old Eli had been found dead as a door nail on his kitchen floor. The old man had had himself a killer of a heart attack and no one had discovered him for three days. But Jon had known— had sensed something was wrong. He'd felt Eli's whenever the wind had shifted and blown past Eli's house before touching his skin. Jon had experienced a feeling—the kiss of death, he called it. It had really given him the creeps.

He'd been the one to call the sheriff's department, anonymously of course, from a phone booth in town, and a deputy had been dispatched to find Eli still clutching his chest as he lay on the cracked linoleum only a few feet from the phone that he'd tried and failed to reach.

Jon still missed the old coot. Eli hadn't seemed to mind that he was different. For as long as Jon could remember, the leathery old farmer had been kind to him, showing him how to whittle on his back porch, or pointing out constellations in the heavens, or letting him have a fiery swallow of his own home-brewed brand of moonshine.

Helluva thing—the old man being dead.

"Son of a bitch." Eli was the closest thing he had to a grown-up friend. He studied the red embers of his cigarette, then took a long drag. He calmed a little as the nicotine hit his bloodstream. Mom would have a fit if she thought he was smoking—really smoking—but he didn't care. He was fifteen, old enough to make some of his own decisions.

He couldn't tell her about this vision tonight because she'd really wig out if she thought he was seeing his own death. She was wigged out enough already. He didn't blame her. It wasn't easy to be the mother of a freak, especially not in a town as small as Hopewell-damn-Oregon.

Wrapping his arms around his knees, he closed his eyes and slowed his breathing, forcing himself to think about his vision and analyze it. His fear had subsided enough for him to consider what it meant and he had to search it through—examine it from all sides—before he could lay it to rest.

In the dream it was night and he was in an unfamiliar city, a busy city that smelled of sea water, gasoline fumes, and something else—pine, maybe? Cedar? Christmas? He was running hard and fast, barely able to breathe, his lungs burning for more frigid air. Cold, mind-numbing fear chased him as buildings, tall, narrow, and looking centuries old, flashed by in a blur. The ground was blanketed with snow that had crusted with ice and he slid all over the place as he forced his legs to pump faster. His muscles began to cramp, his heart pumping in fear. Someone was chasing him—someone deadly—someone with the cunning of a wild animal, a man who could stalk prey in the forest or city, it didn't matter.

Someone who was going to kill him.

Jon swallowed against a dry throat. *Who was this guy?* Try as he might, he couldn't get a mental image of the man, but he knew with cold certainty that the stranger had been searching, looking for him, following him with the deadly and patient skills of a hunter. He wouldn't give up.

Lights blurred his vision—blue, red, green, yellow—
strings of Christmas bulbs framing doors and windows
of the brick houses. Wreaths and sprigs of holly adorned
the grand homes with their paned windows and warm
lights. He raced past them all, hearing footsteps relent-
lessly pursuing him, feeling the hot breath of his enemy
against the back of his neck. His feet tripped and the man
caught up with him, grabbing the collar of his jacket.

Go! Go! Go! Faster!

He slipped out of his stalker's grip.

Faster and faster he ran, gasping for air, sweat drench-
ing his body though snow was falling all over this dark,
unfamiliar town. Far away a ship's foghorn bellowed
through the night.

Sometimes the shadowed man actually caught him, a
sharp hand reached forward, strong fingers clamping
over his shoulder. That was usually when Jon started to
scream, dragging himself out of the nightmare. But the
man's parting words always followed him into consciousness, chilling the marrow in his bones.

"I'm your father, Jon."

Son of a bitch! Jon bit down on his bottom lip until
he tasted blood. His father. *His father?* No way. This was
too damned weird. His father was dead—buried before
he'd been born. James Summers. Killed by a hit-and-run
driver. Or so his mother had insisted. He'd seen the
faded pictures of the thin blond man who was supposed
to have been his dad and the infant who had been his
older sister.

But then there had always been something odd
about that story—something that didn't ring true. His
mother was never able to meet his eyes whenever they
discussed his dad, and she always changed the subject
quickly whenever Jon asked too many questions. Jon assumed it was because she felt somehow guilty about the

accident that had taken Jim's life along with that of Jon's older sister.

He'd never been able to divine into his mother's mind, not once. The gift he'd been cursed with seemed to work best on people he wasn't close to.

Except for these damned dreams.

He squashed his cigarette into the gutter and tried to think. Maybe this was just a bad dream, not really a vision, just a nightmare. Everybody had them, didn't they? But the goose bumps still clinging to his flesh convinced him he was only trying to fool himself. He knew the difference.

Running a shaking hand over his face, he considered waking his mother. He slid through the window and walked to the door of his room only to halt, his hand poised over the doorknob.

Stop being a baby. This is your problem. You've got to deal with it.

All his life he'd run to Kate, cried to her, clung to her, but he couldn't do it forever, especially when he knew how she'd react. Nope. This time he had to handle it himself. He had time. Christmas was still two months away.

Still shaken, he climbed back into his bed, nudged the puppy off his pillow, and stacked his hands behind his head. Staring at the ceiling, he clenched his back teeth together. Nothing was ever unchangeable. The future wasn't laid out in a perfect plan.

Jon was convinced he could alter the course of his destiny. He just had to figure out how.

By Christmas.

Eyes shielded by aviator sunglasses, Daegan O'Rourke eased up on the gas, allowing his old pickup to slow at the Summers place. He couldn't see much, just a long lane that wound through a thicket of pine and scrub oak. The twin ruts were long overdue for a load of gravel, and the house, barely visible through the branches, was some kind of white cottage trimmed in cobalt blue. Neat. Clean. Just as he'd expected.

Daegan grimaced and ran a hand over four days' worth of stubble on his jaw. Dry lips flattened over his teeth. Guilt and apprehension had been his constant companion for the past week, and now as he stared through the grime and dead insects splattered over the windshield, he wished he could roll back time and change things.

He was on a fool's mission. No doubt about it. He'd suspected it from the minute he'd heard Bibi's bullshit story and yet he hadn't been able to tell her to go back to Boston where she belonged. Instead, he'd landed here in Hopewell-damned-Oregon wishing he were someplace else. Anywhere else.

Maybe he should just back up and go home to Montana, because the truth of the matter was he didn't have the stomach for what he was about to do. He'd lost that cutting edge years ago—wasted it on a youthful need for revenge.

But curiosity and guilt had spurred him on and now here he sat in a used pickup planning his next move.

"Hell," he ground out as he drove a little farther, to the next long drive. This house, a sorry hovel, was more visible from the county road that ran straight as an arrow from the blue hills in the distance to the town of Hopewell about five miles in the other direction. Weeds and tall, dry grass already gone to seed choked the lane and scraped the underbelly of his truck as he pulled in. He braked at the open gate. A freshly painted FOR SALE sign had been nailed to the weathered fence, and Daegan decided that he'd just been granted his first break in the ten days since he'd reluctantly started this, his personal quest.

Maybe his luck was changing.

Oh, yeah, and maybe you'll win the lottery, too, you son of a bitch.

His body ached from hours in the truck and he'd have liked nothing better than a beer to cool his parched throat, but first things first. He opened the glove compartment and pulled out a leather pouch. Fingering past a thick stack of bills, he found what he was looking for—several snapshots, old black-and-white stills taken by a private investigator's camera, pictures of a girl who was nearly twenty at the time. Her long hair was caught back in a ponytail, her face clean and fresh scrubbed as she dashed across the corner of School and Washington Streets toward the Old Corner Bookstore Building in Boston. A backpack was slung over one arm and she looked over her shoulder, directly into the camera's hidden eye. Pretty, young, brimming with vitality. Even features, large eyes, and arched eyebrows. Full lips and a wary expression.

He wondered how much she'd changed since then, but then he wondered about a lot of things when it came to Kate Summers, a woman he'd never met.

Yet.

That would have to change.

Stuffing the photos back into the pouch, he located an old receipt for a six-pack he'd picked up at a convenience store in Boise, and with a pencil the previous owner of the truck had tucked into the visor, Daegan scribbled down the number of the real estate agent who'd agreed to list these dry, barren acres. He didn't much care about the land; the ranch would just provide him with the cover he needed until he'd figured out his next move, but the location was perfect.

Location, location, location. Wasn't that the phrase real estate agents always promoted when they were trying to sell you a place? Well, in this case, being right next door to Kate Summers's house, they were right. The location was perfect.

"I'm telling you, Kate, a boy that age needs a father."

A father. Kate's blood ran cold at the mention of the man who had sired Jon—the criminal who didn't know he'd created a son.

". . . any boy that age needs a man around. I'm not just talking about Jon, but because he's well . . . different, you know, and hard to handle, he needs the influence of a strong man even more. Now, I know it's really none of my business, but what're friends for?" Cornelia Olsen asked, her voice blaring from the telephone receiver.

Yes, what? Kate walked around the counter, stretching the phone cord as she opened a kitchen cabinet and found a bottle of aspirin. Even after fifteen years, the mention of the circumstances surrounding Jon's birth made her break out in a cold sweat. As Cornelia continued to ramble on about Kate's teenage hell-on-wheels son, about the McIntyre place next door being unoccupied now that old Eli had died and what did that mean—that more riff-raff would be moving into Hopewell, that's what it meant—about how the weather had turned from a furnace blast two weeks ago to the cool of autumn now that it was nearly November, Kate tossed back the pills and chased them with a gulp of cold coffee. She didn't care about the weather or the McIntyre place. But Jon worried her. He worried her a lot.

Lately he'd seemed edgy and restless, more abrupt than usual. Kate had told herself that it was just adolescence, that he was going through natural changes, physical as well as emotional. But there was more—an undercurrent of tension that was nearly palpable. He was worried, but whenever she asked him about school, or homework, or girls, or whatever she could think of, he clammed up—his latest defense mechanism. Where he used to say too much, letting people know that he could see things others couldn't, lately he'd become withdrawn and brooding. She imagined that he was always looking over his shoulder and wondered what kind of trouble he'd discovered.

Drugs? Sex? Alcohol? Gangs? Weapons? Or was she overreacting? Was it that big of a deal that his grades had slipped and he'd become more sullen?

She stared out the open window to the late October afternoon. Leaves, lifted by an autumn breeze, skittered across the back porch, where Jon's puppy, a black-and-white mutt of indecipherable lineage, lay on an old rag rug. The stalks of corn, now sunbleached and dry, were beginning to tumble down in the garden, where a few red tomatoes were visible through a tangle of pumpkin vines. Half a dozen apples that she'd failed to pick had fallen to the ground to wither and rot in the yellow, bent grass. Fall was definitely in the air, and though she was loath to admit it, Jon had become more of a problem than ever—she cut that line of thinking short. Jon was her son—not a problem—and she'd do anything, *anything* to keep him happy and safe. It was her vow when she'd first seen him, tiny and red-faced. So far she'd kept her promise.

"Never tell anyone that he's not your boy," Tyrell had insisted as she'd held the swaddled infant close to her breast so that he could hear her heartbeat. She'd felt the baby's breath, warm and fragile through her clothes, and a joy had swept through her, a happiness that was kept at bay by the fear that what she was doing was wrong.

"I won't."

Tyrell's tongue had nervously rimmed his lips. Whether it had to do with the adoption or the fact that the IRS was on his tail, Kate didn't know. "The paperwork's in here—it all looks legal." He'd slipped a long envelope into the side pocket of the diaper bag she'd purchased. "When're you moving?" he'd asked, his gaze sweeping over the packing crates and boxes in her small apartment.

"This weekend."

"Still going to the West Coast?"

"Seattle first, then maybe Oregon."

He held his hands up, palms outward. "The less I know, the better."

"What if the family comes looking for him?" she asked in a sudden rush of panic. Now that she was cradling the baby in her arms, she couldn't imagine ever letting him go.

"They won't." Tyrell barked out a laugh tinged in irony. "Believe me, they've worked too hard to keep this all a secret."

"And the father—?"

"Don't worry about him. He's still locked up and doesn't even know he has a son."

"But he could find out."

Tyrell's dark gaze drilled into hers. "Don't let it happen, Kate. For the baby's sake. Leave and never come back."

"My sister lives here," she pointed out, thinking of Laura, how close they'd been, how Laura had helped her through that painful nightmare of guilt and grief after Erin and Jim had been killed.

"Send her a plane ticket. Have her visit you, but for God's sake, Kate, don't ever come back to Boston."

She'd taken Tyrell's suggestion to heart. And she'd never heard from him again.

However, now, years later, one phone call from a neighborhood busybody with a heart of gold and suddenly all the worries she'd lived with, the doubts and fears, came rushing back to slap her with the force of a hurricane. Her mouth was dry and she could barely concentrate on the conversation. *Get a grip, Kate!*

". . . so I just thought you'd want to know," Cornelia was saying so loudly that Kate had to hold the receiver away from her ear. The poor woman, a gossip by nature, was deaf as a stone and didn't realize it. "I'm telling you I wanted to know everything my boys were up to when they were teenagers. Whenever one of 'em wasn't where he was supposed to be, my radar went up, let me tell you. I figured I needed to be the first to find out what was going on. Thought you'd feel the same."

"You're sure it was Jon you saw?" Kate asked, hoping against hope that the town busybody was mistaken. Her fingers clutched the receiver in a death grip, which was silly. Cornelia had innocently mentioned that Jon needed a father figure and here she stood, heart racing, thinking of the faceless, vicious man in Boston whom she'd feared for fifteen years.

"Absolutely, it was Jon. He was down by Parson's Drugstore just twenty minutes ago—"

Houndog cocked his head, gave an excited yip, and leaped off the porch sending the rug flying. Legs scrambling, he dashed around the house. Doom settled in Kate's heart—it looked like Cornelia was right. Again. *Oh, Jon, why?*

"Good luck. It's not easy raising teenage boys, especially without a man to help out. They're trouble. Every last one of 'em."

Slam! The screen door banged shut.

"I'll talk to you later." Kate hung up without waiting for a reply. "Jon?" she called.

"Son of a bitch! Son of a friggin' bitch!" Jon's voice, changing pitch and squeaking, echoed through the few rooms on the first floor.

"What're you doing home so early—?"

Footsteps thundered up the stairs.

Kate steeled herself. *Bam!* Jon's bedroom door slammed so hard the entire house shook. The dining room window rattled. *Great,* she thought checking her watch. One in the afternoon. Score one for Cornelia Olsen and her busybody's nose for other people's trouble. School wasn't officially out for another two hours. But her son was home and in a lousy mood. *Just great.* Her headache increased, pounding behind her eyes.

"Give me strength," she muttered as she headed for the stairs, stopping only when she heard Houndog whining pitifully on the front porch. She stared at the forlorn pup through the mesh of the screen door. "I don't think you want to see him just now," she said to the dog. "I know I don't."

Houndog looked up at her balefully, wiggled, and barked sharply.

"Okay, so you're a glutton for punishment. We both are." She opened the door a crack and Houndog wriggled through.

Sounds of cursing, kicking, and banging erupted from her son's room as she climbed the stairs. The black and white pup streaked in front of her.

She knocked, then pushed the door open.

"Go 'way." Jon lay on his unmade bed, glaring at the ceiling while throwing a baseball up in the air only to catch it again. Books, clothes, CDs, baseball cards, and magazines littered the floor. Shirts and jeans hung out of half-opened drawers and there wasn't an inch of space on the top of his dresser, desk, or bookshelf that wasn't covered with his treasures—everything from model airplanes to books on magic tricks. Houndog bounded onto the bed and sat, tail wagging frantically while Jon ignored him and continued to toss the ball.

"We need to talk."

"Leave me alone."

She sighed, then slid into the room and closed the door. Waiting. He didn't move.

"You're home early."

No answer.

"What happened?"

He made a sound of disgust in the back of his throat, but didn't even glance in her direction. "I ditched."

Hang in there—don't blow this, she warned herself. *At least he's talking, that's an improvement.* Folding her arms over her chest, she rested a shoulder against the door-jamb. "You ditched? Left school?" This was a first. And not good. Not good at all. Somewhere in the back of her mind she was hoping that school had let out early and she'd forgotten, but of course, Cornelia wouldn't have made it a point to call if that had been the case.

"I'm suspended anyway."

Brushing off a size ten basketball shoe, she sat on the chair next to his desk. She was beginning to sweat, but worked hard to remain outwardly calm. "Suspended? This sounds serious, Jon."

"Yeah, suspended," he snarled, mocking her. "And no, it's not a big deal."

"Not a big deal?" Anger surged through her, but she held on to her temper. For now. It was best to get to the bottom of the problem before exploding. "Why?"

" 'Cause that jerk Todd Neider tried to beat me up again. Called me a fag and a weirdo and a freak." Jon swallowed hard and blinked rapidly. "Said . . . said I should be in a mental hospital with the other freaks." Rather than break down and cry, his jaw hardened and she was amazed at the change in him. Until this year he'd never been suspended, never gotten into any serious trouble, even when the kids teased and bullied him, as they always had. He'd cried a lot and been called a sissy and a mama's boy along with the other assortment of cruel names while he was enrolled in elementary school. Whenever there had been trouble, Jon had always run to her, anxious for her protection and love.

Lately, though, since becoming a freshman in high school this fall, he'd begun pulling away, trying to defend himself and distance himself from a mother who didn't understand him. Along with the six inches he'd grown this past year, he'd acquired some pride and a thicker skin.

"Why did Todd try to beat you up?"

"Dunno."

"Jon—?"

"I said, 'I don't know.'" Defiance crept into his voice, and his jaw, just beginning to show signs of whiskers, jutted forward mutinously. She waited and he caught the ball one last time before letting it roll to the floor. "Well, maybe it's because I said he was a stupid dumbass jerk, that he'd end up like his old man—a drunken mill worker who would never get out of this pissant town."

"That might do it," she said, wishing she knew how to handle this situation. When he'd been younger, everything had been easy. Black or white. Good or bad. Wrong or right. Now, the problems blended together and there were no easy answers.

Jon didn't crack a smile. "It's true. Todd Neider's not going to amount to a hill of beans."

"Oh, good," she said, unable to hide her sarcasm. "You told him that? No wonder he was offended."

"He was giving me *shiii*—a bad time about fixing one of the computers for Miss Knowlton. He called me a nerdy-brained freak or something. Anyway, I'd had it, told him off, and he caught me in the hall after class and tried to beat the crap out of me."

"Tried?" Kate asked, wary of the satisfaction that stole into Jon's voice.

"I decked him. Nailed him hard with my fist. In the nose." Jon smiled grimly at the thought of it. Pleasure gleamed in his hazel eyes. "There was blood everywhere, even splattered on Ellie Cartwright's cheerleading uniform and . . . and then he jumped me. Lots of kids had gathered around by that time and then . . ." His voice dropped a little. "Then Mrs. Billings caught us."

"I thought the school called when there was trouble."

"There was some kind of a screw-up, I think. The vice principal was in a meeting so Neider and I were stuck in this room by the office—like a holding tank, I guess—until McPherson got back. Anyway, I got tired of listening to Todd." Jon's expression grew dark again. "He was calling me all sorts of gross names like dickhead and shit-face and—"

"I get the picture."

"Anyway, he said he was going to kill me the next time he got the chance. So I climbed out the window and ditched."

"He has no right to threaten you in any way, shape, or form. And telling someone that they're going to kill you—"

"Big deal." He shrugged on the bed. "He says it all the time. It's just an expression, and you know what?" Jon's eyes squinted up at her.

"What?"

"He'd never do it. It's all just talk because Neider's afraid of me. He's not going to kill me." Jon seemed confident, as if one punch to Todd's nose made up for all the years of being afraid.

"When did all this happen?"

"I don't know." Another lift of his shoulder. "It was just before lunch."

The phone rang and Kate's heart squeezed.

Jon scowled. "Somebody at school probably figured out I was gone."

"Wonderful," she muttered sarcastically, barely able to control her temper. She was angry with him—furious—but it wouldn't help to start yelling. And she was worried—worried sick. She had to remind herself that she was the adult in this discussion. "I'll get the phone and you clean this room. Pronto. You're in big trouble, Jon. Not just with the school, but with me. You can't go around punching someone's lights out even if they are giving you a bad time."

"So what'm I s'posed to do? Call you? Dial 911? Or go cry to the principal?" he sneered under his breath as Kate hurried out of his room and down the stairs.

She grabbed the receiver on the fly, just before the answering machine picked up. "Hello?"

"Mrs. Summers? This is Don McPherson."

Her stomach clenched, as it always did when there was trouble with Jon. She listened as the vice principal told her basically the same story that Jon had. "What makes it worse," McPherson continued, his voice heavy, "is that Jon didn't stay here. He snuck out. That's another day's suspension." She heard him sigh and riffle through a series of papers—probably her son's file, which was growing thicker by the minute. "You know, Jon's had his problems, but he's always been able to deal with them. Until now. Personally, I think it's good in a way. He needs to stick up for himself. But he can't break the rules."

"I know. I'll talk to him."

"You can pick up his assignments; they'll be in the office and we'll start with a clean slate on Tuesday."

She closed her eyes. "It's . . . it's difficult for him."

"I know. But then it's hard for all teenagers today. Lots of pressure. Too much. In Jon's case it's amplified."

Leaning against the refrigerator, Kate rubbed a temple with her free hand. Jon was a good-hearted, smart kid who most of his classmates thought was some kind of oddity. The parents weren't much better. Several had warned their children to stay away from "that peculiar Summers boy." A few others had even said they thought he was a devil worshipper. All because Jon had the ability to see through a window into the future. Sometimes. The window wasn't always clear. Thank God. In all these years he hadn't divined that he was adopted, that somewhere far away he had another set of parents.

"You still want him mainstreamed, don't you?" McPherson asked, bringing up a subject she detested—that of a special school.

"Of course." Kate firmly believed that her son needed to be with kids his own age, even the cruel ones. More than anything, she wanted Jon to fit in. To be responsible. To be happy. Oh, Lord, if she could find a way to make him happy.

"Well, let's not throw in the towel just yet. This isn't a one-sided situation by any means. The other party is just as much at fault. Let's see what the next few weeks bring. There's only, what—six or seven weeks of school until Christmas break? We'll talk then."

She let out her breath slowly as she hung up. She and

Jon had lived in Hopewell for eleven years, ever since she determined that she wanted him to have some of the same happy memories of farm life that she had. Though Jon had never really fit in with his peers, a handful of kids had accepted him. Until last year when Todd Neider and his gang had decided it was open season on "the freak." She cringed at the name. Adolescence was hard enough if one was just like the other kids, but in Jon's case, growing up was hell.

The freak.

Weird how a quality that most kids barely notice when you're younger can be the one thing that defines you in high school. Defines you as a loser, of course.

Back in grade school, kids thought it was cool when he could guess which number Miss Meyers was thinking of. In fourth grade Jennifer Caruso gasped in delight when he told her she'd get the lead in the school play a week before auditions even started. What used to be considered a gift was now a bad stripe, the weirdo factor that turned him from a kid with a talent to a psycho.

Someone should have warned him that it would all blow up in his face, that people would get rattled when they learned about his visions, that they'd stare at him in the grocery store, cross the street when they saw him coming, call him a psycho psychic and a retard.

Like maybe his mother should have had the sense to tell him to crank it down a notch. But she'd always encouraged him to talk about the dreams and images that gripped his mind. When he was little, she'd told him he was seeing "angels" when people appeared in visions. She told him the reason he could read thoughts and see things other people weren't privy to was because he was special.

She should have warned him that "special kids" were the rejects in high school.

She should have told him it wasn't normal to know that your second grade teacher was thinking about the feverishly hot forehead of her son when she left for school that morning. His mother should have pointed out that other kids don't have visions of the shiny green bike they're getting for Christmas, other kids can't smell a snowstorm coming, and they definitely don't have dreams that spell out future events for them months in advance.

Not that he could have stopped the visions from coming, like flashes of light popping from cameras in the dark of a rock concert. Nothing could shut down the flow of his inner sight.

But he could have kept it to himself.

And he had stopped talking about it at school. When kids asked, he told them he couldn't do it anymore, couldn't read their thoughts or see movie reels from the future.

He'd lied.

And he was still pigeon-holed as the kid who could see too much.

The freak.

Out in the hall her footsteps touched the stairs again. The door creaked, but he didn't move from his spot on the bed as his mother paused in the doorway.

"McPherson?" he guessed.

"Yep. He gave you another day's suspension because you ditched."

"Good. I hate school."

"Jon, is it really that bad?"

Instead of answering, he turned his gaze away from her to stare at the wall, where a fading photo of Michael Jordan was partially covered by the mystic, masked eyes of Val Kilmer as Batman, a poster he'd gotten free at the movie theater. The dark, swirling world of the super-hero appealed to him. Something about the fact that Bruce Wayne could put on a mask and become some-one else, a great out when you've got your mother and your principal and half the kids at school on your case.

"Jon?" his mother sat on a corner of the bed and put a hand on his calf. "Something's bothering you," she said, jostling him.

"Just leave me alone, okay?"

"Maybe I can help." When he didn't answer, she added, "Look, I can't fix things with Todd Neider, but I'm not afraid to give Don McPherson a piece of my mind. If you're being treated unfairly at school . . . well, I can push the vice principal . . ."

"Neider is the least of my worries, and McPherson is fair."

"So . . . it *is* something else."

Seeing the genuine concern in her eyes, he turned away. It would be worse to tell her; he hated to scare her. But shouldn't she be warned? It seemed so wrong not to say anything, to sit back silently and watch as the dark danger loomed ahead, a shadow rising over their lives.

He should warn her.

But what could he say? That shadows loomed in their future? That some faceless, nameless evil was on its way to them, chasing him?

"I wish you would talk to me," she said.

"Mom, you can't help. Don't you get it? I lied when I told you that I'd grown out of it. The truth is, it's worse than ever, but it's changed. If someone touches me, I can read their thoughts, things I don't want to know. I get these flashes of what's going to happen to them tomor-row, or next week. And when I go to bed, oh, crap . . ." He pressed his palms to his face, wishing he could hide there. "I'm afraid to fall asleep, afraid to have one of the dreams." God, he hated admitting that he was afraid . . . *hated* it. He was too old to be afraid.

"About what? What are the nightmares about?" she asked.

"There's the nightmare where I'm being chased through a city. Scarier than it sounds. And then the one where a dark figure keeps whispering that he's my father."

Her hands tightened on his ankle. "Sounds very Luke Skywalker. Have you ever thought that maybe they're just normal nightmares. Not that they aren't scary, but—"

His sharp gaze cut off her thoughts. "It's not normal, okay. We both know it. Just 'cuz you don't want to believe it, don't want to think that I'm *different*, doesn't change things. And I'm not 'special,' I'm a freak. And the things I see at night, in my dreams, they scare the sh—crap out of me." He stared at his mother as if he could will her to believe him. "What I see at night. It's coming closer and, I think, I swear, Mom, there's someone evil involved. A guy . . . chasing me."

"Who?" Her eyes were dark with worry as she leaned over him.

He held back the truth, knowing she'd freak if he used the word *killer*. "I can't see his face, but I feel his presence. I can feel him getting closer, his breath on my back. He's coming after me, Mom." He sat up, his heart beating so hard he felt the pulse pound in his ears. "He's on his way, and he's trouble, Mom. Big trouble."

She shook her head, not so much disbelieving him but wanting to ward off the evil. "You're going to be okay, Jon," she said, folding him into her arms. "You know you're safe here."

Once he'd felt safe in his mother's arms, but not anymore. She couldn't protect him from getting slammed by a kid like Todd Neider, and no one, not even his mother, could save him from his nightmares.

"Why do you think I'm having nightmares about my father now?" he asked.

"You're growing up, probably wondering about him."

"You never talk about him." Probably because of the way he died, Jon thought. The accident sounded awful, but sometimes his mom acted as if the world had stopped spinning the day Dad and Erin died.

As usual, his mom veered off the topic of Dad. "You're going to be fine," she said. "Just give things some time."

Leaning into her shoulder, he noted the shadows in the corner of his room, at bay for the moment, but still threatening to rise into inky blackness. His mother meant well, but she couldn't protect him from the future.

From the darkness nipping at his heels.

From the voices whispering of his father.

From the person chasing him through the dark city streets.

His pursuer.

His killer.

Chapter 2

"You new here?" the bartender asked as he mopped up a spill and refilled Daegan's glass when it was only half empty. The Plug Nickel Saloon was doing a banner after-work business. A small crowd was huddled near the television set watching the World Series, others were scattered at tables, talking, joking, and drinking. Cigarette smoke hung heavy despite the fans whirring overhead.

"Yep," Daegan said, deciding to reveal as little about himself as possible.

"Lookin' for work?"

"Nah. I rented the old McIntyre place."

"That scrap of sagebrush?"

Daegan's grin was slow. "Yep."

The barkeep chuckled. "Well, I'll be. Gonna do some ranchin'?"

"Hope so," Daegan drawled, "if I can fix the fence line to keep the cattle in. Wouldn't want 'em wanderin' down the road or into the neighbor's place."

The bartender stopped the fluid motion of his towel on the counter, and his face, big and pockmarked from a bout with acne, creased. "You met your neighbors yet?"

Daegan shook his head and lifted a shoulder as if it didn't matter much even though he was trying to learn as much about Kate Summers as possible. He'd sift through fact and fiction later.

"Well, there's a widow livin' to the south of you."

"She alone?" Daegan asked, as if the conversation bored him though his fingers tightened over his mug.

"Nope. Lives there with her boy." Rubbing his chin thoughtfully, the barkeep added, "She's a looker, that one. Young—probably thirty, maybe thirty-five, good shape and smart. Teaches over at Western Cascade, that's a local two-year college in Bend. Keeps to herself a lot, but then I can't blame her."

"Why?" Daegan asked, though instinctively the muscles at the base of his neck tightened.

"Well . . . it's her boy . . . he's . . ." The bartender sighed loudly and his eyebrows slammed together. Leaning closer to Daegan, he said, "Well, the kid's an odd duck if ya know what I mean. No other way to describe him. He never has really fit in and there are stories about him."

"Yeah?" Daegan displayed only mild interest, though he was hungry for any scrap of information about the woman and her son.

"She's got her hands full with that one."

"Hey, Ben, how about a refill?" a burly lumberjack ex-football type at the far stool demanded. Unshaven, with sprinkles of sawdust in the hair that was visible beneath his hunting hat, he motioned to his glass. "You talkin' about the Summers boy? Goddamned freak, if you ask me. A bonafide *retard*."

"Takes one to know one," another wiry man with leather-tough skin added. His laugh cackled through the saloon and an unlit cigarette jabbed in the corner of his mouth bobbed.

"Shut up, Spencer," the giant returned glumly, and Daegan, glancing in the mirror, caught a glimpse of Kate Summers walking out of the local dress shop.

"Thanks," he said, climbing off his stool and leaving more than enough cash to pay for his beer. So now for phase one, he thought grimly, and the thought settled deep in his craw. He'd never liked playing games and detested lying, but he was about to do both.

"It's now or never," he reminded himself, shouldering open the door and walking briskly to keep up with her pace. She strode along the dusty sidewalk as if she were a woman on a mission, her sun-streaked hair bouncing against the shoulders of a faded denim jacket decorated with silver studs. She was small, not more than five foot four inches, and she didn't look to the right or left. Her keys were clasped firmly in one hand, the strap of a large leather purse thrown over one shoulder.

She must've heard him because, as she paused to unlock the door of her station wagon, she tossed a look his way. Eyes the color of aged whiskey gave him a quick once-over. His gut clenched unexpectedly as she looked away and he climbed into the cab of his truck.

Yep, she was the same woman in the photograph. Her face had thinned in the past few years and there were a few tiny lines near the corners of her eyes. Her skin was more tanned, her hair streaked by the sun, and there was an air to her—the way she carried herself— that he hadn't expected. As if she were a woman to be reckoned with.

She opened the door and threw her purse on the passenger seat when he rolled down his window, then jabbed a finger in the direction of her right front fender. "Looks like you've got yourself a flat."

"What?" she said, but her face fell. Quickly she walked around the front end of her car and her lips tightened in disgust as she spied the deflated tire. "Oh, great. Just great!"

"Need help?" He slid out from his truck's cab.

"Oh, no, I couldn't—" Shaking her head, she turned to face him and again their eyes met. The breath caught in the back of his throat for a second at the depth of her gaze—intense and suspicious.

"I'm used to this," he said. He motioned to her trunk. "You got another tire?"

"Yes, but . . ." She eyed him with more than a glimmer of distrust. "I've changed a tire before."

"Just an offer."

"But I don't even know you—"

"Daegan O'Rourke," he said, managing a grin as he extended his hand. She clasped his palm briefly.

"I'm Kate Summers, and thanks, it's nice of you to offer, but if worst comes to worst, I can always run down to the service station and—"

"No need," he said and leaned a hip against the back fender. "I do this kind of thing for a living."

"You're a mechanic?" Again the tone of skepticism. She stood, hands on her hips, glaring murderously at the car. Black jeans, matching belt and boots, white blouse, and a scowl that was all business.

"No, I'm just a rancher—new around here. But I'm used to fixing broken-down equipment. Afraid it comes with the territory."

"Fine, Mr. O'Rourke—"

"Daegan," he cut in.

She hesitated a beat. "Daegan, then." Still wary, she used her key to open the trunk, shoved some books and paper bags aside, and pulled off the mat to uncover a dusty whitewall that looked underinflated as well.

"Wonderful," she mocked, blowing her bangs out of her eyes and checking her watch.

"It might hold," he said though it was all he could do to concentrate on the conversation when he had a hundred questions he'd rather ask her—a hundred questions about her and her son. Gritting his teeth, he hauled the jack and spare tire from the trunk. "Nothing worse than a car hassle."

"Look, you don't have to—"

"No problem." He flashed her a half-smile. "I'm not in any rush."

Nervously, she waited and he assembled the jack, secured the wheels, loosened the lug nuts with a wrench from his toolbox, and eventually raised the front quadrant of the car. Within ten minutes the Buick was resting on the soggy spare, the jack and flat tire were in the trunk, and Kate was groping for words.

"I don't know how to thank you," she said, squinting against the lowering sun. A dry wind blew down the dusty street, scattering a few leaves and papers and lifting her hair from her shoulders. A few people hurried past, casting only mildly interested glances in their direction.

"No thanks needed."

"But . . ." Shading her eyes, she stared at him as if memorizing the planes of his face. "These days a Good Samaritan is hard to find."

"Believe me, I'm not that good." At least that wasn't a lie. A pang of guilt twisted his gut as he slammed the lid of his toolbox closed and set the battered metal crate in the bed of his truck. "If it would make you feel any better, someday you can buy me a cup of coffee—or a beer. Whatever."

A rattletrap of an old truck passed, windows down, heavy-metal music throbbing. A couple of teenage boys, three sheets to the wind from the looks of them, laughed over the pounding beat of hard rock. Kate watched them drive by and her lips clamped a little tighter.

"It's a deal," she said, glancing back to him.

"Good." He managed half a smile. "Maybe I'll see you around."

"Maybe," she replied as if she didn't mean it, her intense eyes scrutinizing his for an instant. "Thanks again."

"Anytime."

She climbed behind the wheel of her station wagon, slid a pair of sunglasses onto the bridge of her nose, and after one quick, intense glance in his direction, drove off in the same direction as the loud teenage boys. Daegan was left with a gnawing in his guts.

"Damn you, Bibi," he muttered under his breath. Knowing he was about to make a mistake that would follow him for the rest of his life, he climbed into his old Dodge pickup and headed toward the cheap cinder block motel on the edge of town.

"I heard you call out last night," Kate said at breakfast the next morning. Jon, distracted, was pushing a burnt corner of his toast through the glop that had been the middle of a fried egg.

"Bad dream," he mumbled, heavy strands of dark hair tumbling over his forehead as he avoided her gaze.

"Another?" She tried to sound casual when inside she was dying. The scream she'd heard had caused her to sit bolt upright in the bed and fling off the coverlet. She'd been halfway to the door of her bedroom when she'd forced herself to stop and listen over the thudding of her heart and the rush of adrenalin that had pumped through her blood. She'd closed her eyes, counted to ten, and listened, ears straining.

Jon resented her intruding into his life. The last time she'd dashed into his bedroom, she'd been met with quiet hostility that had simmered for two days. Jon had accused her of babying him, of overreacting, of smothering him with her motherly attentions, so last night, she'd stood in the middle of her room, silently counting off the seconds. When he hadn't cried out again or come knocking on her door, she'd gone back to bed and lain awake until the alarm on her digital clock had gone off at six.

"What else would it be?" he charged as she took a sip of her tepid coffee.

"You tell me."

He looked past her to stare out the window, past the oak tree where the leaves were turning color, to the craggy mountains on the horizon. His eyes narrowed, as though he wasn't seeing the sun-bleached fields or stand of pines that separated this patch of land from the McIntyre place. "Okay, so it wasn't just a dream."

She leaned her hips against the counter and clutched her cup more tightly. "A premonition?"

"Yeah." He bit his lower lip as he always did when he tried to puzzle something out. "Maybe."

"Bad?"

"Have I ever had a good one?"

Kate's heart sank. *Oh, Lord, now what?* "Tell me about it."

Lifting a shoulder, he said, "There's a man involved and there's gonna be trouble."

"What kind of trouble?" she asked, her voice steady, her heart beating a million times a minute.

He squeezed his eyes shut as if forcing the vision. "I—I don't know. I can't see anything else."

She reached for the coffeepot on the stove, burned her fingers, and sucked in her breath. *Don't blow this, stay calm,* she warned herself as she added warm coffee to her cup, though she hardly knew what she was doing. Jon was worried; she could see it in the strain on his face. "How long have you sensed this?"

He lifted a shoulder in a shrug. "Just a little while. A week, maybe two. But last night . . . last night it was more than a feeling."

He shoved his plate aside and stood. Houndog scrambled out from under the table as Jon picked up his backpack and slung it over one shoulder.

"You might be wrong. You've been wrong in the past. You know, as a little boy you thought you saw angels."

His head turned swiftly. He glared at her with such intensity, she nearly winced. "I *never* saw angels, Mom, okay? *Never.* Don't tell anyone about the angels or the ghosts or any of that shit—" She raised her eyebrows and he caught himself. "Any of that stuff."

"Watch the language."

He started to say something, then changed his mind. "Look, I shouldn't have said anything about the danger or—"

"You didn't say danger," she cut in quickly, fear touching her lungs with cold, damp fingers. "You said trouble."

"Same difference."

"I don't think so. Trouble is a bad report card, or losing your keys, or making a mistake in your checkbook. Danger is different. It usually means life-threatening or incredible pain or . . ."

"I meant trouble, okay?" He muttered, but he avoided her eyes and picked up a dishtowel on the counter. Wadding the towel into a ball, he tossed it into the sink.

"Jon, what's going on?"

"I don't know, I just get the feeling that . . . that somebody—a man without a face—is after us. I know that sounds crazy, but it's true.

"Do you know who he is?"

Jon shook his head, but his face drained of color and his pupils dilated despite the brightness of the day. Snatching a tennis ball that he'd left on the counter, he kneaded it nervously in his fingers. "But I keep hearing the word *father.* I told you." Her insides curled in on themselves and she gripped the back of a kitchen chair for support.

The criminal.

If only Jon's dreams could be haunted by some other beast. She'd been dodging the truth, and now it was getting to be a problem. Jon didn't know he was adopted; she'd promised not to ever confide in him, but that seemed impossible in today's technology of blood typing and DNA testing. Fortunately Jon had never hurt himself badly enough to need blood or been ill so that he needed an organ or bone marrow or anything else that would require tissue typing and a match. Kate prayed that her luck would hold until he was an adult. Then, if the subject ever came up, she might confide in him. But not now. Not when he was still young and vulnerable.

There were other reasons as well. She was afraid that if Jon found out the truth that his natural parents hadn't wanted him, the knowledge would scar him, shake the underpinnings of his self-esteem, and . . . she had to face it, she was scared of the truth and that he'd want to leave, to search out his "real" parents, to find out why he was different from the other children, if there was a reason, a genetic trait that had been passed from one generation to the next.

She'd thought that he might somehow divine the truth, that with his ability to see into the future, he'd know that she wasn't his blood relative, but over the years, when he'd said nothing, asked no questions, seemed to accept her completely as his mother, she didn't have the heart to tell him. Sooner or later, she would have to, but she wanted to wait until their relationship, so shaky recently, was strong again.

Coward. You're just afraid of losing him!

He was staring at her with confused blue eyes. "Your . . . your father's dead," she said, feeding the lie that had seemed so small and innocent nearly fifteen years ago.

"Is he?"

God, help me. "You know it, Jon. Your father was killed—"

"I know the story that *you* told me, but there's more, isn't there? Things I don't know. What is it, Mom? Was there another guy? Someone you were involved with after James died?"

"No!" she nearly shouted, her fingers curled over the top of the chair in a death grip as she lowered her voice. "There's never been another man."

Still holding the ball, Jon lifted his hands to the side of his head. "I know it sounds weird, but I get this . . . feeling that somehow . . . my father . . . he's alive. I know it's stupid." He shook his head, and Kate bit her lip.

This wasn't the time to tell him there was the other man, the man who had given Jon life because that man, the one who had been in prison, didn't know where Jon was, didn't care, probably didn't even know that he had a son. Or did he? Was he on his way? The trepidation that had followed her around like a deadly shadow for the past fifteen years crystallized into something real and tangible and terrifying.

"See, crazy, huh?" Jon threw the tennis ball down the hall and Houndog took off in a frantic, scrambling streak of black and white. "Maybe Todd Neider's right. Maybe I am a freak."

"Of course you aren't," she said, her mouth feeling dry as cotton. She walked over and tried to give him a hug, but he shrugged her off.

"Don't. Don't treat me like a little kid."

"You are—"

"I'm fifteen! I can get a driver's license in less than a year!" He took a step away from her. "Too old to be kissed and hugged by my mom."

She wanted to protest. A part of her cried out inside, but she didn't say a word and tried not to look hurt. He was right. He was growing up, growing away from her. He probably did need a father. But not the man in Boston. Never him.

Houndog, tennis ball firmly in his mouth, rounded the corner, jumped up on Jon's legs wildly, his bark muffled before he dropped the ball on the floor. The pup's tail wagged furiously as he stared up at the boy, almost daring Jon to toss it again. Jon didn't notice, just shifted his backpack to his other shoulder.

Kate tried one more time. "Look, Jon, I didn't mean to bug you about your dreams, but—"

"Just stop, okay?" His jaw worked in anger and he plowed a hand through his hair.

"Everything's going to be all right," she said, as much to convince herself as him. Inside she was falling apart. Was it possible? After all these years? Could Jon's father have found out about him? The safe little shell she'd built around them was cracking.

Finally Jon saw the dog whining at his feet. In one swift motion, he shot the ball down the hall again. "I don't think so, Mom. Everything's not gonna be okay. I don't want to scare you, but I think we're in for some heavy sh—stuff around here."

"You do?" Her heart knocked crazily.

He nodded. "It's starting. Today."

"What?" She swallowed back her fear.

His eyes narrowed as he stared through the open window again, to the distant mountains and the black clouds that rolled across the sky. The smells of dry grass, dust, and faded wild flowers filtered into the room, and far away a tractor engine rumbled, but Jon, looking into a distance only he could see, seemed unaware of the noises and odors. Absently he rubbed a hand over the muscles of his other forearm.

Kate felt cold as death.

"The danger," Jon said slowly in a voice that was an eerie whisper. "It's coming."

"Oh, God, no." This time he hadn't tried to soften the blow by calling it trouble. This time he had admitted the peril, the unnamed danger that was stalking him.

He swallowed hard, then looked at her, his gaze bright and focused again, as if he were back in the moment. But his grim expression didn't change. "It's coming, Mom," he repeated hoarsely, "and there's no way to stop it."

Chapter 3

Daegan jammed on the brakes and his truck slid to a stop near the dusty front porch of the cabin. "Fixer upper," as the real estate ad had boasted, was more than a little optimistic. "Rustic" was a lie. The place was shot to hell. From the looks of it, old man McIntyre hadn't lifted a hammer, paintbrush, screwdriver, or pair of pliers in years. The cabin was small, with a sagging roof, broken steps, boarded-over windows, and a view of some of the driest acres Daegan had ever seen. The barn hadn't fared much better. Never having been painted, the old structure had suffered from the elements—sun, wind, and rain contributing to the silvering of the siding and the missing shingles.

"Perfect," he grumbled to himself as he surveyed the rest of the ranch.

A pump house, machine shed, chicken coop, and old windmill with missing blades completed the landscape that was nearly devoid of vegetation. No shrubbery or flowers, just a solitary pine tree giving some shade to the house and breaking up the expanse of sagebrush, berry vines, and dirt. Broken-down cars were scattered between the buildings, and tires had been propped against the side of the house or tossed into a nearby corral.

No wonder it had been cheap.

He didn't really give a damn about the grounds, the house, or anything else. He'd lived in worse. He had to remind himself that he was here for a purpose and this ranch was the closest rental available to Kate Summers, the reason he'd come to this godforsaken place. He didn't want to think too long or hard about his mission. Hell, he could be on some wild-goose chase, but he was going to see it through. No matter how painful.

With one final glance at the broken rails of a fence that visibly listed, he unloaded his truck, dropped his meager belongings on the rickety porch, and reached into the cooler for a beer. Opening the bottle with the flat of his hand and the rail, he took a long drink, then rammed a tarnished key into the lock of the front door and walked into his new home, temporary though it might be. The electricity had been turned off and the rooms smelled musty. He lifted every grimy shade and threw open each window, letting in a sharp, dry breeze that cut through this valley.

There was furniture—stained and filthy, the floor no better. The real estate agent hadn't lied. The place needed paint and Lysol, varnish and Windex, elbow grease and lots of TLC. Well, he had a little time. Not that it mattered. He didn't own these hellish acres, he just had to act like he needed to use them for a while. His own place was waiting for him near the Bitterroot Mountains with Cal Hanson tending the livestock. If he ever wanted to return. He really didn't know—not anymore. Not since his meeting with Bibi less than two weeks ago.

Rolling up a yellowed shade, he stared through cracked glass and thought about Bibi, a woman he'd tried to forget for what seemed like a million years. He'd gotten the call and agreed to meet her. Two weeks ago . . .

* * *

Heads—you win. Tails—I lose.

Daegan O'Rourke tossed his silver dollar into the cold night air, watched it spin under the streetlamps, caught it deftly, and flipped it onto the back of his wrist. The eagle. Tails. *I lose.* Of course. This was, after all, a no-win situation. An invitation to disaster. But one he couldn't ignore.

Collar turned against the wind, he watched a jet, lights winking, take off into the frigid night. A few drifting snowflakes fell from the sky, promising that winter in Montana, harsh and unforgiving, was close at hand. Pocketing his coin, he shouldered his way into the lobby of the hotel. He didn't pause at the desk, just made his way to the bar and slid into a booth near the door to wait.

For Beatrice. Bibi. His sultry cousin. A woman he'd tried to forget, but every time her image filtered into his mind, he felt a jab of disgust and guilt that cut him straight to the bone.

What was it that brought her from the comfort of her town house on Beacon Hill to this harsh stretch of land? He'd tried for years to divorce himself from the family that had never wanted him, had pretended he didn't exist, had looked down their aristocratic noses at him, had accused him of murder. And yet Bibi was flying in. A bad feeling settled in his gut.

He ordered a beer from a waitress with an eager smile, then half listened to a country-western ballad he'd heard crackling over the speakers of his old Dodge truck on more than one occasion, not that he noticed much. Life on his ranch in the Bitterroots was pretty much the way he liked it: simple hard work, no game playing, no manipulations, no questions without answers, just survival. He picked at a dish of salted peanuts and wished he could just get this ordeal over with.

The waitress brought him a chilled long-neck and he tipped her heavily as he stared at the door. Waiting. For disaster to strike. He'd barely taken two swallows when he saw her.

Beatrice, lynx coat billowing behind her, expensive perfume in her wake, swept into the bar, glanced quickly around, and then, without so much as a smile, zeroed in on him. She'd aged in the past fifteen years—was a little thicker around the middle, her dark hair tinged red, her makeup a little more severe than it had been in her youth. She was still pretty enough, he supposed, if you liked snobby bluebloods. He didn't. Not anymore. But there had been a time . . .

She slid into the seat across from him and pulled the collar of her coat closer to her throat. Shivering, she motioned to the waitress. "Jesus, this is a gawd-awful place."

He grinned. Bibi never had been one to mince words.

"I thought you might not show up," she said with a brittle smile, then gave him a quick once-over with interested eyes. "God, Daegan, it's indecent how good you look." The waitress came over, and without glancing away from him, Bibi said, "Vodka collins. With a twist."

"Slumming, Bibi?" he asked, once the waitress had disappeared.

"On my way to San Francisco." She fumbled in her purse and pulled out a gold case. Her hands were shaking as she slid out a cigarette and reached for her lighter. Little lines of strain etched the corners of her mouth.

"Montana—any part of it—isn't generally a layover between the coasts."

"I needed to see you, all right?" She lit up, clicked her lighter shut, and with a sigh, let a cloud of smoke filter out of her mouth and nose.

"Better?" he asked.

"Yes," she snapped back. "Much. Not that you care."

He didn't answer that one. Didn't want to lie. He'd had it with lies a long time ago. Tipping up the bottle, he took a long pull. "It's been a while," he finally said.

"Yeah, and I've missed you, too." A drink was deposited in front of her and she fished in her wallet, withdrew a twenty, and said, "Keep the change."

"Thanks!" The waitress, fresh out of college from the looks of her, smiled broadly.

Bibi didn't seem to notice, just took a hasty sip from her drink, as if to settle her nerves, swallowed, then sucked hard on her European brand of cigarette. Swirling her drink, she leaned back against the tufted cushions. "I can't believe I'm here."

"That makes two of us."

Her eyes, a dusky shade of blue, found his and he felt a sudden chill. Bibi had always been the most light-hearted of all his relatives, a girl who had been more daring than the rest of her stuffy family and hadn't let her wealth or social position discourage her from having a little fun. She had accepted Daegan, her bastard of a cousin, the black sheep of the family. Whereas his own half-brother and sisters had detested him, Bibi found him amusing, a ruffian whose blatant irreverence for all things Sullivan fascinated her. Her brother, Stuart, the great manipulator, had used Daegan when he needed him, just as he'd used everyone, including his sister. But that was all a long time ago. Before everything had changed forever. Before they'd crossed the invisible, forbidden line. Now, as she stared at him with pained eyes, he knew that whatever she was going to tell him was bad news. He steeled himself and took another swallow from his bottle.

"I wouldn't have come unless it was important," she said, drawing on her cigarette as if for comfort, then spewing a jet of smoke from the side of her mouth. "I, um, oh, Christ, this is hard." Sighing loudly, she avoided his eyes. "You remember what happened between us?"

A cold lump settled in the pit of his stomach. "I try not to."

"Yeah, I know, me too, but it wasn't that easy for me." Leaning forward, she dropped her head into her hands, her polished nails digging against her scalp, her cigarette burning slowly between her fingers. "Daegan, I don't know how to tell you this . . ."

"Just spit it out." He finished his beer in one long swallow. Every muscle in his body was drawn taut as a bow string and he could barely breathe. He counted off the seconds with the quickened pace of his heart.

"We have a son." Her voice was barely a whisper.

"What?"

"I said, we had a baby together."

"Jesus, Bibi! Are you out of your mind?" There was a ringing in his ears, a roar of denial thundering through his brain. As if a raw winter wind blowing through a canyon at midnight had passed through his soul, he felt scraped bare. Naked. "No."

"Yes, Daegan. No matter how much you deny it . . . you and I, we have a son."

"But that's impossible." God, what was this? His mouth was so dry he wanted to spit. Of all the ridiculous lies—

She lifted her head, and her gaze, saturated with desperate agony, drilled into his. "He's fifteen." She was serious—dead serious, her face beneath her makeup pale as a ghost.

Over the sounds of laughter and clinking glasses, Daegan heard the unmistakable knell of doom. That part of his life he'd tried so hard to suppress, to hide, was about to come roaring back at him again.

Bands of steel seemed to constrict his lungs and he

couldn't begin to comprehend the truth—if that's what it was. The world seemed to buckle beneath him, and all the lies, deceit, anger, and betrayal that he'd left in Boston seemed to chase after him like a relentless shadow. "No way."

"Daegan, why would I come all the way here unless it was true?"

He didn't say a word, just stared at her. His head reeled. Bile burned a hard path up his throat and he signaled for another beer. *No! No! No! There has to be some mistake. Bibi was his cousin, part of a world he detested. No way could they have . . .*

"I should have told you . . . you might have found a way that I could've gotten an abortion—"

"For the love of God, Bibi, what're you saying?"

"But . . . Mother and Daddy found out that I was pregnant and they took charge and . . . I ended up having the baby—a boy—and giving him up for adoption. Oh, God, Daegan, I'm sorry." Her throat worked and tears stood in her huge eyes.

Daegan felt as if the world had jolted to a stop. Bibi could be lying; it wouldn't be the first time. But the haunted look in her gaze and the pinched corners of her mouth convinced him that she wouldn't have made this trip without a good reason. A damned good reason. He closed his eyes for a second, trying to pull himself together. *Think, O'Rourke, think! You've been in tight situations before and been able to work things out, but a kid. Oh, Jesus! She's lying, she's got to be. But why?* When he opened his eyes, the glare he sent her could have cut through steel. "I don't believe it."

"Damn it, Daegan, why would I make this up? Why in the name of God would I lie?" She blinked hard and pride elevated her chin a few notches. When she took a final drag on her cigarette, it shook in her hands.

A son? He had a son? Painful images of his own childhood flashed before his eyes. He'd grown up without a father's love, or recognition, with the cruel knowledge that the man who had sired him had considered him nothing but a mistake, a fluke of improper birth control, a big bother. "Wait a minute, Bibi. This is all too fast. Start over—" But he already knew the time, date, and place. He hadn't been careful. Neither had she. Reckless, wanton, stupid kids. That's what they'd been.

A whining song about love gained and lost played from hidden speakers. The waitress left another beer on the table. When she disappeared, Bibi jabbed out her cigarette and rolled her glass between both palms.

"How do you know it's mine?" he asked.

A twisted smile curved her lips, but there was not a trace of merriment in her eyes. "I know, okay, Buckaroo? I wouldn't pull this out of thin air. Even I'm not that crazy."

He was still trying to find his equilibrium, to put his mind back onto a much-needed even keel. "Your folks—they know?"

"About you?" She shook her head and the dim lights played in her reddish tresses. "Are you kidding? It was bad enough telling them I was knocked up, but if they knew it was you . . ." She swallowed and blinked hard. "So I lied. Said it was some sailor I'd met, a guy named Roy Panaker, and they bought it. He didn't even exist as far as I knew and they didn't check when I told them he was married and had already shipped out . . ." She lifted an elegant shoulder, and with the gesture the fur slipped away from her throat. "It was the best I could do."

"But you never told me."

"I didn't tell anyone. I couldn't. You'd already joined the damned army to avoid jail, Stuart was dead, and . . . I guess I just had to fight this one alone." Burrowing deeper in the lynx, she sighed. "I screwed up. What can I say?"

Daegan's emotions were galloping in every direction, but he took the reins, pulled them back in, and tried to look at this situation objectively. As he always did. This time, it was damned near impossible. "What if I said there's no way I'm ever gonna believe you?"

"But you do, Daegan; I can see it in your eyes."

Another song was playing, a faster one, and some brave couples were twirling around the dance floor, laughing, talking, going on as if the world hadn't stopped on its axis. Daegan rubbed his chin, felt two days' worth of stubble and tried to ignore the roiling in his stomach, the sickness that wanted to consume him with the knowledge that he and his cousin . . . oh God. "Why are you telling me this now?"

"That's the worst part," she said with a sigh. "It was hard, you understand. Damned hard to tell Robert Sullivan III that his only daughter was pregnant and unmarried. Not that the old man had many aspirations for me, but since Stu was dead . . ." Her voice, filled with pain, drifted away, and for a few seconds she followed it, as if lost in the swirl of lies and heartache that she'd lived with for fifteen years. Suddenly she sniffed, blinked hard, and pursed her lips. "Well, I was all they had left and the scandal was too much for the family to bear. You understand, of course."

Only too well. The rich, blue-blooded Sullivans abhorred the least suggestion of impropriety even though their family was riddled with dirty little secrets, deception, and hypocrisy.

Her lips trembled though she tried to smile. "Just think how bad it would have been if they'd guessed the truth—that my cousin was the father? That the bastard sired yet another bastard."

"Stop it!" Daegan whispered harshly. His stomach clenched in pain.

"Okay, that was a low blow." She stared at her near-empty glass. "I'm sorry. Anyway, Mother and Daddy and I finally agreed about something. We all just wanted the baby to disappear—to make sure that no ripple of scandal disturbed the Sullivan waters, so they concocted some story for their friends—about me going away to Europe on some kind of exotic cruise, I think, then Daddy moved me in with an elderly woman who lived in this dive of an apartment on the Cape. She was a grandma type and talked all the time—drove me nuts. Dad hired some lawyer acquaintance in a small firm to handle the legal part. The guy, a lawyer named Tyrell Clark, owed Daddy a huge favor and promised to keep his mouth shut. The adoption was private, and I never saw my, our son—well, not after the delivery room."

She paused and smiled sadly. "I know this sounds schmaltzy, but that experience of actually giving birth . . ." Her gaze touched his briefly, and he remembered her as the younger fun-loving girl he'd first met before years and experience had taught her to become brittle. "It was . . . the most incredible experience of my life. I can't . . . will never be able to describe the feeling." She managed a small, fleeting grin. Tiny red veins showed in her eyes as she struggled against tears.

"But it was an impossible situation," she continued, her speech sounding rehearsed, as if she'd repeated it to herself a thousand times over. "It would have ruined my life to keep him, so I gave him away and I thought it was over. There was no reason to tell you. As I said, no one knows you're the father. Yet."

He leaned back, his head propped up by the back of the booth. She could be lying. Bibi was a consummate liar, but why contact him now? Fifteen years after the fact. His gut instinct told him she was telling him the

God's honest truth, unburdening herself, but he didn't yet know why. He kept his face impassive, waiting for her to put all her cards on the table.

She licked her lips, then finished her drink. "Everything was fine . . . well, as fine as it could be. Then, two months ago, Dad found out he has prostate cancer. It's not bad enough to kill him—at least not yet, but he kind of went through this whole new religious experience. Like he's facing his own mortality and realizes there's more to life than just making money." Her laugh was bitter. "Hard to believe, isn't it?"

"Damned hard." Robert Sullivan was a money-grubbing, self-centered, wealthy son of a bitch who believed that propriety and the Sullivan fortune came before all else in life. Not much better than his younger brother, Frank, Daegan's father.

She ignored his remark and fished in her purse for another cigarette. "Anyway, Daddy's decided he wants my son back."

"What?"

"Isn't that a hoot?" she said without a flicker of gaiety. She had trouble with her lighter, clicked it several times before a flame shot up and she sucked on her filter tip. "He seems to think blood is thicker than water and all that rot and he . . . he wants the kid to come home to Boston and take his place where he belongs. Dad's realized that he'll never have another grandchild and so he's determined to find this one."

"You could have more children—"

She shook her head and her dark hair brushed against her cheeks. "Nope." She looked away and closed her eyes for a second. "I can't believe I'm telling you all this." Biting her lip, she sighed. "Not too long after the baby was born—a few years—I was diagnosed as having endometriosis. That's—"

"I know what it is."

"Anyway, after a partial hysterectomy, I'm through having kids and Daddy won't accept the fact that his blood line will cease to exist. Oh, there's Frank's kids—you included—but none of you really count to him, and the thought that Frank's family will gain control of the Sullivan finances drives Daddy crazy. Uncle Frank and Daddy have the same old rivalry that just won't end, even now. So Daddy's focused on—no, *focused* isn't a strong enough word. It's more like he's obsessed with the kid I gave up. He wants my son back in the Sullivan fold."

"Oh, God." Daegan couldn't think of a worse punishment for some unsuspecting child.

"Daddy hasn't done anything yet, but he will. I can tell. He'll hire the most expensive private investigator in the state to find his grandson. In the course of the investigation, I'm sure the investigator will discover that Roy Panaker didn't exist and therefore couldn't possibly have fathered my child and they'll eventually come up with your name."

"How?"

Her fingers drummed on the table. "Daddy has ways."

"You mean you'll tell him."

"Never!" she said with such vehemence he believed her.

"You're paranoid, Bibi," Daegan said, but he knew she was right. Robert Sullivan, senior partner in the law firm of Sullivan, Black, and Tarnopol, was ruthless and dogged and had often been compared to a pit bull. His pockets were deep and filled with judges, politicians, and policemen. Robert Sullivan, Esquire, knew how to get what he wanted, using methods ranging from bribes to threats to beatings.

If Bibi's story was true, then she was right. Robert would leave no stone unturned in the search for his missing grandson.

His son. Another mistreated and unwanted Sullivan bastard. Daegan's jaw clamped hard and he pushed all thoughts of his own upbringing and his own father from his mind.

"You still haven't explained why you're telling me all this now."

She drained her drink. "I've got my reasons. First of all, it's your right to know about your son."

"Cut the bullshit. If you believed that, you would have told me a long time ago—"

"Okay, I'm telling you because I'm scared. I don't want this kid in my life, all right? I don't want to explain to the boy or to my friends or my family that my bastard cousin and I had an affair."

"It wasn't an af—"

"Doesn't matter. We conceived a child, Daegan. Not only is that kid a bastard, like you, my dear, but the product of some kind of incest as well."

He closed his eyes for a second—to get his bearings. *Incest.* Worse than being born illegitimate and never recognized by your family! No matter what happened, the kid was going to end up scarred for life.

"I can't afford that skeleton to come strolling out of my closet right now."

"Why's that?"

She stared down at her left hand and Daegan noticed her ring and the large diamond that winked in the smoky bar. So the rock was more than just another expensive bauble. "I'm engaged."

"Not the first time."

"No, but this time I want it to last, and Kyle, he's a decent man—a good man who has certain values. It bothers him that I'm divorced, but he handled it and I . . . well, I even owned up to having a baby out of wedlock. That nearly ended our relationship, but Kyle finally accepted that he couldn't change the past. However, if

Dad gets his way and the boy shows up and it comes out that you're the father . . ."

"I get the picture." His stomach sour, he took a long pull on his beer and wished this were all just a dream—a nightmare.

"It doesn't help that I lied."

"Never does."

Glancing at her watch, she hurried on, "You've done a lot of things in your life, I know."

"You've kept up on me?"

"As best I could," she said and he realized suddenly the full potential of this woman, how strong she really was. A victim no longer, one in charge of her own fate. "Now you're a rancher out here in the middle of nowhere, but before that you were a rodeo rider, and before that a tracker who took city slickers on trail rides and hunted game in the wilderness." She pointed a well-manicured nail at his face. "From what I hear, there was even a time when you were a private investigator and you tracked down people. That's what I want you to do, Daegan," she said, staring at him. "I want you to find our son before Daddy does."

"No way! Are you crazy?"

"You have to—we have to!"

"Why? What if we do find him? What then?"

"Hell, I don't know. But I can't have the kid coming back and screwing up my life, not now." She reached across the table in desperation, her fingers twisting into the sleeves of his rawhide jacket. "You hate the family. I know it. You hate your father and mine, so why not thwart them—get even for once? Besides, the kid is yours as much as he is mine."

"The problem is he belongs to his adoptive parents."

"Unless the adoption was botched."

"What good would that do?"

"None. It only helps my father's case. Oh, God, this is such a mess." She let go of him and fell back against the tufted naugahyde seat. "But whoever has my baby, and I think I know who that is, was in on the illegal adoption. I know I never signed any paperwork. The woman who ended up with him knows it, too."

"The *woman*? Not a couple?"

"I don't think so."

Daegan glared at her. He'd never really trusted Bibi. After all, her name was Sullivan.

"I'll pay you," she said. "If you can find a way to keep Daddy from locating the boy, I'll see that it's worth your time."

"I can't promise that."

"I know, oh, how well I know." She rolled her eyes and sighed loudly. "You know, Daegan, your latent sense of morality is a real pain in the ass."

He frowned and weighed her offer over in his mind. If he'd really fathered a kid, then he damned well wanted to know about it, to find the boy, to let him know—what? That his natural mother and father had gotten drunk, slept together, and he was the unwanted result?

Bibi was suddenly impatient. "Just find him, okay? I'll make it worth your while to beat Dad to the punch. Here." She dug in her purse, pulled out her wallet, and found an envelope that had yellowed with age. Looking quickly over her shoulder, she fingered through the packet and retrieved a torn scrap of paper. "Here's the name and address of the attorney who handled the adoption."

"You know him?"

"I made it my business to know of him, but he won't be much help. Problem is about three months after I gave my baby up, Tyrell Clark croaked. He had tremendous gambling debts to pay off and back taxes due, and the stress probably was too much for his heart. I've got the name and address of the law firm that ended up with most of his clients, if that helps you much, and a list of some of his employees, but that's about it."

"More than I'd expect."

"And there's something else."

He hated to ask. "What?"

"I, um, hired some fly-by-night private investigator to check out Clark. I . . . I just had to know something about my kid, and so this guy, his name was Fred Marquette, he, um, he thinks that Clark was paid a lot of money to get rid of the baby and that he just pocketed the cash and gave the baby to a secretary of his, a woman by the name of Kate Summers. At least that was her name then. She could have remarried. I've got a few pictures of her and some information—well, it's all fifteen years old but she was single at the time. Her husband and kid were killed less than a year before."

He contemplated the woman sitting across from him, baring her soul, talking as if this was the kind of thing that happened every day. "I can't believe you went to the trouble of hiring a detective."

She skewered him with a look that told him he'd underestimated her all these years. "I had a baby, okay? I was young and scared, but I wasn't stupid enough not to think that I might change my mind and want to see him someday." Sliding the picture, the scrap of paper with Clark's ancient address, and the envelope across the table, she said, "I don't know a lot about the Summers woman, just that she had to realize the adoption was shady. Fred Marquette seemed to think she was Clark's lover. He had a reputation as a ladies man.

"Maybe she did it for the money. I snooped around my dad's office and found a fifteen-year-old canceled check to Tyrell for legal research services or some such crap. The check was for eighty thousand dollars. Expensive research."

Daegan let out a long, low whistle.

"Please, Daegan, say you'll help me. It's worth twenty-five thousand to me. And if you can come up with a way to keep Dad from finding our son, then I'll pay you more."

"I suppose you'll give me that in writing?" he drawled.

"This is no time for jokes." She checked her watch and swore softly. "I've got to catch a plane." Standing, she wrapped the fur more tightly around her waist. "I would think, considering your background, you'd only be too anxious to find your boy."

"If he's mine." He picked up the picture and studied the faded snapshot as if it held the secrets of the universe. And maybe it did. The photographs had yellowed, but caught a profile of a woman, little more than a girl, with even, well-defined features and brown hair pulled back in a ponytail. Oval face, high cheeks, large eyes fringed by thick lashes. Dashing across a street in sun-bleached jeans, backpack, and sweatshirt, she could have been a college coed for her look of carefree independence. Instead she was the adoptive mother of his son. A woman who had walked on the wrong side of the law and been paid well to do so. But she was also a woman who'd wanted a baby. His baby.

"Oh, he's yours all right. I'll call." Swinging the strap of her purse over her shoulder, she swept out of the bar as quickly as she'd breezed in. Daegan frowned as the doors closed behind her. He was left with the hint of her perfume, a packet of fifteen-year-old information, the knowledge that he could be a father, and the feeling that he was being set up. Big time.

Again he looked at the photos. *Who are you, Kate Summers, and how're you connected to the Sullivans?* She was pretty in that fresh-scrubbed all-American girl way that usually didn't do anything for him. A good cover for a

woman so cold she would be willing to adopt a child
without the proper paperwork. Had she been desperate
for a baby? For money? Or just an opportunist?

He read the information, such as it was. She grew up
in the Midwest until she was eighteen when she eloped.
She and her husband landed in Boston, where she'd found
a secretarial job with Clark. She and Jim Summers had a
baby daughter and shortly afterward both daughter
and husband were killed in a hit-and-run accident. The
culprit was never apprehended and it was speculated
that she took up with Clark—either before or after her
husband's demise. A few months after the accident, she
moved away, presumably with Beatrice Sullivan's son.

"Unbelievable," he muttered, gazing at the picture
and wondering again why she did it—if she did. Probably not for love. So it had to be money. "Damned unbelievable."

Studying her features, he wondered how she'd matured in the past fifteen years and found himself already regretting what he was about to do. *Too bad, lady,*
he thought cynically. *No matter what you did, whether you're
guilty as sin or lily white, life as you know it is gonna change.
You have no idea what you're up against. If the boy's my son,
then you're gonna lose him. You've had your turn. Now it's
mine.*

He finished his beer, scooped up the photo, Tyrell
Clark's old address, and the packet of information about
Kate Summers, then left enough bills on the table to
cover the tab.

The action in the bar was picking up, more people
clustered at the tables and the counter, seven or eight
couples dancing, and the noise and smoke level elevat-
ing. A pretty woman in tight jeans and plum-colored
lipstick sidled up to him. "Buy you a drink, cowboy?"
she offered, showing off a dimple.

"Not tonight."

"Got a hot date?"

Daegan snorted a laugh that held no mirth and stuffed the envelope into the inner pocket of his jacket. "Just business," he said and ignored the sultry but practiced pout that formed on her lips. "Another time."

"Promise?" Her voice chased him out the door to the outside, where a blast of northern wind ripped through his jacket. He walked briskly to his truck, unlocked the door, and climbed inside as tiny flakes of snow began to fall from the dark sky. The sound of a jet's engine blasted eerily through the quiet night, and a lingering hint of Bibi's fragrance followed after him. He watched as the great silver bird took flight and he tried to block out the images of Bibi from his mind. For years he'd struggled to erase the pain of his childhood and adolescence, and now, as he rammed the truck into first and eased out of the half-filled parking lot, his childhood came back to haunt him with a vengeance. Once again he felt the fear. The humiliation. The rage. The thirst for revenge against a family who treated him worse than a stray dog.

He forced all the old feelings back into the dark, locked part of his mind he tried to ignore. What he knew about the Sullivan family could probably destroy them socially, but over the years, he'd tempered his bitterness and he wasn't interested in revenge—the sharp, kick-you-in-the-gut kind that he'd fantasized about as a kid going to a poor man's parochial school.

But that was a long time ago. Another lifetime. A kid he didn't want to recognize or remember.

The silver dollar tucked deep in his jeans pocket rubbed against his thigh as he drove through the night. There was a chance he was a father, that he had a son. A son he'd known nothing about.

The truth will never hurt you. Or so his mother had often said.

Like hell, he thought as he switched on the wipers and remembered growing up poor and Irish and Catholic in Boston. Now he knew that his mother, despite all the rosaries she'd said, all the prayers she'd sent to heaven, had lied. The fact of the matter was that the truth stings. It stings like a bitch.

Kate Summers was about to find out.

Chapter 4

Winter had come early to Boston. A week before Halloween, the first snowstorm of the year had blasted across the Atlantic, whipped Massachusetts Bay to an icy froth, and ripped through the streets and alleys of the city to dump six inches of icy white powder onto the streets—not enough to cripple the town, just enough to clog traffic and become an irritation. The weather forecast had been for a warming trend, but the forecasters were incredibly unreliable even with all their sophisticated satellites and computers, and this storm had caught them with their pants down.

Tonight Robert Sullivan brushed the snow from the shoulders of his wool coat, then hung it in the closet. The house was cold and empty despite the fact that every lamp was burning brightly and there were three maids scampering about, polishing silver that was rarely used, turning down his bed, making a fire in the den, pouring his brandy, and fixing his favorite meals. They would handle any little scavengers who had the nerve to knock at his door in a week and demand candy. He wouldn't have to be bothered.

Rubbing a hand over his near-frozen jaw, he saw his reflection in the Louis XVI mirror. Age was causing his once-robust skin to wrinkle and sag, his eyelids to droop, his square shoulders to slope. Someone had said it was hell getting old, and whoever that son of a bitch was, he was right.

Life wasn't the same as when Adele had been alive. He smiled faintly at her memory and reminded himself again that all the money in the world hadn't been able to save her. His life had been hollow ever since she'd given up her battle with cancer and left him alone nearly five years before. Funny, he never thought he'd miss her as much as he did. Their marriage had become comfortable but staid in the years since Stuart's death and the trouble with Bibi.

He and Adele had slept in different bedrooms and he'd had a string of young mistresses—discreet beautiful women, some of them married, who wanted nothing more than flowers, jewelry, and a little attention. If Adele had known of them, she'd kept the information to herself, never once so much as raising an eyebrow when he came home late or spent the weekend away. She either accepted his excuses of too much work or chose to ignore the obvious. He didn't know which. It was only after her announcement that she'd developed breast cancer that he realized how much he loved her, that he'd broken off with the other women, that he'd remained celibate to the day Adele had passed on. In fact, there had been no other woman since.

He missed her horribly; her void was a real ache that was with him each time he crossed the threshold to this, their home for nearly forty years. Her presence, the scent of her perfume, her gossiping whispers while she talked to her friends on the phone, her thin smile, and her staunch support. Lord knew he'd been a poor excuse for a husband, but she'd never once complained.

And then she'd left him. Only when she was gone did he realize how much he'd loved her, how alone and lost he was without her.

Alone. The word echoed through his brain.

Even his job had lost its luster. Being the senior partner in the law firm didn't mean as much as it once had. He dropped his keys in the glass tray on a table near the door and made his way to the den, where, upon his request, the evening newspaper, a snifter of expensive brandy, and a Cuban cigar were waiting.

This evening would be better than most, he told himself, because he expected company, someone who, for the right amount of money, was willing to help him in his newfound quest. Neils VanHorn, a private investigator of questionable morals, intense hunger for all things monetary, and a reputation for always getting the job done, was joining him for dinner. VanHorn was reputed to be the kind of man who would sell his soul for the right amount of money. Excellent.

Loosening his tie, Robert stared out the window overlooking Louisburg Square and watched as fat flakes continued to fall, but he didn't see the snow or the darkness. In his mind's eye, he pictured a boy, a fifteen-year-old boy with bright eyes, eager expression, cocky smile, and that edge of arrogance that kept the Sullivans in their proper place, an inch or two above the rest of the world. Sullivan blood was running through that adolescent's veins. Blue blood. As much like Stuart's as he would be able to find.

He thought of the boy, the child he'd scorned at birth, the grandson he'd sworn never to meet, and now, it seemed, the only chance for the Sullivan name to be passed from one generation to the next. His bastard grandson. Oh, there were his brother Frank's children, of course. A motley crew if he'd ever seen one. Whining daughters and a son without a drop of starch in him.

Not one fit to run the family empire. Even Alicia's young son, Wade, seemed to take after Maureen's spineless family. Unfortunately, if Robert didn't find someone of his own flesh and blood, first Frank, if he was lucky enough to outlive his older brother, and then Collin, Frank's spoiled dandy of an heir, would inherit the lion's share of wealth that had been tended to and nourished for seven generations. A damned waste, that's what it was.

If only Stuart had lived. Robert blinked hard and fought the old emotions that tended to strangle him each time he thought of his son. So strong. So handsome. So brilliant. Now, there was a boy with starch and sturdy moral fiber. The only one of the next generation. Even his own daughter, Beatrice, had turned into a disappointment not that she had an ounce of her older brother's vitality and brains.

Yet Stuart was the one who had bled to death on that dock, and despite the findings of the investigation, Robert knew who his son's murderer was; someday that bastard would pay. His vengeance would be cold and sweet and untraceable to the family. That's why he'd waited so long.

Besides, there were other, more pressing matters. He had to find his grandson and soon. Not only was Robert's life ebbing away, but his brother, Frank, was pushing that the reins of control be given to first him, and then Collin.

Robert reached for a cigar and bit off the tip. He'd been a fool fifteen years ago, an arrogant, blind fool, and it was time to rectify his mistake.

If he'd learned anything in his seventy years, it was that family meant everything, blood was thicker than water, and that he'd do whatever it took to find his grandson and return him to his rightful spot as heir to the Sullivan fortune.

* * *

Neils VanHorn smelled money. Big money. The kind of money that only comes along once in a lifetime. He sat by the fire smoking goddamned Havana cigars, the two-inch heels of his boots propped on an oxblood leather ottoman, and as he looked at the man seated next to him in a matching wing-backed chair. He knew this was it—his big score.

Over the sharp aroma of cigar smoke and the sweet scent of brandy from the snifter in his right hand, he detected that elusive scent of cold hard cash. Vaults of it. Robert Sullivan, gray-haired, distinguished down to his patrician nose and frosty blue eyes, was loaded. This renovated town house located on Louisburg Square, filled with antiques and oil portraits of old dead Sullivans, reeked of mutual funds, secret safes, stocks, and bearer bonds. Neils felt like he'd died and gone to heaven.

The clock struck half-past twelve and Robert had yet to get down to brass tacks, but VanHorn prided himself on his patience.

"So," the old man was saying, "this situation will have to be handled with the utmost discretion."

Neils was way ahead of Sullivan. "No problem."

"No one knows about the boy. That was how it was supposed to be."

"Understandable, considering the circumstances." Sure, Robert Sullivan had wanted to deep-six an illegitimate grandson just to keep up appearances. It hadn't occurred to him then that the kid might just be the last of the line, so to speak. VanHorn drew hard on his cigar and let out a puff of sweet, aromatic smoke. He feigned interest just to keep the old boy talking while taking a mental inventory of the Persian rugs and flintlock rifles locked behind the beveled glass doors of the gun case. Was that a Renoir mounted over the fireplace or a good fake? "You don't know the name of the couple who adopted him?"

"No . . . I . . . well, my wife was alive then and my son had just passed away, but we thought there would be more grandchildren. Legitimate ones. Beatrice hadn't married, of course, not yet, she was still pining for that sailor—Roy Panaker his name was . . ." His voice trailed off, as if weary from years of disappointment.

"How about the lawyer?"

"Dead. Tyrell Clark. A ladies man with a gambling problem, or so I was told. He was an associate with our firm for a while, didn't get along with some of the partners, and struck out on his own. Always a little on the shady side, Clark eventually got himself into a mess with the IRS and debtors. He popped off not long after the adoption."

Robert's mouth pinched into a little frown. "His practice—what little there was of it—was sold by the government to one of Clark's competitors, a man by the name of Millard Kent. I've tried discussing this with him, but his firm is a little more reputable than Clark's was. No one's talking. I wonder if there are any files." His cold eyes turned to VanHorn. "Sometimes in a case like this, if everything isn't exactly on the up and up, it's better if there isn't a paper trail."

"But the couple had to sign documents, get the kid a birth certificate, go through the proper channels . . ."

Sullivan lifted a shoulder and sipped from his drink. "I'm sure there are loopholes in the process that we can dig up. It shouldn't be too difficult because Tyrell had more than his share of trouble with the bar—his work wasn't always exactly on the up-and-up. He was never disbarred, mind you, but he left our firm with his tail between his legs because he came close."

"Yet you chose him to handle the adoption."

Robert scowled at the remains of his drink. "For just

that reason," he admitted with a long sigh. "I didn't ever want some bastard grandchild showing up on my doorstep with his hand out. I saw all the problems my brother Frank had with one of his, so I thought—and now I realize my complete and utter snobbery about the situation—anyway, I thought I wanted the kid to disappear. He was a cancer, a blight on the proud Sullivan name, you see." He smiled wistfully. "It's funny how your perspective can change when you're facing your maker."

Neils chose to ignore Robert's statement on his own mortality. It didn't have any bearing except that he didn't want the old boy to kick off before this deal was done. "The parents are probably going to fight you."

"Who cares? The way I see it, they were lucky enough in the first place to adopt the boy. Now it's time for him to come home—to his rightful spot."

"Which is?"

"Heir, of course."

"How does your brother feel about this?"

"Frank?" Robert made a scornful sound. "Frank's never understood about family, about right of succession, about the *responsibility* that comes with our station in life. In fact, he's always enjoyed the privilege of wealth, but oftentimes has acted . . . well, common, for lack of a better word."

"He'll find out."

"I know. I plan to talk to him later in the week. But the less you involve my brother and his family, the better."

"Does your daughter know about this?" Neils asked, wondering at the old man's power trip. Arrogantly superior, Robert Sullivan believed that he was right and everyone else was wrong, just because he'd been born first in line. No, that wasn't right; according to his notes, there had been an older brother who had died before ascending to the Sullivan throne. His name—William or Charles or something very British.

"Beatrice." Robert's frown deepened as he left his cigar to burn in a crystal ashtray. "Yes, she knows I'm hiring someone, but it's best to leave her out of this as much as possible. She didn't want the baby then, doesn't want him interfering with her life now. Really, she's quite upset about it. Doesn't understand why I can't just let Frank and his boy, Collin, inherit everything."

"She's not in line?" VanHorn said, lifting his eyebrows.

"She's a woman."

"So what if there were no sons?" VanHorn asked, disbelievingly. This was nearly the turn of the century, for God's sake; no one believed all that women-are-inferior-garbage today.

"Having no sons," Robert said succinctly, "would be a problem—basically unacceptable."

"I'd think Beatrice would be fighting tooth and nail for her own interests"

"Unfortunately, she's not interested in the family business or assets. She's content to collect a check every month and never question where it comes from." He sipped his brandy, set his snifter on a nearby table, and removed his glasses. Polishing the lenses slowly with a monogrammed handkerchief he'd drawn from his breast pocket, he said, "Remember, this arrangement is best left between you and· me. Beatrice and I have already talked. I can't just show up with her child one day and not prepare her, but keep her in the dark as much as possible. I'll handle Beatrice." The old man's jaw hardened.

"Does anyone know where Roy Panaker is?" Neils prompted.

"Not to my knowledge." Robert was suddenly impatient. "You'll have to find him, of course. Set the ground rules. I assume it will be necessary to pay him off, but rather than making him rich, it would be better to dig up a little dirt on him, something unscrupulous you can use to bribe him and keep him in line, so that there's no way he'll risk exposure if he ever finds out about the boy."

"He hasn't been interested yet?"

"Probably has no idea, but I'd like to be reassured that he won't be a problem."

Neils nodded, as if everything Robert was saying was commonplace, that bribery and invasion of privacy didn't matter—which they didn't—it was just the magnitude of Robert's request that blew him away.

"When that time comes, *if* it comes, when you have to talk to Beatrice, let me know. I'll arrange a meeting, but it's best that you don't contact her. There's no telling what she'll do. Unfortunately, Mr. VanHorn, my daughter isn't very stable."

A secret meeting.

What could it be about? What did Robert Sullivan and Neils VanHorn discuss within the walnut-paneled walls of Louisburg Square?

Royce didn't have all the details, damn him. The butler was too discreet to press his ear to the door, too afraid of losing his highly prized title of head servant in Robert Sullivan's household.

The damned hired help. You paid them through the nose, and still they only passed on the bare essentials, information that could be easily soaked in while removing dishes or setting a fire.

But Royce did report that Robert Sullivan had dined at home with a man named Neils VanHorn, a private investigator and not a professional of the stature Robert Sullivan usually hired.

"Let's just say his overcoat was a tad frayed at the cuffs," Royce had said. A tattered coat and boots with holes, for God's sake. Royce had actually spied black spots on the soles when VanHorn had the audacity to prop his feet up on the oxblood leather furniture. Feet up as he'd burned through one of Robert's Havana cigars.

Something was in the air . . . power swirling, spinning in a fierce maelstrom.

And Robert was behind it, manipulating and twisting, always the mastermind, always the ruthless patriarch.

Well, he wasn't going to proceed unchecked.

The old man had to be watched.

Carefully watched.

Robert Sullivan had overstepped his boundaries one too many times.

One more bold step, and he would have to be stopped.

Chapter 5

Daegan O'Rourke propped the phone between his head and shoulder so that he could bang on the splintered window sash to pry the damned thing open. Right now the phone was one of the few things that worked in Eli McIntyre's old cabin, and if Daegan was going to stay here, he had his work cut out for him just making it livable. Which he would have to do, if he was going to stick around here until he met the Summers kid and figured out if the boy was the one. "Okay, Sandy," he told his old friend from grade school. "What do you have for me?"

"Your information panned out." Though he was miles away, back in Boston, Sandy's gravelly voice sounded close and familiar. "Looks like old Robert has engaged the services of one Neils VanHorn, a two-bit private investigator with a reputation for chasing a buck and bending the ethics of the profession."

So Bibi was right; Robert was looking to dig up some old dirt.

"VanHorn is not the sort of guy a man like Robert Sullivan usually employs," Sandy went on. "Makes you wonder what Robert wants VanHorn to do."

He's looking for a male heir, Daegan thought. *A way to sink his claws into some innocent kid, a total power trip.*

"No doubt VanHorn's been hired for something slimy and underhanded," Sandy went on, half-joking.

"You got that right," Daegan said.

Sandy Kavenaugh's instincts had always been on the money. During a stint in the military, Kavenaugh had done some intelligence work, then, once his hitch was over, had opened his own private detective agency. It was Sandy who'd checked up on Daegan's mother, Mary Ellen, whom Daegan hadn't had contact with in years, as well as keeping an eye on the Sullivans, watching each and every one of them, including Bibi. As far as Daegan was concerned, none of them could be trusted.

"Want me to see what I can find out about Van-Horn?" Sandy asked.

"See if you can get wind of what he's doing for Robert Sullivan," Daegan said as he stared out the window toward the Summers place next door. "And keep your ear to the ground for any mention of an illegitimate heir to the Sullivan fortune. Seems my cousin Bibi had a kid some fifteen years ago, and there's something brewing about finding the boy now and naming him in the will."

"Imagine that? Some kid could be a secret millionaire," Sandy said.

At what price? Daegan thought, brushing away a cobweb as he turned toward the bedroom.

"I'll see what I can find on the kid and get back to you," Sandy said.

The kid. As Daegan hung up, he felt his jaw clench at the notion that the kid living in the neighboring ranch could be the one he was looking for . . . his son.

The idea of having a son was still fresh and uncomfortable, like a new boot that was a little too tight and pinched at the toes. He'd never seen himself as a father; never planned to have any children. And never, *never* would he have let a kid of his grow up without a strong male influence.

But the worst of it was Jon's mother. Kate. More intelligent and wary than he'd expected and far more attractive than he'd hoped, there was something about her he found damnably intriguing. Probably because she was forbidden fruit—that was his problem with women. The ones that were off-limits were the most fascinating. His own personal curse. He'd make sure the attraction passed, but wished he knew what to do with her.

In the bedroom he paused and frowned at the stained mattress lying on the floor. Nearby was a half-full bottle of rot-gut whiskey, a carton of cigarettes, and a couple of copies of *Playboy* magazine. Looked like someone was having himself a party. An ashtray that had the irregular shape and mottled coloring to suggest it had been made in some kind of crafts class was filled with butts—several different brands. Daegan smiled. Yep, the old McIntyre ranch must've become the local clubhouse for juvenile delinquents, one of which might well be Jon Summers.

Good. If the kid was trouble, his job would be easier. He walked outside again and a low growl emanated from beneath the dusty floorboards of the porch. Bending on one knee, Daegan peered below into the darkness and found a half-starved dog lying in the shadows. Teeth bared, steady eyes trained on Daegan's throat, the mutt let out another rumbling warning. "That's no way to treat the new tenant," Daegan admonished softly. "Come on out of there."

The hound didn't budge, just snarled.

"Great." That's when he noticed the metal dishes—mixing bowls tucked into one corner of the porch. One was half-full of water, the other was empty. "Someone taking care of you, boy?"

The dog didn't respond, just cowered, looking at Daegan with yellow, distrusting eyes.

Standing, Daegan stretched and stared at the barren acres. The only house close by was the Summers place, located on the other side of a stand of pine. Other neighbors could have made it their mission to take care of old McIntyre's dog, but Daegan had a gut feeling that either Jon Summers or his mother was seeing that the mutt didn't starve or dehydrate. Just the break he needed. "I think you and I are gonna be good friends." *And what about the boy? Is he gonna be your good friend, too? Or is he going to end up hating you for the rest of his life?*

Kate waited impatiently for her sister to answer and glared at the clock. Almost three here, nearly six o'-clock in Boston. Laura would be getting home from work and Kate wanted to talk to her sister in private, before Jon got home from school so he wouldn't overhear any of the conversation. "Come on, come on," she said, pacing by the kitchen window and stretching the phone cord as she walked from one end of the kitchen to the other. Laura, who worked for the state, had access to all kinds of legal documents. Births, deaths, prison records.

Kate had never asked a favor of her sister before. Even though she'd been tempted a hundred times to find out the true identity of Jon's biological parents, she'd resisted asking Laura to look up the information. Whether she felt she was crossing an ethical barrier or because she was just plain chicken to find out, she didn't know. But things had changed now that Jon had begun asking questions about his father. She needed to find out the truth in order to protect Jon.

The recorder picked up on the fourth ring. "Hi, you've reached Laura and Jeremy. We can't come to the phone right now, but if you'd leave a message after the beep . . ." Kate waited impatiently, then asked her sister to call. Now that she'd decided upon a course of action, she was anxious to set it into motion.

Slamming the receiver down, she told herself to remain calm. Nothing had changed. Yet. Kids had bad dreams all the time.

Pouring the final cup of coffee from this morning's pot, she sat back down at her desk to read the last of twenty-five essays she had to correct for her class in the morning. She rubbed her eyes and was reaching for her reading glasses when she heard the rumble of an engine. Peering through the lace curtains, she expected Jon to appear. Rather than waiting for the bus, he'd probably caught a ride with someone, a kid with a car and hopefully a driver's license. He was starting to complain that taking the bus was a drag and only for babies.

A beat-up once-green pickup lumbered up the drive and Kate recognized it at once. Daegan O'Rourke, the stranger who had fixed her tire, stretched out of the cab and she felt a warning increase in her pulse. Tall and lean, a cowboy type in faded jeans, dusty blue shirt, and rawhide jacket, O'Rourke made his way to the front porch.

What could he possibly want from her?

She'd thought of him a couple of times since he'd insisted upon helping her—there had been a raw sexual energy about him, a hidden strength of character that made it impossible for him to take no for an answer. She hadn't wanted his help, but he'd practically shoved it down her throat, and rather than seeming ungrateful, she'd let him change the damned tire. So what was he doing here? Whatever it was he was peddling, she wasn't

interested. Contrary to popular belief, the last compli-
cation she needed in her life was a man.

As she watched him climb the steps, his boots ringing on the old planks, she noticed the determined cut
of his jaw, the blade-thin mouth, the harsh planes of his
face. He looked like a man with a mission and she knew
instinctively that somehow it involved her.

Normally she wouldn't have thought a thing about
opening the door to him. Every once in a while someone
stopped by to ask for directions or with car trouble, but
today, when her nerves were already stretched thin from
worries about Jon, she was suspicious, and as he rang
the bell, she opened the door but stood on the other
side of the screen.

His eyes met hers through the mesh and a quick
smile lighted his face. "So you're my neighbor." His
voice was a deep drawl, his tanned face all blades and
angles honed from hours in the elements. Gray eyes
studied her without a trace of warmth. "How about
that?"

"Neighbor?" she repeated.

Hitching a calloused thumb in the direction of the
ranch next door, he said, "I'm renting the McIntyre
place."

Kate felt a little catch in her breath and told herself
she was being silly. She had nothing to fear from this
man, no reason not to trust him. He'd *helped* her, for
crying out loud, changed her flat tire. She should be
grateful that someone was going to live in Eli's place
and keep it up. Empty buildings often attracted a bad
element. But she couldn't shake the sensation that this
man was the last person on earth she wanted living next
door. He carried with him no air of satisfaction that usually came with ranching. No, this man was restless; a
thrum of energy seemed to hide beneath the tanned
skin that stretched over the strong angles of his face.

All Jon's talk had unnerved her, that's all. *Relax, Kate.*
She opened the screen door.

"How's the tire?" he asked.

"Back on the car. I must've run over a screw somewhere. George, down at the station, found one lodged in
the tread, though I can't imagine where I picked it up."

"So it could be fixed?"

"Yeah, I guess I lucked out."

He hesitated, then rubbed his chin. "I guess it's my
turn to ask a favor," he said, shifting from one leg to the
other. "I'm having a little trouble myself. I was wondering if I could use your phone to call the telephone company. They were supposed to send out a guy this
morning, but he never showed."

Some of the tension in her muscles drained. *You're
losing it, Kate.*

"Sure. I'll go get it." She should have just asked him
inside, but she was still nervous. Even though he
seemed honest enough, she didn't know him. And
there was Jon's prediction to consider—trouble or danger coming their way. "I'll just be a minute." In the
kitchen, she picked up the remote, and as she passed by
the front closet, she reminded herself that her grandfather's rifle was tucked in the corner, unloaded, but a
weapon nonetheless.

As if she needed one.

*Face it, Kate, all Jon's talk has got you wound tighter than
a top and now you're jumping at shadows.* Her heart raced
a little and she silently called herself a fool. This wasn't
the city, for God's sake, and this guy certainly wasn't an
ex-prisoner from somewhere in New England. He
spoke with a western twang, dressed as if he'd been
born in a pair of rawhide boots, and probably had
never seen the eastern shores of the Mississippi.

O'Rourke was propped against the railing, his dark
hair showing streaks of red in the afternoon sunlight.

"Here you go." She handed him the receiver and his jaw slid to one side. He was probably amused by her caution. He inched his wallet out of the back pocket of his faded jeans and found a card, then punched out numbers and waited. "Hold," he mouthed, then hit another number. "I hate these things." Grumbling under his breath, he kept punching, finally stopped and looked at her with steely eyes guarded by thick black eyebrows. "It would help if they'd just connect me to a real person instead of a machine and tape recording—" His head snapped up. "Hell, yes, I'm here. Look, I'm expecting a man to come and hook up my phone . . . what? Oh. Daegan O'Rourke and I live . . ." He turned his back to her and concentrated on the phone call.

She couldn't help studying his backside—shoulders broad enough to stretch the seams of his jacket, trim waist, narrow hips. His jeans were worn and dusty, his boots needed polish, the heels worn down, the back of his neck tanned from hours in the sun. He was frustrated, raking a hand through his hair as he spoke, but there was nothing sinister about him. Nothing suspicious. Just an angry restless man trying to untangle the red tape surrounding Eli McIntyre's place.

"Well, if it's the best you can do, then it'll be fine," he said, his voice edged in irritation. "I'll expect him in a couple hours." As he faced her again, his gaze caught hers and his lips turned downward in agitation. He handed her the phone.

"Everything okay?"

He made a sound of deprecation in the back of his throat. "Looks like the cavalry's decided to come to the rescue after all. Thanks."

"No problem . . ." She heard the bus. The growl of the huge engine was distinctive, and for the first time in her life, she hoped that Jon had caught a ride from another kid and was cruising around town. She didn't want him showing up while O'Rourke was still here, though she didn't really understand why. She wasn't so lucky. Glancing at the road, she caught a glimpse of the mustard-colored school bus flashing through the thicket of scrub pines at the end of the drive. Gravel crunched as huge tires slowed and the doors whooshed open.

Jon, backpack slung over one shoulder, loped through the play of shadows on the rock driveway as the bus lumbered away. Houndog, who had spent the better part of the afternoon waiting at the mailbox for Jon, barked wildly, darting through the woods and flushing out pheasants and grasshoppers in his path.

"Hey, Mom, guess what?" Jon called before spying the truck in the drive and the man on the front porch. The smile on his face, a smile she hadn't seen in days, evaporated when his gaze landed full-force on O'Rourke. "Who're you?" he asked.

"This is our new neighbor, Daegan O'Rourke. My son, Jon." Her lungs suddenly constricted painfully.

Daegan offered a hand, but Jon ignored it.

"What's he doing here?"

"Jon," Kate said sharply though she knew, he, too, had a million questions, all tied into his nightmares. "Mr. O'Rourke just came by to use the phone. He's moved into the McIntyre place and his isn't connected yet."

Daegan leaned against a post supporting the roof. "And you must be the guy who's been stopping by and taking care of old Eli's dog."

The color faded from Jon's face and a wary look settled in his eyes.

"Jon?" Kate's eyebrows inched upward though she shouldn't have been surprised. Jon had been taking more than his share of long walks lately. He missed the old man—the only grandfather type he'd ever known. "Have you been over there?"

"No harm done," Daegan cut in, his gaze never leaving her son's face. "Someone needed to look after the hound."

"Yeah, old Roscoe wouldn't leave after the funeral and so I—"

"You didn't tell me," Kate said, learning more about her boy each day and wondering how she would ever retrieve the reins of control that continually slid through her fingers.

"You would've called animal control," Jon accused her.

"The dog's old, Jon," Kate said softly. "And vicious."

"And he doesn't deserve to be put to sleep! Just because Eli died doesn't mean that Roscoe—"

"It's all right," Daegan said. "You can keep comin' over and seein' him if you want. To tell you the truth, the dog won't have a thing to do with me. I think he'd just as soon rip my throat open than lick my hand."

Jon's eyes narrowed. He looked from his mother to Daegan again, as if expecting some kind of conspiracy. "You mean it?"

"Hold on . . ." Kate interjected. Right now, with the frightening visions Jon had been having, he needed to stay close to home. And she wasn't sure she could trust this stranger. Not yet

O'Rourke offered a hard smile. "I bought some dog food in town, but Roscoe—that's his name, right?" Jon nodded slowly. "Old Roscoe won't go near it. Acts like I'm trying to poison him." He lifted a shoulder. "Maybe I bought the wrong brand."

"He doesn't like anybody."

"Great," O'Rourke said sarcastically. "Just what I need. Another headache."

"You're gonna keep him?" Jon was suspicious.

The cowboy lifted a shoulder. "If he doesn't die on me or take a chunk out of my leg first. Maybe you could come over and show him that I'm okay."

"I don't know," Kate said quickly. This was all happening fast. Way too fast. "I don't think—"

"Oh, come on, Mom, please." Jon was suddenly pleading.

"Something about this doesn't feel right—"

O'Rourke straightened and rubbed one shoulder. "Well, it would help me out. I think Jon might've left some of his things over at the house."

Jon froze and he looked at the ground. Hot color washed up the back of his neck.

"What things?" Kate asked, bracing herself. These days it seemed as if her son had another life—entirely separate from her own. She couldn't imagine what kind of stash Jon was hiding from her, but she was certain she was about to find out.

"Well, I just assumed they were his. A jackknife and a comic book or two, deck of cards, that kind of thing. No big deal. It's just that I'm cleaning things up and I didn't want to throw out anything valuable."

Jon lifted his eyes slowly, studying the man before him.

"Tell ya what, Jon. I'll save them for you, and next time you come over to see the dog, you can pick 'em up. Fair enough?"

Kate watched as Jon's eyebrows flattened into one thoughtful line. "Fair enough."

Daegan extended his hand again, and this time Jon took it, his gaze locking with the uncompromising stare of their new neighbor.

"Good."

For a second Jon just stood there shaking O'Rourke's

hand then quickly yanked his fingers away and his voice was the barest of whispers when he asked, "Who are you?"

"I told you. My name's—"

"I know what you said." Jon's nostrils quivered and a breeze lifted the hair that fell over his eyes. "But you're lying. Who are you and why are you here?"

Kate's muscles flexed. "Jon, Mr. O'Rourke—" Her voice gave out as she saw her son back up a step and lick his lips nervously. The hairs on her nape lifted in sudden premonition and her insides turned to mush. *Oh, God, no.*

"You killed someone," Jon said, his voice shaking, his color bleached away by fear. "You killed someone, didn't you, someone you cared about!"

Daegan held the boy's gaze steadily, didn't even flinch. "What the devil are you talking about?"

"There was a fight and you . . . oh God, you . . . you . . ." Jon blinked hard as he sometimes did when the image he was seeing began to fade.

Daegan shook his head. "Believe me, Jon, I've never killed anyone in my life. Not even when I was in the army." Was this child really his? Were the eyes staring so intently at him O'Rourke eyes—Sullivan eyes? What would happen if the kid ever found out the truth? "Where'd you get a notion like that?" he asked, and refused to be sucked into the emotional whirlpool that threatened to drown him.

Jon swallowed and stepped back, nearly tripping on the porch. He rammed his hands into the back pockets of his baggy jeans. "I, um, don't know, I just—" He shrugged and Daegan felt as if he'd been kicked in the gut. *The kid just knew?* In that second Daegan was convinced that Bibi hadn't been lying; not only did the boy bear a resemblance to the Sullivans, he also had the gift, that special little touch of ESP that had been float-

ing along Sullivan bloodlines for centuries, long before
the witch trials, all the way back to Dublin and rumors
of black arts. Not everyone in the family possessed it;
sometimes it skipped an entire generation, only to show
up later in a grandchild or niece, those with the right
combination of Sullivan genes. This kid, the product of
a union between first cousins, had been cursed or
blessed, depending upon your state of mind.

Daegan loathed the gift himself; it had brought him
nothing but trouble. The feelings were always there, just
under the surface, ready to remind him that he was, in
fact, a Sullivan. Though that special intuition had helped
him when he'd been a tracker, he'd just as soon he
never experienced that tingling sensation of reading
someone else's thoughts again.

"Sometimes Jon . . . he has premonitions," Kate said,
her fingers working nervously on the antenna of the
phone she still held in one hand. Her demeanor had
changed and she looked at him as if she were staring at
the very devil himself. Wariness darkened her amber-
colored eyes.

"Well, this time he's wrong." He needed to ease her
mind in order to keep up his charade. If she doubted
him, his job would be all the more difficult. "I was in a
fight once, with a cousin of mine—a bad fight."

Jon's expression didn't change. "He's dead."

Kate's fingers tightened around the phone. "Is it true?"

No reason to lie. "That's right, but I didn't kill him."

A small, sharp sound escaped her and she covered
her mouth with one hand.

"The police thought you did."

"They were convinced otherwise, Jon." Daegan
rammed stiff fingers through his hair. "It was all over a
long time ago." Daegan offered a smile he didn't feel,
trying to set Kate at ease, then reminded himself that
he had a job to do, one that had to be accomplished

swiftly. Besides, this woman wasn't as lily-white as she pretended to be; she was in on the adoption scam from the get-go. Now, it seemed, she really cared for her boy, hadn't done a half-bad job of raising him, but she'd still walked on the wrong side of the law—a side that was familiar to Daegan. Whatever bonds existed between this woman and boy, they were secondary in importance. At least for now.

He just wished he could wash his hands of this mess. He wondered how he was ever going to tell the boy that he was his father, that he didn't know Jon had existed for nearly fifteen years, that the kid was a product of a forbidden and unloving union? How was he going to explain about an obsessed and dying grandfather, one of the richest men in Boston, a man who had now determined to change the course of the boy's life forever, a man who didn't take no for an answer?

"This sight, does it help you see into your teacher's grade book?" Daegan asked, trying to change the subject.

Jon didn't crack a smile.

"I wish." Kate laughed nervously, her gaze never leaving Daegan's face. If he'd ever hoped to gain his trust, he'd blown it by letting the kid touch him.

He inclined his head. "Thanks for the use of the phone. I'd better go back and see if the guy from the telephone company is really going to show up." His gaze settled on Kate's for just an instant, long enough to see the questions in her eyes, long enough to feel like a heel for what he was about to do.

The boy, not so much as a glimmer of a smile in his eyes, glared at him. Daegan felt a great rending in his soul as he realized his son—the only kid he'd ever bring forth on this earth—not only distrusted him but probably hated him as well. And if he didn't yet, he would soon.

He loped back to his truck and climbed inside. Through the open window, he yelled, "Anytime you want to come over and pick up your things and see that poor excuse of a dog, you're welcome."

Jon didn't answer. He shifted slightly, placing his body between Daegan's pickup and his mother, as if he sensed a threat from Daegan, a threat to Kate.

"Hell," Daegan muttered under his breath. No matter if the adoption had been dirty, this woman and boy cared for each other and they faced the world together alone. Just like he had with his own mother.

He backed out of the drive and wished to high heaven that he'd never laid eyes on Bibi Sullivan or the rest of the damned family. But it was inevitable that they'd met. To Daegan, in his youth the wealth and glitter of his father's other life had constantly drawn him, like the pull of the moon on the tides. Daegan had been doomed from the second he'd learned that he was Frank Sullivan's bastard son, and because of it, a life of privilege and wealth would be dangled in front of his nose like a carrot, only to be yanked away.

He'd come a long way from Boston, a long way from the scared little boy he'd once been . . .

BOOK TWO

DAEGAN

1968–1990

Chapter 6

"He's ... well ... I don't know how to put this delicately, Joanna. Mary Ellen O'Rourke's boy is ... he doesn't have ... there's no man in the picture, if you get my drift. I'm afraid he's illegitimate ... a bastard."

Sister Evangeline, on the other side of the glassed partition, slid a guilty glance in Daegan's direction, and he, not quite six at the time, realized immediately that the ugly word referred to him. After having dared utter the profanity, the good sister quickly crossed herself and turned her attention back to the secretary, a laywoman who was struggling to fill out Daegan's admittance forms.

The nun reminded Daegan of a vulture as she hovered in her dusty habit with the frayed hem. A rosary dangled from a pocket hidden deep in the folds of her voluminous black robe, and her hands, covered with age spots, fingered the worn beads anxiously.

Most of the whispered conversation between the two women drifted into the reception area, and Daegan's mother, sitting next to him on the bench polished by the rumps of truants and worried parents, fiddled nervously with the strap of her purse. She was wearing her best dress, black with white polka dots, and a black hat perched at an angle on her head; her long red hair had been pinned into something she called a French twist, and she'd been extra careful with her makeup, forgoing her favorite cherry-red lipstick for a faded coral.

Across the room, above another bench, was a crucifix, large and life-like, and Daegan concentrated on Jesus's crown of thorns and the painted blood that dripped down his gaunt, serene face. Near the window was a clock, the pendulum unmoving, as if time stopped once a potential student passed through the vestibule of St. Mark's Elementary.

The slow-paced clacking of typewriter keys stopped completely. "So then who's the boy's father—?" the gray-haired secretary, bending over ancient keys, asked.

"She didn't say."

"But if there's a problem at school and I can't reach her—?"

"She gave a friend's name, it's here, listed on the form. Rindy DuBois." The sister's voice again, frigid and superior. Daegan looked through the glass to stare at her pale face and tall, draped body. Her skin, wrinkled already, was further furrowed by the tight wimple that hid so much that not even a strand of her hair showed. Maybe she was bald. She seemed to feel his gaze and he saw it then, a little window into her mind, that opened suddenly to him. *Devil's spawn,* she said wordlessly and returned his open-faced stare with an imperious glare.

He shuddered and his mother whispered, "Don't stare. It's not polite."

"She hates me."

"No, babycakes, she's just trying to help." Mama patted his hand, but she looked nervous—the way she did when Frank called to tell her he wasn't stopping by.

Daegan knew better. His "sight" wasn't complete, and

he couldn't read minds, but he caught glimpses of people's true feelings. He had been able to do this for as long as he could remember, but he didn't tell his mother about Sister Evangeline's thoughts because the one time he mentioned being able to see what people were thinking, Mama had slapped him hard across the face and told him that he was never to mention it again. People would think he was crazy or possessed by demons or something very bad. And it wasn't as if he could look into everyone's thoughts or that it happened all the time.

Now, she stroked the side of his cheek. "You just do your best in school, honey, and everything will be all right."

"*Miss* O'Rourke," the sister's nasal tone was commanding, her hands folded piously as she stood in the doorway between the secretary's room and the reception area. "If you could give Mrs. Bevans your insurance information, that sort of thing, I'll take David down to—"

"Daegan," his mother said.

The sister's eyelids settled downward for a second, as if she was gathering her imminent patience. "Of course, Daegan. I'll take him down to the classroom so he can meet the other children. You know, school started last Monday."

"I—I know; we were out of town . . ." Her voice faded away as if she knew how feeble her excuse sounded. She was lying, Daegan knew. They hadn't been away; she had just been fighting with his father again. She'd wanted Daegan to go to the other private school and Frank had refused to allow it, wouldn't pay for it, so they were here, at St. Mark's.

"Well, you're back now and Daegan's already behind in his lessons. Come on, son, I'll show you to your room. Sister Mae will be your teacher." She swept out of the room and Mama bent down and kissed him on his cheek.

"Don't you worry," she told him, her smile wobbly as

she squeezed his hands. "St. Mark's is one of the best schools around and you'll make lots of new friends."

Daegan wasn't sure he believed her as he took in the dark wood walls, yellowed linoleum floors, cold benches, and glass windows with wire threaded through them. To him, the school was a prison.

"You be good for the sisters," his mother ordered softly.

"I'll be back to pick you up when you're done today, so you won't get lost. Now, run along."

Clutching his lunch pail, he took off after Sister Evangeline, who, after rounding a corner, paused in front of a scratched wooden door. Inside the room, kids were already seated at wooden desks on runners that were bolted to the floor in perfect rows. Each desk with its slanted top was full. Not an empty one in sight. Students in navy and green uniforms twisted their heads to look at him as if he were a curious animal in the zoo.

"Sister Mae, this is Davi—Daegan O'Rourke, the new student I told you about."

"Ah, yes, well, he'll have to sit at the table in the back of the room until we can come up with another desk—or . . . no, Daegan, why don't you share a desk with . . . uh . . . Lucas . . . Lucas Bennett . . . there, Luke B., raise your hand."

Luke, a short freckle-faced kid without any front teeth scowled as he halfheartedly waved at Daegan. With Sister Evangeline shepherding him, Daegan squeezed into one side of the chair. "Be good and pay attention. I want no trouble out of you," the vulture-nun whispered.

"There we go." Sister Mae seemed pleased, her plump face flushed as she smiled.

Duty done, Sister Evangeline slipped piously out of the room.

With a warm smile and bright eyes behind her rimless

glasses, Sister Mae insisted that everyone greet her new charge. "Come on children, let's welcome Daegan. Everyone."

Daegan wanted to drop through the floor.

"Hello, Daegan," the class said in somewhat distorted unison.

"You can meet everyone at recess. All right, class," she added, her gaze all-encompassing once again. "We were starting to learn the alphabet . . . how many of you can recognize this letter?" She pointed to a tagboard alphabet strung across the top of the blackboard. A hand shot up. A girl in the front row with springy curls and a smug little smile slid glances to either side of her, checking out her academic competition.

"Amy?"

"That's a G," she sang confidently.

"I hate Amy Webster," Lucas grumbled. "She's a stuck-up snot."

Daegan smothered a grin and decided maybe Lucas wasn't so bad after all.

"Very good . . . and this one?" Sister Mae pointed again and Amy, waving frantically, practically peed her pants trying to gain Sister Mae's attention again.

Daegan's mind wandered. The room smelled of chalk and floor wax and oil from Lucas's dirty hair, but the teacher seemed kind and so he tried to pay attention, as he'd promised his mother he would. "You're lucky, you know," she'd told him the morning after her fight with Frank about where their son was to receive his lessons. Her eyes had been red-rimmed, her voice lacking conviction. "Not every father would pay for his son's education in a private school."

Daegan wasn't too young to know that Frank Sullivan didn't give anything away without exacting a price. That's the way it had been since the first time he'd laid eyes on his father. Daegan hadn't asked at the time, but he couldn't help wondering just what it was his mother was expected to give for her son to attend St. Mark's.

School turned out to be okay, though as he grew older, he came to understand the full meaning of being branded illegitimate, being the only kid in his class with such an ugly distinction. Everyone had a father and a mother, except for Derrick Cawfield, whose dad had been killed—crushed by crates of frozen fish that had slipped off a crane while he'd been working on the docks.

Daegan, the new kid, had been teased at first, his lunch stolen, spiders put in his desk, taunts hurled in his direction until he proved that even though he wasn't as large as some of the kids in the class, he could use his fists as well as anyone. He suffered two bloody lips and a black eye, but gave as good as he got, and soon he was accepted and the bullies turned their attention and jeers to Max Fulton, a thin boy who'd been born with only one thumb. His left hand had four fingers and some kind of freaky-looking stump. Max was embarrassed about his deformity and kept his hand hidden under his desk a lot of the time. He never missed an answer in class, received A-pluses on every paper he ever turned in, and was the teacher's pet, much to Amy Webster's dismay. The entire class, including Amy, hated Max. Daegan was just glad someone else was taking the heat.

As Daegan grew, he understood more about his position in the world—or his lack of it. His father came and went in the dark hours of the night and seemed a mystery to Daegan. Though his mother insisted that Frank Sullivan was a wonderful man, a good provider, and handsome as the day was long, Daegan didn't believe her. Too often after Frank had spent several hours in her bedroom, she'd ended up crying as he left and every so often Daegan noticed bruises on her arms and neck. Once she even had a black eye, but she didn't blame it on Frank Sullivan. Instead she claimed she'd been clumsy and bumped into a door. Daegan didn't believe her.

Out of a sense of morbid curiosity, Daegan wanted to know more about his father and his family, Frank's legitimate children. Daegan spent hours watching the Lincolns, Mercedes, and Rolls Royces drop off their precious cargo at the private school only a few blocks away. Though both institutions were overseen by the same bishop, there was a definite line drawn between the haves and the have-nots, the factory owners and the workers. Nowhere was the social chasm more visible than the stoplight between St. Mark's Elementary School and Our Lady of Sorrows, a newer brick building built a little higher on the hill, closer to the church and therefore, Daegan reasoned, closer to God. Which was all just as well, he decided, as the years clicked by, because the farther he was from God, the better.

On some Sundays as the church bells chimed, he sneaked up to Our Lady of Sorrows, climbed a big elm tree that shaded the parking lot, and viewed the chauffeured car as it rolled to the front entrance. Daegan always hoped for a glimpse of his father—the man who never saw his mother in the light of day, a tall man with broad shoulders, stiff spine, and copper-colored hair. A man who had never, not even in his late-night visits, ever once slid more than a disgusted glance in Daegan's direction.

His children—real children—were always with him as was his wife, a small woman with a flat chest and lines around her mouth that suggested she didn't smile often. Maureen was never without a wide-brimmed hat that shaded her face, dark glasses to hide her eyes, and a fur coat wrapped around her slim figure. Mama said Maureen Sullivan drank all the time and could barely sober up to stumble into the church on Sunday mornings.

The kids, two girls and a boy, looked more like their mother, all blond and pale, than Frank, whose complexion, Mama said, reminded her of Tony Curtis. Frank's other children, with their polished shoes and expensive clothes, were serious, never talking or laughing together. As the family walked along the sidewalk to the church, they didn't touch or even speak, but at the doorstep, with a quick, sharp command from Maureen, Frank's legitimate children linked fingers and Frank, frowning distastefully, took Maureen's gloved hand in his without uttering a word.

Daegan wanted to puke. So fake. The girls, Alicia and Bonnie, wore perfect dresses with matching hats, and Frank's boy, Collin, was always dressed up in little suits and bow ties. Daegan told himself he was *glad* he wasn't one of Frank's real children, *glad* he didn't have to have a woman like that bossing him around, *glad* he didn't have to wear a stupid-looking tie and prim little suit . . . but he would have liked just one ride in the shiny car. Just one.

Once, when Frank paused to stub out his cigarette beneath the elm, Daegan screwed up the courage to spit on him, hitting him square on the top of his oiled head. Hardly daring to breathe, Daegan then cowered behind the elm's thick trunk.

"Damn birds," Frank growled as Daegan smothered a smile and prayed to God he wouldn't be seen. He hazarded a peek and grinned to himself as Frank wiped his shiny hair with a monogrammed handkerchief. Hucking spittle at Frank was as close to communicating with his father as Daegan had ever come.

Each time Frank planned a visit, Daegan was warned by his mother to always feign sleep, never speak to Mr. Sullivan, and never, ever open the bedroom door, no matter what he heard.

He hadn't been able to stop, though, not when he'd heard his mother moaning and crying one night, whimpering as if she were in excruciating pain. Biting his lip to fight his cowardice, Daegan had climbed off the sleeper sofa, walked boldly across the tile floor, and pounded on the locked door. All noise, crying, sniffing, growling, and squeaking of the mattress, suddenly stopped. The apartment became immediately still except for the constant drip of the kitchen faucet. Daegan's knuckles hurt and he was about to reach for the handle of the door when he heard a round of obscenities.

Daegan froze.

"Dumb little shit," Frank sputtered, the bed making noise again. "I guess it's time to teach that kid a lesson."

"Frank, no—" his mother cried. "He's just worried about me. That's all."

"Well, he's bothering the hell out of me."

"He's just a little boy." Then more loudly, "Daegan, honey, babycakes, you go back to bed. Everything's okay. Go on, now."

Daegan could barely swallow, his mouth was so dry. If he were brave, truly brave, he would open the door and try and protect his mama from whatever Frank was doing to her.

"I hate him lurking around—spying on us, looking at us with those damned eyes. He needs to know how to behave, and for Christ's sake, don't call him anything so sissy as babycakes. You want him to grow up into some kind of fag?" There was a jingle of keys and buckles and Daegan imagined his father, with his bulging arm muscles, reaching for his belt.

"No!" Mary Ellen whispered frantically. "Oh, Frank, no—please, don't hit him, please—"

Daegan's throat turned to sand but he didn't give up his vigil and pounded again. "Mama?" he croaked.

"Dumb little bastard. I think it's time he learned who his father is—how I should be treated, that I pay for that goddamned school he goes to and this shithole of an apartment!"

"No, no, no!" She was panicking, her voice breathy. "Come on, honey, he's quit pounding on the door, hasn't he? He's probably already asleep." Daegan, his mouth tasting foul, backed slowly away. "Here, let me make you feel better," she said in a voice that was low and whispery—an ugly voice Daegan didn't want to think of as belonging to his mother. It made her sound nasty. "That's better, baby. Come on, I'll make you feel good." Again the sound of buckles jangling.

There was silence for a heart-stopping moment. The drip continued. Outside a cat cried, then the hoarse whisper of Frank's voice. "Sweet Jesus," he said. "You know how to do it, don't you? Damn, but you're good. I don't think I can hold back—oh, kitten, oh God." A long slow groan followed, almost as if Frank Sullivan were in some kind of severe, but ecstatic pain. "What you do to me . . . oooh . . . that's it. More, more, more. Take more. That's it, baby. Keep doin' me. That's *iiiit.*"

The back of Daegan's legs collided with the sofa. His jaw worked. Squeezing his eyes shut until they hurt, he fought the hot tears that burned against his eyelids. He should do *something*, anything to save her from having to act this way. Then it hit him. His mother was doing it for him. Because she loved him. How many times had she told him that she was saving her money so that he could have a better life, so that he wouldn't have to work twelve-hour days huddled over a sewing machine doing piecework at a big factory like she did—not that he would, of course. The men didn't sew. They had higher-paying jobs filling boxes, stacking crates, loading trucks, but he—Daegan O'Rourke—would have better because she willed it so. He was, after all, Frank Sullivan's son. The blood flowing through his veins was a wealthy shade of blue.

Shaking, Daegan crawled back to the fold-down couch that served as his bed. Above the cushions a picture of John F. Kennedy was hung reverently next to a portrait of the Virgin Mary with her arms spread wide, a halo glowing around her head.

Daegan huddled under the blanket, his head pushed into the pillow as he tried to block out the sounds of rutting from the bedroom. Fists clenched, he concentrated on the noises of the city—horns blaring, tires spinning, people laughing and yelling from the tavern beneath their apartment, the low belch of a foghorn from a ship in the harbor, the scratch of mice in the walls, anything, *anything* but the moans of pleasure and pain that erupted from the bedroom.

Feeling like a coward, he tried to sleep and woke up later to hear his mother pouring a drink. They—his parents—were standing in the kitchen in the dark, the lights of the city allowing enough illumination so that Daegan, even through nearly closed eyes, could watch them.

Frank was standing behind her, his head was bowed into her shoulder, his arms firmly around her waist, pulling her buttocks tight against him. "I didn't mean what I said earlier—about the boy."

Never did Frank refer to him by name.

"If only you'd love him." Her voice had that forlorn, world-weary tone Daegan had come to hate.

"I've tried to, Mary Ellen, really I have. But he's so different from my other kids. I'm not much good with them, either."

"But Daegan's special."

"Probably. So are the others. Christ. It's all so goddamned complicated."

She twisted in his arms and handed him the drink. "He needs a father, Frank."

"I know, I know, kitten, but it can't be me."

"He's your flesh and blood."

"So you say."

"You know it. He looks just like you." A pause. She stood on her tiptoes and kissed him lightly on the lips. "You love me, don't you?" she wheedled and there was a weighty pause that nearly broke Daegan's heart.

"You know I do."

"Let Daegan know you care."

"I—" He slid a glance over at the divan and Daegan squeezed his eyes shut. "I don't know how."

"But you know what it's like. Your father—"

"Was a self-centered son of a bitch. We addressed him as sir; he never smiled. Since I was third in line, I didn't count much—not even when William was killed. He sent me to boarding school at six and in the summers I was away at camp."

"So you know how it feels to be ignored by your father."

"Listen, baby," he said gently and Daegan chanced opening one eye a crack. "You have to understand something. No matter what I feel about you—or the kid—nothing's ever gonna change." He kissed her on the neck and shoulders before sliding the strap of her negligee downward and pressing his lips to the top of her breast.

Daegan nearly threw up. Why did she let him touch her that way? Why?

"I want you to marry me, Frank."

"I'm already married, you know that."

"Divorce her."

"I can't."

"You don't love her." Another breathless, silent heartbeat.

"What's love got to do with marriage?"

"Frank, please—"

"She'd take me to the cleaners, Mary Ellen."

"You'd still be rich and we could be together."

"You just don't get it, do you? This"—he motioned broadly to the apartment and Daegan—"isn't what it's all about." He glanced around the dingy room and scowled. "I'll get you a better place."

"I don't want a better place. I want you."

"Oh, baby, quit dreaming, would ya? I'll try to be nicer to the boy, get you into a bigger apartment, but I'll never divorce Maureen."

"But I love you." There were tears in her voice, and Daegan cringed.

"That's why I keep coming back."

"But you sleep with *her.*"

"Not much. I already told you, we have separate bedrooms. Most of the time her door is locked."

"And when it isn't?"

"Then I go to her. She's cold as a fish, just lays there like a statue, her legs spread, her eyes shut, her mouth turned down at the corners, but she thinks it's her duty to sleep with me once in a while. I don't really get it, but I do it."

"I wish you never touched her!"

"Do you? Why don't you show me how much?"

She giggled. "Again?"

"That's why I come here, baby." Lifting her off her feet, Frank carried her into the bedroom and kicked the door shut.

Daegan hated the nights his father came visiting, detested feigning sleep at the sound of Frank Sullivan's heavy tread and the smell of smoke, whiskey, and cologne that followed the big brute of a man into the apartment. Daegan always knew when Frank was coming over.

The apartment was cleaner than usual, and he was told to do his homework quickly and eat a hurried meal of macaroni and cheese and creamed corn while his mother spent hours getting ready, listening to Frank Sinatra records, wearing her best dress, nylon stockings with seams up the back—the kind Frank liked—and heels that elevated her four or five inches. She washed and set her red hair, then worked feverishly plucking her eyebrows, and applying foundation, rouge, lipstick, and God only knew what else from a dozen jars and tubes.

When her hair was combed just right and her earrings in place, she splashed perfume over her neck and shoulders, all because Frank was coming over to spend a few lousy hours in her bedroom humping her and drinking whiskey before leaving as quickly as he'd come, slinking down the stairs and driving off in his Jaguar to the three-storied house on the hill to his wife and real children.

His mother didn't like Frank's wife. "Maureen Smythe—a snob, let me tell you. Oh, she gave Frank a son, but the boy's not strong and handsome like you—takes after her side just like those two snot-nosed daughters with pale skin and pinched faces. But me . . . I gave him a beautiful son who looks like him," she'd said proudly despite the tears standing in her eyes. "A strong, beautiful, good son."

Daegan hated it when she called him beautiful, hated it even worse when she reminded him that he was Frank Sullivan's bastard. He wasn't even sure being good was all it was cracked up to be. Being good was a helluva lot of trouble and not much fun.

By the time Daegan was in the seventh grade, Lucas Bennett was already shoplifting records from the local store and some of the kids were making out. Sandy Kavenaugh, a tenth grader who lived in a dingy apartment on the other side of the alley, bragged that he'd gotten all the way to third base with Kristy Manning, but then the girls always fell for Kavenaugh.

It didn't take long for Daegan to discover that walking on the right side of the law wasn't all that exciting.

At eleven, he started stealing cigarettes and smoking them with his buddies in the littered baseball field behind St. Mark's. By the time he was twelve, he was swiping hubcaps while carousing at night and had already sampled from the priest's stock of wine in the sacristy when, as an altar boy, he was supposed to be cleaning up after service. The temptation of sin was opening to him as he reached adolescence and he was embracing every minute of it.

During lunch break in the eighth grade, he was lucky enough to slip into the cloak room with Tracy Hancock— a tenth-grade girl with pillowy breasts as big as cantaloupes. He'd kissed her with his open mouth, felt her lips part eagerly, and had thrilled when his tongue had touched hers. She'd nearly sucked it out of his mouth and he wondered how much farther she would go. He took a chance and she started breathing fast and didn't slap his hands away when he felt her up, his fumbling fingers reaching into her stitched cotton bra and grazing soft, willing flesh. Her nipples felt like warm little buttons and his cock was so hard it ached as it strained against his fly. He couldn't think, just moved with her, and his mind was blazing with the images he'd seen in a tattered copy of *Playboy* that Sam Crosby kept hidden in his backpack and loaned out for a quarter a night.

Tracy panted in his ear.

He pushed up her sweater and tore at the buttons of her blouse, anxiously shoving the white fabric away with his sweaty hands so that he could look at her breasts— and they promised to live up to their reputation. Pale skin with a faint webbing of blue veins just beneath the surface. Her face was red, her mouth open, her eyes glazed as he rubbed a hand right over her bra. "More," she whispered anxiously, writhing on the floor.

He was afraid he might come in his slacks. Impulsively he'd kissed her collarbone and she moaned, her legs wrapping around his middle. Then, with thick fingers, he unlatched her bra and saw the famous Hancock boobs in all their glory. Huge and white, with little pink nipples that stood proudly at attention. Heaven. He was in heaven. She arched upward, inviting him to touch her even more, proud of the biggest bra size in all of St Mark's.

They felt so good. They filled up his hands as he rubbed. "Good, that's good," she whispered from the back of her throat. So hard he felt like he was about to explode, he started kissing her and tasting her and licking at her nipples. With a soft moan, she started moving her hips against him, practically begging for it as he suckled. His blood was pounding in his ears, his crotch aching. Oh, God, were they going to *do it?* Right here in the cloak room with nuns in the lower hallway and pictures of Jesus hung near the door?

He reached under the waistband of her skirt, felt her shiver in anticipation, and touched a warmth so divine he thought he might die and go to heaven. Tracy's fingers worked at his fly. *Oh, God, oh, God, oh*—the sound of leather scraping against wood caught his attention. Footsteps. Coming fast and hard. Tracy didn't seem to notice, she was sprawled beneath him, her legs in knee-high stockings spread wide. Instinctively, he yanked her sweater down, hiding her tits. There was a sharp, judgmental gasp as the hangers and coats parted with a whoosh.

"What're you doin' . . . ?" Tommy Shoenborn, a nee-

dle-nosed little kid with a big mouth and dirty fingernails who was still praying he'd go through puberty
someday, had come searching for his parka and found
them panting and groping on the floor of the closet.
"Oh, my God, oh my God, oh my God! Sister Clare! Sister Clare!" Tommy, a suck-up from day one, stared
down at them. "Daegan and Tracy are fornicating!"

Daegan scrambled to his feet, grabbing Tommy by
his collar and shoving him up against the wall. "Shh!
Say a word and I swear I'll kill you."

Tracy, red-faced and mortified, slapped Daegan sound-
ly, her boobs swaying deliciously before she reached
under her sweater, hooked her bra deftly, and tossed her
hair away from her face. "Stay away from me, Daegan
O'Rourke," she said. "If you ever try that again, I'll send
my brother after you!" She shouldered her way past the
coats and a gaped-faced Tommy and Daegan.

His first sexual experience had cost him. Pitying, reproachful looks from the nuns, extra homework, his
hands whipped with the pointer until they bled, and
about a million whispered rosaries, all acts of contrition
to seek forgiveness for his sins, but with each "Hail
Mary" he uttered, he sent up a silent prayer of thanks to
God for allowing him a chance to touch the spectacular
Hancock breasts.

In a vain attempt to restore her tattered reputation,
Tracy had never even glanced his way again, but the
girls at St. Mark's had been intrigued. Already a curiosity because he was a bastard, Daegan had gained a certain fascination. The girls had all thought he was
naughty and seductive, and with his new prestige as a
nasty boy interested in sex, he'd become suddenly popular. Only a few prim and proper girls hadn't openly
wanted to experiment with him.

The boys had been awed that he'd actually touched

Tracy's nubile body and wanted intimate accounts of the size, shape, and texture of her boobs. Derrick Cawfield, a kid with freckles the color of his short hair, swore that he beat off every night just thinking about the twin pleasure mounds. Even Sandy Kavenaugh, older and the most sexually advanced of all the boys Daegan knew, was impressed. Sandy made it his personal mission to try and feel Tracy up and give her a hickey on one of those incredible tits.

Daegan's teachers were concerned, and the flashes of insight he caught from them told him that they thought he'd never amount to anything. Beneath Sister Clare's patient smile was a thought that bothered him. *Poor dear. He can't help himself. Its a shame he was born to such a loose woman. Such a smart boy, but so willful.*

Sister Evangeline was worse. *Should never have agreed to let him enroll. A bad seed if there ever was one. Devil child, born to a slut who sleeps with a married man. If it weren't for the money Frank Sullivan offered for a new gymnasium, I'd expel him on the spot. God would understand. This one, Daegan O'Rourke, is a child of Satan.*

And Tracy Hancock was no better. Though she never outwardly gave him the time of day again, he saw a glimmer in her mind as she wondered what it would be like to go all the way with him.

Daegan's teachers began advising his mother that he was wandering down the treacherous and painful road of sin.

Sister Mae glowered at him—though he thought she had a curious twinkle in her eyes; priests, after punishing him with a paddle, counseled him on the temptations of the flesh and gave him extra duties around the school, along with long prayer sessions where, on bent knees, he was supposed to be begging the Father's forgiveness, but Daegan had never regretted his experience with Tracy for one second.

As Daegan entered high school and fought against his ever-present lust, the entire situation with his father became too much to bear. He saw Frank Sullivan for the useless son of a bitch he was—a spineless coward who made him sick. Too old to pretend that he didn't know what was going on in the bedroom, Daegan left before each of Frank's visits. His mother always protested violently, having some screwed-up idea that they—the three of them—were some kind of pathetic family, but he just grabbed his worn leather jacket and ignored her pleas as he slipped outside, turned up his collar, and climbed down the stairs past the back entrance to the Cat O'Nine Tails Tavern. He'd rather hang out at pool halls and beer joints even though he was underage than listen to his mother and his jack-off of a father go at it.

Those years he worked a little, stole a lot, and swore that if he ever met Frank Sullivan in the light of day, he'd beat the living shit out of him.

Matter of fact, he looked forward to the opportunity.

Daegan met his cousins for the first time when he was just shy of eighteen. Though he'd known of them for years, seen them from a distance, he wasn't certain that they'd been told about him when one night, out of the blue, Beatrice approached him.

It was near Christmas and he was hanging out at one of the pool halls in South Boston, smoking and telling disgusting jokes, wishing the owner, Shorty O'Donnell, didn't know he was underage so that he could order a beer. The heater rattled as it pumped hot air from vents dark with smoke and grime.

Above the sounds of laughter and scratchy Christmas music coming from a tiny radio near the window, he heard the door open. A bell jangled announcing a new player—a potential patsy. A whoosh of cold air rushed into the room, and even though he was poised over the shot, he swore he heard, *How could anyone stand to be in here for more than two seconds?*

He missed the shot and looked up.

"Would ya look at that?" one man whispered.

Another, the guy with the droopy eye and tattoo of a skull on his arm, let out a long, appreciative whistle. Heads all around him swiveled. Eyes slitted.

Beatrice didn't fit in the cavernous room. Wearing a fur-lined jacket, kid gloves, and matching boots, she didn't look a thing like the rest of the few women who frequented Shorty's. They usually hung around their boyfriends, wore short leather skirts or jeans, sucked on suds, and smoked silently. Their hair was teased, their makeup on the thick side, their teeth not close to being even for the most part.

Beatrice Sullivan's patrician looks reeked of blue blood and money. She spied her cousin and sauntered up to him. "So you're Daegan O'Rourke," she said as he leaned over a pool table marred by neglected cigarettes left burning throughout the years.

"That's right." He made the shot indifferently though his heart was really racing. Why had she come looking for him? The spit in his mouth dried up. The cue ball smacked into the number seven ball, which ricocheted into the corner pocket. He moved around the table, using the chalk, never meeting her eyes, as if he didn't give a damn that she'd obviously followed him. What did he care?

A lot, he realized with a sick jolt. He cared a whole lot more than he should have.

"I'm Beatrice. Everyone calls me Bibi."

"I know." He was starting to sweat. The pool cue slipped in his hands.

"We're related."

He made a deprecating sound in the back of his throat. "Not really. Look, I've got a game to play. There's money involved. You want something?"

"How much?"

"What?"

"How much money's involved?"

For the first time in his life he tried to look into some-one's mind and failed miserably. As he'd matured, his ability, the one he'd cursed so violently, had weakened. "Why?"

"I've got something more interesting to do."

"I'll bet, baby," a thick-headed guy with a flattop yelled.

"How much?"

Daegan thought about the five bucks he had riding on this game. Nothing to her. A fortune to him. "Enough."

"Leave it."

"Sure," he said sarcastically. As he tried to make his next shot, she leaned her hip against the table, directly in his line of view. Her skirt was wool, her legs long, and she looked as out of place here as a five-carat diamond in a bucket of gravel. "I think we should talk."

"Why?"

"Family matters."

He raised an eyebrow, cast her a drop-dead glance, and said, "I don't have much family."

"You'll have less if you don't lose the attitude."

He straightened and folded his arms over his chest, pinning his cue stick between his T-shirt and forearms. "I'm busy."

She laughed. "This is how you spend your nights?"

"I'm asking again. Just what is it you want?"

Her gaze slid around the room, to the other men who were gawking at her openly, like hungry wolves around a wounded lamb. "We should talk in private."

"This is as private as I get."

"That's not what I heard." A wicked little smile played upon lips that glistened a soft shade of pink.

A chorus of "Whoas" swelled around him.

"Maybe you heard wrong."

"I don't think so."

"Look, Beatrice—"

"Bibi."

"I don't see any reason to—"

"Have it your way. I'll be in the car." She checked her watch and Lefty O'Riley, a pickpocket at the next table, greedily eyed all seventeen jewels. "You've got ten minutes." Leaving a cloud of perfume in her wake, she strolled out of the pool hall and the clicking of cue balls stopped. Everyone in the building watched her rump sway as she made her way outside.

"Hell," Daegan growled, glancing at the bills laid flat against the corner of the table, then tossed his stick to the guy he'd been playing and followed her.

"Hey, you can't walk out on a game!" Bill Schubert called.

He didn't reply, just snagged his beat-up leather jacket off a hook near the door and swung outside, where the winter wind ripped through him like a chain saw. His boots crunched on snow that had fallen, half melted, and refrozen. Several men had gathered near a fire that crackled in a trash can, warming fingers that poked through tattered gloves, their bodies wrapped in long coats, their collective breath fogging the air.

A car, a big black Cadillac with smoky windows, was idling in the loading zone. The back door was open. Waiting. Exhaust clouded from the tail pipe and strains of "The Little Drummer Boy" floated from the interior.

I knew he'd come, she said without speaking.

He jabbed his hands into his pockets and crossed the sidewalk.

The distinct impression that he was going to make the single worst decision of his life tonight and there wasn't much he could do about it nagged at him.

Bibi and whatever she had planned was waiting. For him. About to change his life.

Daegan took a deep breath, decided he didn't have much to lose anyway, and ducked in the buttery soft interior of the Cadillac.

Chapter 7

Bibi wasn't alone. Stuart, her older brother, the golden child of the Sullivan family, sat in the driver's seat of the luxury car, drumming his fingers impatiently on the top of the steering wheel. She sat beside him, couched in soft leather and fur.

Already second-guessing himself, Daegan slid into the backseat.

The heir-apparent turned and looked over his shoulder. "I'm Stu." Close-cropped brown hair and piercing blue eyes.

"Daegan."

"I know. Close the door." As Daegan yanked the door shut, Stuart stepped on the accelerator. Tires squealed, slush sprayed, and Daegan began to feel as if he were in a trap—one of those rooms where the walls ever so slowly begin to move closer together, promising to squeeze the living breath out of anyone in their steady, relentless path.

"I suppose you wondered why we came looking for you," Stu said in a voice that sounded as if he were modulating the debate team. He was a lot older than Daegan, over twenty, and smooth as expensive glass. He'd been wearing a tie but it had been tossed carelessly over the seat. His wool sports jacket was navy herringbone, his features definably patrician, and he drove with his hands barely on the wheel, as if by the sheer power of his will the Cadillac responded to him.

Through the city streets they sped, past the tenements and warehouses of Daegan's neighborhood. "You are curious, right?" Stuart prompted when Daegan didn't answer his question. Sullivan's blue eyes met his in the rearview mirror. "You'd like to know why we'd bother looking you up."

"It crossed my mind."

Stu glanced over his shoulder, flashing a thousand-watt smile. "We—Bibi and I—thought it was time you met the family."

Daegan felt a tic stirring in the corner of his jaw. "What if I don't want to?"

Stuart slammed on the brakes. Daegan flew against the front seat. The big car skidded on the ice, nearly turning sideways near an old boarded-up warehouse and fish cannery. "Then you can get out," Stuart said in that same near-bored voice.

"Oh, don't!" Bibi interjected. She pushed on the lighter and was fiddling with a tape in the dash. "And stop driving like a maniac, you're going to kill us all." She placed an arm over the back of her seat and twisted to face Daegan. "It's going to be fun."

"Fun?" Daegan repeated, mentally kicking himself.

"Sure. Collin's going to be there and . . ." Music drifted from hidden speakers. Rolling Stones. Not really an upper-crust band. "Let's spend the night together. Now I need you more than ever . . ."

"Collin?" Daegan's throat threatened to close. His half brother. The boy Mary Ellen had always compared to Daegan. Collin, of course, had always come up short every time in Mary Ellen O'Rourke's biased opinion. He was thin, blond, and pale like his mother, not strapping. Often sick. In her words, "a snot-nosed wimp."

Bibi found a cigarette in her purse. "Yeah, and Bonnie and Alicia, too."

"Your choice," Stuart said as he glanced at Daegan in the rearview mirror with those placid eyes. But in the blue depths, Daegan saw something else, a bit of evil. He didn't have a glimmer into Stuart's mind, but there was just a hint of a smile on his face, a wicked little ghost of a grin that indicated he anticipated a great sport, one in which Daegan would be a primary player.

"Where are we going?"

"As I said, to a party—a very private party." Stuart's eyes, in the mirror, narrowed just a fraction.

"What kind of party?" he asked, more nervous than ever though he'd never admit it.

"One for all the cousins," Stuart said. "Kind of a coming out party. For you."

"Oh, Stu, stop it." Bibi lit her cigarette and took a long drag. "You know, I was wrong. This was a shitty idea."

"Whose was it?" Stu asked.

"It was just a joke," she said, smoke sifting from her nose. "I had no idea you'd actually go for it."

"But it's brilliant, darling," he said and touched her lightly on the cheek.

So they'd cooked this up together, whatever it was, and already Bibi was regretting her part. Not good; not good at all. *Get out, Daegan, get out now while you still have some pride.*

"Where is this party?"

"Out of town. At the lake."

"Daddy's summer house," Bibi said, frowning.

"What's it gonna be, O'Rourke?" Stu demanded. "You think you're man enough to face the family?"

In the deep cushions, Daegan bristled. He'd never been one to turn down a dare, even when he knew he was going to regret it. "As long as my old man's not there."

"Frank?" Stu snorted the name in disgust. "Don't worry. This is a closed party. Invitation only. Uncle Frank didn't make the cut."

"But I did."

"Yeah." There was a smile in Stu's voice. "You definitely did." He twisted the wheel, and they were off again, the smooth engine of the Caddie purring through the night. Daegan had ridden in his share of cars, even though his mother didn't own one, but this was the best. The lights of the city swirled past the shaded glass windows. Music and smoke drifted through the warm interior. He started to relax and listen to the Stones. Maybe this wouldn't be so bad after all.

Daegan changed his mind when the electronic gates of some obscure piece of Sullivan real estate parted and Stuart nosed the Caddie along a snow-crusted lane. Several other cars had passed through the wrought-iron fencing and left deep ruts in the otherwise pristine drifts. Fir trees, their boughs laden with a heavy blanket of white, were overburdened compared to their naked counterparts—stark, leafless maple and oak trees that seemed to lift their black skeletal arms to the sky.

Daegan's mouth was dry and he'd kill for one of the cigarettes that Bibi so carelessly smoked, but he didn't say a word, not even when the forest parted and a house the likes of which he'd never seen before came into view. Sprawled upon the banks of a vast lake, three stories of red Sullivan brick rose upward. On either side, single-storied wings swept away from the tall center. White stone edged each corner, and six or seven chimneys, one of which spewed smoke into the clear evening air, stood like sentinels on the roof. Tall windows glowed in the night, the panes shimmering with ice, black shutters open. A behemoth of a house.

Daegan bit his tongue. So this was how the Sullivans lived. It was enough to make him sick when he thought of the hours his mother put in at the textile mill, how her feet and back ached each night, how she rubbed the knots from her fingers and the back of her neck after getting off her shift, how she waited by the phone, smoking silently, hoping *he* would call.

Stuart parked near the porch behind a new Jaguar. Smoothing the sides of his hair, he flashed Daegan one of his killer smiles. "Show time."

"Oh, Christ," Bibi groaned as she jabbed out what had to have been her third cigarette. Pursing her lips, she offered Daegan a look of apology as they climbed out of the car, then, as if embarrassed, wouldn't glance his way again. The air was crisp, cold, and clear, the night silent. No noise of city, no smell of exhaust, no ever-present throngs of people bustling around. No, this place, in its mantle of white, was serene and stately.

Stuart reached the door and flung it open, motioning gallantly for Daegan to enter. Impulsively Bibi took Daegan's fingers in her hand and squeezed. "If this gets too hairy, let me know. I'll get you out of here."

"I can handle myself," he said, yanking his hand away and stuffing both fists into his front pockets. If this was going to be a sideshow, so be it. He wasn't going to come out looking like a wimp and leaning on a woman.

The interior of the house reminded Daegan of a seldom-used museum. A sweeping staircase rose from the hallway to the second floor, split and climbed to the third. Oak floors were polished to a mirror finish then decorated with rugs that looked like they came from some place in the Far East. Antiques and mirrors, tables and lamps, living plants and paintings of dead ancestors filled the corners. Music was playing through hidden speakers—some classical piece performed by an orchestra. "This way," Stu said, leading them through a short hallway where Daegan heard the first sound of voices.

". . . I don't care; this was a dumb idea. Mummy will kill us if she finds out," the nasal voice of a girl complained. "What is this surprise of Stu's anyway? Really, he can be such a bore."

"If it weren't for Stu, how much fun would we ever have?" whined Collin. Though he'd never met him face-to-face, Daegan had heard his voice often enough at a distance. He gritted his teeth.

"I love surprises," another younger, female voice said excitedly.

"Mummy will skin us alive." The first girl—probably snotty Alicia. Daegan felt as if a rope had settled over his neck. With each step, the noose tightened.

"She'll never know." Collin again.

Hell, this was a crazy idea. What was he doing here? Why had he agreed to come?

"Whatever Stu's cooked up, you can bet it will be good."

Daegan's stomach clenched into a knot of apprehension, and he wondered what had possessed him to leave the familiar and comfortable surroundings of Shorty's Pool Hall. He didn't have to be told that he was about to step into the middle of a three-ring circus and he was the main attraction. He slid a glance in his eldest cousin's direction, but didn't get a clue as to his true motives. Just what the hell was Stuart Sullivan's game? As he had before, he tried to look into the older boy's mind, but to no avail; Stuart's thoughts were as closed to him as a sealed vault.

They walked into a room that spanned the back of the house, and for the first time in his life, Daegan met his half-brother and -sisters. Silhouetted against a brilliant, crackling blaze, Frank's other children were clustered around a huge fireplace faced in marble. For a split second, Daegan thought he caught a glimpse of his own personal vision of hell.

"Oh, shit," Collin said softly. The glass in his hand nearly fell to the floor.

"What's the meaning of this—?" the taller girl, Alicia, asked. Her blue, frosty gaze landed on Daegan with all the warmth of an arctic storm. Her skin was pale, her mouth set in condemnation. "Stuart, how could you?"

Bonnie, smaller than her sister, bit her lip. "That's—"

"We know who he is," Alicia snapped, fury burning in the sudden hot spots on her cheeks. "You said we were going to have a party!" she said, seething as she glared at Stuart.

"We are. A private party." Stuart was as calm as Alicia was enraged. "I thought it was time we all got to know each other."

"Bastard!"

"Not me," Stuart said easily and Daegan wanted to strangle him.

Bonnie just stared at Daegan as if he were the reincarnation of the devil himself.

"We're all family here," Stuart said.

"*Pleeeeease.*" Bibi reached into her leather handbag for her cigarettes. "Give me a break. Family?"

"Sure, we are. Daegan's our cousin and their brother."

"Get this straight, Stuart. He's not *my* brother," Alicia said. She tossed her long, blond curls over her shoulder. "He's—"

"Here. In Uncle Robert's house. Why?" Collin asked, folding his arms over his chest. Slender, with even features and smooth skin, he was dressed in a wool sweater and slacks, his dark blond hair combed neatly.

Bibi clicked her lighter to the end of a cigarette.

Bonnie flopped down on the cushions of a tufted couch and continued to stare at him as if he were an oddity under a microscope—an interesting organism she couldn't hope to understand.

"Because it's time," Stuart said, striding over to the bar and lifting a crystal glass from a dust-free shelf. He sorted through an array of gleaming bottles. "I don't know about you, but I'm sick to death of hearing about him—well, not to my face, of course—but behind closed doors. I thought we should all meet each other and get it over with. Come on, Collin, you have to admit, you've been curious for a long time and you"—his gaze swept back to Daegan—"I know you wanted to see what we're all like. You used to climb up in the tree by the church on Sunday mornings, just to catch a glimpse of us going into Mass."

Daegan wanted to deny it, but just shrugged. No reason to lie. Obviously Stuart had watched him.

"You sneaky little bastard," Alicia spat out. "You were spying on us?" Her voice rose an angry octave.

"Yeah," Daegan admitted, sick of her holier-than-thou attitude

"It wasn't a big deal," Stuart said as he found a bottle of scotch and poured himself a stiff shot. "It wasn't as if you were stripping or running around in your bra and panties, now, was it?"

"Stuart!" Bibi cut in.

"Just pointing out the obvious."

Alicia's mouth rounded in horror. "You're disgusting," she told her oldest cousin, and Stuart had the audacity to grin back at her.

"I don't think so. Anyone else want a drink?"

"No!" Alicia said swiftly.

"Sure." Collin nodded, then tossed back the remains of the one he'd been working on.

"Why not?" Bibi asked.

Stuart's gaze found Daegan's and held. "How about you?"

Daegan knew he should keep a clear head, but he couldn't resist a taste of rich man's fare. Besides, his throat was dry as sand. "Yeah."

"You're pouring him a drink?" Alicia shook her head in disbelief. "Stuart, you can't just haul him up here and—"

"Can it!" Bibi cut in.

"Isn't this illegal?" Bonnie's little eyebrows drew together and she chewed on her lip nervously. "We're not old enough—"

"Highly illegal," Stuart assured her as he passed out the glasses and clicked his to Daegan's. "Welcome to the family," he said mockingly as the fire popped and hissed. "You'll never find a worse set of lying cutthroats, cheats, and whoremongers than the Sullivans of Boston."

"I won't be a part of this." Alicia's body quivered in outrage and her nostrils flared in disgust. "You've gone too far this time, Stu. Too damned far."

Stuart's eyes sparkled. "That's what you love about me, isn't it?" His wink was slow and sexy, and Daegan's stomach revolted when he realized that Stuart got his kicks by manipulating everyone, making them all uncomfortable. He wasn't just playing with Daegan, but the whole damned family.

"It's what I *hate* about you," she clarified.

"Then let me point out that you're a part of it whether you like it or not." Stuart's smile held zero warmth. "Sit down and shut up."

"I will not—"

"Do it," Collin ordered, and Alicia, in all her self-righteous rage, refused, stood her ground, and rested a hip on the polished surface of a babygrand piano. Her jaw was set so tight the skin over her chin was stretched thin. "I think Stuart's right."

"You always think he's right," Alicia charged. "Use your own brain for once, Collin. That is, if you have one."

"I am always right." Stuart seemed to be enjoying himself and he sent an unreadable glance to Collin.

Daegan's skin crawled. There was more going on here than just his personal humiliation; people's emotions were involved—emotions that they all tried to hide and hold secret.

Collin cleared his throat and settled into a club chair near the window. "It's probably time we all got to know each other—"

"No way! I didn't come up here to freeze my ass off and meet the son of some gutter—"

"Don't!" Collin warned, his lips flattening over his teeth in what Daegan assumed was an unusual display of anger. Then, in his most cultured voice, the modulation the perfect mimicry of his sisters, he intoned, "Come now, Alicia, let's not sound common."

"Like him?" She pointed a long finger at Daegan. "He's the son of Daddy's whore, or don't you remember?"

"Nice to meet you, too," Daegan said, unable to hold his tongue any longer. Usually, in a new situation he was quiet, just listened and watched, waiting until he discovered which way the wind was going to blow, but he'd had enough insults for one night. His patience was running thin and anger shot through him. These people—his *family*, if that's what you'd call them—were just a bunch of bickering, petty snobs looking for a night's entertainment to disrupt the boredom of their perfectly planned lives. Who needed it? Curiosity satisfied, he tossed back the scotch, hoping it would be smooth and smoky, but it burned a hot path down his throat and splashed into his already roiling stomach. It was all he could do not to cough and he felt that invisible noose around his neck tightening another notch.

Bibi laughed nervously, but Alicia was far from amused. "I suppose this was your idea," she surmised aloud.

"Yeah, but I was only joking." Bibi tapped the ash from her cigarette into a silver tray.

"So was I," Stuart said with that naughty-boy twinkle in his eye and Daegan decided he wasn't going to stand around and let people talk about him as if he wasn't in the room. He strode to the fireplace, where he warmed his shins and ran a finger along a dark wood mantel that was decorated with antique lanterns and candles. "Who owns this place?"

"Daddy," Bibi said.

"That's open to debate, isn't it?" Collin stared at Daegan with mild curiosity. "The firstborn son of our parents' generation was Uncle William, a war hero in World War II, and killed three weeks before he was going to be married. Since he left no issue, the next in line was Robert, quite a bit younger, but older than the youngest brother. My father. Yours, too, if the local gossip can be believed.

"So, I guess, if we follow the same traditions that have been in the family ever since the old country, most of the estate will pass on to Stu because of his birthright or some such rot."

Stuart laughed and the sound rang through the cavernous rooms. "Unless I die first. Then . . . well, either Bibi gets it or Uncle Frank does. I'm not sure how Grandfather's will was written."

"Like hell," Alicia said, her eyes narrowing thoughtfully. "I'm willing to bet that you know where every dime, nickel, and penny of the estate is and who it goes to. You know, Stuart, just because you're lucky enough to be the firstborn male of the firstborn male—"

"Second born. Remember poor Uncle William," Collin interjected.

"Doesn't matter. I'm just saying that just because Stuart was born first doesn't make him smarter than the rest of us."

"Just luckier," Stuart said. Collin stepped closer to his older cousin, as if Stuart needed protection from Alicia's wicked tongue. Stuart seemed unruffled; if anything, he appeared amused by this little party he'd put together.

Collin finished his drink and set the glass on the bar. "Arguing and picking at each other isn't getting us anywhere."

"Amen," Bibi said under her breath and offered Collin a fragile smile.

"What's the point?" Alicia demanded.

"The point is that we all have a bastard in the family," Stuart said, "and I was just wondering what we're going to do about him."

The imaginary rope around his neck snapped with the flare of Daegan's temper. "Nothing." He'd seen enough. These people were pathetic, all consumed with their family's wealth and not giving a damn about anyone else. He slammed his empty glass onto the mantel and glared pointedly at his eldest cousin. "There's nothing you can do about me and I'm sick of this. If you want some cheap entertainment, go out and watch a porno flick, or laugh at the poor or torture a cat or something but leave me alone." He turned and strode quickly out of the room, his heels clicking loudly against the gleaming wood.

"Wait!" Bibi ran after him.

"He's not going anywhere," Stuart said confidently as Daegan strode out of the room and down the hallway. He couldn't catch his breath in this stuffy old house filled with antiques, hot air, and inflated, prejudiced opinions. What had he been thinking when he'd slid into the seductive interior of the Cadillac?

"Idiot," he ground out, his fist clenching. He slammed it into one of the walls, splintering the old plaster. What a fool he'd been to come here! Why hadn't he listened to his own gut feelings? What twisted sense of curiosity had lured him here? Every instinct had warned him to avoid the Sullivans like the proverbial plague and yet he'd allowed himself to be seduced; he'd wanted to be a part, just for a few seconds, of the family. Well, now he knew what they were made of and he didn't like any of them. Including Bibi.

She caught up with him and grasped his arm. "Look, Daegan, please. Just stop for a second."

He didn't break stride, just threw her off.

"I'm sorry."

"Forget it."

"No, really, Daegan—"

Spinning around so quickly his body slammed up against hers, he grabbed both her arms and pushed her against the wall. A picture of Rose Kennedy rattled and fell to the floor, glass shattering everywhere. Bibi's eyes widened in fear. "I don't want your apologies," he growled, feeling not the least bit of remorse when she tried to pull away and he only pinned her in his punishing grip. "I don't want your excuses, and most of all, I don't want your pity." He let go of her then. "I should never have come here."

"Why did you?" she demanded.

Good question. A damned good question. "I was stupid and couldn't help myself." Walking through the front door, he heard other voices getting closer. Great. Stuart and his flock of ninnies were following after him to see what the poor, pathetic *bastard* would do. "It won't happen again." As he strode down the icy steps, he thought about "borrowing" one of the Sullivan fleet, but decided against it. With his luck, one of them would press charges. It galled him to think that for even one second he had envied them and wanted to be accepted. Well, not anymore. For all he cared, everyone bearing the last name of Sullivan could rot merrily in hell.

The path that led behind the lake house to the indoor tennis court was covered with snow, a smooth white blanket glazed with ice. Cool, pristine, glossy, much like the facade of the Sullivan family.

But that facade was now marred by the appearance of Daegan O'Rourke, the bastard son who had reared his head like the straggly brown weed that poked through the snow cover, corrupting the serene winterscape. Yes, he was an insipid weed that threatened to crack the smooth veneer of the family.

Not that the Sullivans were perfect. They had their share of blemishes. Liars and adulterers, drinkers and cheats. But Father O'Meara was always reminding the parishioners that no one was perfect, that God had made man a flawed creature. Original sin started with Adam and Eve in the Garden. Maybe that explained Frank Sullivan's incredible lapse to have conceived a bastard out of wedlock, let alone encourage the kid by continuing to mess around with his mother.

No sin goes unpunished. But now, were they all going to have to pay for Frank Sullivan's sin? Was this bastard son planning to insinuate himself into the family?

The tennis court was chilly inside, but light flooded the shiny floor at the touch of a switch. A basket of balls would help ease the tension brought on by the unwanted bastard. The nerve of Daegan O'Rourke, coming here and thinking he could possibly belong, thinking he would ever be accepted as a Sullivan when in truth he was a mistake of nature, a stupid accident. Well, he would be hard-pressed to pass himself off as a Sullivan.

A tennis ball lingered in the air as if suspended, then went soaring over the net.

A second ball hovered for a moment before it, too, was slammed onto the court.

Each serve a blow to Daegan O'Rourke.

Each forceful swing a strike at his skull.

Each direct hit a vow of the violent pounding he would suffer if he ever dared tangle with the Sullivans again.

"It won't happen again," Daegan had promised during his hasty exit.

Perfect, because never would be too soon to see the dark, handsome face that resembled Frank Sullivan more than any of his children—his *real* children. If Daegan O'Rourke was smart, he would keep his distance and stay far, far away from the Sullivan clan. He would learn that the Sullivans were a family to be reckoned with.

And if he didn't?

He would have to be stopped.

Daegan didn't see any of the Sullivans for two months. After hitchhiking back to the city from the mansion on the lake, he avoided any place he thought a Sullivan might show up. Which wasn't hard. Before Stuart's little get-together, the whole tribe had acted as if he hadn't ever existed. As far as he was concerned, they could go back to that scenario.

His good luck ran out one blistering cold day in February. He worked after school for a fuel company. Shoveling coal, pumping oil into huge trucks, and stacking cords of firewood were his primary jobs—backbreaking labor that helped keep him out of trouble and honed his muscles.

He didn't expect Bibi to show up, but as he walked away from the manager's office, his meager paycheck folded in his back pocket, he blew on his fingers for warmth and saw her leaning against the fender of a silver Corvette. Several of the guys changing shifts slowed their stride. Whistling, they eyed her long legs and big bust along with the sleek lines and wide tires of her car. Daegan didn't know which was likely to give them more of a hard-on—Bibi's sultry pout or the menacing throb of the Corvette's engine.

"Daegan!" She flagged him down, waving frantically.

Homer Kroft, a forty-year-old guy with a beer belly and oil on his hands, glanced over his shoulder and winked at Daegan.

"Looks like you got yourself an admirer," he said with a low, leering laugh. "Boy what I wouldn't do to ride in that—or on her."

"Enough," Daegan said swiftly though why he chose to defend Bibi's honor was beyond him. She only spelled trouble. Sullivan trouble. After Homer and the rest of the workers had left the shipping yard, Daegan approached her warily. "Slumming?"

"Maybe." She managed a smile.

"What is it you want?"

"To see you."

"Why?"

"I wish to God I knew," she admitted with a vexed little frown that showed how perplexed she was with herself. "I just didn't want you to think that we're all horrible."

"Aren't you?"

She smiled a little and gnawed at her lip. "Not all the time."

"Humph." What was he doing talking to her? "If that's all you wanted to say—"

"No! I mean I'd like to make it up to you."

"Don't bother."

"I—I think we should try to—"

"To what? Be friends?" he demanded, angry all over again. "What is it with you, huh? Didn't you get enough kicks last time?"

"Whether you like it or not, you *are* part of the family."

"Don't kid yourself," he snapped, shoving his face close to hers so he wouldn't have to shout. His hand fisted and he wished he had something, anything, to hit. "My old man has never said one word to me. Not one, Bibi. Oh, sure, he gives Ma some money for the rent, but he never seems to find it in his heart to see that she's promoted to a better job, and when he shows up at the apartment, I make sure I'm out. It's easier that way. He isn't reminded of his mistake and I'm not faced with the fact that my old man is ashamed of me. Almost as much as I'm ashamed of him. And just so we're clear on this. I don't like you or anyone else in the family. I think you're all a bunch of shallow, greedy, overbearing snobs who have nothing better to do than plan your next tennis match and argue about what stupid charitable committee you plan to be a part of. All anyone in the family cares about is money. The truth of the matter is that if I'd had a choice, I'd rather be related to pit vipers!"

She wasn't the least bit unnerved. "Frank's an asshole."

"You got that right."

"If it makes you feel any better, he barely speaks to his other kids. But not everyone's so bad."

"Of course not," he mocked. "You're all a bunch of goddamned saints." With that he stalked off and felt his paycheck in his back pocket. Wages for two weeks' work. Probably not enough to make one payment on Bibi's flashy car. Not that it mattered.

His breath, a short burst of angry air, fogged. In his wake, he heard a car door open and slam shut. An engine roared. Gears clicked. Tires squealed in a sharp U-turn. Within seconds she was driving in the alley next to him, wheeling around the trash cans and crates, her window rolled down. "Can I give you a lift?"

"Oh, sure. How about to Jamaica?"

"I'm serious."

"So am I."

"Jamaica's an island."

"Guess that's a 'no.'"

"Daegan——"

"Listen, Bibi, just step a little harder on the pedal under your right foot and drive away."

"Why do you hate me?"

He barked out a laugh. "Take a guess."

"I said I'm sorry."

"Fine. You're sorry," he said angrily without glancing in her direction. "Listen, I don't even know you and that's the way I'd like to keep it." He glanced skyward, past the sharp angles of fire escapes and the high brick walls scarred by graffiti. Some of the boarded-over tenements were nearly two hundred years old and had once housed Irish immigrants when they first set foot on American soil—Sullivans and O'Rourkes of generations gone by. The Sullivan family had thrived in the new land, working, saving, buying wisely, and amassing a fortune, while the O'Rourkes, for the most part, had become laborers generation after generation. As his mother toiled in the textile factory, so would he in some other dead-end O'Rourke job. He might even drink himself to death as his granddad had.

Clouds, as gray as his thoughts, scudded across a sky that was darkening as night approached.

Bibi was driving beside him, keeping pace, her window rolled down, her blue eyes stormy. She, a Sullivan, would never know an empty stomach or a thirst for money so powerful he was willing to sell his soul to break the cycle of O'Rourke bad luck.

Maybe Bibi, in her need, could offer him a way out, but then he'd have to swallow his much-prized pride.

"What have I done that's so wrong?"

"Set me up."

"I . . . I didn't mean to."

"Cruel joke, Bibi."

"It wasn't supposed to be."

"Sure it was."

"But I didn't know it," she said. "Really, Daegan, don't despise me because of Stu's perverted sense of humor."

This was a mistake. "I don't despise you."

"You act like it."

For the love of God, he nearly felt sorry for her. What was wrong with him? She was putting on an act, using her endless female charms to try and find a way to humiliate him again.

"What if I told you I want to know you?" she demanded.

"I'd say you were a bored rich girl looking for a cheap thrill."

"I'm not."

He didn't answer, just kept walking. What a sight they must look, him greasy and tired from a long day at the fuel company, her impeccably well groomed as she wheeled her expensive car through the narrow, refuse-filled alleys. A cat scrambled out of their path and watched from the top of a trash bin.

Bibi sighed loudly. "I do understand, you know. I don't fit in either. Never have. Stuart and Collin are always together, laughing and talking and keeping secrets. Alicia's a first-class bitch and Bonnie's just a kid."

"What do you care?" he threw back at her and the question ricocheted through his mind. *What do you care, O'Rourke? Why even keep up this conversation?*

"I don't like being left out."

"It's not so bad." Christ, the irony of it. Now he was trying to make her feel better about some tiff she'd had with her shit of a brother and cousin. "Why don't you go and lay all this on Alicia?" He reached into his jacket pocket for a pack of cigarettes and shook one out.

"We don't get along."

"What a shame." He couldn't keep the sarcasm from his voice.

"I was hoping we could be friends."

"No you weren't. You're not that stupid."

"You really are a bastard, you know that, O'Rourke?"

The same old bad taste climbed up his throat. "So I've been told."

"Don't take it to heart."

He jabbed a cigarette into the corner of his mouth. "Why're you interested?"

"Because you're part of the family—the interesting part," she said boldly. "And I want to know you better."

"Why?"

Her smile was sincere. "Believe it or not, I think I like you."

"Jesus, quit kidding yourself!" He clicked his lighter to his cigarette and, as the tobacco caught flame, drew in a deep calming drag. "You just find me amusing right now."

"Maybe, but that's good enough for me," she said as she gunned the engine and the Corvette leaped forward, nearly knocking him over as she sped through the alley.

"Getting to know me is a mistake," he muttered, but she was already gone, the taillights of her expensive car flashing bright red in the alley ahead. His eyes thinned against the smoke as he thought. No doubt she'd be back. She had that stubborn look about her, one that said she didn't give up easily.

So what the hell was he gonna do with her?

He wasn't wrong. A week later she showed up, waiting for him after work, her rear propped against the hood of her shiny car as he ended his shift and started walking home.

Homer Kroft nudged him in the ribs with an elbow. "Looks like you got yourself a little piece of uptown."

"Shut up."

"When you're through with her—"

Daegan spun then, grabbed the older man's arm. "Give it a rest, man!" he ordered, his teeth clenched so hard they ached.

"Okay, okay." Homer raised his hands in mock surrender. "Jesus H. Christ, back off." He wandered off toward the bus station and Daegan approached his cousin.

"I thought I told you to leave me alone," he growled as he walked up to her, ignoring the wolf whistles from some of the guys during the shift change.

"I can't."

"Why not?"

She cocked her head to one side and smiled. "Oh, I don't know, maybe I'm just a natural masochist. I can't help but hang out with people who don't like me."

"I never said that." Or had he? He couldn't remember.

"Then let me buy you a cup of coffee or a drink or something." She opened the car door.

He laughed. "I'm not going to fall for that again."

"You can drive," she said, holding the keys in front of his face, letting the metal dangle and clink provocatively before his eyes.

He didn't know what to say. Was she joking? The car was powerful and fast. His throat went dry with anticipation. His fingers itched to grab the keys. "You're not serious."

" 'Course I am."

"But—" He looked down at his greasy overalls and felt worlds apart from her. The way he wanted it.

"Don't worry about it. The car's been dirty before." His heart started pounding hard and fast at the thought of wrapping his fingers around the steering wheel, tromping on the accelerator, and feeling the surge of power that came with all that horsepower. Then he thought of his mother. Nothing the Sullivans gave was without a price—a high price.

"What do you want, Bibi?" he asked suddenly.

"Just to get to know you."

"Oh, hell!"

"I'm not lying," she said, and he touched her then, grabbed her wrist and tried to see into her mind, but the door was closed and the only impression he received was the quick beat of her pulse and the sensation that she was hoping to do something wild and unconventional, something that was against all of Daddy's rules.

Seduced beyond his power to say no, he licked suddenly dry lips. *This is a mistake, O'Rourke,* his rational mind insisted, but desire overruled logic and he lost the mental battle. He stared into her eyes and realized she knew she had him just where she wanted him. "Where would we go?" he asked.

Her smile hinted at sex and mystery. "Wherever you want, Daegan. It's your call. I'm just along for the ride."

Chapter 8

"You're making a fool of yourself. *En garde!*" Stuart lunged at Bibi, the tip of his foil nicking her shoulder as she parried, her fencing shoes squeaking on the old hardwood floor of the gym.

"What else is new?" Thrusting forward, she tried to gain the advantage, but he dodged her blow and she sliced at empty air. Again. Damn, but he was good. Always a natural athlete, Stuart had continually bested her at sports, academics, popularity, conversation, you name it. Several years older, with the edge of testosterone to keep him at an advantage, Stuart couldn't help making her feel that she, his younger sister, was vastly inferior. Yet she kept trying to beat him, no matter what the contest, so today she'd agreed to this stupid fencing match Of course, she was losing.

"I've seen you with O'Rourke," he said, clicking his tongue. "Bad form."

"Seen me?" she repeated, stunned just as his foil drew a nasty line down the front of her metallic plastron. She'd thought she'd been sneaky, that no one besides her and Daegan had a clue.

"Ah, ah, ah." With a final lunge, he won the match "Never let an opponent destroy your concentration. Sorry, Bibi. You lose." He tossed off his mask and gloves. His foil clattered to the floor. Snagging a towel from an ancient hook near the window, he swiped at the sweat that had drizzled from his scalp and flattened his usually neat hair. "As for O'Rourke, you'd better leave him be. He's trouble."

"I don't think so." Bibi fingered the button on her foil, bowing the thin blade. It had taken all of her nerve to seek Daegan out again and his reception to her had been about as warm as Nantucket Sound in December, but slowly he'd come around, met her for coffee a couple of times, only insisting that she let him buy. He'd become less hostile, not so damned brooding and cynical, and she'd seen past his facade, through his tough act to a glimmer of the boy behind the guarded and wary mask, a side to him that she'd found refreshing. "Besides, he doesn't even know I'm alive," she lied, walking over to the window and staring outside through the thick glass. The private gym was spread over the top floor of their house. From this, the fourth floor, she stared down to Louisburg Square, where the first pale rays of sunshine were slanting through branches of trees just starting to leaf.

Stuart rotated the kinks from his neck as Bibi pulled off her mask. "Oh, I bet he knows you're alive and has probably estimated how much you're worth. He's under-educated but far from stupid. We're the ones who should act as if he doesn't exist."

"Change of heart?"

"I just don't like you getting involved with him."

She tossed her hair off her shoulders. "I'm not involved with him or anyone else."

"Don't lie, Bibi." Leaning a shoulder against the old

window ledge, he rubbed his chin and sighed. "You're so poor at it. Anyway, I've seen you with him and so has Collin."

"Collin?" Her head snapped up and she caught a naughty glint of amusement in her brother's eye.

"That's right. He wasn't too pleased, called O'Rourke a . . . let me get this straight . . . 'a dumb-ass lowlife who just wants to see what it's like to get into a rich girl's pants and drive a car he'll never be able to afford.'"

"What?" Bibi whispered, horrified. It was one thing for Stuart to know what she was doing, but not Collin. At least not yet. So far, nothing had happened between Daegan and her. Not that it would. What she did with him was no one's business.

"Well, something along those lines." He scratched a shoulder. "Collin hates the bastard. Somehow thinks he might usurp his right as Frank's firstborn or something." His smile was cold. "Silly, isn't it? Just like his old man."

"You started it by taking Daegan to the summer house."

"And it was fun, admit it. The collective look on our cousins' faces was priceless! I thought Alicia was going to shit her silk drawers, and Collin, damn but he was nearly apoplectic."

"What about Daegan? How do you think he feels?"

"Who cares? Oh! I get it. *You* care. Perpetual friend of the underdog, righter of wrongs, doer of all that is good in the world."

"Not really."

"But that's what you'd like us all to think now, isn't it?" Stuart said as he scooped up his foil as well as hers and hung them neatly in the glass case at the far end of the cavernous room. Weapons of all shapes and sizes were displayed in the cupboard. He fingered a particularly wicked knife with a curved blade. "You'd like us all to believe that you have lofty goals when even you know that you're a fake."

"I'm not—"

"Oh, shove it, Bibi. You don't have to prove anything to me. I know how your mind works and love you anyway." He locked the cabinet and turned to face her, his features set in that superior, don't-question-me-as-I'm-damned-close-to-being-a-deity expression that she'd come to loathe.

She bristled. "Don't you have better things to do than spy on me?"

"It's in all our best interests, and mine specifically, to keep an eye on you."

"Afraid I might soil your reputation?"

"Don't you know me by now?" Stuart's lips stretched into an easy leer. "If anyone dirties my name, believe me, it'll be me and I'll do the deciding of how, who, when, and where." His voice was suddenly oily, as if he found the thought of crossing whatever moral line he'd drawn in his head seductive.

"I thought you wanted to get to know him."

Scowling, he draped the towel around his neck and settled onto a bench of the exercise unit, doing leg curls as he stared at the ceiling. As children, they'd shared their deepest secrets in this room where they'd played, worked out, and sought sanctuary whenever the pressures of being solid, upright Sullivans had become too great. Bibi had practiced ballet at the barre until she'd become too tall and gangly, and Stuart had polished his tennis and squash strokes against the far wall in this room that smelled of generations of Sullivan sweat mingling with lemon-scented oil that was used to wash the floors and walls.

The weights clicked softly with each push of Stuart's muscular thighs. "I guess you have a point," he admitted in un-Stuart-like fashion. "I would like to know him—to find out what makes him tick. Hey, would you add a little weight—ten pounds, I think," he said as Bibi, trained from her youth to do whatever he asked, adjusted the pins in the heavy bars. "I guess he's interesting in a perverted kind of way."

Stuart was sweating again, his face reddening as he kept pushing on the weights. "Why do you think Frank keeps a mistress for twenty years but completely ignores her kid—his bastard? Why, when it's common knowledge that he's got this . . . well, this other family for lack of a better word . . . are we forbidden to talk about it? Why doesn't Aunt Maureen divorce him or force him to give the slut up?"

"Pride."

"Stupidity, if you ask me."

"Maybe she takes lovers herself," Bibi mused and Stuart laughed out loud.

"Can you imagine Maureen doing it with anyone? I think it's a miracle that she's got three kids. That means she had to have sex with Frank at least three times." His face twisted in revulsion and he said in the high falsetto he used to mimic his aunt, "How messy!"

"Stop it." But she couldn't help smiling. Aunt Maureen put the tight in uptight. "You're the one who's perverted."

"Yeah, but I have to work at it. With Frank it comes naturally—kind of like a gift. Maybe from God."

"You're wicked," she teased and his gaze settled into hers in that heart-stopping way she found so unnerving. Sometimes it was as if he could read her mind, see past the barriers she'd so carefully erected, and find his way to the darkest part of her soul.

"So are you, Bibi. And it doesn't stop there. You're as perverted as the rest of us." His smile had disappeared and he was suddenly dead serious.

"Don't turn this around on me—"

"You can't have him."

Her heart stopped.

"It's not decent. Practically incestuous." He said the word as if it tasted delicious. "I think you're fascinated with him because he's the forbidden fruit, you know, kind of like Eve in the Garden of Eden with the snake and the apple."

"And where do you fit in this scenario?"

"I'm the snake, of course."

"And Daegan's the apple?"

"Right . . . and Collin, he's Adam, isn't he?"

"Don't be silly," she said, flushing.

"If you say so. Just be wary of the bastard O'Rourke."

"I feel sorry for him, okay?" Bibi lied as she shook her hair away from her face.

"Sorry for him? For the love of Christ, why?"

"He's poor."

"But free."

"Free?"

"Hell, yes. *He* doesn't have the responsibility of being a Sullivan. He doesn't have to come at anyone's beck and call, does he? Just hangs out in pool halls and bars until he gets kicked out, keeps the hours he wants, and doesn't have to worry that someone isn't the right social station." Stuart let the weights drop with a clang. "That's freedom. Something you or I won't ever feel."

"But he doesn't have any money."

"Maybe he doesn't need it. Maybe money's just a trap to keep a person in line."

"Wait a minute. For years you've been telling me that wealth is freedom."

He climbed to his feet, snatched his towel, and started for the door. She was right on his heels. "I hate to admit it, but maybe I was wrong," Stuart said. "Just for a week, I'd love to feel what it's like to be my own master—dirt poor but able to make my own choices in life. Just for once"—he said, opening the door to the winding steps leading downstairs—"I'd like to tell Dad to 'fuck off.'"

She could barely believe her ears. Stuart liked to use foul language behind his father's back, but he'd never seemed so vehement before, so angry. Even now, after a strenuous workout, his muscles were bunched, his jaw tight.

"So why're you giving me so much grief about seeing Daegan?" she asked, her finger trailing on the rail as they hurried down the stairs.

"Because you're getting *too* involved. Losing your objectivity. All winter long you kept going and visiting him. Instead of looking at him clinically, like a lab specimen, you're beginning to think of him as family . . . or possibly more. He'll start to get ideas."

"I think he's interesting, that's all."

"Oh, sure!" Stuart made a sound of amused disgust and stopped at the final landing, where he turned and faced Bibi on the stair above him. "O'Rourke's dangerous as hell. You'd be smart to stay away from him."

"And you'd be smart to stop spying on me."

"Would I?" His gaze smoldered for a second, raking down the front of her, as if her fencing jacket and breeches were made of clear plastic wrap. "Careful, sis, you're playing with fire."

"That's right, Stu, and you can't make me stop."

He hooked an eyebrow skyward and clucked his tongue. "A challenge, Bibi? You're throwing a challenge in my face? Haven't you learned anything yet?" His eyes sparkled with a fierce anticipation. "I never lose."

* * *

"Frank's coming over tonight and I think it would be nice if you stuck around." Mary Ellen was seated on the faded stool in front of her vanity and tilting her head this way and that as she twisted her hair and pinned it to her head. The radio was playing softly. Neil Diamond's voice warbled through the small rooms.

"Why should I stay?" Not that he was really interested,

"We have a lot to discuss. You're nearly finished with high school; it's time to think about college and Frank promised to—"

"I don't want his money."

"Don't start with me," she warned. "He's paying lots for Collin to go off to Harvard—"

"That's different."

"You're his son—"

"I'm not!" he said harshly. "Don't you get it? God, Ma, what would it take for you to understand? He doesn't claim me and I don't want him." The song ended and a DJ started talking about local news.

"Hog wash." Mary Ellen snapped off the radio.

"I'm serious, Ma. The minute I turn eighteen, I'm outta here. We've already talked about it."

"But I didn't think you meant it." She pasted her most wounded look on her face as she slid big gold hoops through her earlobes, but Daegan didn't let it get to him. Not this time. It was better if he left—better for her, better for Bibi, better for him. Life was more confusing than ever. He grabbed his house key and reached for his jacket. "Don't go," she begged forlornly.

"I have to," he said, turning and seeing, in the mirror's reflection, the pain in her eyes. She was scared. Frightened of losing her only son and certain that the man she'd let mistreat her for nearly twenty years would throw her out once his bastard was on his own. She would no longer have the golden chain looped around Frank Sullivan's neck forcing them to be together, but Daegan figured it was for the best.

He reached the door when it banged open and the bane of their existence strode in. Red faced, his nostrils quivering with rage, he cast one quick look at his mistress before zeroing in on Daegan. "Who the hell do you think you are?"

"Frank?" His mother's voice wobbled, but Daegan was on the balls of his feet, smelling the fight that had been simmering between him and his old man for as long as he could remember. All he wanted was one good shot.

Mary Ellen stepped out of the bedroom. "Frank, honey, please—"

"Let him say his piece," Daegan cut in.

"Do you know what the boy's been up to?" Frank demanded, his eyes focused on Mary Ellen. "Do you? I'll tell you what. He's been hanging out with Robert's daughter. Even showed up at the lake house last winter, confronted Collin and the girls." He hooked a meaty thumb at his chest. "At my kids. Do you know what Maureen did when she found out?" He shook a fist at Daegan. "She's talking to her damned lawyer, some hot-shot divorce attorney in Manhattan! You know what that means?"

Mary Ellen's face changed. Hope gleamed in her eyes. "That you'll finally be free."

"Yeah and broke. She's gonna wipe me out."

"But then we could be together. Oh, Frank."

He stared at her as if she'd said she'd just been visited by aliens from Mars. "Are you nuts? You think that's what I want? To what? Marry you? For the love of God, woman, sometimes I swear you don't have a brain in that pretty head of yours. I've told you over and over again that it's out of the question."

Daegan hated him.

Mary Ellen's voice was weak and she stood in her best green dress, her hair washed and brushed, her eyes glistening. "I—I don't understand," she said but everyone in the room knew it was a lie.

"Ma, forget it."

"Sure you do, babe. You understand, you just don't want to admit it. All these years you've been sitting here waiting for something to happen between me and Maureen, but even if it did, nothing would change." A muscle in Frank's jaw was jumping wildly, like a caged beast hurling itself at the gate. "I'll make it clear for you, so that even you can get the picture. Maureen will put up with you and him"—he pointed a blunt finger at Daegan—"as long as you know your place, keep quiet, stay away from the house and from my kids. She doesn't care if I screw my brains out with you or anyone else—"

Mary Ellen gave a little squeak of protest.

"But she doesn't want it thrown in her face. So you and your kid better not—"

"Stop," Daegan growled, turning on the man who had sired him.

"Say what, boy?"

"I said stop yelling at my mother and get out."

"Daegan, no," Mary Ellen warned.

"*Me* get out? Now, that's funny. Real funny." Frank shook his head as if he couldn't understand the boy's stupidity. "I have news for you, kid. I pay for this place. That's right. I pay for the rent, your schooling, and buy your ma a new dress or underwear whenever she needs it. I'm good to her."

"Bull."

Frank took a step toward him. "Mary Ellen, you'd better shut your boy up."

"Get out," Daegan said, not budging. He was closer than he'd ever been to his father and he wasn't backing down. Not this time.

"I'm not going anywhere."

"Of course you aren't, Frank," Mary Ellen said, reaching for his arm. "You just got here, honey."

Daegan's stomach churned and his fists clenched at his sides.

Frank shook Mary Ellen's clinging hands away. "You know, boy, I can do what I damn well please because not only can I kick both of your sorry asses out of here, but I can fire your ma as well, make sure she gets no references so that no one else will hire her. I can do that— make your lives a living hell."

"You already have," Daegan said, unable to control his tongue.

"You ungrateful little shit, I should whip you into showing some respect!"

"And I should cut off your balls."

"No! Oh, God, no! Don't, Daegan, don't do this," Mary Ellen begged. "You don't know what you're saying." Then she turned to Frank. "He's just a boy."

"Yeah, and he needs to learn a lesson I should've taught him a long time ago."

"No, no, no. Stop. Please, just stop," she whispered. Mary Ellen was crying now, huddled in a corner, tears and black mascara running down her face, but Daegan couldn't control the rage that had been burning in him for years.

He hurled himself at Frank Sullivan, his body slamming into that of his father. They reeled against the wall. A chair flew out of the way. Frank bellowed. Mary Ellen screamed.

"You little prick!" Frank's body was hard and heavy, honed from hours working out in a gym. His fist crashed into Daegan's face, then a left cross connected, snapping Daegan's head backward and sending him spinning to bounce off the wall. Plaster cracked. His mother wailed. The metallic taste of blood filled Daegan's throat.

"Stop!" Mary Ellen cried. "Please, Frank, for the love of God!"

Stunned, Daegan rounded and tried to land another blow, but Frank came at him with two left jabs to the stomach. Daegan doubled over and Frank kicked him hard between the legs. Pain, like fire, roared through his crotch. He bit back a scream, fought the tears that burned in his eyes. Spitting blood, his head and groin throbbing, he staggered to his feet and stood on rubbery legs.

"Daegan, don't. Frank, please—" Mary Ellen was sobbing loudly and hysterically as Frank, his eyes burning like hot coals, advanced on his son.

"I should have done this a long time ago, kept you in line. Your ma sure as hell didn't."

"So come on," Daegan encouraged, his mouth already swelling. "You've wanted to for years."

"You stupid kid."

"Come on!" Daegan swung at his father, but Frank ducked.

"Oh, God, no, please—Frank, baby, don't," Mary Ellen pleaded.

"I tried to talk her out of havin' you, ya know," Frank swore. "There was a doctor who would have helped us out of the jam we were in, but the damned church doesn't believe in abortion and I'm not riskin' goin' to hell, not for the likes of you. But you," he said, breathing hard and staring at Mary Ellen, "you should have given him up, like I told you. Saved us both a lot of embarrassment."

"Screw you!" Daegan yelled.

"Oh, you have, kid. And let me tell you this, so you'd better get it straight. You are not and never will be my son. Let me put all this in terms you'll understand so that we'll be clear on it, okay? Your mother, she's my whore."

"Oh, no, Frank, you don't mean it," Mary Ellen said, then stared at Daegan. "This is all because you've riled him up."

Frank wasn't finished. "She does what I want when I want and how I want. A good woman. Knows her place. I take care of her and she appreciates it." He said it as if he meant it, as if he really cared about her in his own weird way. "But you, you've been a pain in the butt since the day you were born. Nothin' I can do about it, but you stay away from my kids. Do what you want with Robert's, but keep away from mine."

"You stay away from my ma."

"Daegan, no!" Mary Ellen wailed.

"What?" Frank said. "Don't you get it, kid? Without me, your ma's nothin', just a pretty woman who's getting older—a woman who no other decent man would look at because of her useless kid. If it wasn't me keeping her, it would have to be some other guy—someone who might not be as nice as me. She'd be another man's whore."

Daegan came around again, this time landing a bone-crushing blow to Frank's face that jarred him up his entire arm. Blood sprayed from Frank's nose. With a shriek of pain and outrage, Frank let loose, pummeling Daegan's belly so hard he heard his ribs crack. Like a bloodied heavyweight contender, Frank landed blow after blow, ignoring Mary Ellen's screams and the sounds of voices outside.

Daegan spat on his father.

Frank swore and grabbed him by the front of his jacket. "You dumb little bastard."

"Frank, don't, oh, dear God, don't!" His mother was sobbing.

Crack! Pain seared through Daegan's face as his father's fist slammed into his nose and blood spurted. Daegan spun back against the wall and slithered to the floor. "Don't get up," Frank, breathing hard, ordered.

Daegan struggled to his hands and knees and his mother screamed.

"You never learn, do ya kid?"

Breathing hard, Frank hauled Daegan to his feet. His legs were like jelly and Frank laughed. "Yeah, you're not as tough as you think you are."

His mother was out of the corner and clinging on her lover's arm, wailing, trying to keep Frank from hitting Daegan again. "For the love of God, Frank, don't hurt him. He's your son, your flesh and blood."

"Humph." Eyes deep with rage burned into Daegan. "Then it's my duty to show you your place. Now, you miserable punk, if you ever so much as look at me or my family again, I'll kill you."

"Try," Daegan goaded through teeth that rattled and he spit again, a bloody wad of spittle splashing Frank in the face.

Frank's fist balled and blasted into Daegan's face. Daegan dropped to the floor.

Mary Ellen shrieked. "You've killed him, oh, God, Frank, look what you've done! Baby, oh, baby." She was on her knees beside Daegan, touching him, her tears splashing on him.

"Leave him alone," Frank ordered.

"But he's hurt—"

"I said, leave him alone."

Blackness threatened to overtake Daegan. He saw his father yank his mother to her feet. "Now I came here for a reason. Let's get to it."

"I can't. Not now—Daegan needs a doctor." She was white and scared and it was all Daegan could do to stay conscious. "We have to help him."

"You have to take care of me," he reminded her. "The kid'll be okay. He's out of control, Mary Ellen, he needed to be taught a lesson."

"No, Frank, I can't—"

He lifted her off her feet and staggered into the bedroom. "I hear 'no' at home," he said, throwing her into the room and slamming the door behind him; but still the ugly words seeped through the door. "From you, I expect 'yes' and 'whatever you want, baby.'"

"But Daegan—"

Slap! The sound echoed through the room and was chased by a horrifying shriek. "Frank, don't!" Slap. Another wail.

Daegan dragged himself to his feet, spitting and coughing and thinking of the gun that he'd hidden in the mattress of the hide-a-bed. His mother was screaming and Frank was spouting obscenities. "The boy will be all right, but the sooner you take care of me, the quicker we can call a doctor."

"No, no, no!"

Slap! "Undress."

"Frank, what's happened? We have to see about Daegan—"

Slap! Thunk. "I said take your clothes off, goddamn it, or you'll get the beating of your life!"

"You wouldn't," she said, her voice quavering in fear. Daegan wanted to throw up. He struggled to his knees and wretched up blood.

"Don't, don't, don't, please, no—" she screamed and fabric tore.

"You're in for the fuck of your life, baby," Frank snarled.

Daegan, fighting the blinding pain, crawled to his bed. He reached the couch and felt up inside the frame where he'd taped the gun. His mother screamed and sobbed. Head pounding, he didn't think of anything other than he had to end it. Once and for all. They couldn't go on this way. Now or never.

Slap! Flesh hit flesh and his mother whimpered, but Frank was feeling better. "That's more like it," he was saying and Daegan imagined him doing all sorts of vile things to his mother. "See, honey, oh, God, that's it . . . oh God." The springs began to creak, faster and faster.

"No!" he yelled, but his voice was only a whisper and he felt impotent, unable to help the woman who had brought him into the world. Gritting his bloody teeth, Daegan wrapped sticky fingers around the gun and dragged it from its hiding place, then crawled painstakingly across the floor.

The bedroom door wasn't locked, and still on all fours, he willed himself into the room and saw his father half-dressed and grunting, rutting like an enraged animal atop his mother. Her best green dress was in tatters, tears stood in her eyes, and her face was already starting to bruise where he'd hit her. Using the door frame for support, Daegan pulled himself upright, standing on legs that threatened to give way. He caught a glimpse of the pain in her face, of the feeling of hopelessness that was her life just before she glanced in his direction.

"Daegan, no!"

Frank stiffened. "What the hell?"

She let out a scream that echoed through the room. Frank twisted so that he could see the doorway and

Daegan, sagging against the frame, the gun shaking in his fingers. Fear jelled his father's features. "Jesus Christ, kid, what'd'ya think you're doin'?" He started to scramble off the bed.

Someone pounded on the front door. "Hey—what's going on in there?" a loud male voice demanded.

Mary Ellen grabbed the comforter covering her breasts. "Daegan, don't, put that down—" she shrieked, sliding to the floor in a tangle of bed sheets. "NO!"

Daegan squeezed the trigger.

Chapter 9

Bam!

The gunshot blasted through the apartment.

Frank dove off the mattress. The bullet zinged past his head and wood splintered in the old oak headboard of Mary Ellen O'Rourke's double bed.

Frank hit the floor with a thud, his eyes wild with terror, his legs tangled in sweat-soaked sheets.

Mary Ellen wailed.

Someone pounded on the front door. "Hey—hey! What's going on in there? Cy, call the goddamned police! Hey, are you all right in there? Mary Ellen? Mary Ellen!"

Frank tried to roll his huge body behind the bureau. "For the love of God, woman, get him to stop!" His eyes widened as he stared at Daegan. "Don't do it boy! Make him stop! Jesus, Mary Ellen, make him stop before he kills us all."

"Hey! Miss O'Rourke, what's going on in there? Are you okay?" Voices outside, more of them.

"Oh, shit!" Frank yelled. "Sounds like the goddamned Fourth Battalion!"

His mother was shaking on the bed, holding the tattered quilt around her, crying in wretched, incoherent sobs. Daegan took a step toward her but her lips curled back in disgust. Frank was dragging himself to his feet. "I should have you up on charges!"

"NO!" Mary Ellen cried.

In the living room there was the sound of an axe ripping through wood.

"Oh, God, now what?" Frank zipped his pants and looked furtively to a window.

In the distance sirens began to scream.

"Shit, what a mess."

"The police," Mary Ellen whispered.

"I gotta get out of here."

Crash! The lock gave way. Footsteps on the stairs. Daegan glared at his father and for the first time realized that his eyes were hot and wet with tears. "You sick bastard, you leave my mother alone."

"No, Frank, don't leave," Mary Ellen cried, a huddled, pathetic woman shamed by all who loved her.

Mike O'Brien, a big, strapping man with thick red hair and beard, strode into the room. Bouncer for the Cat O'Nine Tails, he was used to outbursts, brawls, knife fights, and even an occasional gunshot. "For the love of Saint Peter, what happened here?" Meaty hands planted on his hips, he raked his gaze across the mess that had been Mary Ellen's bedroom, only to stop when he saw Frank cowering in the corner. "Well, if it ain't Mr. Uptown. Looks like ye found yerself a helluva mess this time and you—" He turned to glare at Daegan. "What were ye thinkin', eh, boy?"

A siren split the night and Frank was sweating. "I can't have the police involved. If Robert finds out—"

"Shakin' in yer boots, are ye?" Mike laid a big hand on Daegan's shoulder. "Too bad ye missed, son," he said as he strode to the closet door, ripped down Mary

Ellen's chenille robe, and tossed it to her. "Better get yerself dressed, Mary girl. I think ye got some explainin' to do. You, too, ye sorry bastard," he added to Frank, then shooed everyone out of the room to allow Mary Ellen a little privacy. There was a crowd gathered in the living room. Gawkers from the bar downstairs. Soon, the police, weapons drawn, raced up the stairs.

Daegan, his face swollen, his head thundering, dropped onto the couch that was his bed. The second he'd pulled the trigger, he'd experienced a personal epiphany. He'd wanted to kill or maim his father, but he'd missed. In a heartbeat he realized how he'd nearly ruined his life as well as his mother's. If he'd killed the tyrant, he would have ended up in jail and Mary Ellen O'Rourke would have been kicked into the street.

No charges were ever filed. Frank swallowed his pride and called his brother. Thirty minutes later, at two in the morning, Robert Sullivan swooped in wearing a three-piece suit, starched shirt, and impeccable tie. His hair, salt and pepper, was neatly trimmed and combed. He even smelled of expensive aftershave. All business, he observed his brother through frosty eyes and acted civil to Mary Ellen and Daegan only for the policemen's benefit. A criminal lawyer, as oily as the eels pulled out of the bay, accompanied him.

As Mary Ellen smoked and answered questions in her softest voice, Robert was encouraging and kind; he even offered Daegan a sympathetic smile, but all the while, Daegan suspected, he was manipulating everyone in the room. Using his friendly, let's-just-keep-this-little-disagreement-between-us-friends smooth talk and his deep pockets, he handled the police and the onlookers.

Dazed, his head throbbing, Daegan heard words exchanged. Robert's low voice was filled with concern for all involved. He shook his head and Daegan only caught a few of his words. "Unfortunate misunderstanding . . . accident . . . a tragic miscommunication that we should all forget . . . the poor boy. Growing up . . . well, you know. Thankfully nothing was seriously damaged."

Cash was quietly slipped to the police and a few others, including Mike O'Brien, who looked as if he didn't want to take the hundred-dollar bill being offered, but ended up tempted by greed. With an embarrassed glance at Mary Ellen, Mike tucked the folded bill into the deep pockets of his sturdy overalls.

Still shaking inside, Daegan knew instinctively that he'd crossed an invisible moral line. When he'd picked up the .38, he'd shaken off his shackles of childhood and become an adult. Never again would he live the way he had.

From now on, he was on his own. He would pave his own way, play by his own rules, and disregard all the heretofore time-honored dictates of God, country, mother, and the Family Sullivan. He was his own man, able to level a gun at his father, ready to take the consequences for his actions.

After the police and Frank, escorted by a silently seething Robert, left, Daegan began to pack. Mary Ellen didn't even try to stop him, just sat in a chair at the kitchen table, smoked, and watched him with wide, wounded eyes. She looked old and haggard, her hair mussed, her makeup long since faded. Her legs straddled the corner of her chair and Daegan noticed that her once slim ankles had begun to thicken from years of hard work, age, and the inevitable effects of gravity.

She played with her cigarette, rolling the tip around in an old ashtray he'd won for her at a county fair by shooting wooden ducks in an arcade. Somewhere along the way, thankfully, his aim had lessened and he hadn't killed Frank. It seemed as if Mary Ellen was fresh out of tears, but as he hefted his duffle bag to his shoulder and looked at her one last time, she swallowed hard, her lips folding in on themselves.

"I'll call."

"Sure." Defeat edged her words.

"I will."

She didn't believe him—he could read it in her eyes though her mind wasn't open to him. Her shoulders drooped and he guessed that she was still in shock that he'd tried to kill the man she loved. When he touched her lightly on the shoulder, she closed her eyes and clenched her jaw. As he brushed a kiss across her cheek she let out a soft little moan of dismay, but she didn't reach for him. On wooden legs he walked out the broken door that Mike O'Brien had fixed with old plywood.

Unbelievable.

Daegan O'Rourke had attempted the unthinkable, a crime against a Sullivan.

Attempted murder.

Although no word had leaked out officially, murmurings of the bullet fired by O'Rourke had rasped through the hallowed halls of the Sullivan estates and stately townhomes. The buzz was that the bastard boy had a violent temper. A shot had exploded in the night, the bullet narrowly missing Frank Sullivan.

A close call. Far too close, but then again that bastard boy had always exuded trouble.

Too bad the shooter couldn't have been arrested. It would be such a relief to have him behind bars and out of their faces for ten or twenty years, though it wasn't possible. If Frank had to testify at trial, the fact that Daegan was his bastard son would inevitably be revealed, leading to a conundrum far worse than having the shooter listed as a runaway.

Still, it was ludicrous, *so wrong* that a person who didn't belong, a boy who had no right to be near the Sullivans, could wield so much power. The power to embarrass. The power to intrude. The power to kill. One could only hope that Daegan had learned his lesson, that he wouldn't tangle with the likes of Frank Sullivan anymore.

And so far so good. According to family scuttlebutt, O'Rourke was into the wind, missing since the incident. Not that anyone was beating bushes trying to find him. His own mother, Mary Ellen O'Rourke, the only person who seemed to care one iota, seemed to accept that he was gone for good. Gone far, far away from Boston and the world of trouble that would be his if he insinuated himself into this family again.

Why don't you just drop off the face of the planet, Daegan? Make it easy on all of us and just disappear?

Daegen spent the first night sleeping behind a Dumpster, the next in an alley near Shorty's. Cold, dirty, tired, and filled with a burning hatred for the man who had created him, he kept walking around the south side of Boston. After nearly a week on the streets, huddled in doorways or unlocked cars, spending what little money he had on one meal a day, he found an apartment over a service station where the owner, a rotund man with piglike jowls and beefy hands, eyed Daegan and decided to let him pump gas in trade for his rent.

Counting himself lucky, Daegan managed to juggle his hours, still putting in a forty-hour week at the fuel company, but not having much time for school. He managed to scrape up enough credits to graduate and the State of Massachusetts handed him a diploma. He could almost hear the nuns who had been his teachers sigh in collective relief that he was out of the revered educational system.

To keep things simple, Daegan didn't see his mother, or Frank, or anyone from the family besides Bibi. Not that he wanted her around, either. But she was a stubborn thing, and for some reason he couldn't quite fathom, she found him interesting. Daegan figured it was some kind of sicko guilt complex or fascination with the black sheep of the family.

"I don't think this is healthy," he told her when she tracked him down from work and showed up at his dingy apartment soon after he'd moved in.

"Why not?"

He'd unpacked his old duffle bag, and the few clothes he owned were strewn on the stained mattress. "I don't like feeling like some freakin' animal in a sideshow."

"That's not why I'm here."

He raised a disbelieving eyebrow. She was standing just inside the door eyeing the place as if she thought it needed dousing with disinfectant, which wasn't too far from the truth. Time-worn varnish on the door. The windowsills had peeled, exposing old wood. Yellowed linoleum that looked like it was laid in the twenties was cracked and curling at the corners, and the sink, shower, and toilet were darkened by rings and rivulets of rust.

The Ritz it wasn't, but it would do. For now.

"Okay," he said, sitting on the edge of the mattress, exposed box springs squeaking in protest. "Enlighten me, why are you here?"

"You don't have to ridicule me. Believe me, that I can get at home." Strolling into the room like she owned the place, she reached into the large bag she was carrying and withdrew a bottle of champagne. "I thought we should celebrate your freedom."

"With that?" he asked dubiously.

"Compliments of my father," she said as she dropped the bottle on one of the grimy counters.

"Uncle Robert sent it?" He didn't bother hiding the sarcasm in his voice. He really didn't understand what Bibi's fascination with him was and yet the street ran two ways; though he was loath to admit it, he was intrigued by her and everything she represented.

"Well, he doesn't really know. I sort of borrowed it."

"And how are you going to sort of give it back?"

"I'm not. I figure he owes me." She peeled off the foil. "Got any glasses?"

He just stared at her and she lifted a shoulder. "I guess not."

"Crystal isn't a top priority."

"Fine." She bit into her lower lip as she worked the cork from the neck of the bottle with supple fingers. Pop! The cork rocketed across the room and frothy champagne slid down the green neck of the bottle. "Here. You first," she said, holding her prize out to him.

Staring up at her, he grabbed the bottle and took a long pull. Why not? She was here. He'd never tasted hundred-dollar-a-bottle booze in his life and there was nothing stopping him. He handed the champagne back to her and watched as she held the bottle up and sucked, her long neck working.

"It's good, isn't it?" she said, eyes bright.

"It's okay."

Her laughter filled the rat hole of an apartment. "More than okay. It's divine."

"God might not agree." He took a long swallow. Effervescent wine slid down his throat. Something told him he was being foolish, consorting with the enemy, going to end up detesting these few happy minutes for the rest of his life, but he ignored the warning and enjoyed himself for the first time in weeks.

They drank until there was nothing left and she, seated beside him on the tattered mattress, held the bottle upside down and caught the last drop on her tongue. "Ah, well, all good things have to come to an end."

"So they say." He was feeling a little lightheaded but he wouldn't admit it. When he looked at her, she was prettier than he'd originally thought. Sleek hair, wicked little I-know-what-you're-thinking smile that curved her full lips and large eyes capable of turning a dark shade of blue.

"Gotta run," she said as she glanced at her watch. "But I'll be back."

"Will you?"

"Umm." Nodding, she fished in her bag, found a tube of lipstick, and painted her mouth a glossy shade of plum. "If you'll let me."

"I don't know."

"Why not?" she asked innocently, eyes round, eyebrows elevated.

"I don't trust you."

She looked wounded. "Why not?"

Flopping back on the mattress, he sighed. "Figure it out, Bibi. Your last name's Sullivan."

Stuart wanted to lash out and at anyone for anything! Rage stormed through his bloodstream and he let out a string of oaths that would have sent his mother right to her grave. All because of his sister, his damned, fool-hardy, let's-dance-with-the-devil sister!

Bibi was out of her mind! No two ways about it. She wouldn't leave O'Rourke alone. Stuart had kicked himself a thousand times over for getting involved, but now the damage was done. She was enthralled by the bastard.

"This is your fault, you know," he said to Collin as they drove to the lakeside house. It was summer now and the roads were wet from a warm rain.

"My fault?" Collin chuckled. "You blame me for everything. What Bibi does is her business."

"Is it?" Stuart wasn't convinced. He shot his cousin a look that could cut through granite. "You're the one who started all this with your talk about him!"

"But you took it one step farther, didn't you? I just mentioned him to Bibi. You're the one who decided to contact him and make sport of him." Collin sighed and shook his head. His blond hair gleamed pure gold even in the cloudy day. "You'll never learn, Stuart. Never."

"I know, I know. I fucked up this time. Believe me I've lived to regret it." He stepped on the throttle and his Porsche leaped forward, the speedometer pushing ninety, rain singing beneath the wide tires.

Collin sighed and fiddled with the radio until he found a song he recognized. Old Janis Joplin tune. Just the kind of heart-wrenching gritty rock that Collin favored, though few people knew about that side of him that he so jealously guarded. There was Collin the perfect, the A student at Harvard, a member of the crew and debate teams, a man never without his argyle socks . . . unless you came across him after midnight when he was on the prowl. "So why blame me?" Collin asked.

"You know she's in love with you. Has been since she was about six, I think."

"We're cousins, for God's sake." Collin laughed nervously.

"Since when would that stop you?" Stuart asked, his thoughts dark. "Besides, it's kind of a family tradition. Sullivans have been screwing Sullivans since they first landed on Plymouth Rock."

"We weren't on the *Mayflower*," Collin reminded him. "You keep forgetting that."

"A real blight on the family name." Stuart braked for a corner and the tires squealed a bit. Collin didn't even seem to notice.

"Not the only one," Collin said, leaning back against the passenger seat, his hands tapping in rhythm to the song on the radio. His fingers were long and strong. Graceful and supple from years of practicing piano, violin, and guitar. "Remember—Great-great-great-great-aunt Corinne was—"

"Burned at the stake, I know. A witch. Could read people's minds or some such rot. I think you missed a great or two in there somewhere."

"Probably. And not burned at the stake. Just accused of being a witch. I think someone else was flogged for witchcraft, but his or her life was spared." Collin's expression turned dark. "It looks like you're going to be in charge of this family someday, so you should get the history right." He reached into the glove box and found a pair of sunglasses he'd left in Stuart's car nearly a year ago—last summer. "I wonder why O'Rourke took a pot shot at Dad."

Stuart laughed dryly. "He missed, didn't he? Point-blank range. My guess is that he wasn't really trying, but then maybe his aim was off. He's probably never been skeet shooting."

"Nor fenced or read Thoreau, or caught an opening on Broadway, either," Collin said without the slightest trace of a sneer. He slid the aviator glasses onto the bridge of his patrician nose though the day was already gloomy.

"Never suffered through the Russian Ballet or had the opportunity to learn French in Paris."

"Poor unfortunate wretch."

"A lucky stiff if you ask me. He can do what he bloody well wants. Like try to shoot Frank Sullivan."

"Probably missed on purpose."

"My ass. He hates your old man."

Collin's lips curled slightly. "Don't we all?"

"So why don't you pick up a gun?"

With a slow smile Collin said, "There are better ways to get back at dear old dad, don't you think?"

"And you know them all."

Collin's laugh was downright dirty. "Not only know them, but practice them daily."

"If you're lucky."

"I usually am," Collin assured him as Stuart rounded the final bend and eased the Porsche through the open gates. Robert and Adele had already moved to the lake for the summer, and this was their first party of the season. Stuart had offered to pick up Collin as he'd been trapped with late finals, so they'd driven up together.

"The least you could do is offer Bibi some encouragement," Stuart said. "Maybe then she wouldn't be so interested in O'Rourke."

"That would be cruel."

"Why?"

"Because I don't love her—not like that." His lips pinched at the corners.

"What's love got to do with anything?"

"For Christ's sake, Stu, forget it. If you're so interested, you do it."

"Hell, Collin, she's my sister."

"She's my cousin!"

"So?"

"Oh, for the love of God. There's no way I'm going to lead Bibi on."

"Sure you will. Come on, it could be fun."

"Fun?" Beneath his sunglasses, Collin's eyes narrowed. "I don't think so."

"Think about it," Stuart said.

"What do you want me to do? Kiss her? Feel her up? Get into her pants, for Christ's sake? What are you, her fucking pimp?" He was angry now, his usually calm expression changed by fury. Blue eyes were narrowed, lips grim and flat, nostrils flared. Outraged. Just the way Stuart liked to see him.

"Just show her some attention."

"Seduce her?"

"There are worse things you could do."

"I don't think so!"

Stuart parked near the garage. He yanked the key from the ignition and Collin shoved open his door. "Wait." Clamping strong fingers over his cousin's arm Stuart said, "Just be kind to her, okay? Don't lead her on, but give her some hope so that she gets over O'Rourke."

"False hope, you mean."

"We could make it more interesting."

"I don't need more interesting, Stuart. Or don't you remember?"

Stuart wasn't listening. As the oldest, he'd always been able to get his sister and younger cousins to do his bidding. Sometimes he asked them, other times he threatened, but his true skill, his talent, was in manipulation. "Come on, Collin, give the girl a break. It won't take long and you might enjoy it. Right now O'Rourke's new and interesting, but she's really hung up on you."

"Great." Collin rolled his eyes. But he was weakening. As he always did.

"This . . . intrigue she feels for O'Rourke will pass of its own accord, but we're just giving it a little push."

"*We?*"

"Well, you, really."

Muttering under his breath, Collin fell back against the seat. "I don't know why I let you talk me into all this nonsense."

" 'Cause you love it. Now, listen. It'll be easy to turn Bibi's head from the bastard. She's had this crush on you since she was six." Now that his quarry was in no danger of escaping, Stuart could remove his hand from Collin's upper arm, but he let it linger, reminding Collin just who was boss. "Oh, I know she's been with a couple of other boys—infatuations that passed. She's always been way ahead of the girls her age. Once Mother caught her making out with Donny Cheltham on the dock. The top of Bibi's swimsuit was off and Donny had a boner so big his Speedo couldn't hide it."

"Your mother told you this?"

"I was there," Stuart said, and he felt a familiar rush in his bloodstream at the thought of Bibi and Donny groping and rolling around in the hot summer sun, their bodies slick with sweat and suntan oil. "They just didn't know it."

"So now you're a peeping Tom."

"Always have been and you know it. You like it."

"Let go of me." Collin ripped his arm away, stood, and straightened his tie. "You're depraved, you know that, don't you, Stuart?"

Stuart slipped the keys in his pocket. "A fucking deviant and proud of it."

"Oh, hell!" Collin's mouth lifted at the corner. His fury dissipated quickly, as it always did. That was the problem with Collin; he didn't really know how to hold a grudge. Unlike his old man. Unlike almost everyone else lucky enough to be a part of this family.

Bibi watched him walk into the room with Stuart. Tall, lean, sexy. Collin had always appealed to her. As kids they'd played together, and later as he'd grown, he'd become her friend and confidant, but then adolescence had taken hold and he'd spent more time with Stuart than her. The larger her breasts became, the more defined her waist, the less the boys wanted to be around her. A few years ago, they'd been an exclusive threesome, never letting prim and tattletaling Alicia into the group, but slowly Bibi, too, had been weaned. Now Stuart and Collin were best friends.

Bibi tried to reach him. Sometimes Collin was just plain cold, as if his thoughts were elsewhere, as if he had problems he couldn't share with her, but other times he was friendly and she was reminded of the boy she'd grown up with.

Tonight, he nearly blinded her with his smile. Alicia was playing the piano, hoping to impress them all with her perfect rendition of some classical piece—Chopin, Bibi thought idly. The parents were gathered in the living room, where they were sipping martinis. Bonnie was near the fire, curled on a sofa and reading a book.

"Isn't this a rowdy group?" Stuart observed as he eyed the hors d'oeuvres arranged on a tabletop. Snagging a prawn wrapped in bacon, he plopped it into his mouth.

"The rest of the guests are supposed to arrive around eight." Bibi didn't like the thought of putting up with another boring party with friends of her family, but she had no choice. This was a command performance.

"Maybe we can all be drunk by then," Stuart said so that only she and Collin could hear. He smeared some salmon pâté onto a tiny cracker.

"Fat chance," she said. "Some of us aren't old enough."

"There are ways," Stuart told her and slid a glance at Collin as he took a bite from the cracker. "Meet us in the pool house after everyone arrives, so you won't be missed. Nine-thirty."

Collin shot him a look that could kill.

Bibi ignored it. "Why?" She couldn't help the excitement that crept into her voice. They were finally including her again.

"It's a surprise," Stuart told her. "Don't tell the girls." His gaze moved to include Bonnie and Alicia. "Make sure you come alone."

Bibi slipped out of the house unnoticed. Collin and Stuart had left a few minutes earlier, not together. First Stuart had wandered onto the flagstone deck and not returned. After hanging around the dessert table and talking with a couple of older guys, Collin had made his exit as well. Now, Bibi, making sure that no one was paying any attention to her, headed for the powder room, then once she was in the hallway, slipped through a door to the servants' quarters and out a back way near the laundry room.

A light drizzle had deigned to mist over the Sullivan party and wisps of fog clung to the black surface of the lake. She made her way to the pool house by memory, having spent every summer of her life here. The lights outside didn't illuminate the grounds near the wing that housed the maids who lived with them in the summer, but Bibi was still able to run through the shadows, past a laurel hedge and around the edge of the pool that, with its submerged light shining, shimmered an electric shade of aqua in the night. The pool house was unlocked and dark.

"Anybody here?" she whispered, her eyes adjusting to the dim light.

"For God's sake, come in and close the door!" Stuart's voice bounced off the walls.

The lock clicked behind her and Stuart drew all the curtains then snapped on a small lamp near the bed. A tiny pool of light cast warm shadows over the floral bedspread and matching chairs. "I can't believe we're sneaking around like a pack of thieves."

Collin emerged from the kitchen. Balancing a wicker

tray that was loaded with three filled glasses, he said, "Don't we always? Face it, Stu, it's our lot in life." A look passed between them that she couldn't read and Collin handed her a glass filled with amber liquid.

"It's silly," Stuart said, anxious to be his own man. For the past few years he'd been pulling at the bit, wanting more. Soon he'd graduate from college, then he'd put in a stint at law school and finally be able to step into the shoes that had been fashioned for him from the day of his birth.

"Silly, but necessary. Cheers." Collin let him pick a glass from the tray, took another for himself, and tossed the empty wicker tray onto the bed. He clinked the rim of his glass to both Stuart's and Bibi's. "To the Three Musketeers."

"Is that what we are?" Bibi asked as she sat on the edge of the mattress.

"Sure." Stuart took a swallow from his glass and sprawled in one of the side chairs. "Always have been."

"Not recently."

"Maybe that's all changed," Stu said cryptically. "Come on, Bibi, relax. Drink up."

For a reason she couldn't name, she felt a speck of indecision. She wanted desperately to be close to them both again and yet there was something wrong here. Something that she couldn't put her finger on.

"I thought this is what you wanted," Stuart prodded.

"It is," she said, reaching for her purse and finding a crushed pack of cigarettes. She lit up and calming smoke curled down into her lungs.

Collin stared at Bibi over the edge of his glass as he took a healthy gulp. His eyes were mesmerizing and Bibi's throat was suddenly as dry as the Sahara in summer. Without another thought she sipped from the glass, felt the blended scotch burn a fiery path down her throat, and waited for the alcohol to hit her bloodstream. She needed that warmth now and it came quickly in a familiar rush. After the fourth or fifth swallow she felt her muscles soften and her doubts flee. She was with Stu and Collin again. What could possibly go wrong?

She wasn't aware of time, didn't even think that they might be missed from the party, but after a while—during the second or third drink and a like amount of cigarettes—Stuart, known for being able to hold his liquor and keep a level head—said he'd make a brief appearance back at the main house and field questions. If anyone asked about Bibi or Collin, he'd say they took a walk down by the lake or some such nonsense. No one, with the exception of Alicia, would doubt him for a moment. He breezed out through the back door and Bibi leaned back against the pillows of the big bed, used occasionally for weekend summer guests. She took a final drag of her smoke and squashed it in a bedside tray.

"Refill?" Collin asked, gathering up her half-drunk glass.

"I'm fine."

"Yes, Bibi, that you are," he said softly before disappearing into the kitchen. The way he said her name made her tingle inside, though she mentally called herself a fool. He was her cousin and therefore off-limits, but ever since she'd been a little girl, when he'd carried her across a creek, keeping her party dress clean while his own trousers had become sodden and muddy, she'd looked up to him. They'd been playing where they shouldn't have, down by the swollen waters of Bright Creek on their grandparents' property.

They lost track of time laughing and throwing rocks into the stream, and Stuart, realizing they were late, had yelled at them to hurry back. He'd crossed the

water easily, by hopping from one slippery rock to another and was racing up the bank to Grandmother's big
stone house on the hill. This was the day Bonnie was to
be baptized into the church. Bibi had nearly fallen in
the creek and knew she couldn't make the leaps that
Stuart had. She'd started to cry when Collin, tucking
his shoes and socks into his pockets, had carried her
across the rushing water. But as careful as he'd been,
mud had splashed up his pant legs, and by the time
they'd returned to Grandma's house, Collin was in deep
trouble. His mother nearly fainted at the dirt and water
stains on his new suit pants, and Frank, loving father
that he'd always been, was furious with his son.

"Good for nothing!" he roared, his face mottled red.
"Why don't you ever use that brain that God gave you?
Huh?"

"I'm sorry."

"Sorry's not good enough!" Frank spewed and Bibi
was suddenly scared. Uncle Frank's face was twisted
evilly. He looked like a monster.

"I messed up."

"Bend over."

Everyone stopped talking. Only the wind sighing
through Grandma's lilac tree made any noise.

"I said—"

"No! Father, please—"

Frank lunged at his son and threw him down on the
grass with such force the air rushed from Collin's lungs.
"You'll do as I say! Now stand up, bend down, and grab
your ankles."

Collin fought tears of shame. "I—I can't."

"Be a man for once!"

Shaking, Collin struggled to his feet. "Now!" Frank
bellowed.

Collin's face drained of color. "But sir, I'm too old—"

"Not too old to go playing like a two-year-old in the mud. Well, if you're gonna act like one, then you're gonna have to be treated like one."

"Frank," Grandma admonished softly.

"It's good for the boy," Grandpapa had stated, his pipe clamped firmly between his yellow teeth. "Give him character."

"It was my fault!" Bibi cried.

Frank cast his niece a harsh look. "No doubt, but it doesn't matter. Collin can think for himself. He's made us late, kept the priest waiting, made us all look like fools. This is just to make sure it won't happen again. Now, boy, if you know what's good for you, you'll grab your ankles."

"Please, Frank! Not here." Grandma Sullivan intervened.

"Stay out of it, Bernice," Grandpapa said, watching the display with grim determination. "Collin needs to learn his lesson."

Aunt Maureen looked away and fiddled with a long strand of pearls. Bibi's parents didn't say a word; they made it a practice to stay out of other people's business.

Face flaming in shame, Collin bent over. In front of all his family, Frank spanked him with a Ping-Pong paddle. He bit his lips and fought tears as his father, red-faced and smelling of brandy, whacked him ten times, each smack echoing in Bibi's heart. Sweating from the effort, Frank finally dropped the paddle and took a long, triumphant swig from his glass. "Now, go upstairs and change and never . . . do you hear me, never, let some little girl talk you into disobeying me or your mother again." Collin, swallowing hard, marched in silent mortification from the patio. "And say a hundred Hail Marys while you're at it."

The back door banged behind Collin. Frank, as if

suddenly aware of the reproachful eyes cast in his direction, rolled his palms to the sky. "What?" When no one said anything, again he shouted, "What?"

"It was a little harsh," Maureen said.

"It was wrong! Collin didn't do anything but give me a piggyback ride!" Tears ran down Bibi's face.

"You shouldn't have put him in that position," her father said. "Let's get in the car." Robert focused his gaze on Frank. "We'll meet you at the church. Come on, Stuart."

For the first time Bibi saw her brother, standing by the gazebo in Grandma's rose garden. His face was white and he glared at his own father with hard eyes. "Don't ever treat me that way," he said to Robert.

"I won't. Now, let's get a move on."

The children lagged behind their parents, and before climbing into the car, Stuart looked at Bibi with eyes that drilled into her soul. "I'd kill him," he whispered, conviction edging every word. "If Frank were my father, I'd shoot him dead."

"What can we do about Collin?" Bibi whispered.

"Nothing." Stuart cast an angry look over his shoulder. "We can't do anything yet. But someday—"

"Stuart. Bibi. Please! Get in the car." Their mother Adele, was adjusting her hat in the front seat. "Let's make sure our side of the family doesn't look like Frank's." She shuddered and Bibi slid into the plush interior of the Mercedes. She knew her mother considered Frank to be a ruffian even though he'd been raised in the same family as her husband. "Sometimes there's bad blood in the family," she'd said often enough. "A throwback to some Neanderthal. That's the problem with Frank. He's filthy in mind and body!" For the most part, Adele kept her thoughts to herself and held her tongue. Family unity above all else was the motto she held dear to her heart. She'd been taught from an early age to bear incredible personal pain if it meant not compromising her social position or that of her family. But once in a while even she couldn't hold her tongue.

They drove to the church, and Bibi, biting her lower lip, her head bent in feigned prayer, waited. Eventually Frank, Maureen, and their brood arrived, but Collin wouldn't look at her, nor would he catch Stuart's eye. He knelt at the pew, eyes cast downward in the centuries-old church and never so much as risked a glance in her direction.

It was later at Frank's house as she was walking by the door to the den, looking for Stuart and Collin, that she overheard a conversation between her uncle and father. They were seated by the fire, swirling their drinks and smoking huge, smelly cigars.

"The boy needed to be taught a lesson," Frank insisted, obviously defending himself.

"Not in front of the entire family." Robert puffed angrily. His back was to her but Bibi saw the cloud of blue smoke he created. It rose to the ceiling like odoriferous mist.

"Look, Bobby, you do what you think best with your kids and I'll handle mine." Frank stood and walked to the mantel.

"The way you 'handle' the other boy?"

Bibi just stared at her uncle with wide eyes. *What* other boy? Frank had only one son.

"Let's not talk about him now."

There was another son? But where? Bibi's mind was racing in circles.

"Why not? Don't want the whole family to hear?" Robert said. "Think about it, Frank. Of course you don't. Just like Collin didn't need to be humiliated in front of his cousins."

By this time Alicia, her white dress without so much as a spot, sneaked up behind Bibi. "What're you doing?"

she whispered, then looked through the crack between the door and the casing and saw the men inside. "Boy you're asking for it."

Bibi inched away from the door. "Do you have a brother?" she asked. "I mean, besides Collin."

"No."

"But Daddy asked Uncle Frank about his other boy."

"Oh." Alicia tossed her long hair over a shoulder. "Him."

"What—him?"

"It's nothing," Alicia said, her superior attitude back in place, though she avoided Bibi's curious gaze. "Excuse me Mother wants me to practice my Mozart." With that she scurried away in a rustle of white lace, her footsteps retreating to the parlor.

Later, Bibi caught up with her brother and demanded answers. She explained what she'd overheard and Stuart, curse him, didn't seem the least bit surprised. He was forever keeping secrets from her.

"It's about the bastard," he finally revealed.

"The what?"

Stuart's eyes gleamed. "What'll you do for me if I tell you?"

"Just tell me!" she demanded, and after a little teasing he regaled her with the sordid tale of Frank's whore and bastard son, Daegan O'Rourke, her other boy cousin who was scandalously illegitimate, not that she could be expected to understand everything this meant. From the look on Stuart's face when he whispered the information to her in the attic of Frank's house, Bibi understood that something wicked and nasty had gone on.

Now, years later in the pool house, as Collin returned with a refill of her drink, she gazed up at him and saw the young hero he'd been to her when he'd taken a beating that should have been hers. She ignored her half-smoked cigarette as he took a seat in the overstuffed chair and propped a foot on the matching ottoman. He seemed uncomfortable.

"Something's bothering you," she said.

"Something's always bothering me."

"Why?"

He lifted a shoulder, dismissing the subject, then took a long gulp of his fresh drink. If he wasn't careful, she thought, he'd get himself drunk. Unlike Stuart, Collin couldn't hold his liquor.

"Maybe I can help."

"Oh, Bibi," he said with a long sigh as he lolled his head back and she watched the glorious length of his throat. "If you only knew."

"I'll trade you my secret for yours."

A blond eyebrow shot skyward and he skewered her with a look that made her want to squirm against the pillows. "You've got a secret?"

"More than one."

"Interesting." He glanced to the shadowed doorway on the other side of the bed, then, leaving his drink on a rattan end table, climbed to his feet. "Tell me, Cousin, what are they?" Walking slowly, he crossed to the bed and stopped, looming above her. His crotch was at eye level and she tried not to stare and wonder if he was getting hard. Something in his manner had changed and the air in the room seemed close and thick. She had trouble breathing. She thought she heard a door creak open, but couldn't really tell over the hammering of her heart. "Do these secrets have anything to do with me?"

She swallowed hard, then took a long drink. "Maybe."

"Don't you know?" He reached down and tangled a finger in her hair, tugging a little. Deliciously painful.

She could barely breathe. "Collin—"

"Don't."

"I have to," she admitted, knowing it was the time to unburden her heart.

"I don't think—" It was as if he were struggling with himself, waging some inner battle. Because they were cousins—related—he had to deny any feelings he had for her. That was it!

"Just listen," she pleaded.

He sank onto the bed and his face was barely inches from hers. "What, darling?"

Her heart was thudding like a jackhammer, her breathing raspy and shallow. Had he really called her darling? Did he, too, care more than he'd admitted. "I—um . . ." Oh, God, what could she say? She smelled the expensive Kentucky blend on his breath, felt his finger slide from her hair along her chin to rest at her lips.

"You don't have to say anything."

"I *want* to, don't you understand. It's something that I . . . that I've been thinking for a long, long time."

"Oh, God."

"Collin, I—"

"Just do what you want to, Bibi," he said in a low voice that she barely recognized, a voiced filled with defeat.

She reached forward tentatively, her arms encircling his neck. "I want to kiss you."

"You don't know what you're asking," he said, closing his eyes.

"Just let me." She pressed her lips to his and felt him shudder. Her fingers dug into the muscles between his shoulders and he groaned. He wanted her, she could feel it! As if the wall of doubt he'd erected had suddenly fallen into rubble, he kissed her back. Hotly. Hungrily. Fiercely.

"Is this all you want? Just to kiss?"

She could hardly think between the alcohol and the magic of his touch. "Yes . . . no."

"Make up your mind, Bibi. It's now or never."

"I want to—to—"

"What, darling?"

"Love you," she said weakly, saying the words that had hovered in her mind for a dozen years.

He groaned as if in agony, then twined his hands in her hair, jerked her face close to his, and kissed her so hard she couldn't catch her breath. As if giving into a temptation he'd been denying for far too long, he slowly began unbuttoning his shirt, displaying a chest of raw muscle without any disturbance of hair.

She was suddenly frightened, but his skin, glistening in the light from that single bulb, beckoned her.

"We can do anything at all. We're all alone." He threw off his shirt and he was bare to the waist, all tight skin and corded muscles. With a half smile, he glanced to the open door and dark hallway that led to the kitchen.

"You think Stuart will be back—"

"Not for a while," Collin said, though his voice was strangled. "Don't think about him." His dusky gaze found hers again and he circled her lips with a finger that smelled vaguely of smoke.

She touched the tip of her tongue to his skin and a soft moan escaped him. Inside she was turning hot and sticky and liquid, like honey warmed over open coals. She took more of his finger into her mouth, sucking loudly, making sensual noises that seemed to arouse him.

"That's right, baby," he whispered, one hand tangling in her hair as he pressed soft lips to hers. His mouth was open, his tongue quick.

Hot jets of passion spurted through her blood and she kissed him eagerly, tumbling back onto the bed as he pushed her down. His hands were strong, suddenly rough as he tore at the buttons of her blouse.

The first niggle of doubt pricked her cloudy mind. "Collin?"

"This is what you want, isn't it?" he said. The fabric parted and her breasts, tucked into the demure cups of a cotton bra, were exposed. He rubbed her chest hard with the flat of his big hand and her nipples peaked.

"Yes, but—" Where was the tenderness? The love? A dull roar started in her ears, sounding like the din of the sea, the same roar she heard whenever she was in trouble.

He ripped the blouse from her torso and she'd never felt more naked in her life. He was kissing her sloppily, wet and anxious, his fingers fumbling at the back fastening of her bra. This wasn't right, she thought wildly as the hook gave way and he yanked the scanty fabric down her arms.

He was touching her, groaning, breathing fast, and yet it was as if he wasn't really there, as if only his body was in the room, that his soul had departed.

"Collin, wait—" she whispered as his sweaty hands kneaded her back.

"Why?"

"I don't know. I don't think . . ."

"Don't tell me you're a tease, Bibi." He pulled his head away from hers to stare at her with condemning eyes. "Not you. Not with me."

"I said I just want to love you."

"You will," he said in a breathy voice, but glanced over her shoulder, as if he expected someone to barge in on them.

"I mean, I want to, really I do, but—"

He stood suddenly then and glared down at her as if she were a piece of meat—rotten and foul. "Get up."

"No—" The roar in her ears was deafening, and she noticed that when he looked at her breasts, his expression didn't change, even though she'd been told before how spectacular they were. Large and full, crowned with big dark nipples, the two boys who had been given the privilege of viewing and touching them had raved about their beauty. Collin didn't seem to notice, or to care, even when she crawled to the side of the bed and stood directly in front of him. No playful tweak, no guilty glance. Nothing.

"You can't have it both ways, Bibi. Either you want to do it with me or you don't. We can end it now or we can go all the way. It's up to you." His voice was cold and harsh as a judge meting out a sentence.

"But you don't want me," she accused him, swallowing hard, feeling hot tears shimmering in her eyes.

"Of course I do."

"No, something's wrong."

He closed his eyes for a second, as if he was mentally counting to ten, trying to gain some self-control.

"You're not the same."

"You're right," he admitted as she covered herself with her hands. He glanced again to the doorway, as if he were attempting to find answers to their dilemma. "This is hard for me, too. I'm not sure it's right."

"Because we're cousins."

"No," he said, hesitating and biting his lip as he had during childhood whenever he was faced with hard decisions. "Because I care about you." He seemed sincere, though he didn't meet her gaze. "I don't like the idea of using you."

"You won't."

"Oh, Bibi—"

"I won't let you." Sadness converged on his feature and he squeezed his eyes shut, as if his sudden attack o nobility were too much to bear. This was the Collin sh loved, this was her hero. "It's all right."

"No, Bibi, you don't understand."

"Sure I do." She shifted, holding a breast in each hand, rubbing the hard tips of her nipples against hi chest, letting him gaze down at the huge pillow mounds. "I love you." She wound her fingers in his an raised his hand, guiding him to her nipples, then sh moved sensually, using her hand and his, feeling tha little hot tickle of desire deep between her legs as she al ways did when she massaged her nipples. "Touch me Collin, touch me all over and love me," she whispered throatily.

"It's not just you and me," he protested.

"It is right now. Let me love you."

"Bibi, don't do this." She dropped his hand and ra her fingers over his shoulders, feeling the power withir his muscles as he kissed her. But the kiss had no life an his fingers had stopped kneading her breast. His sud den attack of conscience had drunk up all his desire But Bibi knew how to get it back. She kissed him hun grily, then let her tongue slide down his chin, neck, an breastbone. She didn't stop until she reached his fly and dropping to her knees, she slid the button and zip per open with deft, well-practiced fingers, only to find that he wasn't hard, that he was as limp as a wet dishrag

"What?" she asked, gazing up at him.

His face was twisted in silent agony and his eyes glis tened as if he was fighting tears.

"Collin?"

"You don't have to do this," he said, swallowing as hi fingers played in her hair.

"Why not?"

"It's not right."

"Probably not," she admitted, "but I can make you feel better." His hands curled into fists. She thought she heard the scrape of a shoe against the tile floor. But that was silly. They were alone and he didn't flinch, just stood over her, his eyes trained on the darkened hallway.

Sometimes being able to look into another person's mind was a pain in the butt—a damned curse. Worse yet, Daegan couldn't control this gift—not one bit. Whenever he least expected it, he'd get a glimmer— just a hint of what someone was thinking—not enough to do any good, but a glimmer nonetheless. He'd never be able to make his living reading palms or predicting the future and yet he had to live with the knowledge that he was occasionally offered glimpses into another person's soul, as he was now.

It was Bibi who was calling out to him. He heard her voice in his dreams, and tonight after work he'd gone to the pool hall, lost a little money, and drunk more beer than he usually did, then he'd staggered home, kicked off his shoes, stripped off his shirt and jeans, and fallen facedown on his bed when he heard her voice, panic-stricken and pained, bouncing off the walls in his mind. He'd told himself that he was drunk, that he was imagining everything, but he'd barely drifted off when the racket on the other side of his door drove him back to consciousness. Someone was pounding frantically on the ancient, peeling panels, rattling the lock, trying to wake the damned dead.

"Hell," he muttered, blinking at the illuminated face of his clock as he snapped on the light. Two-thirty. He'd have to be downstairs with the pumps turned on at six.

The pounding continued making a horrendous racket. Forcing himself to his feet, he rubbed a calloused hand over his face. He knew before he opened the door that Bibi was on the landing at the top of his stairs.

"Oh, Daegan," she cried as the door swung open. She burst into the room smelling of smoke, liquor, and perfume. Dropping onto a corner of his mussed bed, she cradled her head in her hands.

"Bibi?" He plowed his fingers through his hair and massaged his eyes. "Do you have any idea what time it is?"

Waving off his question, she shook her head. "I'm so stupid, so damned stupid!" she wailed, her voice filled with pain. "Oh, God, what am I going to do?"

"What're you doing here?"

"I needed to get out, to get away . . ." Her words were slurred and he realized dully that she was as drunk as he. A dangerous combination.

"Away from what?"

"Them!" She spat out the word as if it were vile then started to sob, deep, soul-wracking sobs that shook her whole body. Wrapping her arms around her waist, she began to rock back and forth, forward and backward and forward again. Over and over.

He had no choice but to try and help her, to calm her down. "Come on, Bibi, what is it?" he said, sitting on the bed beside her and draping an arm over her shoulders.

"Collin." She looked as if she might gag. "And Stuart."

"I thought you liked them."

"I did. Oh, God," she wailed. "Oh, God. Oh, God. Oh, God." She was white as a sheet. "I've been such a fool, such a goddamned stupid fool."

"Hey, slow down, tell me what happened," he said, yawning.

"I can't." She shook her head quickly.

"But you came all the way down here—"

"Just hold me, okay?"

"Sure." His arm tightened around her and she leaned into his shoulder, her tears hot as they drizzled from her eyes to his bare skin. As dull as he was, he knew that touching her was precarious, that she was hurt and he was nearly naked, that just the smell of her was causing a tightening in his gut and he was getting hard. Her breath whispered over his chest, ruffling his chest hairs. Determined to keep the stiffening in his groin at bay, he gritted his teeth.

"Can I stay with you?"

"I don't think that would be such a good idea." His little apartment wasn't as bleak and austere as when he'd first moved in, but it was still a far cry from what she was used to. Though there was a secondhand throw rug on the floor, sheets and blankets on the bed, a stick or two of furniture, it was still a hovel—a dirty little apartment over the top of a service station. But then, even if he lived in a mansion, he wouldn't think her staying with him would cause them anything but grief.

"Please. I just need to be away."

What could he say? She obviously needed a friend and he—he needed a smoke. "Fine. You . . . you can sleep here. I'll take the chair."

"No. Please, Daegan, hold me tonight," she begged, clinging to him. "Please, just hold me. I need someone."

"But—"

"I'll be good, I promise."

"You are good," he said.

"Then, please, hold me and protect me."

Though his ale-soaked mind warned him that he was playing with fire, he sighed and turned off the light. They tumbled into the sheets together, sharing a pillow, and he swore that the swelling between his legs and his hot-blooded sexual urges wouldn't get the better of him. He'd hold her, assure her, maybe even kiss the back of her neck, but that was all. He didn't need the pain and agony of having slept with his cousin and yet she was so soft, so warm, so vital. When he pressed his lips to her hair and told her to sleep, she turned to him, her luscious mouth open, her arms circling his naked torso.

"You care about me, don't you?"

"Of course I do."

"And you think I'm . . . sexy."

"Too sexy." God, what was she doing? His head was pounding with desire, his cock hard as the rock of Gibraltar. "Go to sleep, Bibi."

"Do you want me, Daegan?"

"Go to sleep." His brain was on fire.

"Do you want me?"

"It doesn't matter what I want." He tried to think past the beer still clouding his judgment and the warm woman in his arms. His heart throbbed in his ears.

"I want you."

"Shit!"

"I mean it."

"Bibi, go to sleep or leave." His mind was saying one thing, his body, hot and anxious, another.

"You don't mean it."

"Please, no—"

But she was kissing him already, her lips warm and soft and wet against the skin of his chest. "Let me," she whispered in a breathy voice that reminded him of a summer breeze.

"Oh, God, don't—"

She lowered herself slowly and his fingers tangled in her hair. With quick, hot ministrations, she rimmed one of his nipples with her tongue and the world began to spin.

"For the love of Mike—Bibi, please don't—"

Her fingers dipped in the waistband of his jeans and skimmed his fly. He closed his eyes. The zipper opened with a quick, sharp hiss. His mouth was dry and his cock aching to be stroked. His insides turned to jelly as her breath, like the wanton air from the lungs of Jezebel, swept across his belly. His jeans slid to the floor and Daegan was lost. Forever.

His arms tightened around her, and mentally cursing, he gave himself into the passion drumming through his blood. He kissed her long and hard even though he knew there was no turning back.

Chapter 10

Daegan opened one bleary eye and ran his tongue around teeth that were far from slick. His mouth tasted like the inside of a garbage can and his head throbbed. He'd drunk too much and then stumbled back here and . . .

Turning onto his side, he saw her and his stomach curled in on itself. He nearly retched all over the bed.

Bibi! Oh, hell, no!

He shot out of bed and made a startled sound of panic as the seduction crept into his mind in glorious, horrifying, sickening images. Bile rose up the back of his throat and he had to fight to keep from losing whatever was left in his guts. He tried and failed to block out how once he'd given into her anxious ministrations, he'd lost all inhibitions. They hadn't stopped at making love once, oh, no. Theirs had been one helluva drunken sexual marathon.

Fool! Idiot! Stupe! What the devil were you thinking? The contents of his stomach churned again. If only it were all a dream—a nightmare. He couldn't believe that he'd had sex with his cousin. Shuddering, he stepped farther away from the bed, putting distance between her warm, naked body and his and feeling a stranglehold of guilt tightening around his throat. For the love of God, what had he been thinking?

He'd made love to a Sullivan.

Disgust scraped at his soul. Stark naked, he walked to the sink in the bathroom and saw his reflection in the chipped mirror mounted over the faucets. He looked worse than he felt, and yet it seemed to him that an invisible vise had clamped his head in its steely, unforgiving jaws and the pressure on his brain, as the vise was tightened, made him feel that he was about to explode.

He had to be perverted for sleeping with her. Depraved. Abnormal. All of the above. A real sicko. And he couldn't really blame the situation on the booze. He'd wanted Bibi. He stared into bloodshot, guilt-riddled eyes and sneered, "You stupid bastard."

He was no better than his monster of a father. Using and abusing women. Splashing water over his face, Daegan tried to think. He had about fifteen minutes to get to work, fifteen lousy minutes to figure out what he was going to do about Bibi as well as the rest of his life.

He thought of their coupling and spat into the sink. It was as if once he'd crossed the forbidden threshold, he hadn't been able to get enough. Her body welcomed him, and in his drunken state, he hadn't even bothered with a rubber! "Goddamned fool," he ground out.

Grinding his teeth at the recollections that kept picking at his brain, he quickly showered, hoping the hot water would erase the memories, knowing that he'd have to face her sooner or later. He stayed in long enough for the tank to drain and the temperature of the weak spray to drop. What could he say to her? What could he do? They would never be close again.

Throwing on his brown, grease-stained uniform, he slowly counted to ten, ran fingers through his wet hair, and found the courage to open the bathroom door. A cloud of steam followed him into the living area where Bibi slept. The smell of stale booze, cigarettes, and sex filled the room, and he opened a window just as a train rattled on tracks not far away. It was still dark outside; not quite six o'clock, the air smelled early-morning fresh. The eastern sky was beginning to streak with the hint of dawn.

Sooner or later he'd have to face up to what he'd done, but she appeared so peaceful and untroubled as she slumbered, as if the world couldn't hurt her, that he didn't have the heart to wake her and remind her that he, along with Stuart and Collin, the three men she should have been able to trust, had used and abused her.

Oh, Jesus, what was he going to do?

He lit a cigarette from the pack she'd left on the file cabinet he used for a nightstand. Smoking silently, knowing he was already late, he watched the sun rise. He should rouse her, he supposed, but he didn't. Instead he tucked the blanket under her chin, brushed a stray lock of hair off her cheek, then stubbed out the smoke and hurried downstairs to turn on the lights and start the pumps. He could take a break around ten, check on her, and tell her that last night had been a big mistake, that he hadn't known what he'd been thinking, that he liked and respected her but couldn't be her lover.

He muttered an oath under his breath. Anything he could say sounded twisted and depraved and trite.

Locking the door behind him, he took a big, bracing gulp of air, then hurried down the stairs. Like it or not he had to turn his attention to the job at hand. A big tanker-truck was already waiting, the driver anxious to fill the underground tanks. The idling engine rumbled smoothly, exhaust filling the air with the heavy scent of diesel. Cupping his hands around the end of a cigarette he was lighting, the trucker disregarded the bold NO SMOKING sign posted near the front door.

"Hey, whaddya think I'm doin' here?" the driver said, clicking his lighter shut as he spied Daegan. A cloud of smoke rolled out with his words. "I don't got all effin' day, y'know."

"I'll just be a minute," Daegan said, unlocking the front door and snapping on the lights in the service bays as well as the reception area by the cash register. Ignoring his throbbing head and the fact that the thick stench of diesel was playing havoc with his sensitive stomach this morning, he searched for the invoice sheets for the gas that was expected to be delivered from the distributor, found a clipboard, and half ran outside. With the quick motions of someone who was familiar with his task, he unlocked the covers to the underground tanks. Soon gas was flowing from the truck through a huge hose.

A car pulled into the pump area and the bell mounted over the door chimed loudly. Daegan dashed to help the first customer and tried not to notice that in the side lot, parked between a rusted-out shell of a Pontiac and a Volkswagen van that still sported a faded peace symbol and psychedelic art work, was Bibi's Corvette—metallic silver that sparkled in the dawn and looked as out of place as a yacht in a moorage for fishing dinghies.

"Fill 'er up," a familiar and grizzled face ordered as Daegan approached the driver's side of the old Chevy wagon parked at the pumps.

What was the old coot's name? Preston? No, Prescott. Oliver Prescott, that was it. "Sure thing."

"Nice wheels." Prescott shifted a match from one side of his mouth to the other as he gazed at Bibi's car. "Yours?"

Daegan slid a quick look at the Corvette with its gleaming finish, leather interior, and expensive tape deck. "I wish."

"You and me both." Prescott laughed in a rasp until he began a coughing fit that brought tears to his eyes and rendered it impossible for him to dig into his wallet to extract some bills. Finally, he was able to pay. "Well," he said, handing Daegan a twenty, "you and me both can keep on dreaming about expensive cars and fancy women, eh?"

Daegan's mouth turned to sand and he thought about Bibi. What was he going to do with her? She hadn't said what had happened to her earlier in the evening but he'd gathered that somehow she'd been humiliated by Stuart or Collin or both. No doubt she wouldn't feel much better this morning when she remembered everything they'd done last night and realized that Daegan, too, had taken advantage of her.

That's not the way it happened, he reminded himself but couldn't help feeling guilty as sin as he made change for his first customer. He should have been in control. She'd come to him for comfort and ended up with sex. Shit, what a mess.

By the time the mechanics showed up and he could break away, it was nearly eleven. Bibi was still in bed, the blankets drawn over her breasts, her eyes fixed on the stained ceiling tiles.

Daegan felt like an intruder in his own home. All the flaws—the dirty windows, grimy, cracked floor, noisy heat register that hissed and chugged no matter what he did—seemed to mock him.

What could he say to her? Nothing. They could no longer be friends. They'd crossed that barrier along with a dozen others when they'd let their bodies join in pure animal pleasure.

"This wasn't supposed to happen," she whispered, her lower lip quivering.

"I know." He couldn't move, acted as if he'd been nailed to the interior of the door.

"You shouldn't have let it."

"I know."

"Damn it, Daegan, is that all you can say?" she demanded, tears filling her gorgeous eyes.

"I'm sorry."

Blinking rapidly, she sniffed and ran the back of her hand under her nose. "Not half as sorry as I am."

"It won't happen again."

"Damn right it won't." Her voice changed and she pursed her lips to each other as if fighting to hold herself together. "Do you know what they did to me?" When he didn't answer, she turned to face him and the blankets shifted a little, showing off a hint of her cleavage. Daegan kept his eyes focused on her face. "Stuart and Collin, did I tell you how they set me up?"

"You didn't say anything."

"Well, I guess it doesn't matter now," she said, drawing her body into a sitting position, her expression dull as she held the flimsy sheet over her body. Shoving a hank of hair from her face, she said, "God, I need a cigarette. Hand me my purse, would you?"

He did as she asked, depositing the leather bag on the bed near her, and she scrounged deep in the purse's interior, drawing out a pack of Viceroys and lighting up. Shooting a stream of smoke in the air, she closed her eyes.

"I've always had a crush on Collin."

"You don't have to tell me this." The less he knew of what went on between the Sullivans, the better.

"Yes, I do." She sighed wearily. "That's why I came over here in the first place."

"No, Bibi, look, I don't want to hear it."

"Well you're going to. It's the price you've got to pa for . . . for . . . for doing what you did to me."

He cringed, but stood his ground. What they'd done they'd done to each other, but he felt too guilty to argu about semantics. "If that's what you want."

"I don't know what I want! That's the problem." He voice wavered again and he was afraid she was going t break down altogether, but she was made of stronge stuff this morning. She tucked her knees close to he and wrapped one arm around them, messing the shee that was her only covering. "What I need right now i for you to understand why I was so desperate, such basket case, last night."

"It won't change things."

"But it'll help me." Smoke drifted from her nostril "We were alone, the three of us—Stuart, Collin, and I– for the first time in a long, long while. Daddy—Robert—

"I know who he is. We met."

"You have?" Questions darkened her eyes. "When?"

"When he was convinced that I tried to kill Frank."

"Oh." She hesitated and he thought for a momen that he might be spared. Instead she just shook he head, bit her lip, then kept on talking. "Daddy threw party at the lake house last night, the same kind he doe every year when he and Mummy move up for the sun mer. It was a drag and Stuart, Collin, and I made our selves scarce when all the guests arrived and starte drinking. No one even missed us."

She smiled bitterly, but her eyes were brimming wit unshed tears again. "We hid out in the pool house, wher we drank some of Daddy's booze and . . . got a little drunk I guess." She shoved a hank of hair from her eyes, an her brow furrowed in concentration. "Some of the de tails are fuzzy, but we were all having fun, then Stuar had to leave, to make sure that no one got suspiciou and came looking for us. Collin and I were pretty well ripped already, and like I said, I've had a crush on him for a long time. I kissed him and he kissed me back and one thing led to another." She stared at the floor. "I got the impression, I mean, I thought he *wanted* me. He, uh, he let me believe that he cared but . . ." She blinked against her damning tears. "I, uh, sensed something was wrong, that he wasn't excited, that he wasn't really paying attention to me, but I thought that if I . . . showed him how much I cared . . ." Her voice drifted off and she seemed to forget that Daegan was in the room. Her cigarette burned neglected in her fingers. "I, um, tried my best to arouse him but it wasn't working, and then I knew what was wrong." She took in a long, shuddering breath. "We weren't alone."

A length of ash fell to the floor. Daegan didn't move. Bibi didn't notice. She wasn't in the room any longer; she was far away, staring at the linoleum, but not seeing, reliving her mortification of the night before.

Her voice was barely a whisper. "Stuart hadn't really left. He was in the hallway watching us, observing every intimate detail, hearing every word and . . . and Collin knew it. He couldn't perform because he was self-conscious, but they both were going to let me go through with it, both listened as I begged Collin to make love to me, watched as I . . . well, as I tried all sorts of tricks with my hands and mouth." Tears slid down her cheeks and chin. "I was such a fool."

He lifted his empty hands and felt like a heel. Every male she'd trusted the night before had taken advantage of her, including him. "If I could change things, I would," he said gruffly.

"Me, too." Tears rained from her eyes. "How can I ever face them again?" Her voice was so small, it broke his heart. She lifted the cigarette to her lips.

"You weren't to blame."

Blinking rapidly, she sobbed. "I guess I'm a lousy se
ductress."

"Not so lousy," he said, the irony in his words audi
ble.

"Oh, God, Daegan, and then you and I—"

"I know, I know."

"How could they do it to me? How could I be so
damned stupid and naive to let them use me for . . . for
some kind of weird sport?"

"Don't blame yourself, Bibi. Collin and Stuart,
they're as much to blame. More. They used you. I—I
used you."

"No, I think . . ." Her pretty face drew into a knot of
concentration. "I think I used you." She raised her eyes
to his. "You tried to stop it."

"But I didn't."

"I wouldn't let you."

He felt a sad smile tug at the corner of his mouth. "I
could've been stronger. You didn't rape me, Bibi."

"Oh, God!" She dropped her cigarette into an open
beer can and hiccupped loudly, crying hysterically.

He crossed the room and drew her into his arms.
She flinched, but he didn't let go, just whispered into
her hair, telling her over and over again that things
would work out even though he didn't believe his hol
low, soothing words. From that moment on, he knew he
was damned. Forever. Her hair smelled of perfume and
smoke and he held her until she was in control, until
the hiccupping sobs subsided. He whispered platitudes.
"Everything's gonna be all right. It's not the end of the
world. You can put this behind you." But he knew the
words were all lies.

"If only it were that easy." She let out a long, tremu
lous breath then abruptly stiffened. "Let me go."

His hands dropped to his side and Bibi pushed him
aside, as if suddenly his touch was foul.

"This—this—everything—it's got to stop. Got to," she said, tossing off the covers, unafraid to let him see her nude again. He turned his head and she threw on her clothes, stepped into her shoes, and gathered her purse and keys. "I'm sorry, Daegan, about everything," she called over her shoulder as she fumbled with the lock and let herself out. He heard her footsteps retreating down the staircase as she half ran to her car. But even as she dashed away, he realized that it wasn't over. Far from it. This was just the beginning. In the keen insight that sometimes warned him of the future, he sensed that because he'd slept with his cousin and committed one of the most scorned taboos of all, he was in for the worst trouble of his life.

Guilt stole after him all day. He kept expecting to hear from someone, anyone connected with the family, and was jumpy, always looking over his shoulder as he loaded coal into several trucks.

Nothing happened. The day was extraordinarily quiet, a cool summer afternoon with enough of a breeze to chase away the smog. After work Bibi wasn't waiting for him. No one stopped by his apartment as he changed his clothes. Even his mother, who was shunning him in the hope that he would see the evil of his ways and return, didn't break her silence.

By evening Daegan was able to breathe a little. He wandered over to Shorty's, drank some beer, and won nearly a hundred bucks playing nine ball. Though his conscience still twinged with guilt, he figured things would work out; that sleeping with Bibi hadn't been the end of the world.

Or so he'd thought until, like the sharp crack of Satan's whip, retribution lashed out at Daegan O'Rourke with all the fury of hell.

Walking home from the pool hall that night, fists burrowed deep in his pockets, the fingers of his right hand curled possessively around his meager winnings, he ducked through the familiar alleys that skirted the water-front. There were only a few people wandering through the narrow streets and a thick fog had rolled in off the harbor. Hardly a light blazed in any apartment window. Even the hookers and pimps seemed to have disappeared.

Maybe it was the fog, laying thick and cold along the shoreline, or maybe most people had more sense than he did. Probably a combination of both.

A foghorn moaned in the darkness.

Sidestepping garbage cans and puddles, he noticed a dog lying in a doorway. The animal let out a low, threatening growl. "It's okay," Daegan told the mutt, but the animal wasn't watching him. His ears were cocked, his golden eyes fixed somewhere behind Daegan in the soupy darkness.

The hairs on the back of Daegan's neck raised.

He picked up his pace.

The dog let out a deep bark and Daegan sensed rather than saw his attacker. Quick footsteps chased after him. Daegan started to run, but he heard the sound of rushed breath and felt a silent and deadly hatred oozing through the night.

"You're a dead man, O'Rourke!" The voice was familiar—smooth and polished with years of education.

Stuart.

Daegan's muscles bunched reflexively. He smelled a fight. All of his lovemaking with Bibi flashed through his mind as he turned and Stuart, breathing hard, emerged from the mist. Wielding a thick black crowbar, he walked forward at a slow, determined pace. "Now, you listen," he said, rage contorting his aristocratic features. "I'm gonna beat the shit out of you and leave you lying in your own blood so that the pathetic beast back there

an have a crack at you." He thumped the crowbar
menacingly against his free hand. Then, quick as a
nake striking, he swung.

Daegan ducked, but the bar connected, smashing his
aw with a sickening crunch. Pain screamed through his
ace. Blood spurted from his mouth. His legs wobbled.

"You deserve to die, O'Rourke." Crack! Another
low. Sharp. Fast. Daegan's head snapped backward.
His legs turned to jelly. He spun around and his head
lammed into the cold concrete.

The dog was in a frenzy, snarling and barking and
creating a ruckus.

"Stay away from her! You stay away from her!" Stuart
icked him hard in the gut. Daegan's body curled into a
all. "Bastard!" Stuart roared. "You dirty, rotten, fucking
astard!" Stuart's voice rose an octave. Daegan fought a
ickening wave of nausea and looked up through eyes al-
eady swollen. In the darkness Stuart, his face distorted
n a savage, brutal fury, towered over Daegan. Still hold-
ng the crowbar in one hand, he slid a deadly, thin-
laded knife out of his pocket with the other. "I should
ut your black heart out right now! Bibi trusted you."

"Yeah, like she trusted you."

Another vicious kick. Daegan's ribs snapped. Pain,
ot as liquid fire, shot through his chest.

"*I* didn't screw her!" Stuart screamed, waving the
ruel knife high in the air. Its wicked, narrow blade
linted blue in the watery glow of the streetlamps.

"Didn't you?"

"No way."

"It doesn't have to be physical," Daegan said, his head
eginning to clear. His jaw throbbed, his ribs ached, but
le was getting his bearings. "You can screw up someone
vorse by messing with her mind. That's what you did to
our sister."

"You don't know anything." Stuart lunged, the kni[fe] thrust forward.

Daegan rolled to his right and onto the balls of h[is] feet. "Don't," he warned thickly, through teeth th[at] were soft in his gums. Blood drained from his mou[th] and his eyes were mere slits.

"I'll cut you to ribbons, maybe even fillet those ill[e]gitimate balls of yours."

"Try it," Daegan suggested, ready for the fight.

They were circling in the alley, Stuart's Sullivan-bl[ue] eyes shining brightly, his lips tight over perfect teet[h] his expression grim and dangerous. "You're a fo[ol] O'Rourke."

"Yeah, but I don't play peeping Tom while my siste[r's] making it with my cousin."

"You cocky little prick." Stuart flew at Daegan, b[ut] this time Daegan was ready for him. With a sharp kic[k] he swept Stuart's legs from beneath him, ducked th[e] slice of the knife, and landed on his own feet. Stua[rt] went down. The crowbar clattered from his hand, b[ut] he managed to hang on to his more deadly weapon.

"Drop something?" Daegan asked, snatching up th[e] metal bar and swinging it over his head.

On his feet in an instant, Stuart warned, "I'll hav[e] you up on charges."

"Fine."

Stuart's blade swished through the thick night a[ir] carving wildly, nicking Daegan's ear. Blood gushed an[d] Daegan swung downward, glancing a blow off Stuar[t's] shoulder. Stuart let out a howl of pain and fell to h[is] knees.

"Hey—knock it off down there," a gruff voice yelle[d] from a window three stories up. "Break it up. People a[re] trying to sleep!"

The dog was barking like mad.

Daegan threw himself at his cousin, grabbing Stuart's midsection and hurtling them both to the ground.

"Stop it, man," Daegan ordered but Stuart sliced upward, the blade connecting with flesh.

Daegan's restraint fled. As Stuart uttered oaths and kicked, Daegan grabbed his wrist and pushed it backward until the knife clattered to the ground and the bones snapped.

"Jesus Christ! I'm callin' the cops!" the man in the window warned.

Stuart screamed in fury and pain just as Daegan connected, his fist slamming into his cousin's jaw. He didn't stop. As Stuart struggled, Daegan hit him again and again until Stuart stopped moving, just moaned in agony. Blood and bruises discolored what had once been even, patrician features and he lay face-up on the asphalt, his eyes rolled back in his head, his breathing raspy. Daegan's rage dissipated as he realized what he'd done. "Oh, God." Daegan stopped—his bloodied fist raised in the air. His own breath was quick and shallow. Blood was everywhere and Stuart looked as if he might be dead.

"Shit!" Daegan grabbed the knife and snapped it in half over his knee. Then he dropped both pieces near Stuart's form and ran to the nearest phone booth. His hands shook as he tried to find change in his pockets, then quickly dialed the police.

"There's been a fight, down by the docks, near . . . near . . ." Oh, damn, where were they? He tried to think, get his bearings, but all he saw was Stuart's white face staring sightlessly up at him. "I think it's by Taylor's Mill on the waterfront. One of the guys is beat up pretty bad. He looks dead. You'd better send an ambulance." Then he thought of the cross street and rattled off its name before slamming down the receiver, wiping away the blood with an old gas rag he had in his pocket and taking off at a dead run, covering the few blocks to his apartment. He'd have to go back, to turn himself in—to explain what had happened, how Stuart had attacked him for sleeping with his sister. Oh, hell, what a mess!

With shaking hands, he poured himself a beer then saw his reflection in the mirror. His face was bruised and battered, his eyes blackened slits, his hands swollen, half his earlobe missing, and he could barely breathe, his ribs hurt so bad, and a deep nasty scratch, where Stuart's little knife had reached him, arched from his shoulder to his navel.

As best he could, he cleaned himself and doctored his wounds using hot water, iodine, and strips of gauze.

He'd have to deal with the police, and if they didn't have him up on charges, which would be a miracle, he'd leave Boston. There was nothing left for him here. He'd lost Bibi as a friend by taking her as a lover. His mother had chosen Frank Sullivan over her only son and the rest of the family would despise him after Stuart was hauled to the hospital and named the bastard black sheep as his attacker—or worse yet if he died.

Daegan's life would be over, not that it was much of a life anyway. It was time to move on, head west. His only regret was Bibi, but she was better off without him. He'd sever all connections with this city, including his mother, his poor Irish roots, and his accent. In the West there were vast acres of land, room to move, a way of life so far removed from Boston that he'd erase every painful memory he'd ever collected.

He was folding clothes into his old duffle bag when the police arrived. A detective and sergeant, both of whom looked like they'd been on the force for a hundred years, were still pounding loudly on his door as he yanked it open. The younger man, Detective Jones, was redheaded and nervous, forever popping his gum, but the older guy, Sergeant Claud Traskell, was calm, his baleful hound-dog eyes penetrating as he announced that Stuart Sullivan had been found near the docks, his body beaten practically beyond recognition, a hunting knife broken and left near his hand. His heart had been beating when the paramedics had gotten to him, but he'd died on the way to the hospital.

Daegan's legs nearly gave way. Panic took a stranglehold on his throat as he read the censure in Traskell's eyes. *Dead?* Stuart Sullivan was dead? Holy mother of God, no! Even though he'd told himself it was possible, he hadn't been prepared. He couldn't believe that Stuart was dead—Stuart the golden boy, Stuart the heir, Stuart the great manipulator.

Grief and fear settled like lead on his shoulders. He clamped hard on his jaw, willing himself to appear stoic when inside he was falling apart. Stuart—*dead?*

Leaning against the wall for support, Daegan only half listened as the sergeant read him his rights and clamped a pair of handcuffs around his wrists. There was nothing he could do.

Daegan O'Rourke was the Boston Police Department's number one suspect in the murder of Stuart William Sullivan.

BOOK THREE

BOOK THREE

KATE

1995

Chapter 11

"Stay away from him, Jon," Kate said, a cold frost burrowing deep in the folds of her heart after Daegan O'Rourke had driven away from the house. *Who was he and what had he done? A killer? Dear Lord!* She found that impossible to believe. Nervously, she shoved a stray strand of hair from her face and watched as the dust settled back in the drive. He was too close. Too damned close living at the McIntyre place. "Don't go near him, ever again."

Jon, eyes trained on the empty drive, bent down and scratched Houndog behind his ears. "I won't," he said, his young jaw tight, his eyes trained on the driveway, "but I promised Eli I'd take care of Roscoe—"

"Don't argue with me," she said testily, shaken inside. "Tell me what you saw."

"Nothing."

"But you said—"

"It wasn't a vision," he admitted, kicking at the gravel in the drive as if he were embarrassed. "Just a feeling. I can't really explain it."

"Just stay away from him."

"I promised, didn't I?" Jon said tightly, belligerence traced in the angles of his face.

"Yes, I know."

"Don't freak out, Ma. We'll be fine," he muttered.

But she was freaking out. Big time. All of Jon's worries about the future had finally gotten to her, and his accusation that Daegan had killed someone had turned her blood to ice.

"The dog will be fine," she said, her voice sounding distant to her own ears. "O'Rourke will feed him. Now, listen, I don't want you setting one foot on the McIntyre place again. Not until we find out more about our new neighbor." She'd call Laura back and throw Daegan O'Rourke's name into the loop, though how he was connected with the East Coast was beyond her. She'd listened and she hadn't heard a trace of Bostonian accent in his speech pattern, checked the license plate of his truck, and noted that it was registered in Montana, scrutinized him, and hadn't noticed anything other than country ways and ranch charm, except for the feeling—just a shimmer of intuition—that he was deadlier than he looked, that if pushed hard, he'd push back just a little harder.

Despite all his rugged country-boy allure and regardless of the fact that he'd played the role of Good Samaritan, Daegan O'Rourke was a man to avoid.

Looking over her shoulder and shivering a little with premonition, she let herself into the house. Was Daegan the stalker in Jon's nightmares? Or was it someone else . . .

Daegan unlocked a cheap hutch he'd bought in town and pulled out the file he'd begun on Kate Summers and her son, Jon. It was empty for the most part; there wasn't a lot of information. After Bibi had originally contacted him, it had taken nearly a week to track down Kate, which wasn't long, considering that she had wanted to disappear, but all he'd had to do was contact some friends he'd made in the investigation business, Lana Petrelli in Boston and Foster Investigations here in Oregon. Lana had come up with the birth certificate of Jon Summers, the death certificate of Kate's husband and daughter, and some records through the DMV about bought and sold cars. The paper trail had led him to Oregon, where Foster had picked it up.

Daegan had called Bibi, checked with some real estate people in Hopewell, and lucked into the McIntyre place—if being able to rent this dump was lucky. To maintain his cover, he'd bought two horses and a few head of cattle at a local livestock auction, which he could either sell or move back to Montana at the end of this. The scheme seemed elaborate and contrived, but he felt it necessary to gain Kate and Jon's trust. To do so, he had to look and act like a legitimate rancher—which wouldn't be too difficult. Though he'd never much liked lying, it often came in useful, and over the course of his lifetime, he'd developed a talent for avoiding the truth when necessary.

But how, if Jon did turn out to be his son, would he ever be able to get past the lie? What would he do about the boy? About his mother? Damn it all to hell, this wasn't supposed to happen. When he'd severed ties with the Sullivan family, he'd intended never to look back.

The kid had changed all that.

The man was a liar. Jon knew it. He'd felt it. *Seen* it the moment he took Daegan's hand.

Now, as he lay on his bed and tossed a baseball in his hands, he barely heard the song on the radio. Everything faded at the memory of the sensation, the vision, that had sizzled through his brain, only to disappear as quickly as it had come.

Just a short glimpse into Daegan's past, short but vivid.

In his mind's eye he'd seen a bloodied unmoving man sprawled in a dark alley. Pain, fear, and rage had streaked from Daegan's body to his. In a split second, Jon had witnessed a brutal fight. Knuckles and an iron bar had smashed into flesh. Bones cracked. Skin broke. Cartilage had crumpled. A horrendous series of blows had torn flesh until blood ran in the street.

Even now, hours later after shaking his new neighbor's hand, Jon felt the aftermath, the residual thrum of adrenaline coursing through Daegan's body. He felt the ache in his own teeth as if they'd been loosened, smelled the deep, primal scent of a fight in the cool night air.

It had been a long time ago, yeah, but it had happened.

And O'Rourke had lied about it. The other guy had died.

Jon raked his fingers through his hair and switched off the radio.

Who the hell was Daegan O'Rourke?

And why do I feel so in tune with this stranger's distant memories?

Snatching the ball in midair, Jon sat up, rolled it under the bed, and went to the window. Two squares of gold light, windows at Eli's old place, glowed through the trees, and Jon wondered what Daegan O'Rourke was doing now. What was the man even doing here, in nowheresville Hopewell, Oregon?

Cheek to the cool glass, Jon let his eyes fall to the dark spot below the trees where he'd worn a shallow path to the McIntyre place over the past few years. He could steal over and no one would know. Sure, he'd promised his mom he'd stay away, but then there was Roscoe to consider. The dog was still so freaked by Eli's death that he wouldn't come out from under the porch, except when Jon was there.

Going over there would be a mission of mercy.

Besides, no one had to know if he slipped over once in a while to check on Roscoe or visit the horses.

Or spy on the stranger with the scent of death in his past.

Kate answered the phone on the second ring. "Hello?"

Far away, her sister Laura's voice was rushed, as if she was out of breath. "Hey, hi!"

"Laura." Kate felt an immediate sense of relief and of longing. Right now she would have done anything to see Laura and be wrapped up in her optimism and care-free spirit. Stretching the cord so that she could peek from the kitchen to the living room, she made sure that Jon was nowhere nearby, then heard his footsteps over-head in his bedroom followed by the sound of bass throbbing. For the first time in her life she was grateful for the loud, hard-rocking beat of Metallica.

"Hey," Laura was saying, "I got your message and it sounded like you were way beyond stressed."

"I am. Oh, God, Laura." Kate, suddenly weary, leaned her sagging shoulders against the kitchen wall. How could she even begin to explain something she didn't under-stand?

"What's wrong?" Her sister's voice had lost a little of its normal lilt.

"I need your help."

"That's a switch! You usually come to the rescue when I need something, not the other way around." Laura laughed with a touch of irony and Kate remembered some of the times she'd had to bail out her way ward, rebellious sister. "Anyway, rest assured your wish i my command. What's up?"

"It's—it's about Jon."

"So what else is new?"

"This time it's different," Kate said.

"Then it's not about kids calling him a freak and al that shit, right?" Laura asked, her aunt antennae on constant alert. Laura, with no children of her own, ha always been Jon's champion.

"No . . . well, there's that, too, but right now the teas ing and taunts aren't at the top of my priority list. Wha I want is for you to do some snooping—through th State of Massachusetts's files."

"Snooping?" Laura said and the laughter in he voice faded.

"Yes."

"Uh-oh, I smell something underhanded here. I'n not sure I can help you out, but hold on a minute, wil you? I need to get to the desk so I can write this down. There was a pause, muted conversation, and then Laur was back again. "That's better. Jeremy and I just got bac from the gym and I'm sweating like a pig even thougl it's still snowing out here. Can you believe it? Befor Halloween and six inches of fluff on the ground. Thos trick-or-treaters are gonna freeze their little tushes off.

Kate could barely listen to Laura's well-meaning bal ble and anxiously tapped her fingers on the phone.

"Okay, now, what was it you wanted?"

"I need all kinds of information on Jon's birth, if yo can get it, and I'm not talking about the phony birtl certificate. I need the real thing."

Laura let out a long, low whistle and Kate coul imagine her digging long fingers anxiously through he red brown curls. "I thought you were never going to tr and dig up all that mess."

"I don't want to, but I have to." Deciding she had no choice, she quickly brought Laura up to date. Her sister, usually jovial, just listened and didn't bother cracking one joke. "So," Kate finished, "I want to find out Jon's real birth mother and father, and if the father has a criminal record of any kind."

"I don't suppose you have any names, any place to start?"

"I'd tell you to check with whatever law office took over Tyrell Clark's cases, but I doubt that he kept files on Jon's case," she said, glancing out the window in the direction of the old McIntyre place. She couldn't see the house through the thick copse of pine trees, but wondered about her new neighbor. "And while you're at it, maybe you can also check out the background of the guy who's renting the ranch next door. His name is Daegan O'Rourke. He doesn't look or sound like he came from anywhere near Boston, but then people can change in fifteen years. Just see if he's connected to this in any way. He drives an old truck—a Dodge, I think—and at one time it was green. The license plates are from Montana, but I didn't catch the numbers."

"Montana's a long way from here."

"I know, but it's a start, isn't it?"

"Just because you have a new neighbor—"

"It's more than that. Jon shook his hand and freaked out, accused the guy of getting into a fight and killing someone."

"Geez."

"Yeah. O'Rourke denied it, of course, said that he got into a bad fight with his cousin but he didn't kill him." Her insides were churning again. She couldn't believe that she was discussing this—the fact that a possible murderer, someone connected with Jon—might be living next door. "I'd tell Sheriff Swanson, but he'd just laugh at me. His kid and Jon don't get along—"

"Calm down, Kate. Take a deep breath and tell me about him."

"Okay, okay." Kate closed her eyes for a second and snatched at her rapidly fleeing composure. Losing it wouldn't do anyone any good. She had to remain in control, keep her wits about her. "This guy is white—probably Irish, I'd guess if any part of his story is true—about thirty-five, give or take a couple of years. A little over six feet, six one or two maybe. He's probably a hundred and eighty or ninety pounds. He's lanky but has wide shoulders, clean-shaven, has gray eyes and dark brown hair, almost black but with streaks of red. He dresses and talks like a rancher or cowboy and has the lingo and swagger and faded Levis and cowboy boots down. But it seems more than a coincidence that he showed up when he did."

"He came to your house?"

"Yeah, to borrow the phone. The telephone company hasn't installed his yet."

"Sounds like a criminal to me," Laura mocked.

Kate counted to five in her mind. Her sister had never been as serious as she and more than once Laura had accused her of being melodramatic. "And he changed a flat for me."

"Now I'm really worried."

"Well, I am, Laura. I think he should be checked out."

"You think he's lying? About what?"

"I wish I knew. Maybe he's okay, just who he says he is, but the timing's all wrong." Winding the phone cord around her fingers, she tried to picture Daegan O'Rourke as a cold-blooded killer, as the father of her son, as a man bent on evil. True, there was something suspicious lurking in his steely eyes—a shadow of deceit—or was it her imagination. Lately, with all Jon's defiant antics, she'd lost her usual cool head and perspective. "I'm just nervous," she admitted. "All this is happening too fast. Way too fast."

There was a pause before Laura said, "You know, Kate, maybe you should do the checking personally."

"But I need—"

"I mean just be friendly to him, instead of suspicious. Is he single?"

"Damn it, Laura, I don't know; I didn't ask," Kate shot back, unable to hide her agitation.

"That's the first thing I would have found out. From your description of him, the guy sounds . . . interesting."

"As interesting as a desert sidewinder!"

"You don't know anything about him except that Jon thinks he was involved in a fight."

"Not just a fight. Murder," Kate said angrily. For years Laura had suggested that she start dating, seriously dating, that being single and raising a son on her own was too much for Kate. Which was ridiculous. It was time to set Laura straight. "Look, even if he was just a regular guy, the most eligible bachelor on the face of the earth, I don't have time for a man—"

"Oh, for God's sake, Kate, give it up," Laura snapped. "When are you going to get off this guilt trip you've been taking and let go of Jim? He's been gone for nearly sixteen years. He's not coming back and it doesn't mean you didn't love him if you happen to find someone else."

"I'm not looking."

"Well, you should, for crying out loud! You're young, Kate, not ready for spinsterhood. My advice is quit looking at this new neighbor as a potential threat and think of him as a possible love interest."

"I don't want—"

"Have you ever thought maybe that's what's wrong

with Jon?" Laura demanded. "Look, I hate to be blunt, but you're having a lot of trouble with him now, aren't you? Fights? Ditching school? Out and out rebellion? Maybe he needs a father figure."

"And you think Daegan O'Rourke's a good candidate," Kate ventured testily. "You haven't even met him."

"Okay, not O'Rourke—maybe this guy is bad news—but *someone*, Kate. If not for Jon, then for yourself. You've dedicated your life to that kid and he's gonna be gone in a few years. What then?"

"I don't know," Kate admitted. She'd worried about Jon's leaving herself. Not only for her. But for her boy.

"Quit trying to be such a damned saint and live a little."

Live a little. Laura's personal credo. Where Kate had always looked to the future, planned her life, kept an eye over her shoulder hoping the past wouldn't catch up with her, Laura had lived for the moment, unconcerned about the thunderclouds gathering in the distance.

"This guy bothers me, Laura."

"You let him bother you. Because Jon had a bad dream. Slow down and take a deep breath. You're borrowing trouble."

Kate ignored the jab. For years Laura had called her a worrywart. "Okay, okay, but listen to this. I noticed something else about O'Rourke. One of his earlobes, his left one, I think, isn't as big as the other."

"Geez, Kate, haven't you noticed? No one's perfectly balanced."

"I know, but this guy's ear looks like it was sliced."

"Like in a knife fight?" Laura was clearly skeptical.

"I suppose."

"So what? Was it bleeding all over your living room carpet?"

"No, I mean it might have happened a long time ago."

"For the love of God, Kate, listen to yourself. So he lost part of his ear. Big deal. Remember, Dad was minus a couple of toes because of some accident when he was a kid. And O'Rourke admitted to the fight with his cousin, didn't he? Maybe he was cut then. You're beginning, no, I take that back, this isn't the beginning, you've always been this way."

"Which is?"

"Paranoid. For nearly fifteen years nothing has happened, and Jon's been wrong with his premonitions before, hasn't he?"

"Yes, but—"

"So don't worry about the new neighbor and I'll run some checks, see what I can find out. Luckily, he has a somewhat unusual name."

"If it's his real one."

"Well, if it isn't, then we're in trouble," Laura said, "but let's not think about that, not just yet, okay? I have a couple of friends in another department who have access to the prison records, but I bet this guy never set one foot east of the Great Divide. So take it easy. Have a glass of wine, take a hot bath, do whatever it is you do to unwind and I'll call you back in a few days. Everything's going to be all right," Laura said as she hung up.

"I hope you're right," Kate replied to the empty line. "Oh, Laura, I hope to God you're right."

But she didn't believe her sister for a minute. There was trouble brewing, big trouble, and Kate would bet her last dollar that it had something to do with Daegan O'Rourke.

Jon sneaked through the trees and hiked his collar up around his neck. The moon was riding high and a jillion stars spangled the sky, but it was cold, colder than

a well digger's butt, as Eli used to say. At the thought o
the old geezer, Jon gritted his teeth as he made his wa
through the trees and across a field of dry grass an
weeds. He'd walked this way a hundred times befor
when Eli was alive, and now, since meeting O'Rourke
he couldn't stay away. Oh, sure he'd promised hi
mother that he'd keep off the McIntyre spread, but h
hadn't. Three times since O'Rourke had first shown up
Jon had made a nocturnal visit. He'd sat in the shadows
petting Roscoe, watching O'Rourke through the shade
less windows. The guy read a lot, had himself a lapto
computer that he used, talked on the phone, watched
little television, the news and Letterman, before turn
ing out the lights after one.

He didn't do anything all that suspicious and seeme
to be taking good enough care of Eli's old hound. Yet . .
there was something about him, something that wasn'
quite right.

He snapped on a twig and Roscoe let out a quie
"woof" before scrambling from beneath the porch and
loping toward Jon.

"Here ya go," Jon said, digging in his pocket and giv
ing the dog a biscuit. Carefully, he wandered around th
house. The lights were on in the kitchen, and O'Rourke
was pouring himself a beer. From the darkness, Jo
watched him move from the kitchen to the living room
where, without bothering to snap on a light, he propped
stockinged foot on a battle-scarred coffee table, sippe
his beer, and watched the tube. Bluish flashes illumi
nated his angular face, and if Jon were prone to believ
ing in such nonsense, he would have thought O'Rourke
looked like a devil.

Why he kept coming over here, he didn't under
stand. It was one thing when Eli was alive. They'd spen
hours together talking, gazing at the ever-changing sky
playing guitar and harmonica, and telling stories—Ol

Man McIntyre had more stories about growing up poor on the Great Plains than anyone. Jon had confided in Eli, admitting that he had a crush on Jennifer Caruso and that's why Todd Neider was always trying to beat him up. Because of Jennifer. Eli had chuckled, telling him there was no fool like a fool for a woman.

God, he missed the old coot. That's why he probably kept hanging out, that and the new colt that had suddenly appeared in the paddock two days before. Jon had always had a thing about horses, but his mother had refused to let him have one. Though indulgent in about every other way, she'd put her foot down when it came to buying a horse. They'd had plenty of arguments and he'd offered to buy one with his own money, but she'd been adamant, saying that he'd no sooner get the animal than want a car and that, he admitted, was probably true.

But O'Rourke's colt fascinated him. Jon knew enough about horses to tell that the chestnut-colored quarter-horse was worth some money while the other nag—a gray gelding—was just a work horse, sure-footed and easy-tempered, without the fire of the colt.

Whistling softly, he reached into his pocket and found an apple that he cut into two pieces with his jack knife. The trusting gray ambled over, eagerly nuzzling Jon's palm, but the colt shook his head and snorted nervously, his two white stockings flashing.

"Come on," Jon whispered. "Otherwise you're going to lose out to Greedy again." Extending a hand, he felt a smile play upon his features as the temperamental animal flattened his ears but reluctantly edged closer. "That's it."

The colt stretched his neck and swept the apple from Jon's open palm in one quick movement. Teeth grinding the apple, he backed away.

"His name is Buckshot."

Jon nearly jumped out of his skin! Heart pumping wildly, he whirled and found O'Rourke standing less than ten feet away from him. He'd managed to slide into his boots but hadn't bothered with a jacket, and his arms were crossed firmly over his chest.

"Jesus!" Jon whispered.

"You like the horse?"

Jon was thinking fast. Now that he was caught, what could he do? Run? But O'Rourke could call his mom. His mouth was dry as dust, his palms sweaty. "He's . . . okay,"

"You want to ride him?"

"No!" Jon lied. He had to get out of here and fast.

"Too bad. He could use the exercise." Was this guy for real? Jon's teeth began to chatter. "Cold?"

"Yeah."

"You want to come into the house and warm up? I got coffee and maybe some of that instant cocoa."

"No . . . oh, no." Jon shook his head vehemently. This guy was still the enemy; he knew it in his bones, and yet he seemed decent enough.

"What're you doing here?" O'Rourke asked, and any hopes Jon had of getting away with this without his mother finding out disappeared.

"I, uh, used to come and visit Eli. And Roscoe."

Daegan glanced at the dog sitting obediently by Jon's sneaker. "He likes you a helluva lot more than he likes me." His gaze moved up to study Jon's face. "You weren't spying on me, were ya?"

"What? No way!" Jon's heart began to pump wildly again. Shit! Why hadn't he heard the guy approach? He'd been so into getting Buckshot to respond that he hadn't heard the door open, the screen creak, boots on the porch, or the snap of a twig. It was like the guy just willed himself out here like a damned ghost or something.

"But you have been here before?"

"No, I swear . . ." The look on O'Rourke's face called him a liar. "Well, yeah, a couple of times."

"Your mom know you're here?"

"No!"

"And you'd like to keep it that way?"

Jon shrugged. "She wouldn't like it."

" 'Cause you called me a murderer."

"And she doesn't like me sneakin' around at night."

"It could be dangerous." O'Rourke rubbed his jaw and stared at the moon. "You want your stuff back?"

"Oh." Jon shook his head. "If Mom found it, she'd kill me."

"I doubt it." O'Rourke shook his head. "I'd guess she'd do just about anything for you."

" 'Cept buy me a horse."

O'Rourke's laughter thundered through the night and Jon physically jumped. "Your mother's a smart woman, Jon. These animals are nothing but trouble."

"You think?"

"I know."

"But you have 'em."

" 'Cause I'm a fool, I guess. They can't go the miles of a pickup, need to be fed and groomed, kept healthy, and are general pains in the butt, but, yeah, I like 'em."

"I, uh, better get going," Jon said.

"Next time you want to see the horse, stop by and talk to me first."

"Sure," Jon said, knowing there wouldn't be a next time.

"And Jon?"

Here it comes. This is the part where he's going to let me know that it's his duty, hard as it might be, to call Ma and tell her that I snuck over here. "Yeah?"

"You're too young to drink."

"Oh."

"And cut back on the smokes." His eyes were sharp and fixed on Jon. "You'd better get back home before your mom figures out that you're gone. Then both of us will have a lot of explainin' to do. I don't know about you, but I'm not in the mood for a lecture."

With that he turned and headed back to the house, and Jon was left with the bad need for a smoke and the dawning realization that Daegan O'Rourke might not be so bad after all.

Chapter 12

Kate didn't expect to see Daegan again, especially not at the local coffee shop where she usually stopped on her way back from the college, but there he was big as life, smiling at the waitress who was refilling his cup. One long jean-clad leg stretched into the aisle by the table and the sleeves of his cotton work shirt were rolled up, showing off tanned, muscular arms. A five o'clock shadow darkened his jaw, and he seemed at ease in the worn mock-leather booth.

She nearly hesitated at the door, but as if he'd sensed her arrival, he swiveled his head at the sound of the door opening and sent her a crooked half-smile, one that suggested they shared a secret—a private secret. Her stupid heart fluttered and she called herself six kinds of fool. This was the one man—the only man in all of Hopewell—that she should avoid at all costs.

"Kate!" His voice was friendly and smooth, his gray eyes warmer than she remembered. "Have a seat."

The last thing she wanted to do was to be trapped in a booth with him and be caught trying to make idle conversation. He was too full of restless energy for her, too starkly rugged, too damned male. It had been nearly a week since she'd last seen him, and in that time she'd calmed a bit. Laura hadn't called with any mind-numbing news that he was a serial killer or child moles-ter or even traffic violator, but still she had to be wary. He'd admitted that his cousin had died as the result of some kind of fight—who knew what other secrets he kept hidden behind his easy smile?

Before she could take another seat, other customers in the little café had twisted their necks to view her. Rather than give them more room for gossip—it was hard enough knowing that most of the townspeople viewed her as an oddity because of Jon and his strange premo-nitions—she walked up to O'Rourke's booth and plopped down on the opposite seat. She didn't even protest when he motioned for a waitress to bring her a cup of coffee.

"Small world," he said with a devilish glint in his eye.

"Small *town,* or haven't you noticed?"

A corner of his mouth lifted. "Just the way I like 'em."

"You've lived in the city?" she asked innocently, though her nerves were stretched tighter than fence wire. What was she doing pumping him for information? What could she possibly expect to learn?

"Nah, but I've been in enough of 'em to know that I'm a country boy at heart." Again that country-boy charm.

"Are you?" She leaned back in the seat and was about to ask him where he was from when the waitress, Tami Lynde, daughter of the shop's owner, brought a cup of coffee and asked Kate if she'd like anything else.

Wishing she'd never stepped foot in the door, Kate declined and then felt her back stiffen when she spied Carl Neider, Todd's father, saunter through the door. He was a huge bear of a man with hands like meat hooks, the start of a beer belly, and a flat face covered by a dark beard beginning to streak with gray. His eyes were wide-spaced, small and mean, and when he smiled, he showed off a mouthful of gold crowns.

"Friend of yours?" Daegan asked when she watched Neider take a booth on the other side of the café.

"Hardly." She poured a thin stream of cream into her cup and listened to the sounds of quiet conversation, rattling utensils, and the squeaking of a slow-turning ceiling fan mounted high over head. "His son Todd is a big kid who's taken delight in humiliating Jon. Called him names, picked fights with him, bullied him—you name it. All the usual." Watching the clouds roll up in her brew, she sighed. "I can't just blame him, of course. Sometimes Jon asks for it."

"No one asks to be humiliated." O'Rourke's eyes narrowed on Neider as he sipped from his cup, and again Kate felt that underlying current of energy, that raw force that was a part of this man. His jaw clamped tight and Kate decided she wouldn't want to cross him. Not ever.

From the back behind the counter, the short-order cook yelled at Tami over the sizzle of the fryer.

When Daegan focused on Kate again, all the warmth had evaporated from his eyes and she felt that same premonition of fear—of danger that seemed to lurk just beneath his "good ol' ranchin' boy" surface.

"You're right," she said. "Anyway, Jon's bigger now, able to take care of himself better. Hopefully he's smarter, too."

"Is he picked on for no reason or is it because of that sight he's got—because he sees things others don't?"

She didn't move and the cup she'd been raising to her lips stopped in midair. Clearing her throat, she set the steaming mug down and frowned. "You're very direct."

"You brought it up."

She couldn't argue the point. Resting her elbows on the table, she folded her hands and dropped her chin on her linked fingers so that she could hold his gaze without flinching. "That I did, Mr. O'Rourke, and the reason I did is because the things that have been said to Jon, the cruel remarks, the vicious jokes, the hateful names wound deep. It doesn't matter that the person who hurls the taunts his way is jealous or scared or feeling inferior. All those ugly words are painful. They scar. Not only him, but me, too, because I love him."

All through her tirade Daegan stared at her. His gaze never once moved from her face, and his lips, already thin, creased into a hard, uncompromising line.

"Do you know what it feels like to be called names—to feel out of place—to think that you're not as good as the rest of the kids?"

A shadow passed behind his eyes, a pain-filled shadow that quickly disappeared. "Afraid so," he drawled. "Maybe it's a rite of passage. Part of growin' up."

"It shouldn't be."

"Amen."

She lifted a shoulder and sighed. "So that's why I get a little defensive and overprotective. My mother bear claws begin to show and my instincts tend to work overtime and get me into trouble with my son."

"Why?"

"He seems to think that I'm in his way," she admitted, though she knew she shouldn't confide in him, shouldn't trust him with any secrets close to her heart. "He's convinced that I should keep my nose out of his business."

"Maybe you should."

"He's only fifteen."

"How does his dad figure in?"

She nearly choked on a swallow of coffee. "His fa-

ther?" she repeated, astounded that this man would
bring him up. "His father's gone. Jim died before Jon
was born."

"I didn't know . . . and he had no stepfather?"

"I never remarried," Kate admitted, then drained
her cup. This conversation was getting personal—too
personal.

"Why not?"

"What about you?" she said, turning the tables on
him. "Is there a Mrs. O'Rourke?"

He shook his head. "I'm not the marrying kind."

That, she believed. "Neither am I," she said, fishing in
her purse. "I mean I was, with Jim, but . . . well . . ." She
found her wallet and pulled out a couple of bills. "I
guess he was just a hard act to follow and I didn't have
all that many offers. Lots of men—at least some of the
ones I dated—considered Jon extra baggage. Can you
imagine? The fact that he has this sight made it all the
worse. But it's worked out just fine," she assured him.
"Jon and I are all right." She slapped the bills on the
table.

"I'll buy," he insisted.

"Thanks, but I'm used to paying my own way," she
replied. "Fact is, I like it that way." With that she swung
out of the restaurant and made a beeline to her car.
Being around O'Rourke was just too unsettling. He was
too direct, too restless, and too damned sexy. His eyes,
so deep and gray, his hands, big, calloused, the backs
dusted with dark hair, his jaw firm and square. For crying out loud, she'd never, never looked at a man so intently since Jim.

Calm down, she told herself and ignored the pounding
of her pulse. He was just a man. Nothing to be afraid of.
At least not yet. She climbed into her station wagon and
jammed her key into the ignition. Her new neighbor
had learned more than she'd intended to tell him about

Jon today, but now it was her turn. As she checked her rearview mirror to back out of her parking spot, she made a note to call Laura tonight and find out what her sister had dredged up on a would-be cowboy named Daegan O'Rourke.

So now what are you going to do, O'Rourke, kidnap the boy?

Daegan dug his heels into the old gray he'd bought at a local auction and glowered at the fence line, as if he gave a good goddamned what happened to this place. The sorry rusted wire and rotted posts weren't any of his concern—just part of the lie, a lie he was getting damned sick of.

The truth of the matter was he was looking beyond the fence and through a scraggly thicket of pine and spruce, to Kate Summers's house. The trees veiled his view, but he caught glimpses of the white 1920s vintage cottage with its wide back porch and blue trim. The yard, dry and spotty, was partially obscured by a row of raspberry canes and a vegetable garden. An apple tree stood near a weathered building that was probably a pump house or woodshed, and a long, sun-bleached rope dangled from one of the lower branches. He spied the path Jon used to sneak over here and couldn't stop a smile. The kid was sly, but Daegan had felt the boy's eyes on him while he was watching television, known he was being observed. He'd let it go on long enough for Jon to trust him and see that he was just another lonely bachelor rancher.

Ha! Another lie. Daegan couldn't hardly open his mouth without veering from the truth these days.

He needed to approach Kate again, but he hadn't figured out how. After lucking out and meeting her in the café, he hadn't seen hide nor hair of Ms. Summers, so now it was his move. If he could come up with one. Flattening her tire, pretending to need the use of her phone, waiting at the coffee shop where he knew she stopped after work—he'd played out all his "coincidences." Now he'd just have to call her up and pretend to be interested in her. Trouble was, he might not be pretending. She was starting to get to him, Kate Summers was. Complicated and pretty, she wasn't the type of woman who usually attracted him. Smart women with sharp tongues, deep thoughts, and stormy pasts were usually too much trouble. But Kate was different. And she was the adoptive mother of his son.

He gritted his teeth and fought a headache. Christ, what a mess!

Usually riding cleared his head, though he rarely saddled up an aging plow horse that he'd saved from the glue factory such as this gray. Years ago, he'd discovered the thrill of racing across acres of open land astride a swift horse. In his early twenties, after his brush with the law, a hitch in the army, and a brief career as a private investigator, he'd pointed his nose toward the western horizon. He'd landed in Albuquerque, then drifted through Laramie before ending up in western Montana, where he served as a guide to tenderfoots. Eventually he'd saved enough money to buy his spread in the foothills of the Bitterroots, the first place he'd ever felt was home.

And now he was here, astride an old nag, glaring at a ridiculous excuse for a fence while contemplating just what to do about the boy. His son.

So now what?

He could just wash his hands of the whole situation, but then he remembered Robert and Frank Sullivan. His back teeth ground together. There was no way, no way on this earth, they were going to get their pampered, rich hands on the boy. His boy. Kate's boy.

For the first time in six years he hungered for a smoke.

Who would have thought he would have ended up here, staring past the swaying branches of scraggly pine trees, wondering how he was going to approach a woman about giving up her son?

"Son of a bitch," he grumbled, yanking on the reins and heading back toward old McIntyre's house.

Ever since meeting Kate at the cafe and admitting to himself that, yes, Bibi's wild story about Jon's conception was beginning to hold water, he'd picked his way carefully. Kate had obviously been shaken by Jon's insistence that Daegan had murdered someone and she was still wary when he'd met her in the restaurant.

In the meantime, while thinking up an excuse to see her and Jon again, he'd kept busy. He'd set things up here—cleaned the place, made room for his fax machine, files, and computer to keep linked with his ranch in Montana, while ordering feed and veterinary supplies for the animals he'd bought. The old dog had deigned to stick his nose out from under the porch, but snarled every time Daegan came a little too close.

Now, Daegan clucked to the horse and ignored the blast of arctic wind that ripped down from the mountains. He needed more information, the kind he could only get from her. A jab of guilt pricked at his mind when he thought of how he was going to use her, how he hoped that she would learn to trust him, so that he could strip her emotions bare to her bones when he stole her boy from her. She'd never trust a living soul again. That thought shouldn't have bothered him. She deserved it, didn't she? She'd asked for it when she'd taken money and a child that didn't belong to her.

But she loved the boy. Done right by him.

Maybe he was going soft inside, but no matter what she'd done in the past, how many laws she'd broken to end up with Jon, she obviously would walk through hell for him. What more could a mother do? "Shit," he growled, imagining himself as the cause of a gut-wrenching agony that was soon to darken her whiskey gold eyes.

Nudging the gray, he decided that somehow, some way, he'd have to speak with Kate alone; try and find out if her son was really adopted, even though she'd already claimed the boy was sired by her dead husband.

He knew that she'd grown up on a Midwest farm until the death of her father, then, because of her mother's neglect, she and her younger sister, Laura, were cared for by an aunt and uncle. Kate married her high school sweetheart and they moved to Boston, where she worked as a receptionist/secretary for Tyrell Clark, the attorney Bibi had mentioned. Tragedy had struck swiftly. Soon after her one-year-old daughter and husband were killed, Kate had left Boston and moved to Seattle, where she worked part-time, took care of her young son, and managed to earn herself a master's degree in English.

From Seattle, Kate had headed south to Oregon and ended up in this miserable small town. Now an English professor, she taught writing to freshmen at a community college in Bend.

As she'd claimed, Kate Summers had never remarried. But her declaration that the boy was fathered by her late husband was false. Either Kate's gestation period was eleven months, the boy was fathered by a lover she'd slept with after old Jim had passed on, or the kid was adopted and the papers were phony.

Lie number one.

The reins slipped through his fingers and he scowled at the yellow blooms of tansy ragwort that persisted in growing on this rocky scrap of land. An ugly weed and deadly to cattle, tansy seemed to grow where nothing

else would take root. A hardy, unwanted pest—kind of
like bastard children.

Adjusting his hat, he turned the collar of his jean
jacket around his neck. The wind was picking up, au
tumn crisp in the air. Heavy-bellied clouds rolled over
the sky, threatening rain for the cracked, parched earth

It looked like Jon didn't even know he was adopted—
had no concept that there was an entire family that was
suddenly interested in him.

If Kate only knew what she was up against. He didn'
know how he was going to battle the Sullivan money
power, and influence, but at least he realized he was in
for a fight. Kate Summers didn't have a clue—or, he sur
mised grimly—a prayer. Yep, he'd have to tread lightly
but at the same time he'd have to move fast. If he'd
found Kate and the boy so quickly, so would Robert.

That same old empty gnawing scraped at his guts
Whenever he pitted himself against the Sullivan family
he felt it eating away at him.

But this time he was determined to win.

And Kate Summers will lose.

Guilt knifed through his heart, but he ignored the
wound. What happened to Kate was too damned bad
She'd started it a long time ago.

Daegan had always sworn that if he ever made the
mistake of fathering a child, intentionally or by acci
dent, he'd be a part of the kid's life, but then he hadn'
counted on his one night with Bibi producing anything
other than a bad taste in his mouth and a shadow of guil
to chase after him all his days.

He couldn't very well just kidnap the boy as Bib
seemed to think was the answer, and no court in the
country would give him custody. And what the hel
would he do with a near-grown handful of trouble who
could see into a man's soul?

Disgusted at the turn of his thoughts, he steered the gelding across a dry gulch that had the nerve to call itself a creek, and headed back toward the cabin. A rabbit scurried out of the horse's path and dust kicked up beneath his hooves as Daegan's gaze never strayed from the fence line. He noted the posts that needed to be shored up and the spots where rusting barbed wire was stretched out of shape.

From the house, the old dog let out a sharp bark.

The gelding snorted and his ears pricked forward. Daegan looked up, squinting against a gust of wind and the grit that came with it. Corralled near the barn was Buckshot, a mean-spirited colt and his only possession on the ranch worth owning. But the horse wasn't alone. Jon was in the paddock with the colt, trying to fling a rope around the animal's neck. Daegan's insides clenched.

Hell, what did he think he was doing?

He kicked his horse and the gelding responded.

The kid had balls of steel, Daegan would give him that. Who would have thought he'd trespass again after the scare Daegan had given him the other night?

"Idiot," he ground out, though he felt a stupid sense of pride that the boy had disobeyed his mother and wandered over this way. "Come on," he urged the horse.

Jon managed to swing the rope over Buckshot's neck, and as the colt sidestepped, the foolhardy kid threw himself onto the horse's back.

"Jesus H. Christ," Daegan muttered under his breath as he pressed his knees into the gray's sides. Was Jon trying to get himself killed? Daegan didn't want to shout, for fear that he would startle the bronc.

But it was too late.

Buckshot exploded in a fury of flashing hooves and dust.

Astride the stubborn colt, without a bridle or a lead

rope snapped onto the halter ring, just a little bit of bal
ing twine wrapped around Buckshot's thick neck, Jo
grinned widely. *Fool of a kid!*

The horse shot skyward, leaping and bucking and
trying to throw the hundred and fifty unwanted pounds
from his back. The dog ran back and forth on the fa
side of the fence.

"Damn it all to hell." Just what he needed! Jon acting
half-brained astride that devil of a colt. Daegan leaned
forward and his mount galloped across the arid field
sending up a cloud of dust. Before his horse stopped
Daegan jumped off, vaulted the fence, and was running
across the corral. "Hey, now, calm down," he said as
Buckshot lowered his head and kicked up his heels
again. Jon, his face the color of skim milk, slid down
Buckshot's neck, but clung on. "For the love of Jesus—"

Daegan had learned respect for rodeo horses long
ago. He had the scars and stiff joints to remind him jus
how dangerous a colt on a rampage could be. "Whoa
fella," he commanded softly as he reached for Buck
shot's halter; but the horse reared high, kicking out hi
front legs. Steel-shod hooves sliced the air. Daegan
lunged forward. Thud! Pain jolted up his arm. He sucked
in his breath. "Hang on, Jon."

The boy looked over at him for the first time, and hi
pale face bleached whiter for being caught in the act.

With an ear-piercing whistle, Buckshot bolted. Jon
pitched forward. *"Nooo—"* he cried, but slammed into
the dirt. *"Shiiit!"*

Daegan's stomach clenched. Every bone in the kid'
body had to have been jarred loose, especially his shoul
der.

Daegan leaned down and Jon tried to scramble away
He winced. "Oh, crap."

"Are you all right?"

"Does it *look* like I'm all right?" Jon said angrily, tears beginning to form in his eyes.

"It looks like you were a damned fool, playin' around with that colt."

"You said I could ride him!"

"With me around! Damn it, Jon, you could've been killed!"

"Yeah, well, I wasn't." When Daegan tried to touch him, Jon jerked away. "Leave me alone."

"Believe me, I will. I just want to see if anything's broken."

"I'm fine," Jon shot back.

"Your ma know you're here?"

He tried to lift his shoulder, then sucked in his breath.

"Let me take a look at—"

"It's okay! Just leave me alone." The boy's eyes, though frightened, were bright with hot defiance.

"I don't think I can do that. Seein' as you're on my place—"

"So sue me."

"I just might," Daegan said, ignoring the throb in his arm as he studied the boy and called his bluff. "Trespassing's against the law—"

"You said I could come over and see Roscoe anytime—and besides, you had some of my stuff!" Belligerence, bluff, and bravado all emanated from the kid in hot waves.

"That's why you're here?"

"Yeah."

"And the horse—"

Jon frowned and gnawed at his lower lip. "Mom won't let me ride."

"Why not?"

"She thinks it's dangerous."

"And you just made the mistake of proving her right. Come on, let's have a look at what damage we've got here."

"I'm okay."

"I'll be the judge of that."

"I said I'm okay! This isn't a big deal." He struggled to his feet, biting back pain, his lips pale but his eyes once again dry. "I gotta go."

"I'll drive you."

"I can make it on my own."

Daegan glanced over to Buckshot, who stood, muscles quivering, at the far corner of the paddock.

Daegan thrust his chin in the direction of the mule-headed colt. "All you had to do was ask, y'know."

"And you would've let me?" Clear blue eyes stared up at him. Penetrating eyes. Sullivan eyes.

"Alone? Hell, no!"

The lips tightened into a line Jon couldn't suspect reminded Daegan of his unwanted relatives. "See?"

"Not without me supervising." Slapping his hat on his thigh, Daegan straightened. "I would've started you off with something a little tamer—like old Loco, over there. After you handled him, okay, we would've switched to Buckshot.

"Now, come on, I think we'd better get you home." He offered the boy his hand. It was ignored. "I asked before—your ma know you're over here?"

Silence. Guilty, white-lipped silence.

"Didn't think so. My guess is she doesn't even know you're gone."

"How'd you know that?" Jon asked, his eyes narrowing suspiciously, as if he suspected that he was in the middle of some kind of conspiracy against him.

"She home?"

"Doesn't matter."

The kid had a chip the size of Nebraska on his shoulder, and Daegan nearly smiled. He reminded him of himself at that age. Then that cold, unfamiliar fear settled into his stomach. "It might be best if I take you in the truck. That way if your ma's all bent out of shape and worried sick about you, she can get mad at me instead."

Jon hesitated. "You'd take the heat?"

"Didn't say that. Just said it would be diffused a little. Come on, now."

"No way." Breath whistling past his teeth, the boy stood, then the color drained from his face, and if Daegan hadn't been there to catch him, he would have passed out completely.

"Great." Daegan didn't waste any time, just carried Jon to his truck and the kid had the good sense not to resist. He grumbled a little when Daegan started up the old Ford, but then was silent as he leaned against the passenger door and stared through the grimy windshield.

The lane was filled with potholes and the truck jostled and jolted. "You forgot your stash," he said.

"Can't keep it at the house anyway." Jon scooted lower in his seat. "It'd be best if Ma didn't know what it is."

"Figured as much."

"You aren't gonna tell her, are you?"

"What? About the *Playboy*s and the booze? If I was going to say anything, I would have. I didn't rat you out about sneaking over to my place, did I?"

"No," Jon said suspiciously.

"And I'm not going to."

Jon let out his breath in a rush, and Daegan realized he'd just climbed a huge hurdle toward gaining the kid's trust. He set the emergency brake. "Your mom *is* home?" Daegan clarified over the frantic barking of the pup. What would he do if she wasn't around? Take the kid to a clinic? Try and do a little first aid on the boy himself? From the looks of Jon's scowl, that wasn't going to happen.

"She's here."

Daegan parked his truck, letting it idle, and the kid shoved open the door and escaped. Daegan had no choice but to follow.

The screen door flew open, and Kate, in old jeans and a green sweater, rushed onto the porch. "Houndog, hush!" Her hair was pulled into a loose ponytail that seemed to be falling apart, and her expression was confused, worried. "Jon? But I thought . . ." She glanced into the house as if her eyes had deceived her and he would appear in the doorway of the kitchen instead of in the front yard. Her eyes rested on Daegan for an uncomfortable instant before her gaze crashed full force on her son again. "What's going on? Are you all right?"

"Fine," the boy said, his eyes trained on Daegan, daring him to say anything.

"He was thrown from one of my horses."

"One of your *horses?*" The corners of her mouth drew down and the wariness he'd witnessed the other day appeared in her eyes. "Jon?"

"I'm okay."

"But you were supposed to be upstairs—I was in the kitchen—I didn't hear you leave . . ." Again her eyes, the color of whiskey in the sunlight, pinned Daegan. "What was he doing on your horse?" There was a small, involuntary tightening of her muscles. "For that matter, why was Jon at your place?"

"I think he came over to look after the dog. You'll have to ask him. I wasn't at the house when he decided to see if he could tame Buckshot."

"Buckshot?" Her eyebrows lifted a little. "Jon, what the devil's going on here?"

"I snuck out." He walked to the porch and leaned

heavily against the rail. Sweat beaded on his upper lip. "So what?"

"So what?" She threw her hands to the heavens. "You're already grounded because of the suspension last week and the fight and—" She cut herself off, glanced at Daegan again, and blew a few strands of sun-streaked hair from her eyes. "Look, before I go flying off the handle again, I guess I owe you an apology," she said without much conviction. "I don't know what he was doing at your place, but I'm sorry if he inconvenienced you. Thanks for rescuing him."

"You might want to have his shoulder looked at. He landed pretty hard."

"It's fine!" Jon said.

"Maybe," Daegan admitted. "Could just be bruised."

"And he didn't rescue me, okay?" Jon glared at his mother. His color was all wrong—the summer tan now a milky shade and his lips were bloodless. He was hurting, whether he wanted to admit it or not.

Kate was having none of his martyrdom and show of false courage. "Let's take a look."

Eyes flashing defiantly, Jon gritted his teeth as she lifted his T-shirt and gingerly touched his skin. He sucked his breath in a hiss of pain as his back and stomach were exposed. Obviously embarrassed, Jon avoided Daegan's eyes as his mother examined him. A dark scarlet blush climbed steadily up his neck to burn in his cheeks.

Kate frowned. "Already bruised." Letting the T-shirt fall back, she said. "We'd better run to the clinic for a couple of X-rays. Get in the car, Jon. I'll find my shoes and purse."

"I don't need X-rays," Jon said vehemently. He scowled at Daegan as if he'd been betrayed.

"Better safe than sorry."

"I'm okay, Mom."

"What possessed you to go joy riding?" Turning to face Daegan, she folded her arms under her breasts. "Or was this your idea?"

"He didn't know about it," Jon admitted. "I was just lookin' after Roscoe and I saw the horse and—"

"Oh, Lord, Jon, don't you know any better? Let me grab my keys . . ."

"Geez, Mom, I'm not a baby!"

Her temper snapped. "Then quit acting like one. Don't argue with me!"

"I'm not a little kid, all right?" An angry look crossed his young features, and Daegan gleaned that the war between mother and son ran deep. They might love each other, all right, but Kate was probably overprotective. The boy was trouble waiting to happen. A bad mix. Daegan knew it all too well.

It was time to leave. "I hope he's okay," he said, then pointed a finger at Jon's chest. "Look, Jon, you're welcome to come over and see the dog any time—but you might be a little careful around Buckshot."

"He won't be around Buckshot again."

"It would be all right, if I was there. Let me know what the doctor says." He touched the boy on his good shoulder, half expecting him to pull away. Instead, Jon froze, his eyes turned dark, and he stared at Daegan as if he'd never seen him before this split second.

Daegan's insides jelled.

"Who was the guy you killed?" Jon asked, and Kate, who was already opening the screen door to the house, paused.

"I told you. No one. The closest I came was a knife fight with my cousin years ago and it was bloody. That's how I got this . . ." He motioned to his ear, where the lobe was missing. "But—"

"He died."

Shit. "I told you that before."

"But not later, like you wanted me to think, but right then and there."

Daegan saw the fear in Kate's eyes and knew he had to nip this in the bud. "That's not quite the way it happened. It was ugly. My cousin jumped me from behind."

"Why?" Jon demanded.

Daegan shook his head. "He was mad at me. We were both young and full of piss and vinegar. He came at me with a crowbar and a knife, and by the time it was over, we were both busted up pretty bad. To tell you the truth, I was afraid I had killed him, with his knife." Kate was staring at him with wide, horrified eyes and a piece of Daegan's soul seemed to wither a bit. "As I said, we were both hurt pretty bad, but I made it to a phone and called the police. By the time they got there, he was dead."

"So you—you—"

"Dear God." Her hand flew to her mouth.

"No. I left him alive. But the police questioned me over and over again. Fortunately there was a witness who claimed he saw me run to the phone booth and another couple of men came along, two-bit thugs probably, who robbed my cousin and finished the job." He looked away and rubbed the back of his neck in agitation. "If I hadn't run to call the police, maybe I could have saved him. Maybe not. Maybe that makes me guilty of murder. All I know is I'd give anything to relive that night again," he said with conviction. "There isn't a day goes by that I don't wish I could change things. But I can't. I have to accept that."

"Jesus," Jon whispered, whether in awe or revulsion, Daegan couldn't tell. The boy's threat worked and Daegan dropped his hand.

Kate's breath whistled between her teeth. "Go inside," she said to her boy. "And I've already warned you about the language."

"Wait a minute, Mom. Didn't you hear what he just said? O'Rourke—"

"Go inside," she repeated. "Do it! Now."

Jon scrambled through the front door.

"I don't know what to say," she admitted, biting her lip. "Your story is—"

"Ugly."

"Yes, and to be truthful, it scares me." Wrapping her arms around her middle, as if protecting herself, she stared him straight in the eye. "I think it would be best, for all of us, if Jon stays here where he belongs. If he wanders your way again, please, just send him home."

Daegan stood his ground. "It's too bad you had to find out my deepest secret," he said and he meant it. Telling her too much about his fight with Stuart, giving her a glimmer into his private life, was dangerous.

"So is that it? Nothing else?"

One side of his mouth lifted. "You expect something worse than me being hauled into jail for questioning in a murder?"

"No . . . I guess not."

He didn't believe her. She had trouble meeting his eyes. Now, it was her turn. "What about you?" he asked.

"Me?"

"Any skeletons in your closet?" he asked as a lonely hawk circled overhead and the wind seemed to die for an instant. He counted out the beats of her heart in the pulse at the base of her throat while she hesitated and looked away toward the mountains to a spot only she could see.

"None that I can share," she finally said.

"What happened to Jon's father?"

"What?" She jerked. He had her attention now.

"How did he die?"

"An accident. Hit and run," she said, swallowing

hard. "He and my little girl were walking and they were both killed." Her voice was the barest of whispers, and Daegan experienced the unlikely need to wrap his arms around her, to hold her and comfort her, to lie and tell her things would be better when he knew they were only going to get worse. Much worse. Instead he scowled at the ground and rammed his hands into his pockets. "Jim never even saw Jon."

"That's a shame. Your son's a good boy. His father would have been proud."

She stared at him as if he'd just said the world would come to an end in ten minutes. Her fingers fluttered nervously and she wiped them on her jeans. "Yes, well, I, um, need to get Jon to the doctor." She started to head to the house, but stopped. "You know, sometimes Jon, he—well, he says things he shouldn't."

"He's a boy. They tend to do that." Daegan saw the questions in her eyes, and behind her, through the screen, he noticed the boy's pale face staring at him through the mesh. "Don't we all?"

He started to turn back to the truck.

"Mr. O'Rourke?"

"Daegan. I thought we were past that. We're neighbors, remember?"

How could she forget? He could be a murderer. The criminal. The man who may have sired her son. His comment that Jon's father would be proud of him nearly caused her knees to buckle. Her throat so dry she could barely speak, she said, "Daegan, right. This fight with your cousin—where did it happen?"

"Back home."

She didn't let up. "Which is?"

"Canada. A little town in Alberta, near Calgary. Good luck with the boy." Daegan turned and walked back to his tired-looking pickup and Kate watched him leave, not moving, just staring after the battered old Dodge as gravel spewed from its balding tires and the engine growled, leaving a plume of blue exhaust in its wake.

Jon let out a long, low whistle, the pain in his shoulder momentarily forgotten. "Did you hear that? He all but admitted it."

"I heard," Kate said, rubbing her arms to get rid of the goose bumps that rose on her flesh. She was suddenly cold as death. Who was Daegan O'Rourke really? Stranger, neighbor, sexy-as-all-get-out cowboy, and possibly a murderer.

The criminal.

If so, why was he here? What did he want? If he'd intended to take Jon away, he'd had ample opportunity this afternoon.

Maybe he was just an innocent cowboy with a colorful, though shady, past.

Sure. And she was the Virgin Mary.

"My friend's still looking through some of the old documents and files, but so far we haven't come up with much," Laura said, sounding as if she were in the next room instead of over two thousand miles away in Boston. Kate fingered the cord and leaned a shoulder against the refrigerator. Through the window she watched as Jon, his arm in a sling, threw the tennis ball across the yard for the puppy, who merrily gave chase. "There were dozens of kids born around Jon's birthday in the greater Boston area. I started with the date on his doctored birth certificate and went forward and backward a week, though you're certain he was only days old when you got him."

"Positive of it," Kate said. "The umbilical cord stump didn't fall off for days."

"Okay, so I'm sorting through, trying to find out if

any of the infants were born to single mothers, but my guess is that whoever doctored the certificate somehow managed to get into the computer data as well."

"Wonderful," Kate said sarcastically.

"I'll keep looking."

"Thanks." She rubbed the top of a pumpkin she'd picked from the garden, the one chosen to be this year's jack-o'-lantern. "What about the cowboy?"

"Since he claims to be from Canada, I'll check with immigration to see if anyone named Daegan O'Rourke ever changed his citizenship. That'll take a while.

"As for him starting out around here, there were several Daegan O'Rourkes, if you can believe that, born in the greater Boston area thirty to forty years ago. None of them has a criminal record that we can find or a physical description. We're still checking to see if any have moved or stayed in Massachusetts. It'll take a couple of days, maybe even a week or so."

Kate groaned and leaned her head against the wall.

"Sorry, Kate, but my friend and I have to do this on our free time."

"I know. Thanks."

"So are you still convinced that the cowboy next door is someone to avoid?"

"Definitely," Kate said, but wondered if it were possible. Jon already had developed an attraction-aversion to the man and even she found him interesting—in a purely male-female way. But that was crazy. She'd never gone for the faded jeans and worn-down boots type, never found any of the men in town overly attractive, but Daegan O'Rourke was different, he stood out in a crowd. She didn't admit her feelings to Laura, but otherwise she filled her in, including explaining about Jon's interest in the man, his accident with the horse, and conceding that they'd been lucky. Jon's shoulder had only been bruised, his pride wounded more than anything else. But then there was O'Rourke to deal with—whoever he was.

"Let me get this straight," Laura said. "You think that Daegan might be Jon's father. Why? Because of some silly premonition? Do they look anything alike?"

"A little," Kate said. "The coloring's about the same except Jon's eyes are a clearer blue. O'Rourke's are gray—flinty."

"Not enough, Kate."

"Okay, so there's some resemblance, I think. The shape of the face and skin tone. Jon's hair is a little lighter."

"Oh, for God's sake. That's not enough. Jon's left-handed—what about O'Rourke?"

"Don't know."

"And Jon's dimple?"

"O'Rourke doesn't smile much."

"Then you don't have much to go on and you might ask yourself something. Assuming that O'Rourke is Jon's father—and that's a helluva assumption from the sound of things, but we'll go with it for now—why would Jon's dad show up all of a sudden out of the clear blue, fifteen-plus years after the fact? Wasn't he supposed to be some kind of violent lowlife? From what you're telling me, you have a cowboy who's maybe a little rough around the edges, who was jumped by his cousin and ended up hurting him—maybe even killing him by accident, but really, all things considered, he sounds like a good enough guy."

"Good guy," Kate repeated, though some of what Laura was saying echoed her own thoughts. So far O'Rourke had only helped her—with her tire and with her son. He wasn't even angry that Jon had wandered over to his place uninvited and taken it upon himself to ride one of the horses. All in all, he'd been a model neighbor. "That cousin ended up dead," Kate pointed out, her stomach churning.

"Okay, okay. What was the cousin's name?"

"He never said."

"It would help if we had a little more information to go on."

Kate tapped her fingers against the wall. "I know, I know. I just don't think I can bring it up again."

"Maybe you won't have to; Jon seems to be doing a pretty good job of it himself."

Outside, Jon threw the ball high into the air and Houndog ran around in circles, his head pointed skyward. Could Jon really be Daegan's son, or was she just grasping at straws? What had Jon said—something about a good man and a bad one showing up here? Maybe Daegan was the good. She shuddered. Who, then, was the bad?

Chapter 13

"You're a freak, Summers, a fuckin' weirdo!" Todd Neider yelled through the open window of his truck. A cigarette was jabbed in the corner of his mouth and two of his friends were wedged into the front seat with him.

Here we go again, Jon thought miserably. He just kept walking, hoping upon hope that his mom would be home when . . . and if . . . he got there. But he still had two miles of long, lonely pavement before the turnoff to his house. He swallowed back his dread and kept his eyes fixed straight ahead to the mountains in the distance.

"Always shootin' off your mouth, claimin' to see into the goddamned future. You're a psycho!" Todd laughed and the other goons joined in. Tromping on the gas, Todd laid a patch of rubber from tires screaming for mercy. A choking plume of exhaust spewed into the brisk afternoon air.

Jon felt a second of relief until the brake lights glowed hot red and tires squealed again as Todd did a quick one-eighty and headed his way again.

"Bastard," Jon swore under his breath. Involuntarily his hands curled into fists. Engine growling, the old Chevy looked like a huge metallic monster bearing down on him with the intent to do damage, serious damage.

Jon jumped into the dry ditch. He hit the dirt as Todd, the wheels of his truck spraying gravel from the shoulder, shot past. Hoots and brittle laughter followed.

"Jesus!" Jon whispered. He'd jammed his shoulder and pain ricocheted down his arm. Climbing to his feet, he started running, grass seeds clinging to his hair.

Again the truck spun around and within seconds Neider's truck had caught up to him. "Hey, Jonnie-boy, ain't you gonna tell me my future now?" he leered as his friends snickered nervously.

Clenching his teeth together, Jon wondered why he'd been stupid enough to get into a fight with Todd again at school. Why wouldn't the big jerk just leave him alone? He slowed his pace but kept walking. *Don't let him beat you. Remember—he's a mental midget.*

"Scared?" Todd taunted. "Hell, we haven't even started yet."

Though he was shaking inside, Jon ignored the bully, refusing to give him one inch of satisfaction.

Todd eased the truck into the oncoming shoulder so that he was close enough to touch Jon. Acrid smells of cigarette smoke and beer wafted from the cab. "You can't run away from me."

Jon bit his tongue.

"Come on, freak, what have ya got to say for yourself?"

Just keep walking

"Shit!" A car coming the opposite direction forced Todd onto his side of the road. The driver of the sedan laid on the horn as he roared by and Jon wished to God that the driver would stop and end this torment. Todd was gonna kill him—beat him up so badly he'd never be the same. Well, he intended to give as good as he got. Inside he was shaking, outside he hoped his face was set in stone.

Sweat covered his back and palms.

When the car disappeared far behind them, Todd drew his pickup close again. "Ya know, Summers, everyone thinks you're a mutant—some kind of throwback." Todd kept pace with Jon on the long lonely road and Jon gave himself a swift mental kick for missing the bus. But then this torment had been worth it as he'd captured a few minutes to talk to Jennifer alone.

"Maybe he's the missing link," Joey Flanders said in a voice that cracked often. Joey didn't bother Jon because Flanders was just a coward who lived vicariously through Todd's mean streak. Jon could handle Joey.

"Yeah, or maybe he's just a dumb-shit." Dennis Morrisey was the son of Preacher Fire-and-Brimstone Morrisey. If Reverend Morrisey had had any idea his son was out carousing, smoking cigarettes, and swilling beer, Dennis would have had to scrub the church bathrooms with a toothbrush for the next six months. The Reverend had been in the army and believed in strict punishment. He didn't worry Jon at all.

That left Todd—a blowhard and a bully, but mean enough to be a problem. Physically, Jon didn't have a chance against him, but mentally he could outsmart him every time.

"Why don't you and me have it out right here?" Todd suggested and again the other boys laughed. He flicked his cigarette at Jon, hitting him in the cheek. Ash and the butt fell into the dry weeds and Jon stomped quickly to put out the ember before it caught on the bleached grass.

"God, Neider, you're such a cretin! What do ya want to do, start a grass fire that won't quit 'til it hits the river?" Jon stopped dead in his tracks and faced Todd.

Throwing out his chin rebelliously, he silently dared the older kid to put up or shut up.

"I don't give a shit."

"That's 'cause you are one." Swiping the ash from his cheek, Jon narrowed furious eyes on his tormentor. Since their last fight he couldn't hold his tongue. The words just tumbled out. "Why don't you go home and cry in your bed like you do when your old man beats you?"

"You little prick!" Todd's color was suddenly high, his deep-set piglike eyes horror-stricken. "My old man never lays a hand on me—"

"Sure he does and you blubber like a baby for him to stop. But it never does any good, does it, Neider, 'cause your old man just takes off his belt and keeps hitting you over and over again, calling you a no-good until he's so drunk he passes out."

Flanders and Morrisey had become silent as death. Todd's mouth worked but no words came out. The pickup idled in the dying sunlight and Jon turned toward home.

"You're a liar, Summers!"

Jon kept walking. The truck wasn't far behind.

"Hear me? A fuckin' liar!"

Jon glanced over his shoulder and the old Chevy rolled to within inches of him. Todd's face was purple with shame and Jon knew he'd gone too far, that he'd told one of Todd's secrets, one Jon had seen when the older boy had grabbed him by the shoulder one day.

"And you're a blowhard, picking on me so that you can feel better because your old man knocks you around."

"That does it!" Todd jammed on the brakes. Tires screamed. Wheels locked. The pickup shimmied and Todd jumped out, leaving his vehicle idling noisily. "You pushed me too far this time, Summers," he warned, his big, meaty fist clenched so hard the knuckles showed white. "Time to learn a lesson." He swung wildly. Jon ducked and started running. The other boys yelled, egging Todd on.

Todd, breathing hard, couldn't catch him, but flung his body into the air, hitting Jon's midsection and throwing them both to the ground. Twisting, Jon hit the dry earth of the ditch, and his shoulder, the one he'd injured before, seemed to crack. A bolt of pain speared through his shoulder, wrenching his arm back. He screamed.

Bam! Knuckles blasted his cheekbone. His bones seemed to melt. He couldn't move. Crash! His nose crumpled. Blood gushed. Pain exploded behind his eyes. Crack! His head snapped back against the ground. A moan ripped from his throat and he choked on his own blood.

"I knew you were a wimp!" Neider crowed.

Jon tried to squirm, but Todd was too big, too heavy, pinning him to the hard ground, his sour breath flowing over his face. "Fag!"

Jon kicked and hit back, scratching, reaching up, trying to get rid of the huge mass crushing his chest.

He heard voices—Dennis and Joey—yelling wildly. "Hey, Neider, that's enough."

"Shit, man, you're gonna kill him."

Todd didn't listen. "You slimy little bastard, I'm gonna teach you a lesson you'll never forget." Todd climbed drunkenly to his feet, then hauled back and kicked Jon hard in the groin.

Jon wretched, his body recoiling.

A knee to the kidneys. Blackness threatened his vision.

"Stop!" a loud angry voice ordered.

"What the hell? Who the fuck are you?" Todd suddenly swore. "Hey—hey! Keep your hands off me!" he bellowed in real fear.

Blinking up through bloodied eyes, Jon felt instant relief. Daegan O'Rourke had Todd by his collar.

"What's going on here?" he demanded, his eyes gray as storm clouds, his lips blade thin.

"Let go of me!" Todd said, taking a swipe at him.

Daegan had Todd on the ground in an instant, one arm twisted behind his back, a knee pressed hard to the boy's spine. "I'll sue you!" Todd screamed.

"Yeah, and I'll have you up on charges for assault so fast, your fat head will spin."

"You don't scare me." Todd was squirming, trying to break free, but couldn't move.

"Well, I should," Daegan muttered as the two other boys flew from the cab of the truck and scattered. "Who are you, boy?"

"Leave me alone!"

"Yeah, like you left him alone?" Daegan said, motioning with his chin to Jon. Once again he hauled Todd to his feet and the boy looked so scared Jon thought he might pee his pants. "You're gonna tell me what's going on and who you are, or I'm calling the police as well as Jon's mother."

Jon struggled to one elbow and his knees.

"You okay?" Daegan asked, and Jon nodded, refusing to let him know how battered he felt, denying the urge to break down and sob for his mother like he wanted to. "Good, now, kid . . ." Again he focused his hard gaze on Neider, though it seemed to Jon that some of the edge had left Daegan, as if he realized he was dealing with a boy and not a man. "You made a serious mistake messing with Jon here, because if you mess with him, you mess with me, and believe me, that's a mistake you don't want to make twice."

"Yeah, and who're you?" Todd managed, wiping his chin as Daegan let go of him.

O'Rourke's lips twisted into a smile that was positively evil. "Your worst nightmare. I'm a friend of Jon's here, and I'm taking it as my personal mission to see that he doesn't get beat up by small-town toughs who like to bully smaller kids."

"He . . . he asked for it," Todd stammered.

"Right." Daegan walked over to Todd's truck and withdrew the keys from the ignition. With a rumble and a clunk, the old motor died.

"Hey—wait a minute. What're you doin'?"

Despite his pain, Jon had to swallow a smile.

"Making sure you have time to think—so maybe next time you won't go driving around, all liquored up picking on kids."

"No way, man. Those are my keys—" Todd wailed and to Jon's amazement Daegan hurled the prize high into the air.

"No!" Todd roared, giving chase, trying to climb the fence as the metal keys glinted in the sunlight, jangling as they fell into the knee-high grass and weeds of Doc Henson's unmown field. "You fuckin' bastard, I'll—"

"You'll what?" Daegan asked, his fury returning full force.

Neider had the good sense to shut up.

"Go ahead," O'Rourke prodded. "You were about to threaten me. What exactly did you have in mind?"

"I'll . . . I'll . . ." Todd shook his head and stared longingly at the field.

"What you won't do is pick on this boy anymore." Daegan glanced at the two other boys, who were far away, still running, trying to make good their escape. "And that goes for your friends, too." He planted his hands on his hips and looked tough as old rawhide. "If

I hear of this happening again—not just to Jon but to anyone else—believe me, I'll come looking for you."

"But my keys—"

"Hope you have an extra set." Daegan turned his attention to Jon. "Come on, let's get you home. Need some help?"

"No," Jon said and followed him to his beat-up old truck. He slid across the bench seat and stared out the cracked passenger window. Daegan shifted into first and they rolled past a red-faced Todd, who shouted obscenities until Daegan stepped on the brakes. Then he was silent.

O'Rourke gave a satisfied snort and found the gas pedal again. "Nice guy," he observed.

"If you like creeps."

"Look through the glove box. I think there's a rag in there. I can't guarantee how sterile it is, but unless you want your mom to faint dead away, you'd better clean yourself up." As Jon scrounged in the overflowing compartment, O'Rourke asked, "What did you do to that guy to make him so mad?"

Jon thought that one over as he discovered an old stained rag and began wiping off the blood that had congealed on his face. How much could he trust this guy? True, he hadn't ratted him out, hadn't told Mom about the girlie magazines and the booze, and sneaking over there in the middle of the night, but still . . . He checked the side view mirror and saw that Todd was out of sight. Slowly he let out his breath.

"He was gonna tear you limb from limb."

"Maybe he didn't need a reason." Jon winced as he touched his cheek with the rag.

O'Rourke seemed to consider it as he found second gear and the fence posts started clipping by at a faster rate. "Usually when a guy's that mad, there's a reason."

"He hates me."

"Why?"

Jon lifted a shoulder, then folded the rag and touched his nose. He nearly jumped out of his skin and his head began to throb. Rolling down the window, he said, "It's 'cause I'm different." He sniffed and blood slid down the back of his throat. "You know, I can see things."

"Like you did with me?"

"Yeah." He sighed. "This is gonna just keep going on and on."

"No way."

"You gonna stop him?" Jon asked, sarcasm in his voice as O'Rourke slowed the truck in order to turn into the lane.

"You bet I am," Daegan replied, surprised by his own sense of conviction. "He won't bother you."

"You don't know Todd."

"I've known a lot of Todds over the years. They're all the same. Scared deep down. If he tries anything again, you let me know."

"Oh, yeah, sure," Jon replied with a frown that reminded Daegan of Bibi's pout. "You think I should run like a crybaby to you?" Incredulity and sarcasm mixed in the boy's words.

Daegan lifted a shoulder. "It's your call, Jon. You can either stand and fight, run, or ask for help."

"I want to stand and fight. I already have."

The truck bounced through a pothole. "Then you'd better learn how to do it so that next time you don't get the living shit knocked out of you."

"Oh, dear God," Kate whispered as she slammed on the brakes. Jon was climbing slowly out of the cab of O'Rourke's truck. Blood stained the front of his shirt and ran down his face. His eyes were swollen, his face battered, and he limped noticeably. Her heart in her throat, she shoved the car into park and scrambled into the yard amid the excited barking and jumping of Houndog and Jon yelling at the pup to back off.

"Jon?" Her gaze traveled to O'Rourke before landing with full, worried impact on her son. "What happened? Jon, oh, honey, are you all right?" The pup came over to greet her, but she barely noticed and turned frosty eyes on O'Rourke. "What's going on?"

"I'll be fine," Jon growled back. "And it wasn't his fault." He motioned to Daegan. "He saved me."

"But—"

"I said I'll be fine." She tried to reach for him but he stood back and blinked fiercely, as if just the sight of her caused his eyes to fill.

"We've got to get you to a doctor."

Jon grimaced.

"I would've taken him, but thought we should round you up first," O'Rourke said. His expression was dark and grim.

"What happened?" She couldn't hide the censure in her voice.

"The town bully seemed to want to use Jon as a punching bag. I caught up with them down the road a piece."

"Yeah and he gave 'em hell!" Jon said proudly.

"That Todd Neider again?" Kate asked and her blood began to boil.

That kid had been giving Jon fits for months and now the arguments and shoves had escalated to a full-fledged beating.

"A foul-mouthed sucker if there ever was one," Daegan observed.

"Yeah, it was Neider," Jon admitted, leaning heavily against the side of O'Rourke's truck. "And his friends. I'll . . . I'll be okay."

"This isn't going to end, is it? We have to stop it."

"Can't argue with that," O'Rourke agreed.

She tried to reach for her son again. "Where does it hurt?"

"Where doesn't it?" Jon asked through cracked, swollen lips. His face was bruised and he held his already-injured arm around his middle.

"He's been lucid, never fell asleep, so I doubt if he's concussed. But he might have a cracked rib or two."

"Nothin's broke," Jon insisted.

"I think we should let Dr. Wenzler determine that. I'll get a wet towel and some bandages so you can clean up, then we'll go." She was halfway up the steps to the front porch.

"Where?" Jon asked.

"To the clinic, of course."

"I don't need to go—"

"I don't know where you get this aversion to medical treatment, but it's not working with me. I'm taking you to see the doctor." She sighed loudly. "I've been worried sick about you and now look . . . Please, Jon, don't give me any grief about this. We're going to the doctor and that's that."

"She's right," Daegan said, staring at Jon with eyes that seemed to see past the teenage barriers her son had so recently and painstakingly erected, the barriers that forced her to keep her distance. "See what the doctor says."

Jon hesitated, running his tongue around the inside of his mouth, seeming to weigh things in his mind. Sullenly, he asked, "You comin'?"

"Not my place."

"It wasn't your place to bust up the fight, either. But you did." Jon was laying down a challenge—testing O'Rourke. Why?

"Your mom and you can handle this."

Jon's lips rolled in on themselves, the way they always did when he fought tears. With a proud lift of his chin, he said, "I'd like you to be there."

Thunderstruck, Kate was at a loss for words. In all her born days, she would never have expected Jon, who only a few days ago had insisted this man was dangerous, that he'd killed someone, to invite him to join them on a trip to the clinic. "You guys decide." Her eyes met O'Rourke's for an instant and she caught a glimpse of something more than just neighborly concern—a deeper unspoken emotion—a glimmer he hid all too quickly. "Your call," she told him, knowing instinctively that getting closer to him was a mistake of immense proportions. But what could she say? He'd saved Jon, hadn't he? "I'll be right back." She unlocked the door, headed for the bathroom on the first floor, and found a clean towel in the linen cupboard. What were they getting into with O'Rourke? she wondered as she twisted on the faucet and dampened the rag.

Grabbing a second dry towel, disinfectant, and some bandages, she tried to shake the worry that had been with her the past hour. Though Jon was hurt, none of his injuries appeared life-threatening. Finding Jon with Daegan was upsetting, but it seemed as if the guy had actually saved her son from getting the living tar beat out of him.

"Let's go."

Jon's intense gaze landed on their new neighbor. "Well?"

"Don't force Mr. O'Rourke, Jon. He just moved in and has a ranch to run and—"

"I'll tag along. If it's okay with your ma."

"Sure. Fine, whatever," she said, lying. She didn't want this man anywhere near her or her son, but now was not the time to wage that particular battle. "Here, Jon, let me clean you up—"

"I can do it." He snatched the towel out of her hand and refused to let her touch him.

Hot embarrassment climbed up her neck. "All right, you handle it, but let's get a move on." She was already on her way to the still-open door of her car. "As soon as we get back from the clinic, I'm going to call Carl Neider and—"

"No!" Jon was vehement.

"What? You want to take a chance on this happening again?" She looked across the roof of her Buick and stared flabbergasted at her son, who was still bleeding, his eyes swollen. No telling what else was wrong with him and he was arguing with her about ratting out the beast who had done the damage! "You bet I'm going to call him."

"You can't do it, Mom," Jon insisted.

"But look at you—"

"It'll only make it worse. Mr. O'Rourke already shook him up, flung his keys into Henson's field, and told him to lay off, so just leave it at that." He hobbled to the car, yanked open the back door, and rolled into the seat. "Let me take care of it."

"I'm not sure I can do that."

Daegan stretched into the front seat next to her and she wished he would disappear. The last thing she needed was this tall, raw-boned cowboy seated close to her, destroying her concentration and, whether intentionally or not, wedging himself between Jon and her.

Doors slammed and she backed the Buick around O'Rourke's pickup, wondering if her life—hers and Jon's—would ever be the same.

* * *

"For the love of Mike, what happened to you?"
Dr. Wenzler, a petite woman with graying hair and kind
eyes, asked Jon. She wore a lab coat two sizes too big
with a stethoscope stuffed into a front pocket. "Get into
a fight with a grizzly?"

"No," Jon said, squirming a little.

"Another boy—another bigger boy," Kate said, grateful that Jon hadn't insisted Daegan accompany them
into the examining room. It was bad enough that he
was waiting for them in the reception area, though, surprisingly, the thought wasn't all that unpleasant. He was
probably thumbing through an old copy of *Parenting*
and wondering how he'd ended up in the pediatric
wing of the clinic.

"I 'spose you gave as good as you got," Dr. Wenzler
said as she gently touched the swelling on his face.

Jon was seated on the examination table, dressed
only in his boxer shorts, and he was obviously embarrassed that Kate was in the room. "I did okay," he
replied, avoiding the doctor's probing gaze.

"So I should be expecting another patient?" she
teased, flashing the beam of a penlight into Jon's eyes.
"Here—look over my shoulder to that dot on the wall.
That's it." Once finished with his face, she ran experienced hands over his shoulder and ribs. "Lucky for you
nothing appears to be broken, but we should take some
X-rays over in the lab building just to be sure." She
glanced up at Kate. "Linda will walk you over and then
bring back the films. I don't think we'll find anything,
he looks fine, but I'd rather be safe than sorry."

"Me, too."

"I'll meet you back in this room in a few minutes,"
she said, then was gone, her voluminous lab coat billowing out behind her like a sail catching the wind.

"I don't know why you're making such a big deal of

this," Jon grumbled, wincing as he struggled with his sweatshirt.

"Because it is, Jon. When someone starts causing you bodily harm, believe me, it's a big deal."

He pulled on his jeans. "Just promise me that you won't call Neider's dad."

"Can't do that."

"Sure you can. If you loved me, you would."

"I'm not going to get into this;" she said, her nerves strung tight as bow strings. She wasn't going to allow a fifteen-year-old kid to manipulate her. "You know I love you."

There was a knock on the door and Linda escorted them through a labyrinthine maze of corridors, out a back door, and past a lab to the X-ray room. "It'll be just a little while," Linda assured them and Kate picked up a battered magazine while Jon fidgeted in the chair beside her. She couldn't help wondering how O'Rourke was enjoying himself.

Pretending interest in a year-old edition of *Field and Stream,* Daegan watched the hallway through which Jon and Kate had disappeared. It had taken forever for the tiny woman he assumed to be the doctor to take the chart from the basket on the door of Jon's room and enter. A little while later she'd returned, without the chart, and issued instructions to a pudgy blond nurse who immediately thereafter shepherded Jon and Kate down the hallway and out the back. Probably for tests or X-rays.

He glanced at his watch. He hated clinics, emergency rooms, and anything that had to do with medicine. Sitting around waiting, smelling antiseptic, watching people in white scurry around behind glass partitions, bothered him.

When the hallway was clear, he stretched, saw that no

one behind the window separating the secretarial staff from those waiting to be admitted was paying him any mind, and on the pretense of searching for a bathroom, he ambled down the hall. But he paused at the door from which Kate and Jon had emerged then slipped inside.

The chart was on a counter. Without a moment's hesitation or sting of guilt, he picked the file up and started scanning it.

Date and place of birth? His heart stopped. The date in February was close enough and the kid had been born in Boston, Massachusetts. His stomach clenched. That information fit into Bibi's story.

Blood type? B negative. The same as Daegan's. Only about 15 percent of the population had Type B, throw in the negative, and that made it even more rare. Yep, it looked as if Jon was his son.

He scanned the file and ignored the rage of emotion that blasted through him. The chances were downright slim that, given all his information, the boy was fathered by someone else. There was no more denying it. Bibi's blood type was O positive; he'd already checked.

He read the entire file quickly, thinking it was his right as a father. *A father.* Oh, God. He dropped the file back where he'd found it, sneaked out of the room, found the restroom, and still reeling with the knowledge that there were no more doubts, he finally returned to the waiting area.

Impatiently, Daegan checked his watch, drummed his fingers on the arm of the plastic couch, and wondered what would be his next move.

Now that he was certain of the truth, the game had just changed.

Chapter 14

"I swear to God, Mom, if you call the police, I'll leave," Jon said, his voice deep with conviction. He swept his algebra book off the dining room table and it flew, pages fluttering, old assignments littering the floor as the book skidded across the floor.

"Pick it up." Kate couldn't stand the out-and-out rebellion from her son. It seemed that as each day passed, he became more vocal.

"Not until you promise that you won't call the police or Neider's dad."

"Pick it up, Jon. The book belongs to the school and even if it didn't—"

"Geez, Mom, you can't be getting the police involved in this," he said, but reached down and scooped up the mess. Houndog cowered under a chair in the living room and whined pitifully.

Kate gritted her teeth and slowly counted to ten. Deliberately she removed her reading glasses and placed them on the table next to her stack of unread essays. They'd found an uncomfortable peace since returning from the clinic, but Kate had sensed that the calm was temporary, that beneath her boy's battered body a storm of emotions was raging, ready to explode.

The battlefield was the dining room table, she seated on one side, he on the other. While he attempted homework, she read a stack of essays that needed to be graded. For years they'd been able to work this way, together but independently, at the old table, sharing a bowl of popcorn or a joke, but no longer; it seemed they fought more than they agreed. And the tension was only getting worse.

Kicking back his chair, Jon struggled to his feet. His face was discolored, nose broken, two black eyes making him appear to be wearing a mask. His shoulder was strained, but no ribs had cracked, so Jon was bruised and battered but not yet broken. He'd miss at least a couple of days of school. "Neider's old man beats him."

"That doesn't surprise me," she said, anger surging through her blood. Carl Neider was a foul-mouthed blowhard who spent more than his share of hours on a stool in the local watering hole. "Maybe children's services should be called."

"Oh, Mom, no! Don't you get it? Just leave him alone."

"Like he left you alone?" With as much patience as she could muster, she leveled her eyes at her boy and said, "You were beat up, Jon, but you lucked out. You could have been seriously hurt, even maimed and crippled for life—"

"But I wasn't! I hit him once too, y'know."

She bit back the urge to yell at her son with his bruised face and black eyes. "He stalked you in his car. If it's not you, it'll be someone else. He has a history of violence and he has to be held accountable, or helped if that's possible."

"Daegan'll make him stop."

Kate nearly laughed. If the situation weren't so dire,

the consequences so great, she might have allowed herself a smile. As it was, she couldn't. Stretching out of her chair, she crossed through the living room to the dark fireplace. "I thought you were so sure that O'Rourke murdered someone," she said, sorting through the few dry logs in the basket on the hearth. "Weren't you convinced a couple of weeks ago that there was trouble and danger coming our way, that a man, a good man or an evil man, was coming?"

"Daegan's good." Jon crossed his arms over his chest, his eyes, deep in bruised sockets, sparking defiance.

"Since when? Because he saved you from getting pulverized?"

"Yeah! What would have happened if he hadn't been there?" Jon demanded and Kate felt cold as death inside. Jon was right. Ever since Daegan had stepped foot in Hopewell, he'd done nothing suspicious, been nothing but neighborly and well intentioned. So what if he seemed charged with a restless energy, like a man who was constantly on the run and looking over his shoulder? What did it matter that he was sexy as all get-out and realized it? Even if he had some skeletons buried deep in his closets, who knew and who cared? Jon was right. So far O'Rourke had proved a trustworthy and concerned neighbor. Nothing more.

She tossed a chunk of mossy oak onto the blackened andirons and searched the mantel for a match.

Jon edged into the living room. "Why do you hate him so much?"

"I don't hate him. He just worries me, that's all."

"Well, I like him."

"Do you?" Her heart sank. Until recently, Jon had never attached himself to anyone but her. He'd had his share of teachers who had been fond of him and a coach or two—usually fathers of other boys—who had been kind to him when a lot of people in town treated him as a pariah, but she'd never heard that ring of conviction and awe in his voice when he'd spoken of another adult.

Daegan O'Rourke, whether he intended to be or not, was now a rival for her child's affections.

"It's because of me, isn't it?" Jon said. "Because of what I said about him. About him killing someone."

She found a match, struck it against a brick in the fire box, and held the sizzling flame to kindling she'd stacked earlier. "I just don't know him, Jon," she said.

"Well, maybe you should."

Her head snapped up and she met her son's pained, hostile gaze. The same thought had been nagging her, though she'd been loath to admit it. She just hadn't faced the truth because it scared her and not just a little. Daegan and her reaction to him were all wrong. She couldn't—wouldn't—get involved with him and yet she'd felt it more than once, a simmering attraction that was downright dangerous with the wrong man. And Daegan was definitely the wrong man.

But Jon's point was well taken and there was no reason she couldn't be more neighborly than she had been, less suspicious. "All right." She stood and dusted her hands. "If you handle all the ghosts and goblins that knock on our door tonight, I'll visit Mr. O'Rourke."

Jon snorted in disgust and eyed the platter of cupcakes, decorated with orange frosting and candy corn that sat, at the ready, on the table near the door. Houndog had moved, plopping himself directly underneath the table, hoping that a scrap would fall. "We don't ever have any trick or treaters, Mom. I don't know why you bother."

"Because the year I wasn't ready, we'd have legions of kids ringing the bell."

"In your dreams," he muttered under his breath.

It's not my dreams that worry me, she thought as the fire sputtered and hissed. *It's yours.*

As he walked down the icy streets of Boston, Neils Van-Horn was a man on a mission. He believed firmly that opportunity knocked only once on a man's door and right now opportunity was trying to beat his damned door down. This was it. The big time. His hands itched at the thought of how much money he was going to make in the next month or so. Bending his head against a blast of raw wind, he ground his teeth together. Soon he'd give up this frigid climate, buy himself a thirty-foot sailboat, and spend his time in the Caribbean.

He found the Irish pub, a dark cavern-like den where whiskey and ale were served with raucous noise and great fanfare. Darts zipped through the air in one corner of the establishment, and glasses clicked behind the bar. Waitresses in white blouses that showed off enough cleavage to give every guy in the place a hard-on swung through the crowded tables. Smoke clouded the air and laughter and gravelly voices vied for air time with muffled music—ballads of some sort.

VanHorn took a corner booth in the back away from most of the noise and other patrons. He ordered a pitcher of the house's special ale and waited, dropping his gloves into the pockets of his coat and unwinding his scarf before hanging everything on a wooden peg sprouting from one of the support posts.

By the time his companion arrived, he was sipping from his second glass, warm inside and bolder than he should have been. "Have a seat," he invited, eyeing the woman in her mohair jacket and expensive perfume. Even in the dinginess of the pub, she remained wearing tinted glasses, her makeup flawless, her expensive jew-

elry in sharp contrast to the ambiance of the surround-
ngs.

"Remind me why I'm here," she said, sliding a glance
around the room with obvious disdain. She was still
standing, as if deciding if he was worth her time.

"Because you want to be informed," he said evenly.
He enjoyed playing both ends to the middle even
though it was dangerous. "You don't like it when other
people are manipulating you."

"As you are now?"

"I'm just here with information." He took a swallow
and let that settle with her.

"When you called, you said Robert was up to something." "That's right." He enjoyed seeing her try to
wrestle the information from him and in a quick instant
he saw a trade in the future. What he knew exchanged
for a night in her bed. He bet she slept on perfumed
satin sheets. In his mind's eye he caught a glimpse of
her long legs strapped around his torso.

"What is it you think is so valuable?" She didn't bother
hiding the irritation in her usually well-modulated voice.

He played with a matchbook, tapping each corner
on the table, watching her nearly squirm out of her skin
while she pretended to have the patience of Job. "You
know that his daughter had a bastard son about fifteen
years ago. She gave him up for adoption."

The full, red lips pinched ever so slightly.

"Of course Robert, he didn't want the kid, nor did
Bibi. Now, it seems, he's changed his mind."

A beat. She touched the edge of the table, and her
eyes, behind those dark shades, never left his face, as if
she was trying to figure out if he was lying to her. "So?"

"So he's paying me to find the boy."

"Why?"

"Seems as if he's had a grandfatherly change of
heart. Thinks it's time the kid took his rightful place as

a Sullivan. You know, inherit everything that should have gone to Stuart."

Carefully, she slid into the booth opposite him. He filled the empty glass the waitress had left for her.

"Why are you telling me all this?" she asked. "What's in it for you?"

"Robert's paying me well."

"To betray him? I don't think so. If I called him now you'd be off the case like that." She snapped her fingers.

"But you won't call, will you?" He settled back against the seats. "Because I'll let you know what's going on."

"For a fee."

His gaze skated down her slim figure. What would it feel like to have some uppercrust woman in bed? Were they ice-cold statues, or did they breathe living fire? This one, he was certain, was definitely hot-blooded.

"How much?" she asked, and without so much as blinking behind her four-hundred-dollar dark glasses, she dug in her purse and withdrew her checkbook.

The oldest trick in the book. "Uh-uh. Shame on you." The leather book was halfway out of her purse, but she paused. "I only deal in cash. Small, unmarked, untraceable bills, lots of them, preferably with Alex Hamilton's face printed on them, though I'm partial to Andy Jackson's as well."

Her mouth twisted into a seductive smile that he found impossible to resist. She settled back against the tufted seat and licked her lips. "Why Mr. VanHorn," she breathed and he was instantly so hot he wanted to pull on his tie. "It looks like you're a man after my own heart."

"Okay, so I believe you." Daegan rubbed an ache from his shoulder and winced as he held the receiver to his ear "The boy's mine. I saw a chart with his blood type."

Bibi sighed gratefully. "Thanks for all your faith. Now, what're you going to do about him?" Daegan heard the worry edging her voice and he wondered how he'd ever found her vaguely attractive. It wasn't so much a matter of looks as of attitude. The fact that she wasn't interested in her own child was unnatural.

"I figure I've got several options. I can tell everyone the truth and—"

"Oh, God, don't do that. If that woman finds out that Jon stands to inherit a fortune, then she'd let Dad claim him or try and blackmail me or—"

"She won't do either," Daegan said with conviction. In his encounters with Kate, he'd started to change his opinion of her. She didn't seem the least bit concerned about money. "I don't know why she got involved in the first place, but I can tell you firsthand that she loves that kid more than anything."

"I didn't say she didn't care about him, but just because she loves him doesn't mean she doesn't have a mercenary streak in her. Face it, Daegan, we all do. My guess is she split the eighty thousand dollars Dad gave Tyrell. Maybe she got the short end of the stick, but don't make her out like she's some kind of goddamned saint."

"None of us are."

"Just so we understand each other," Bibi said and he heard her click a lighter. She let out a long breath. "Option one's out, what's number two?"

"I stake my claim as the natural father."

"That's worse yet. You'll have to name me as the mother and Kyle will never forgive me."

Now we were getting to the nitty-gritty. "How is lover boy?" Daegan asked, not even remotely curious.

"Fine, so far. He adores me, Daegan. For the first

time in my life someone really loves me, but if he found out that the baby I'd given up was . . . was conceived with my cousin, I think . . . I think I'd lose him." Her voice actually shook with emotion and Daegan felt like a heel, as he did each time he was reminded of his one night with Bibi.

"If he loves you, he won't care what happened in the past."

"You're a great one to talk," she said, sarcasm lacing her words. "The original 'love 'em and leave 'em' guy."

He bit back a hot retort and decided she had the right to her bitterness. "Now that I'm in this, Bibi, I won't be able to leave it alone."

"Your job was to find the boy and come up with some idea of how to thwart Daddy."

"It may not be possible."

"Oh, Christ, Daegan, anything's possible, don't you know that by now?"

He glared out the window to the dark night, caught his reflection staring harshly at himself, and wished to heaven that there was an easy answer. "What do you want from me, Bibi?"

She let out a long-suffering sigh. "I want the same thing I gave you for fifteen years. My life. With no complications."

"I don't think I can promise that."

"Well, do *some*thing. Find out what secrets the Summers woman is hiding, get some dirt on her so that we have some leverage."

"In case we have to resort to blackmail or extortion?" The thought burned like hot lead in his stomach.

"Exactly. She's got to have something she'd rather keep secret, something we can use as bargaining power."

"For what?"

"For her to get lost—more lost than she's ever been—but hurry up. We don't have much time. Dad's going to talk to a private investigator, I'm sure of it, and once that happens, it won't be long before the you-know-what hits the fan."

Its gonna be worse than you know, Bibi. He sensed an apocalypse the likes of which the Sullivans had never seen before. "Does Collin have any idea that this is coming down?"

He heard her little catch of breath. "Collin doesn't have a clue," she said with more than a trace of acrimony. "But then, what else is new?" He heard her neatly manicured nails tapping thoughtfully on the other end of the line. "I think, and this is no goddamned joke, okay, I think you should steal the boy and take him to Canada or Europe or Mexico, somewhere outside the jurisdiction of the United States. Look, if you do this, I promise that when I inherit everything from Dad, I'll set you and the boy up for the rest of your life."

"Can't do it, Bibi," he said.

"But—"

"Leave it to me. I'm going to handle this my way."

"And what way is that?"

"I'll let you know when I figure it out." Slamming the receiver down, he swore long and hard. That old Sullivan chain seemed to be coiling around his neck again and he couldn't shake the feeling that he was being set up. A headache pounded behind his eyes.

He walked through Eli's pathetic cabin to the refrigerator he'd recently leased. Everything in the few musty rooms was rented, the old furniture, if that's what you'd call it, stored in the garage. He had only the bare essentials. Just enough to get by for a few weeks—however long this might take.

Snagging a beer from the refrigerator, he twisted off the cap and walked onto the back porch, where, through the trees, he saw lamplight glowing at the Summers place. He wondered about Kate, how he was going to deal with her, then thought of Jon. How was he getting along? He looked like hell. The Neider kid had taken care of that. How was a boy like Jon going to handle Todd Neider and the other hotheads who wanted a crack at the kid who was different, the boy through no fault of his own could see into a person's life?

Daegan knew from past experience what a curse that could be and thanked the powers that be that his own gift had faded with the years. If only Jon could be so lucky. *Jon.* His boy. The one he should claim, but couldn't.

Kate's son. Her reason for living.

"Son of a bitch." He leaned one shoulder against the rough post that supported the roof and listened as a coyote let out a long, lonesome howl. One of the horses neighed nervously and the wind tugged at his shirt tails.

A low growl emanated from the floorboards.

"Come on out from under there, Roscoe," Daegan ordered as if he expected the ornery animal to obey him. "Come on, boy. Give it a rest."

Another growl and deep-throated bark.

"You're the ugliest and most unfriendly mutt I've ever come across," Daegan allowed as he remembered another dog hidden in the shadows, a dog that had growled and threatened to attack when Stuart had stalked him on the waterfront all those years ago.

Stuart, the great manipulator, who had ended up dead. Why the hell would he remember that night now? After over fifteen years?

As he turned to walk back inside, he heard a car jolting down the dual tire tracks of his lane. A visitor? The hairs on the back of his neck rose as headlights splashed twin beams over the dry grass of the backyard. He half expected Todd Neider's old man, equipped with a tire iron or baseball bat, to leap from the car intent on breaking bones or balls, or that someone Robert Sullivan had hired to find his illegitimate grandson might appear.

Instead he recognized Kate's old Buick as it ground to stop near the barn. He felt an unexpected warmth deep n his center and called himself a fool. Whether he wanted to or not, he was going to end up wounding her worse than even he could imagine. With a curse leveled t himself, he took a swallow of beer as she threw open the door. Light from the car's interior played in the golden strands of her hair. Daegan's jaw grew tight. He had no business noticing her hair or anything else about her, especially in light of his last conversation with Bibi.

Pocketing her keys, she nudged the car's door shut with her heel and approached the porch carrying a platter of some kind of cupcakes. "I think I owe you an apology," she said without much of a preamble. "No, I know I do." She shook her head, as if this humble gesture wasn't in her nature. "Happy Halloween."

The scent of her perfume—jasmine, he guessed—carried on the cool wind that teased at her hair as she handed him the plate.

"Halloween. Hell, I'd forgotten. Thanks." Eyeing the jack-o'-lantern cupcakes, he set the platter on the seat of an old rocker well past its prime. "Look good."

"The batter was." A ghost of a smile whispered over her lips. "If you want to know the truth, I feel pretty ridiculous bringing them over, you know, like I'm going to a PTA bake sale or something. It's—it's really not my style. Jon told me the idea was lame, but we don't have many trick or treaters clear out here and I thought you might like them and . . . to tell you the truth, it was just an excuse to tell you I appreciate the fact that you might have saved my son's life."

My son's, too.

She stuffed her hands into the pockets of her jeans and rocked back on her heels as she stared up at him. Jon hasn't had a lot of men in his life. My dad died years ago and then Jim and . . . aside from Eli McIntyre no one's ever taken an interest in him."

Don't tell me this. I don't want to know. "Is that so?"

"Fact is, he scares most men off."

"Then they're fools." His throat was suddenly parched and he took another swallow. Her eyes, in the dark, seemed larger, a liquid gold that shimmered.

"Probably." She lifted a shoulder. "As I said, there haven't been all that many. And out here . . . it's pretty isolated, no close neighbors, town so far away."

"I thought maybe you liked it that way," he said, deciding she'd unwittingly presented him with an opportunity to get to know more about her.

"No," she said with a shake of her head. "The price was right and I was tired of the city."

"You're not from around here?" He knew better, of course, but wanted to hear her version of the story.

She leaned a hip against the porch rail. "No. I grew up in the Midwest—Iowa—got married and moved to . . . well later my husband died and Jon and I moved to Seattle where I finished school. Once I got the job at the community college, we settled in here. Haven't moved since."

"So you like it here?"

A breath of wind tugged at her hair. "It has its moments both bad and good."

"Every place does," he said, then held up his bottle. "Join me?"

She hesitated, then shook her head. "Not tonight but thanks." Her gaze touched his for a fraction of an instant before she quickly glanced away. In the span of that single heartbeat he felt a tightening in his gut he didn't like and couldn't control.

"I think Jon's a helluva kid."

"Do you?" Pride flickered in her eyes. "So do I." Tilting her head, she studied him with inquisitive eyes.

"He needs to learn how to fight."

"Or avoid them."

"Hard to do when an ass like Neider hunts him down."

"You offering to help him?" she asked as little furrows of worry gathered between her eyebrows.

Daegan lifted a shoulder. "Why not?"

"No, the question is 'why'? Why would you bother with a kid you barely know?" she asked, pushing herself upright. Some of the old distress he'd witnessed before tightened the corners of her mouth.

"I just don't like seeing a kid used as a punching bag. It's not good for his self-esteem." He finished his beer and set the empty bottle on the rail.

"You don't know a thing about—"

"I know what I saw," he cut in swiftly, his temper snapping. "Your boy was getting the crap beat out of him. Either he learns to defend himself or he's gonna end up in the hospital if that Neider kid has his way."

"Jon seems to think he won't be bothered again."

"I wouldn't bet on it. That's one mean son of a bitch, lady, and he gets his jollies by picking on smaller kids in front of his friends. If I were you, I'd enroll my kid in karate, wrestling, and boxing lessons, then I'd swear out a complaint and press charges and let his folks know that you won't put up with this kind of backwoods attitude!"

"Jon doesn't want me to talk to the police."

"Jon's a kid. What does he know?"

"You don't have to live with him."

"True enough, but if I did, you can bet that I'd be the boss."

"Do you have any kids?" she demanded, stepping closer.

Jolted, he just stared at her flushed face and the way

her fists were planted on her hips. She didn't know what she was asking . . . or did she? "What?"

Waving impatiently, as if scooting away a bothersome insect, she said, "Just because you're not married doesn't mean you don't have a kid or two living with an ex-lover somewhere."

He couldn't prevent the slow, dangerous smile that crept across his jaw. *If you only knew.* "No way."

"Is that right? Then you must be 'Dear Abby' or have some license that makes you an authority when it comes to raising teenagers."

He held her gaze steadily, refusing to flinch beneath the anger that seemed to radiate from her in waves. "I believe in telling it like it is, lady, and it looks to me like your kid could use some instruction in defending himself. His mama isn't always gonna be around to bail him out nor will he be able to depend on help from a stranger like he got from me the other day. Now, did I hear you wrong or did you say you came over here because of some apology?"

"You're pushing it, O'Rourke."

"I didn't start this."

She elevated a disbelieving eyebrow.

"You're standing on my porch," he reminded her. "Without an invitation."

Color swept up her neck and her lips compressed in a silent fury he found fascinating. The night seemed to close in around them, dark and seductive. He noticed the sweep of her eyelashes against her cheek, the way her lips curved into a sexy pout, the angle of her chin as she glared up at him. Dangerous thoughts crept into his mind and he wondered how her lips would feel against his, how easily her body might press against the harder contours of his muscle and bone. *You're getting in way over your head, O'Rourke. Remember why you're here, what's supposed to be happening.*

But it was too late. Much too late. Already that age-old chemistry was stirring in his blood, and desire, so long dormant, was awakening, starting a fire deep in his loins, sending warm jets of want through his limbs. He wondered what it would be like to make love to her all night long, only stopping when dawn was peeking over the horizon and they were exhausted.

"About that apology," she said and she seemed to have trouble breathing. Her eyes moved to his lips again, and he was damned sure she was wondering what it would feel like to kiss him.

Don't do it. Be smart.

"I was coming over to thank you for saving Jon's skin today, for stepping in and helping out. Despite what I said earlier, I'm thankful you were there to break it up. I, um, I . . . Oh, God, this isn't easy. I've told Jon to stay away from you, that he shouldn't trespass or bother you." She gathered in her breath. "But it wasn't for all the right reasons."

"You're afraid for him. Because he said I killed some-one."

"Yes," she admitted, her eyes searching his.

It was all he could do to keep from reaching forward and dragging her close to him. His jaw worked. His heart began to pound. "Look, Kate, I'm not going to stand here and pretend that I'm a saint, because I'm not, but you have to believe me, I'm not a cold-blooded killer."

She looked up at him with soft whiskey-colored eyes. "I'd like to believe it."

Yearning and self-loathing throbbed through his veins because he was going to lie to her, and damn it, if she didn't leave soon, he'd try to kiss her and things wouldn't stop there. "Do, Kate." He reached forward and brushed a strand of hair from her cheek, his finger-tips brushing her skin, the fire in his blood nearly boiling. Despite the deception, despite the knowledge that he'd lied to her from the start, despite his own convictions that getting involved with her was unthinkable, he couldn't back away. His words—so treacherous as they reached his own ears—echoed into the night. "Trust me," he said, when he couldn't even trust himself.

Chapter 15

Fifteen years.

She folded her long legs, salon-tanned against her tennis whites, and sipped the bottle of Perrier, oblivious to the flurry of activity at the juice bar of Boston's most elite racquet club. The dreadful news from VanHorn had thrown her for a loop, distracted her to the extent that she'd pounded through her lesson with the tennis pro. It had been a wasted session; Vito had worked his cute derriere off calling out instructions and bounding around energetically, but her mind had been stuck on images of Robert Sullivan signing his fortune over to some wide-eyed orphan boy. A regular Oliver Twist.

For fifteen years there had been yet another bastard child running around out there with no one the wiser, and now, Robert Sullivan had hired this seedy investigator to track the boy down. Robert must have lost his mind, thinking he needed to look outside the family for an heir. It was utter insanity, and the most unfortunate part was that Robert, as patriarch, still pulled the strings. If he wanted to pass his fortune on to a clown from the circus, not a soul could stop him.

She knew about these things. God knew, she was the only Sullivan with a head for numbers, though it wouldn't take a financial genius to realize that Robert's assets were the ones worth inheriting now that Frank Sullivan had run his share of the business into the ground.

Damn Robert for searching out this bastard child . . . and damn Bibi for getting herself knocked up by someone who must have been a complete and utter loser. Bibi had always played the forlorn bleeding heart, adopting strays and sighing over kittens and puppies. Who knew she'd turn out to be such a slut, too, having a secret baby. Everyone had always wondered about Bibi the year she'd dropped out of sight. Off to some camp . . . or was it a student exchange program abroad? Whatever the lame story, it had reeked of cover-up, though at the time no one really cared enough about Bibi to pursue it.

Glossy red fingernails tapped the green bottle of mineral water as she considered this new development. The old patriarch who should leave well enough alone and his stupid daughter who should have crossed her legs. Morons.

Not to mention the private detective who thought he was going to take her money and play her against Robert Sullivan. She felt sullied having had to spend thirty minutes with VanHorn. Washing down the bitter taste in her throat with the mineral water, she wished she could swipe out VanHorn with as much ease. Such an unpleasant man with beady little eyes and yellowed fingernails flicking nervously over that matchbook. He thought he was going to gain a small fortune and a modicum of control if he found the bastard boy, but he was wrong.

He didn't realize he was messing with a Sullivan, but he would soon learn. Oh, he'd learn.

* * *

"Pull yourself together!" Kate stared into the foggy bathroom mirror, barely able to see her reflection through the condensation. Standing in a towel, her wet hair dripping to her shoulders, she silently reminded herself that Daegan O'Rourke was off-limits, the worst man in the world for her and yet . . .

Trust me. Those two words had chased each other around her mind all night long. She'd barely slept a wink. A sense of foreboding, like the collection of storm clouds on the horizon, had been with her ever since she'd left Daegan standing on his porch, the light from one window throwing the hard-edged contours of his body in stark relief.

Brushing her teeth, she reminded herself that Daegan O'Rourke was the kind of trouble she didn't need.

She heard the phone jangle in the kitchen. Quickly, she rinsed and wiped her mouth, then slipped her arms through the robe she'd hung near the door. On the third ring, she flew out of the room and was halfway to the kitchen when Jon, from his bedroom, yelled down at her.

"Hey, Mom, it's for you!"

"I'll catch it down here. Are you about ready?"

"I'm not going." She heard the squeak of his mattress as he rolled back into his bed. She didn't blame him, but she had mixed feelings about it. True, Jon would be the laughingstock at school, the object of much speculation and gossip, and Todd Neider would probably rub it in, but he had to walk through the hallowed doors of Hopewell High sooner or later, and facing his classmates wasn't going to get any easier as the days passed.

"Wait a minute, Jon, don't you think—"

"Mom, I look like hell and I feel worse," he yelled through the open door of his room.

"Fine—we'll talk later." This was no morning for a

fight; besides, the restless feeling that something was wrong, or missing, trailed after her as she hurried to the kitchen and cinched the tie of her robe tight around her waist.

Snagging the receiver, she shoved aside the uneasiness that shadowed her mind. "Hello?"

"Where were you—across town?"

"Very funny, Laura," she said, smiling at the thought of her sister. If only they didn't live so far away. Right about now she could use some of Laura's quirky bursts of sunshine.

"Hey, I think I got some information for you," Laura said brightly.

Kate's heart stilled. Her fingers clamped around the receiver in a death grip.

"About Jon?"

"No, about O'Rourke. I wanted to ease your mind. Doesn't look like he has a prison record, at least not here in Boston."

Kate's knees nearly gave way. She leaned against the ladder back of one of the kitchen chairs. "You're certain?"

"Yep. If he was ever charged or indicted, I can't find it, and he certainly was never sentenced. I checked the records going back forty years."

Kate let out her breath.

"So you can relax around the new neighbor."

Relax? Around Daegan O'Rourke? No way. Just because he didn't have a prison record didn't necessarily clear him of all bad intentions, but she felt her pulse jump a little and some of the barriers she'd built around her heart seemed to give way. "Did you find out anything about him? Did he come from Boston or ever live there? Was one of his cousins killed and—"

"Hey, slow down," Laura said, laughing, and Kate imagined her green eyes filled with mischief and amusement. "I'm still checking. I've weeded out a couple guys who couldn't possibly be your cowboy—"

"He's not mine," she said swiftly.

"Ooh, touchy about that, aren't we?"

"Go on," Kate replied, surprised how quickly she'd risen to Laura's bait.

"There are still two guys in the mix who fit the physical description and are about the right age. One guy was illegitimate, born to a Mary Ellen O'Rourke in South Boston and that's all I know about him. He left town before he was twenty. The other guy is the sixth of ten, a working-class family who moved in the mid-seventies. I'm still looking into it."

Slowly, they were getting closer to the truth. "I owe you."

"I know, I know. You always owe me. That's why our relationship works so well. Hey, look, I've got to run. I'm on my break and have about forty-five seconds to get to a staff meeting. I'll talk to you later."

"Thanks." Kate hung up and her heart buoyed a little, even though there was still something wrong—an emptiness this morning.

Thoughtfully she poured a cup of coffee from the pot and walked to the bottom of the stairs. "Jon?"

No answer. Maybe it was just as well. Give him today and maybe tomorrow to heal, then wait until the weekend was over before he returned to school.

Rotating the kinks from her neck, she walked to the front porch and felt vaguely uneasy. Even Laura's good news or a fresh cup of coffee didn't help shake the sensation. Opening the door, she felt a rush of winter-cold air. Outside the sky was as gray as the worry playing with her mind. Thick, black clouds brought the first drops of rain just as the bus slowed at the mailbox then picked up speed again.

Again the uneasy sensation and suddenly she knew

what it was. The dog. She hadn't seen or heard Houndog all morning. She gave a short sharp whistle and listened for an answering bark. All she heard was the gentle pounding of the rain as it started to pour. "Houndog! Come on, boy!" Setting her cup on the table by the platter of cupcakes, she mounted the stairs. Jon was in his room alone. "Have you seen the dog?"

Stretching, Jon yawned and his eyebrows slammed together. "He's not here?"

"Not in the house."

"But—oh, yeah, maybe I left him outside."

"When?"

"He started scratching at the door and whining, like he does when he hears a possum or cat, so I let him out. He took off like a streak across the front yard, barking his head off."

"So you left him outside?"

"He wouldn't come back when I called, so I figured he'd be all right."

She bit her lip. Apprehension knotted her stomach. "When?"

"I don't know. Last night sometime." He rubbed his face and his eyes locked with hers. "Geez, Mom, what? You think something happened to him?"

"Probably not," she lied.

"So where is he? It's not like he ever wanders off." He threw off the covers, and dressed only in his boxer shorts, he searched in the pile of clothes near the foot of the bed for something to wear. Frowning, he came up with a pair of wrinkled jeans and a sweatshirt.

"I think I'll look outside."

"We'll find him, Mom."

Was it her imagination or did she hear a little hint of anxiety in his voice? "Of course we will," she lied as she hurried downstairs and into her room. In seconds she was dressed and outside, sidestepping the puddles that were already beginning to collect and calling Houndog's name. Jon, wearing a Mariners' hat, joined her and together they searched the wet acres, trudging through grass and mud, hoping against hope that they'd come across the puppy, alive and somehow trapped so that he couldn't free himself. But why then wouldn't he whine or bark?

Silently praying that he hadn't been hurt by a passing car or truck, she checked the road and stood in the thicket of trees that sheltered the house from the county highway. Where would the dog run off to? Would someone pick him up? Was he hurt somewhere . . . or was it worse? "Don't borrow trouble," she told herself as she felt the drip of rain soak the hood of her sweatshirt. *Oh, Houndog, where are you?*

She searched the undergrowth and heard Jon's voice, edged in worry, as he called for his dog and best friend in the world. Around the house and past the rosebushes with their dry leaves and blossoms gone to seed.

Fear congealed in her heart when she walked around the woodshed and saw the pumpkins smashed against a pile of old flagstones. "Did you do this?" she asked but Jon just stared at the seeds and stringy orange pulp that dripped from the pumpkin shells.

"Neider," he whispered.

"You don't know that."

"Who else?"

"I . . . I can't imagine."

"Damn it, Mom, of course, it's Neider." His jaw thrust forward, he blinked hard and fought a brave but losing battle with tears. His discolored face twisted into a determined grimace. "You think he . . . he killed him?"

"Of course not. Why would he hurt an innocent animal?"

"Neider doesn't need a reason. He's just mean."

"We don't even know it was Todd. Come on, let's go

inside." But as they turned, they both saw the walls of the pump house—the time-darkened wood covered with graffiti.

HAPPY HALLOWEEN FAG
CRY BABY
COCK SUCKER
FUCK YOU, SUMMERS

Ugly, filthy epithets all aimed at Jon and written in neon orange and stark black.

"Oh, Lord," Kate whispered, reading the slurs and hate. "This has got to stop. Come back in the house," she ordered, marching up the steps not really knowing what she would do, but convinced that the police had to be involved. Jon could scream bloody murder for all she cared, but she was going to dial Sheriff Swanson and explain to the authorities everything that had happened. She'd just reached for the phone when she heard the sound of a truck pulling into the lane.

Nerves strung tight as new barbed wire, she ran to the front of the house and thought about grabbing the old rifle she had locked in the closet. *Look what I've come to,* she thought, her heart hammering wildly as she recognized Daegan's truck through the blinds. "Thank God." Flinging open the front door, she ran across the porch and would have willingly thrown herself into his arms if they weren't already full with a wiggling mass whom she assumed was Houndog. "No!" she cried just as Jon rounded the corner.

"Bastards!" He was across the yard in an instant and taking Houndog from Daegan's hands. Tears mingled with the rain as they drizzled down his face.

"At least he's not dead," Daegan said, a dangerous fire burning in his eyes. "I found him on the back porch tied and drugged, I guess."

The dog had been shorn, scratches evident in his naked, mottled skin, only his face and tail showing more than clumps of fur. On his shaved body, the same filthy words had been sprayed.

"I'm gonna wash him."

"No," Kate said, "not yet. Take him into the car and we'll go visit the sheriff." Outrage searing through her blood, she turned to Daegan. "Would you be willing to sign a statement about Todd Neider assaulting Jon and then discovering the dog this morning?"

"Absolutely."

"No!" Jon protested then looked down at the shivering, drowsy dog in his arms. "Fine. Let's go. Just let me wrap him in a blanket."

"I'll drive," Daegan said as Jon ran into the house. A muscle worked overtime in his jaw. "I guess it's time I met the sheriff anyway."

". . . a shame about the pup, there . . . we'll investigate, of course, but since you have no proof it was the Neider boy, there's not a lot I can do," Sheriff Swanson said. Fit, trim, with a clipped silver moustache and thick glasses, the sheriff leaned back in his chair and tapped his fingers together. Daegan had grown up not trusting the law and he stared at this military-looking man through suspicious eyes. Swanson was trying hard to placate Kate and she was having none of it.

"It's more than a shame and it's more than criminal," she said through tight lips. "It's downright cruel and immoral and it's got to stop!"

"Hey, I'm not disagreeing with you, Kate. I'll send a deputy out to take pictures of the vandalism, and we've already got shots of the dog." He stared at the little pup shivering in Jon's arms. Between the shaved, painted mutt and Jon's bruised and swollen face, they made a

pitiful picture. Just looking at his son caused fury to
burn through Daegan's blood, and whether the sheriff
did anything or not, Daegan sure as hell planned to visit
Neider's old man. "As for the charges of assault," Swanson said, eyeing the signed complaint on the desk, "I believe you. Todd's an ornery character, but the two other
boys, Morrisey and Flanders, they're usually not into
much trouble. Why, Morrisey's father's a minister down
at the First Christian—"

"Just because his old man spouts the word of God
doesn't mean he can't get into trouble," Kate said
swiftly.

"I know, but—"

"Those two—Morrisey and Flanders—weren't throwing any punches," Daegan said, unable to keep his
mouth shut a second longer. Content to drink the sheriff
department's sludgelike coffee, he'd rested his hips
against the window sill and nodded in confirmation
whenever the sheriff had glanced his way. He'd let Kate
and Jon tell their side of the story, but when it became obvious that the law would rather just sweep this "little incident" under the carpet, Daegan had decided to stand
up and be counted. "But they were egging him on. And
if they say different, they're liars just trying to save their
own miserable hides. Cowards, they took off running
when I showed up. But the Neider kid, he's the ring
leader, the one who needs to be horsewhipped himself."

"I'm afraid that's a little harsh."

"Right," Daegan said sarcastically. "We'll save the
whip for his old man." To hear Jon tell it, Carl Neider
spent too many nights drinking down at the Plug
Nickel. If he escaped a brawl at the tavern, he usually
came home mean as a wounded rattler and ready to
strike. His primary target was his son. In turn, the oaf of
a kid took out his frustrations on smaller boys, primarily
Jon.

Swanson smiled at the thought of whipping one of the regulars he had to lock up on Saturday nights. "Neider's a mean cuss when he's had a few too many, but he's had a hard row to hoe, what with his wife walkin' out on him when Todd was barely two."

"Doesn't make it right, Swanson. Lots of people raise kids alone these days."

The sheriff promised to look into matters but Daegan wasn't satisfied. "Not exactly a ball of fire," he remarked once they were back in the car and headed to the veterinary clinic on the edge of town.

Doc Martin, a short balding man with a horseshoe of snow-white hair and freckles on his pate, took one look at Houndog and scowled fiercely. "Who did this?" he asked, taking the shivering pup from Jon's hands.

Kate exchanged glances with her son. "We're not sure yet."

"Well, whoever it is, he's one sick individual, isn't that right, Houndog?" Running expert fingers along the dog's body, Doc Martin poked and prodded gently, took Houndog's temperature, looked into his eyes, and pronounced him none the worse for wear.

"He's traumatized, naturally. Who wouldn't be? Just because Houndog here is an animal doesn't mean he doesn't realize when he's been mistreated. Isn't that right, fella?" He stroked the pup behind his ears. "Boy, I'd like to get my hands on the jerk who did this." Shaking his head, he looked over the tops of reading glasses. "I might just get out my own razor and can of paint."

Daegan grinned. "Not a bad idea," he said.

"Just leave this little guy here overnight and we'll clean him up and make sure he's all right," the vet suggested.

By the time they returned to Kate's, it was nearly noon. Daegan parked his truck and turned off the ignition. Over her protests, he walked them to the house, pausing at the pump house where he stood in the wet mashed-down grass and read the graffiti hastily sprayed on the graying siding. His jaw hardened and Kate watched as a transformation took place. No longer the affable rancher, Daegan, eyes narrowed, muscles tensed, appeared dangerous, even deadly.

His gaze moved to the ground surrounding the old building and to the garden before settling on the horizon. "You know, Jon," he finally said, as if he'd come to some inner decision, one that made Kate's blood run cold. "If you'd like, you can come over to the house and I'll teach you a few things."

"Yeah?" Jon was interested.

Kate didn't like the hard glint in Daegan's eyes. "Like what?"

"To ride a horse, for one." That seemed safe enough.

"Would you? Really?" Jon's black-and-blue face split into a grin.

"Yep, but we'll start with Loco before we move on to Buckshot."

"Why couldn't your horses be named Midnight and Scout? I'd feel a whole lot better," Kate said, still nervous. A soft mist had begun to fall and a breeze stirred her hair.

"That's the way they came." He glanced over at Jon again. "I'll also teach you how to shoot a rifle."

Her gut clenched. "Wait a minute, I don't like guns. Not even BB guns." She couldn't let this man—this stranger—start running her son's life.

"Neither do I," he admitted, turning his gaze back to her and staring hard. She felt as if a raw wind had rushed past her soul. "But living out here, Jon needs to learn to respect how guns work and what kind of damage they can inflict."

"I don't know," she said, still caught in his mesmerizing steely eyes.

"Mom, come on!" Jon insisted, seeing a chance to work with weapons as a once-in-a-lifetime opportunity.

Daegan wasn't finished. He dragged his eyes from hers and motioned through the trees to his house. "I was thinking about putting up a punching bag in the old barn, too. Do you have weights?"

Jon shook his head.

"You might want to start with those at first."

Kate felt as if she were losing control, of her son, her life. Aside from the outside forces physically attacking Jon, here was this man who was working some kind of magic on him and her. Maybe he could be trusted, but maybe he couldn't. The jury was still out on Daegan O'Rourke, and even though he'd acted in her and Jon's defense with nobility in the past few days, she wasn't convinced that she could trust him. Not completely. Not yet. "Let's just slow down a minute, okay? I'm not letting you turn Jon into some kind of . . . Rambo."

"Ah, Mom—"

"Shh!" she said. "This isn't how we live our lives, Jon. We're not survivalists or—"

"Maybe you should be." Daegan was serious and she felt a frisson of cold fear slide down her spine. "This"—he motioned to the ugly words scrawled on the wall—"won't end here."

"Oh, God."

"It's just the beginning."

"How do you know?"

"I was a kid once, too. Had my share of fights. Knew guys like Neider." His eyebrows slammed together and his eyes thinned to a distance only he could see—a distance that looked past time. "Jon just needs to learn to defend himself, that's all."

"Yeah, Mom, why not?"

"No guns," she said firmly. "If you want to teach him

about wrestling or boxing or whatever . . . that's okay
but no firearms."

"Mom," Jon protested.

"Don't argue with me, Jon. Go on in and clean up
and I'll make lunch—"

"But I want to—"

"Now!" she said, at the breaking point. With the anxiety she'd felt over Houndog, the fear for her son's
safety when it came to Neider, the worry about his
dreams, and now these new frightening emotions that
gripped her every time she was with Daegan, her patience was running thin.

For once Jon didn't push the issue, and shoving his
hands into the pockets of his jacket, he turned on his
heel and headed for the house. When he'd rounded
the pump house and was out of earshot, she said,
"You're scaring me, you know."

"You should be scared."

"Because of Todd Neider or because of something
else?" she asked, the words tumbling after each other.
She felt the cool mist against her face and the wind tug at
the hem of her jacket. He stared at her long and hard, as
if weighing what he knew about her in his mind. His gaze
flicked to her lips and she realized in a heart-stopping
second that he was going to kiss her.

The back of her mouth turned to cotton and she
licked her lips as his head lowered and his breath ca-
ressed her skin. "I'm just telling you to be careful, Kate.
You can't go around being a Pollyanna, believing that
everything will turn out right just because you want it
to."

"I'm not."

"Then give the boy a chance. Cut the apron strings, let
him learn to defend himself."

She swallowed hard. He was so close she could see
the streaks of blue in his eyes, noted when his nostrils

lared with a breath or when his pupils dilated as the day grew darker. Unspoken questions hung between them and that raw, restless energy that was part of him seemed to pulse. It was all she could do to step away and clear her throat. "I—I should go in. I promised Jon lunch. Would you like to—I mean, I have plenty. Oh, for the love of God, listen to me. What I'm trying to say is would you like to eat with us?"

A shadow crossed his face for a second as if he were wrestling with some inner torment, but he nodded curtly and shrugged. "Sure," he said, turning away from the damning obscenities. "Why not?"

A dozen reasons, you idiot, his mind scolded, but he ignored that harsh, irritating voice. His son had been through a lot; he just wanted to make sure Jon was okay. And besides, the more he knew about Kate and her deal with Tyrell Clark all those years ago, the better. Right?

Wrong. Right now Daegan felt as if he were treading water and getting nowhere fast. It was coming up on decision time and he'd have to figure out just what he was going to do. He could tell Kate the truth, warn her about the Sullivans, admit that he was Jon's father, but if he did, she'd never trust him again. Of course that shouldn't matter. But it did. It mattered a helluva lot.

Carl Neider's place made old Eli's homestead look like a palace. The house was a shabby single-wide mobile home that was thirty years old if it was a day. With a rusted trailer hitch still attached, as if the owner were contemplating a quick escape, the aluminum home stood on concrete blocks drenched in rust and surrounded by weeds. Two skinny cats were huddled in the corner of a small lean-to porch of tarpaper and silvered wood. Scattered throughout the yard were pieces of old cars— rusted-out radiators, wheels, dashboards, and stacks of bald tires. Long grass going to seed was clumped around the two rickety steps leading to the front door.

Daegan slid his toothpick to the corner of his mouth as he observed the arid acres Todd Neider called home. Patches of scotch broom, tansy, and sage brush were interspersed with a few thin-barked oaks and jack pines whose naked branches danced in the wind.

The sky was an ominous shade of gray, and Daegan could almost smell the scent of disenchantment that had settled into the cold earth on these few rundown acres.

Daegan felt a pang of pity for the kid—this place was every bit as disheartening as Mary Ellen O'Rourke's old apartment over the Cat O'Nine Tails Tavern in South Boston had been.

Well, it was showdown time. He parked his truck behind a massive black pickup with huge tires and a string of lights mounted above the cab. Two rifles rested on the gun rack mounted over the seat. One mean machine; probably owned by one mean *hombre.* Good. Daegan had been ready to take on Old Man Neider ever since he'd seen Todd trying to beat Jon to a pulp.

Now or never. Since Daegan didn't have much faith in the local law, he wasn't about to let matters lie.

He rapped hard on the door and waited until the giant of a man, six-four and pushing three hundred pounds, appeared in the frame. Dressed in a tight T-shirt and dusty jeans, he loomed above Daegan, the same roughneck who had shown up in the café that day, but this time Daegan got a better look at Todd Neider's old man. His face was messed up—a broken nose and scar under one eye, the result of one too many fist fights, Daegan guessed. A tattoo of a snake wrapped around a heart decorated one meaty forearm and a wad of tobacco filled one cheek.

"Yeah?" Neider growled, crossing both arms over his chest.

"You Todd's father?" Daegan asked without preamble. The guy didn't look much for small talk, which was just fine with Daegan.

"Who's askin'?"

"Daegan O'Rourke." Daegan thought about extending his hand, but didn't. This wasn't exactly a social call and they both knew it.

The behemoth stared down at him and shot a stream of tobacco juice into a cluster of weeds. "So you're the bastard who threw my kid's keys into a field of cow shit?"

"That's right." Daegan didn't even wince at the name. Neider couldn't guess how close he was to the truth and it really didn't matter. This was Jon's battle and Daegan was going to savor fighting it.

"Whaddaya want?"

"You to keep your boy from picking on other kids, including Jon Summers."

"That little piece of faggy shit? He's a fuckin' retard, not worth botherin' about." Neider waved, as if shooing aside a pesky horse fly.

"Just tell Todd to lay off."

"Or what?"

"He'll have to answer to me again." Daegan managed his cruelest smile, one that had been known to worry bolder men than this hulking beast.

"What's it to you, O'Rourke? None of your business."

"Jon's a friend of mine."

"Ha! Sure. You're just out for a piece of his ma's ass, like half the men in the county. She's a cold bitch, that one. If I were you, I wouldn't waste my time."

Daegan's teeth clamped over his toothpick. Every muscle in his body tensed. His right hand fisted, and for one quick second, he thought about throwing the first punch. Instead he pinned Carl Neider with a look as cold as ice. "If I were you, I'd be worried sick that a mean son of a bitch might nail my boy the next time he tries to make trouble." He crunched the toothpick into two halves and spit them out on the steps. "As for Mrs. Summers, all she wants is her boy left alone."

"Then maybe she shouldn't raise such a pansy. Christ, that kid's weird. He hears voices or sees visions or some such crap. Probably speaks in tongues and handles snakes, too. It's freaky, just out-and-out freaky. But that's not the worst part. That kid doesn't know when to keep his mouth shut—keeps botherin' Todd at school."

"That's not the way I hear it."

Neider grinned, showing off stained, tobacco-flecked teeth in sad need of a dentist. "Then he's a lying son of a bitch."

"Carl, honey?" a woman's voice slid through the open door.

"In a minute," he shot back.

"I haven't got all day," she pouted.

"I said 'in a minute.'" Turning his attention back to Daegan, he continued, "You got anything else you want to say?"

Daegan's smile was grim as death. "I'm just here to warn you, Neider. Tell your boy to ease off, 'cause if he doesn't, I won't wait for the law; I'll handle him myself, and next time it won't be just a quick kick in the butt and a game of hide and seek with his keys."

Neider made a sound of disgust but his tiny eyes narrowed.

"I'll haul his ass to the county jail myself and make sure Swanson deals with him. Then I'll call social services, see if they think Todd needs help or more supervision or maybe a father that doesn't try to beat the living tar out of him when he's tanked up."

"You scrawny fuck, get off my land!"

"Just tell Todd he better stay away from Jon, his mother, and his damned dog." Daegan glared up at the ugly ox. "Believe me, Neider, I'm not just screwin' round. If I hear of him botherin' anyone—*any*one—I'll take it personally."

"Christ, you've got a bug up your butt." Carl's thick brows drew together as if they'd been pulled by a purse-string, and his breath, smelling of stale beer, drifted over Daegan's face as they squared off. "Oh, I get it," the bigger man said with a leer. "You've got the hots for the kid's old lady, don't you? So you're out stirrin' up trouble about her boy. Trying to look like a damned hero to her. It won't do no good. She don't let anyone near her. Likes to keep to herself. Better men than you have tried, O'Rourke, and no one's ever landed in her bed. There's running bet down at the Silver Horseshoe, the first on of a bitch who fucks her wins two hundred bucks!"

Daegan nearly jumped out of his skin. He rolled onto the balls of his feet, his fingers curled, his muscles itching to pummel the sick bag of wind.

"Don't get yourself all worked up about a piece of ass you can't have and a kid that's a crappy little misfit," Neider advised. "What's going on between the boys, that's their business. You stay out of it, O'Rourke."

"No way," Daegan said as Carl lumbered down the two steps and poked a thick finger at Daegan's breastbone.

"My boy fights his own battles. If someone's giving him shit, he gives it right back, only a little harder. That's the way he was taught, that's what makes him tough, and that's why that whiny little Summers kid is such a wimp. Now take a hike. You're trespassin' here."

"Just so as we understand each other, Neider."

"Carl? You comin'?" A tall willowy woman leaned against the door frame. Wild blond hair framed a face that had once been pretty. Long legs were covered only

by the hem of a T-shirt that was big enough to lop ove
one tanned shoulder. "You got a friend?" she wheedle
holding a cigarette between long, slim fingers.

"He was just leavin', and no, he ain't no friend."

"Too bad," the woman said, looking longingly a
Daegan, her soulless eyes sliding down his body an
resting for a moment on his fly. With a sigh, she saic
"See ya around, sugar."

"Go back into the house, Flo," Neider ordered, his fac
flushing to an ugly purple color. "And you, O'Rourke, ge
the hell off my property before I kill ya."

Cold steel presses into the shoulder blade—the gun
The weapon's brutal potential freezes him in place
He's going to kill me. He's thinking about it. The man'
thoughts are clearly transmitted through the nose o
the pistol.

Just kill the boy now and be done with this . . .

"That's where you're wrong," Jon tells him in a voic
that sounds as aloof as the snowflakes that drift pas
them. "Kill me now and you'll never be done with this
You'll be paying for the rest of your life."

How do you . . . ? Stop messing with my head!

"Just shut up," the man says with a low growl, bu
keeps the gun stabbing into his back. Still prepared t
pull the trigger, still tempted to end it all now. A hanc
clamps hard on Jon's left shoulder as the man presse
closer, cloaking Jon in his evil.

"You left without your jacket, son." The man's voic
oozes with paternal concern, loud enough now fo
other people to hear. The two women decked i
hooded jackets and boots cannot smell Jon's panic a
they walk right by and duck into the door of a boutiqu
strung with white lights. "You can't run around ou

here without a coat," the man says, performing for passing shoppers. "You'll catch your death of cold."

Jon twists his neck to turn toward the man, but unforgiving metal stabs deeper into his shoulder, keeping him in line. The man is a shadow behind him, but Jon is able to make out the bubble jacket around the man's fist, loosely concealing the pistol pressed within inches of Jon's life.

The pistol.

No running from a gun . . . no escape. A prisoner again.

The wind tears over them, shrill and sharp, freezing the tears of frustration gathering in Jon's eyes. He came so close. He nearly slipped away from this man . . . so close. And yet, he is back in the man's grip, gun to his back. Trapped again.

Kill him now . . .

The man's thoughts seep through the broad palm of his hand on Jon's shoulder.

Kill him now and collect the money . . .

"No! No, don't!" Ducking the gun, Jon dove for the ground and found his face and hands sinking into soft sheet. His bed. Damn!

He rolled over and sat for a minute, waiting out the thrumming in his ears, the roar of his racing pulse, the shrill terror of the dream. It was his first glimpse of the man's motives, the first time the dream of his pursuer had spun on so long, though Jon wasn't sure that was a good thing. After all, the ending sucked. A gun to his back with the man behind him licking his chops about killing him.

For money. What was that about? Ransom money? And why would anyone hold him for ransom when his mother could barely pay her Visa bill, let alone scrape together the kind of payoff that would make kidnapping worth the risk.

He slung the blanket over his shoulders, went to the window, and stared out at the moon, barely visible through the tangled tree branches. The inky sky above him was as vast and dark as the morass of his nightmare. Who was the man, his pursuer . . . his killer? And the strange city, lit with Christmas lights? It was a far cry from Hopewell, Oregon, or even Bend with its downtown streets crowded with tables and pedestrians in the summer. No, the dream took place in a location as foreign to Jon as the icy fear instilled by his pursuer.

A gust of wind shook the bare branches outside Jon's window, bending the tops of tall fir trees down the lane. That was when he spotted it—a parked vehicle. Adrenaline shot through Jon as he scrutinized the dark hunk of metal near the road—a truck.

Todd and his guys? Were they back to cause more damage?

Squinting into the night, Jon recognized the truck as Daegan's. Yeah, definitely Daegan's, parked in a weird spot, as if he were keeping watch. Guard duty.

That was all right by Jon. If Daegan wanted to help fend off Todd Neider and his gang, well, he could use the help. But even a big guy like Daegan O'Rourke had his limitations.

Too bad. No one, no one could save Jon from his dreams.

Wind rattled through the old pickup. The sky was dark and gloomy, night settling like a shroud over the land. Parked at the end of his drive with a clear view of the Summers place, he settled in for the night. Daegan had slept in worse places and he didn't plan on getting much shut-eye anyway. Whoever was terrorizing Jon and Kate was gonna get caught red-handed. He was going to see to it personally.

Through the trees he noticed the lights of Kate's house, imagined her walking through the rooms in little more than a robe, her hair pinned up from a recent bath, her skin flushed and warm, her voice soft.

What was her routine? What did she wear to bed? What did she look like without any clothes when the suspicion left her eyes? He swallowed hard, tried to think of anything but her naked body, but try as he might, he saw her in his mind's eye, slowly disrobing, showing off proud, full breasts with big, rosy nipples, long legs with a thatch of brown curls at the apex.

Muttering under his breath, he scowled into the darkness and shifted on the seat, his jeans suddenly too tight. Hell, this was getting him nowhere. He couldn't afford to think of her as anything but an obstacle.

So why're you freezing your tail off here trying to protect her and her son? Not because she's an obstacle. Face it, O'Rourke, the woman's getting to you. Whether you admit it or not, you want her.

Gritting his teeth, he pulled a small flask of whiskey from the glove box, took a sip for warmth, and settled in. It promised to be a long night.

Chapter 16

"What's with you, O'Rourke?" Kate demanded, stepping over puddles to stand near his truck. The night was still for once, only a breath of wind and a million stars jeweled the sky. His pickup was tucked in the night-dark shadows of a thicket of pine and oak near the end of his drive, right next to her own mailbox and lane.

He rolled down the window and offered her that same damning, lazy smile she found so disturbing. "No law against sitting here, is there?"

"Not that I know of, but it's a little crazy." She felt a twinge of foolishness. After all, the man was on his own property. "But I know you've been out here every night for the past week. Why?" she asked, prickly and anxious. She'd spied his truck at the end of the drive the night after Halloween and hadn't thought much about it until she'd gone to bed and wondered why he'd park the rattletrap near the road, as if he were guarding his place—or hers.

When it happened night after night, she'd become concerned and a little nettled. Jon had started visiting him after school and she hadn't been able to stop her son from making a daily trek across the fence and through the trees to the old McIntyre place. By the time she returned from work, her son was usually home again, listening to music, playing with Houndog, or even doing his homework. As she fixed dinner, he'd talk to her as he once had, regaling her with stories about Daegan O'Rourke, who taught Jon how to box and wrestle, change a tire, ride a horse, even change the oil in his pickup. All Jon's worries about some dark and foreboding man seemed to have been forgotten.

Kate tried to convince herself that everything was as it should be, that the biggest concern for her son's safety wasn't some criminal of a father hell-bent to find his boy—no, the danger was more immediate and in the form of Todd Neider's fists. So she'd let him develop a friendship with the man who swore up and down he wasn't a killer, the neighbor who had been kind enough to fix her flat tire and bail her son out of the whipping of his life.

Daegan glanced up and down the road. "I'm just being cautious. Thought I'd make sure Todd got the message."

"So you've appointed yourself our own personal sentry?"

"I have trouble sleeping anyway."

"Look," she said, shivering. "I appreciate your concern, but we can take care of ourselves."

The stare he sent her silently called her a fool, and she rubbed her arms, remembering the graffiti that she'd painted over, the dog's cruel haircut and paint job that had been cleaned by the vet, and Jon's bruised and battered body. "Okay, so maybe we've had a little trouble."

"I think it should end."

"So do I—"

"You want to join me?" he asked.

"No, I—"

The driver's door creaked open and he slid across the bench seat just as headlights flashed down the highway. Daegan fastened his gaze on the approaching car, and Kate, wondering if she had any brains left, climbed in. The car passed, spraying the interior with a wash of light before roaring past.

Inside the truck, Daegan offered her an old army blanket that she draped over her shoulders.

"Warmer?"

"Yeah." What was she doing, for crying out loud? One part of her mind screamed she was dancing with the devil, taking a horrendous risk by being alone with him, the other part—that traitorous feminine side of her soul—was seduced by being alone with him in the dark, watching a ribbon of road in the moonlight.

She felt his eyes studying her—as if looking for flaws. Her cheekbones, chin, neck. Her pulse throbbed at the base of her throat. "I don't know what I'm doing here."

"Sure you do," he drawled, leaning against the passenger door. "You wanted to get to know me better."

"Pardon me?"

"Jon's been coming over and you want me to tell you how it's going."

"Maybe."

"And you want to find out what makes me tick. It makes you nervous that your son's spending so much time with a man you hardly know." He paused for a second and added, "And it makes you nervous to be in here with me. Nervous as hell." To prove his point, he touched that jumping pulse with the tip of a finger.

The air in the cab seemed suddenly close and she couldn't breathe, couldn't think of anything but the skin touching hers.

"I—um, just don't know how to take all this interest

in my family," she admitted, deciding to go for broke and find out his reaction. "In one of his premonitions, just about the time you showed up in Hopewell, Jon saw a man, one he couldn't identify, who was looking for him."

"And you think I'm the guy?" he asked, withdrawing his hand, his eyes flattening in the darkness. She sensed his change of mood, his silent anger.

"I don't know."

"But you do believe someone is coming?"

"Oh, God, I wish I knew."

Another vehicle appeared moving slowly, one headlight dimmer than the other. An old truck. Her heart froze and Daegan shifted, every muscle rigid as the pickup didn't slow down, just rolled past.

"Oh, Lord," she whispered, "now you've got me jumping at shadows. How long will you keep up this vigil, or whatever you'd call it."

"As long as it takes to convince me that Neider won't bother Jon again."

"That may be a while."

"I've got time," he said, his voice hard-edged. "Tell me about the man who Jon thinks is coming."

She hesitated a second, unsure how much she could trust him. Outside an owl hooted softly. "That's just it, I don't know," she said.

"But you're scared."

"A little."

"Don't be," he said in a voice that was rough. He slid closer to her and placed a strong arm over her shoulders. "I'm here."

"I know but—"

"I'm on your side," he said, his breath ruffling her hair. "I want you to know that, Kate." Was there a hitch in his voice—a new edge? "I won't let anything happen to Jon."

Something inside her broke, a dam that held back her emotions, a sturdy wall that she'd built brick by brick, assuring her that she could keep her distance, stay clearheaded, keep all relationships on an even keel. Somehow Daegan had found a crack in the cement around her heart. She swallowed hard as he turned her head with one finger so that she was forced to look into his eyes.

"Trust me, Kate," he whispered, his breath fanning her lips, and her heart, suddenly fragile, threatened to break.

"Oh, Lord—"

He kissed the side of her mouth and she quivered. He kissed her cheek and she let out a ragged, whispery breath. His arms surrounded her, gathering her close, and she didn't protest, didn't argue against his needs or her own.

His mouth claimed hers in a kiss that stole the breath from her soul. She opened her mouth to him willingly and he took what she offered, his tongue sliding past her teeth, touching, exploring, mating with her own.

A soft moan escaped her as he shifted, his weight pressing her downward, his powerful arms holding her close. Her heart pounded, echoing in her ears, and old, long-dead desires heated her blood.

"Kate," he whispered and his voice sounded desperate. "Kate . . . no . . ."

An engine rumbled and Daegan lifted his head. "Hell," he ground out, releasing her suddenly, his muscles coiled as the beams of headlights split the darkness and an old car without much of a muffler slowed near Kate's drive.

Daegan reached under the seat but the car passed, moving on noisily, and Kate sagged against the driver's door. "What's that?" she asked, her heart hammering, expecting him to hold up a gun of some kind.

"A weapon."

"What kind of weapon?"

"A deadly one."

Metal glinted in the night and her heart nearly stopped until she realized that he was holding a wrench. She laughed nervously. "Just don't tell me you've got a gun in the glove compartment."

"Okay, I won't," he agreed but the edge to his words only made her more anxious.

"I think I'd better go. I guess if you want to lose sleep out here, there's nothing I can do about it."

"Guess not."

She reached for the door handle, but strong fingers wrapped around her wrist. "Kate—"

Her breath caught in her throat.

"Anytime you want to visit me again, the door's open."

"I'll remember that," she said, scrambling out of the cab and taking deep breaths of cold midnight air. Wrapping her jacket around her, she walked quickly away and vowed that she wouldn't return to the truck. Being alone with Daegan was too dangerous.

"Are you out of your mind?" Frank lit a cigarette and flopped into a chair. Red-faced, a little gray sprinkling the hair at his temples, the youngest Sullivan brother was beginning to show signs of age.

Robert looked past his brother to the open door, where his secretary was standing helplessly, motioning that she'd tried to stop Frank from bulldozing his way into the office. "It's all right, Louise. I was about to go home anyway. Please, close the door."

She did as she was bade, and when they were finally alone, Robert folded his hands on the desk in an effort at patience. "What are you talking about?"

"You're trying to find Bibi's kid? After all these years? For the love of Jesus, Bob, why?"

"He's blood. The only grandson I'll ever see."

"Big deal." Frank shot a stream of smoke from the corner of his mouth. "Big fucking deal."

"It is to me."

"Why?" Scratching his eyebrow, Frank studied his brother through the smoke curling toward the ten-foot ceiling of the law office.

Robert felt the old rivalry grow between them again, as it had since they were children. Frank resented being born last, behind him, behind William. Since William had died young, only Robert stood in his way of inheriting everything—and now Robert was looking for a new heir? Frank was feeling cheated again.

"You don't know what it's like to lose a child."

"So this is about Stuart."

"There's no hell on earth that measures up to the loss of a son. That he was murdered..." He could barely say the word and scowled down at the folder still open on his desk.

Slowly he closed the file and set it aside. "Your boy did that."

"Not mine. That bastard's not mine, I never claimed him, Bob, didn't give him my name. Hell, how do I know Mary Ellen didn't get herself pregnant by someone else and say Daegan was mine?"

"Enough!" Robert spat out, disgusted. "He was yours all right, looked more like you than his mother; had the cursed sight, too. Just like William!"

"You know a lot about him." Frank's eyes narrowed, as if he were calculating what his brother was up to, and he took a long drag on his smoke.

"I make it my business to know as much as I can about every member of the family. Legitimate and illegitimate."

"Except Bibi's boy."

"Yes," he admitted, standing and walking to the liquor cabinet, where he poured two snifters of brandy. "That was my mistake. I listened to Adele and thought it was best for the family if the child disappeared."

"And you were right," Frank said, accepting the drink. "It's now when you're making your mistake." He took a long swallow and waited for the brandy to hit his belly. "You know how I handle bastards, don't you?"

"By raping their mothers and nearly getting killed by a bullet?"

"The kid was a freak."

"Whatever happened to him?"

"Don't know. Don't care." Frank scowled. "I thought you kept track of everyone remotely associated with the family."

"He slipped through my fingers. Doesn't his mother keep in touch?"

"She swears she doesn't; but she's probably lyin'." Frank shifted uncomfortably in his seat. "I don't see much of her these days. After the night that O'Rourke tried to shoot off my balls . . . Well, let's just say I've moved on to younger, tighter ass."

"Despite the fact that I advised you to be more discreet. That your philandering almost got you killed."

Frank's lips thinned. "No one tells me what to do. No one."

Not even you.

He hadn't said it, of course, but it was there, hanging in the air, unspoken and a challenge. Robert felt the old animosity between them raise its ugly head, baring greedy teeth.

A sick feeling unwound in Robert's insides. His brother had been out of control, drinking and cavorting, for far too long. It was an embarrassment, a stain on the family reputation. All the more reason to search for someone else to carry on the family name—a responsible heir.

Frank leaned forward a little in his chair and swirled his drink. "You know Collin resents you trying to find Bibi's kid. He sees it as a threat; as if you don't trust him. Or me."

"I don't."

"But you'd put your faith in some fifteen-year-old bastard?" Frank stubbed out his cigarette.

"That remains to be seen." Robert felt empty inside as Frank finished his drink in a flourish. They'd never been close, not even as children. His own kids had experienced a special bond for a while, or so it had seemed, and then they, too, had drifted away from each other. Before they could reconnect, Stuart had been killed.

"Be careful, Bob," Frank warned as he stood and adjusted the cuffs of his jacket. "You're playing with fire, here. I'd hate to see you get burned."

"I won't," Robert said calmly. Frank had never scared him. Worried him, yes, but never frightened him. If anything, he was more determined than ever to find his grandson.

Things were quiet. Too quiet, Kate thought as she tapped the eraser tip of her pencil on the corner of the desk in her little cubicle optimistically called an office in the English Department of the community college.

Ever since the incident with Todd Neider nearly two weeks ago, life had settled into its same, slow, normal pace. Except that Daegan O'Rourke had entrenched himself into their lives, and each day he was becoming more important to Jon.

And to you. Whether you admit it or not, Kate, you can't ig-

*nore the undercurrents that charge the air whenever he's around.
Even though you've never been stupid enough to wander back
to his pickup at night again, it's there, simmering between you,
a dark fascination that shouldn't exist.*

Headache brewing, she slid her reading glasses off
her nose and rubbed her temples. She noticed him in
ways she'd never noticed another man, the way his shirt
stretched across his shoulders, the fact that his belt was
worn on the third notch, the flare of his nostrils and
furrowing of his brow as he concentrated, and the way
his faded jeans hung low on his hips. He didn't bother
shining his boots or mending a torn patch in his Levi's
and seemed unaware that he always plowed both hands
through his hair when he was frustrated. She'd caught a
glimpse of his sense of humor—cynical though it was—
and wished she knew more about him and the past that
he never shared with her.

Don't borrow trouble. So he'd shown up when Jon was
freaking out about danger coming their way, so he just
happened to be around whenever there was a crisis, so
he'd gotten into a fight with his cousin, so he claimed
never to put down any permanent roots. So what?

*So you're beginning to fall for him, Kate, and that's scary.
Damned scary.* She'd never let herself become interested
in another man, not since Jim had died. The old pain
and guilt gnawed at her again and she remembered the
last morning she'd seen him, how they'd argued when
she'd said she had to work late, how he'd left the apartment so angry he'd slammed the door hard enough to
break the doorjamb. He hadn't wanted to pick up Erin
from the babysitter, it was his night to play basketball
with some friends, but Kate had been adamant, they
needed the money—overtime that she could make
working for Tyrell Clark.

In the end he'd acquiesced, as he always had, and on

the way home had been struck by a speeding car. Erin, who had been in his arms, had died instantly. Jim had survived the ambulance ride to the hospital, where he, too, had given up on life before Kate had time to say good-bye or to tell him how much she loved him.

"Mrs. Summers?"

A soft voice jarred Kate from her thoughts, and she saw one of her students, Renee Wilson, tentatively sticking her head in the airless room.

"Are you all right?" Renee asked, nervously biting her lower lip.

For the first time Kate realized that tears were tracking down her cheeks. "Fine . . . I'm fine. Come in, Renee, please," she said, clearing her throat and dabbing at her eyes with a tissue she plucked from a box on the shelf.

"I don't wanna bother you. If this isn't a good time—" Renee was edging away, looking embarrassed enough for the both of them.

Kate gave herself a swift mental kick. What had she been doing, breaking down here at the college? "Don't be ridiculous. That's what I'm here for. Sit down. Please." Sliding an old oak chair on rollers toward the door, she brought herself back to the present and shoved all her maudlin, painful thoughts aside.

Renee, in leggings and a cowl-necked sweater, dropped reluctantly into the seat and left the door ajar, as if she hoped to make good her escape. "I need to talk to you about my grade," she said, fidgeting with the spiral binding of her notebook. "I—I . . . you gave me a D on my last paper because I turned it in late, but I don't really think that's fair."

"You might be right," Kate agreed, leaning back in her desk chair until it squeaked in protest. She worked hard to walk the thin line between being a tyrant, a teacher who demanded that all her students never break a solitary rule, and being a pushover, an educator who let the kids walk all over her. "Let's hear your side of the story. Convince me."

"Oh, God," Renee whispered, then seemed to collect herself by drawing in a huge breath. "Okay, I was sick two weeks ago, you know, with that flu that's going around. I even have a doctor's excuse—"

"This isn't high school."

"I know, but I got real far behind, and I tried to catch up and get everything in, but I didn't have time to finish reading *To Kill a Mockingbird* and I really didn't understand the little girl, Scout, and so . . ."

A shadow passed by the open doorway and Renee lost her concentration.

"So I didn't have enough time to do it right. I should have come to you and asked for an extension, I guess."

"That probably would have been a good idea," Kate agreed, studying the girl's worried features. She thought about Jon and his own problems at school, how much she hoped the teachers would bend a little when it came to his issues. "Look, Renee," she heard herself saying as she flipped through the pages of her calendar, "I'll give you until Monday to rewrite it, okay, but I can't go beyond that date, and I'll have to keep in mind that you should have handled this differently; that's only fair to the other students."

"So I can't get an A?" Renee asked weakly.

"You'd have to really knock me out. I mean *really* bowl me over."

Renee rolled her eyes. "Oh, sure," she said with more than a touch of sarcasm, then shrugged and said, "Okay, okay, I'll try. Thanks!" Slinging the strap of her beaded tapestry bag over her shoulder, she slid out of the door more quickly than greased lightning.

Kate decided to call it a day. Jon was probably already home and she couldn't help being on edge. It was Friday, and from past experience, she knew that he was more likely to be in trouble at the end of the week rather than the beginning. She looked forward to relaxing at home

And seeing Daegan.

That thought was particularly irritating. Ever since the night alone in the truck, she'd had trouble nudging his image out of her mind. It seemed to haunt her, over and over, night and day. "Get a grip," she told herself. "He's just a man. Nothing more. Nothing less."

And yet her heart told her differently.

"What do you mean, there's no one named Roy Panaker?" Robert Sullivan looked as if he was going to wet his pants right here and now in the middle of his den with its cherry-paneled walls.

"Just what I said. There wasn't any kind of navy man from deckhand to admiral stationed here fifteen years ago." Neils helped himself to a cigar in the open humidor and bit off the end. He loved to rattle the old man because Robert Sullivan was such a damned snob.

"Beatrice told us that—"

"Beatrice lied, Sullivan. I'm telling you I've been over this a hundred times. No Roy Panaker."

Robert's color wasn't good to begin with; now it was pastier than ever. His voice was barely a whisper. "Then who is the boy's father?"

"Good question," VanHorn said, reaching for the crystal lighter. "Damned good question. Next time we meet, I'll know."

"How?"

"I guess I'll have to talk to Beatrice."

Aristocratic features pinched together in silent disapproval. "She probably won't tell you anything. If she's kept this a secret for fifteen years, I don't know why she'd say anything different now."

"Maybe she doesn't know who the father is," Van-Horn suggested and watched as Robert digested this little piece of information. It stuck in his craw and caused a horrid flush to spread across his cheeks.

"Of course she knows."

"Then it's one helluva secret because she took a big chance coming up with a phony sailor. Her story could have been checked out without too much trouble years ago."

"We—we had a lot on our minds," Robert said quickly, though he was bothered, and Neils suspected that the old man prided himself in not letting anything get past him, knowing what was going on behind the scenes. This time, his daughter had duped him.

"I know, you had to avoid a scandal and find a way to get rid of the evidence. Well, the only thing I can figure is that Beatrice lied to protect someone . . . someone she cared a lot about." He clicked the lighter and drew quickly on his cigar, sending quick little puffs to the ceiling. "I wonder who that guy could be?"

"Maybe it doesn't matter," Robert said with obvious irritation. "You just need to find the boy."

"I'm going to," VanHorn said, enjoying his brief moments in Robert's elegant home on the square. Warm. Stately. Sophisticated. Oozing with generations of culture and refinement. Certainly a cut or two above his little bungalow in the suburbs. But not for long. Neils planned on striking it rich and Robert Sullivan was going to help him. "I think there's a good chance that when I find out who made the mistake of siring the boy, I'll locate him."

"I don't care about the father, damn it. Just my grandson!"

Oh, but I do, you self-serving old geezer. I do. Once I find the father and unlock a few secrets, this gig is going to be worth a hellava lot more than the paltry fee you're paying me.

"Don't worry, Mr. Sullivan," Neils said, "I'll find him if it's the last thing I ever do."

Chapter 17

"Jab, back away, then jab again. Quick. No wasted motion. Like this." Daegan's voice could be heard over the steady, cold drip of the rain. Kate followed the sound, her boots crunching on the wet gravel as she crossed the yard to the open doorway of Eli McIntyre's dilapidated barn.

Quietly, she slipped inside but neither Jon nor Daegan was aware that she was standing in the musty shadows away from the circle of light thrown by one bare bulb.

Raindrops pounded on the tin roof, and water gurgled through the gutters. The smells of grain, dust, and horses drifted in the stagnant air of the sagging barn. A punching bag, still moving from a recent onslaught of human fists, hung suspended from one of the sturdier rafters.

Daegan's shirt was thrown over a bale of hay, and despite the cool temperature of the air, sweat sheened on his bare torso. Sinewy muscles gleamed under the harsh illumination, and his hair was damp. Quick as a mountain lion, he struck. Once, twice, three times he smashed

the canvas bag. Thud, thud, thud. Muscles strained, flex-
ing and unleashing with swift bursts of power, and Daegan
danced around the bag, head ducked, shoulders
hunched, always attacking.

"You see, Jon, you've got to keep moving, just out of
reach and then—" He stepped quickly to the bag and
threw a furious combination of punches. Muscles gathered and stretched in quick succession. Kate watched in
fascination as he, concentrating on his opponent,
stepped lightly over the floorboards. His feet were bare
and energy pulsed beneath his skin. Thick dark hair
covered a chest of corded muscles, and the shadow of
his beard darkened his square, determined jaw. He
glared at the punching bag as if it were the enemy, as if
he were convinced that he could knock it spinning, off
its chain.

"Now," he said, wiping his brow with a strong forearm. "You try again."

Jon, his back to Kate, elbows on his knees as he
watched, had been sitting on the half wall that separated the stalls from the feed bins. Tightening the laces
of his gloves with his teeth, he hopped down and waited
as Daegan tied the strings.

"Okay, give it your best shot." Jon set his jaw. His eyes
narrowed on the bag, and Kate didn't have to be a mind
reader to know that her son was envisioning Todd Neider
in his sights. "You bastard," he growled, then started flail-
ing wildly, like a drowning man trying to swim.

"Hey—wait, slow down a tad."

"You said to hit quick."

"Yeah, but you've got to maintain control. You can't
go at it like you're killing snakes." Daegan chuckled and
the sound was surprisingly heartwarming—as if he had a
kinder side that he managed to hide. "Okay, try again
and concentrate." Planting his feet, Daegan held the

bag steady with one shoulder, and Jon started again, already learning, mimicking Daegan by rolling onto the balls of his feet and shuffling quickly around the bag. "That's it," Daegan encouraged him, a hint of pride in his voice.

Kate rested a shoulder against the open doorjamb and felt the November wind tug at the hem of her skirt.

"Come on, keep comin', show me what you've got."

Wrapping her arms around her middle, Kate watched the exchange. Jon in T-shirt and navy sweatpants that were way too small and Daegan, all raw muscle and bone, tall and lean, his jeans hanging low enough that she saw his flat abdomen, navel, and the stripe of dark hair that delved beneath his belt.

The back of her throat turned desert dry and a flush of warmth stole through her blood.

At that moment, he caught sight of her. His gaze shifted, and he looked at her with dark, brooding eyes. *Oh, God.* In one heartbeat a current of pure sexual energy passed between them, a force so strong it caused her diaphragm to slam against her lungs. She took a step backward, as if she could move away from the intensity of his gaze.

"Kate." It sounded like a caress.

"Mom?" Jon looked up and an expression of irritation clouded his features. "What're you doing here?"

"Looking for you."

"I left you a note."

"I know, that's why I'm here." His face had healed a little and he didn't look quite so miserable. The bruises under his eyes had changed from a deep purple to a sick shade of green, not much better, but at least indicating that he was improving.

"We're working," Jon said.

"I see."

"What did you think of our boy here?" Daegan asked, the corner of his mouth turning up as he grabbed his shirt and stuffed his arms down the sleeves.

Our boy. Just a turn of phrase, but one that caused a fleeting image of them as a family—Daegan, Jon, and her. But that was crazy, impossible, a silly fantasy. "What do I think? That I wouldn't want to meet either of you in a dark alley."

"Oh, Mom," Jon said, rolling his eyes.

"It's true. I'm just a defenseless woman, after all."

"Just the kind I like," Daegan teased as they walked to the door.

"Can't I stay awhile longer?" Jon asked, and before Kate could protest, Daegan shrugged.

"Sure. I'll buy your mom a drink."

"I don't know, I think we should—"

"Come on, Kate, what would it hurt?" he asked, his flinty eyes searching hers. "Nothing fancy, but I've got a couple of beers in the refrigerator or I think I could even scare up a bottle of wine."

It seemed too intimate, too close. With his work shirt open, its tails flapping in the stiff breeze, the scent of rain mingling with that particular male musk that she'd begun to associate with him and the invitation in his gray eyes, she couldn't resist. "One drink," she agreed, "but then we've got to go."

"It's Friday," Jon pointed out.

"Thank God," she said under her breath, thankful that another week of school had passed without any incident. Jon turned quickly away and dashed back to the area beneath the dusty lightbulb and immediately began punching in earnest.

"I'm glad you're here," he said softly and her heart began to pound. Ever since the night in the truck when he'd kissed and touched her, she'd avoided being alone with him, tried to maintain her distance. She'd even called her sister twice, determined to find out something about him, but so far Laura couldn't help her determine if he was lying, if, instead of growing up on a ranch in Canada, he'd lived in Boston. But all her worries seemed far away as Daegan laced his fingers through hers and tugged on her hand. Together they dashed across the yard between the barn and house. Holding up her skirt with her free hand, feeling the fresh wash of rain in her hair, avoiding puddles that had already formed in the uneven ground, she felt fifteen again. There was something steadying in his grip, a comfort from feeling his calloused fingers twined in hers.

Their boots thundered up the few worn steps, and when they reached the porch, he didn't let go. His other hand circled her waist. Pressing against the small of her back, he pulled her closer to him. She gasped, uncertain, and he hesitated just a second, his gaze steady and bright as it locked with hers, then his mouth crashed down on hers with a hunger that snatched the breath from her lungs. Hot, wet lips assailed hers, and she didn't have time to protest, couldn't think. He was hard and wanting, his breath as shallow as hers.

Don't! Don't! Don't! she told herself, but didn't stop him, couldn't deny the heady warmth of desire that surged through her own blood.

His tongue touched the seam of her lips and they parted, allowing him entrance, opening as a flower to the sun, anxious and needy. He wound his hands in her hair and she closed her eyes, hoping the kiss would go on forever, knowing that the turn of her thoughts was dangerous. This was a man she couldn't trust, didn't know, but all her doubts slipped into the shadowy recesses of her consciousness and her arms circled his neck, holding him close, feeling her breasts, through her jacket and blouse, crush against him.

He lifted his head and regarded her with smoky eyes.

"Kate," he said roughly, his breath as uneven as her own, his hands shaking slightly when he released her. "Sweet Jesus." His gaze still burned with a restless, hungry fire, and he turned quickly away, placing both hands on the old, sagging rail, and shaking his head as if arguing with himself. "Damn! Damn! Damn!"

Kicking at a post that didn't seem to need much help in falling over, he said, "I didn't mean for that to happen."

"Neither did I."

"Shit!" he growled, furious with himself. When, exactly, had he lost his self-control? The first moment he'd seen her walking along the sidewalk when she'd let him change the tire that he'd flattened earlier? Or later, when she'd been wary of him, distrust evident in her amber eyes as she'd let him use her phone? Or still later when Jon had accused him of being a murderer? Or had it been the night in the truck when he'd kissed her and touched her and fantasized about making love to her?

Raking stiff, angry fingers through his hair, he knew that he'd made a mistake of irrevocable proportions when he'd taken her into his arms and kissed her again. He'd done it on impulse, and yet he'd never expected the reaction that tore at his soul—not just physically, though that was a big part of it, but emotionally as well.

"Look, maybe I—we'd better go."

"No!" he shouted without even thinking, then caught himself and more quietly said, "Please, stay." Staring into the night, he tried to find some way to explain himself, but couldn't. "Look, I just—I had no idea—oh, for the love of God—" Looking into her wide golden eyes, he was lost. He wanted her more than he'd wanted a woman in a long, long time, maybe more than he'd ever wanted a woman. Because she was forbidden, the mother of his son, the woman he was doomed to de-

stroy, he couldn't forget her. His fingers curled over the
rail until he felt splinters in the heels of his palms.

He had to be cursed. This hot-blooded attraction to
her was sure to be his undoing, but he felt helpless to
fight it, and leveling an oath at himself, he reached for
her again. "Damn you, Kate," he whispered. "What are
you doing to me?"

His mouth crashed down on hers, hot, cruel, punishing lips, and again Kate yielded, her bones seeming to
melt in his hands. Hot desire flooded through him and
all he could think about was the ache in his groin and
the sweet, warm comfort she could give. He pressed her
up against the window, her back pinned against the old
watery panes, one of his hands reaching lower to cup a
buttock.

She trembled against him, and a yearning, as old as
time itself, stretched between them. So hard he couldn't
think straight, he tightened his fingers. Through the folds
of her skirt he felt the swell of her buttock, his finger-
tips grazing the soft inside of her thigh.

She moaned into his open mouth and he pressed
harder, his heart thundering, desire pumping through
his blood and pounding at his temples. She smelled of
rain and summer roses, her breasts rising and falling
with each of her torn breaths. In his mind he saw her
lying naked beneath him in a field of spring flowers,
her body drenched in sweat, her supple flesh quivering
with want as he spread her legs and storm clouds roiled
overhead.

"For the love of God," he whispered, slamming his
eyes shut, leaning against her, but letting go, giving up
his anxious hold on her rump, tearing his lips away
from her hungry mouth. "Kate . . . I—"

"Don't," she said, with a voice so low he barely recognized it. She placed a finger against his lips. "You don't
have to say anything, I understand—oooh." Unable to

resist such sweet temptation, he sucked her forefinger into his mouth, his tongue working of its own accord, his gaze delving deep into hers. She licked her lips, then drew her fingers slowly away from his lips. "This . . . this can't happen."

"You're right," he agreed, though his cock was straining against his jeans and he was so hard he thought the buttons of his fly might give way.

"There's Jon to consider—"

"Right. Jon."

"And . . . and I can't get involved—"

"Neither can I." He kissed her again and the passion sparked between them, alive and catching fire, searing through every argument their rational minds devised. "Kate, sweet Kate," he murmured against her open mouth as he parted her jacket and his fingers felt the firm hard strain of her breasts beneath her blouse. "Oh, God." Through the fabric he touched the button of her nipple, straining and hard. Wanting.

Lowering himself, he kissed her there, through the cotton, wetting the fabric as she leaned against the window. Her fingers wound in his hair as he reached around her, drawing her closer, taking more of her into his mouth. Soft moans escaped her lips and her legs seemed to widen in their stance. Her heat enveloped him and he thought of undressing her and making love to her over and over again, until dawn spilled its splendid light over the valley.

She moaned and he dropped to his knees, pressing his face into the folds of her skirt, smelling its sweet fragrance, wrapping his hands around her legs. She seemed to pulse in his hands.

"Daegan—oh, Daegan, please . . ." she whispered and he stopped again, moving his arms upward to surround her waist, still holding her close as he tried to re-

ain the composure that had rarely failed him throughout his life. But with her, with this one woman, that fierce,
dependable self-control slipped through his fingers and
he was suddenly lost with wanting. The thought eroded
whatever pride he had left, and this time, he told himself as he gritted his teeth and straightened, when he released her, he wouldn't be so weak as to draw her into
his arms again. Slowly he stood, closed her jacket, and
stepped away from her. It was all he could do to keep
his distance.

"I—I think I should go."

He nodded, shaken to the roots of all that he'd held
as true. He'd spent the better part of his life convincing
himself that there wasn't a woman who could touch
him in the way that he'd just been touched. For years he
was determined that no woman would ever change his
way of thinking, but Kate had proved him wrong. So
very wrong.

She cleared her throat and glanced into his eyes for
a fleeting second. "I'll take a raincheck on the drink."

"Fine," he agreed, then laughed mirthlessly when he
heard the plop of raindrops on the old shingles of the
roof. He watched as she ran across the yard and disappeared into the barn. By the time she and Jon emerged,
Daegan's breathing was more normal, his heartbeat a
more even rhythm. He waved to the boy and his mother
and wished to God that he'd never made the mistake of
kissing Kate Summers.

Kate spent the night staring at the ceiling, watching
the shadows shift against the curtains and wondering
where the common sense that she'd honed since she
was eleven had flown. Didn't she know better? Didn't
she remember?

Grabbing her robe from the end of the bed, she

padded into the kitchen and poured a glass of juice. A
she sipped, she stared through the glass to the black
night and the rain drizzling down the panes.

She remembered her mother, Anna, a beautiful
woman who had been widowed far too young. Abruptly
their idyllic life on the farm was over. Anna couldn'
work the acres herself or pay the mortgage, so she sold
the rolling fields, the duck pond, the old barn with it
swallows and owls, and the rambling two-story farmhouse
The small family had been forced to move to the city.

With two daughters to support, Anna juggled two
sometimes three jobs, and when she wasn't dead tired
she dated lots of different men, few of whom Kate ever
met. But she did remember the one man—Riley had
been his name, Pete Riley—the man who had changed
the course of her life irretrievably.

Big and brawny, with a thick brown moustache and
long sideburns, he was a truck driver, on the road a lot
but when he was in Des Moines, he and Mama would go
out dining, dancing, and drinking. He was loud and
sometimes would stumble on the stairs. Kate always sus
pected he was drunk, but Mama always said he was just
a little clumsy.

One late summer night while Kate and Laura were
sleeping in their bunk beds, Riley brought Mama
home. They were loud—laughing and talking, bumping
into the walls—and woke Kate from the fitful sleep tha
overcame her whenever Mama went out late at night.

"Shhh, you'll wake the girls," Mama said when the
door slammed shut.

"No way." Footsteps. Riley's heavy tread. Kate frowned
and slipped through the open window to the fire es
cape. She hated Riley and his loud ways. His voice was
too gruff, and sometimes when Mama wasn't looking
he'd touch Kate on the shoulders or neck, sometimes
her face. One time, when he'd come over before Mama

got off work and let himself in with his own key, he'd insisted Laura sit on his lap, and while he talked to her, he played with her hair and shifted around a lot, rubbing himself on her. Laura tried to climb down, but Riley held her firmly in place, and only when Mama burst through the door did he move sharply enough to send Laura careening to the floor.

Music from the stereo drifted down the hallway and seeped into her room. "Come on, baby, light my fire . . ." Jim Morrison's voice seemed to wrap around Kate like a deep mist and Kate stared down the metallic stairway four stories to the deserted alley below. In the streetlight she noticed a cat sliding through the shadows and from inside the apartment there were sounds of an argument. Not the first. Recently Mama and Riley argued as often as not, and Kate found herself wishing again that Daddy were still alive.

Kate closed her eyes and rocked on the cold metal grate. She didn't want to hear the fight, didn't want to be afraid, but the voices, angry and loud, chased through the apartment and out the window to surround her.

"You're a tease, that's what you are, Anna, acting like some goddamned virgin when you got two half-growed daughters. Well, I'm sick of it, y'hear. Damned sick of it."

"Shh, Pete, the girls will hear—"

"So let 'em. Who cares?"

"Look, maybe you'd better go now."

Yes! Leave and don't ever come back!

"Is that what you want, baby? 'Cause if I walk out that door, I'm not comin' back through it. That's the last you'll see of Pete Riley."

Kate crossed her fingers and prayed.

"Of course not, Pete, but be reasonable . . ."

"They're asleep, they'll never know." Then there was quiet and Kate shivered, imagining them kissing and touching. This was how it always went, Mama would say no, and Pete would change her mind and somehow she'd make him happy and he'd leave before morning Mama always looked tired and unhappy the next morning, sitting in her bathrobe, staring into her coffee cup and sometimes crying. For Daddy. She'd admitted that she still missed him every day.

So did Kate. Living in the city was exciting, the smells of exhaust mingling with the sweet aromas wafting from restaurants and bakeries, the cars, trucks, bicycles, and motorcycles wheeling through the streets, so different from the slow pace of the farm, where she and Laura would help Mama weed the garden, or watch as Daddy plowed and harrowed a new field.

She missed the rattling old clunk of the tractor—the one that always broke down and made Daddy so mad, and the sound of the rooster crowing before dawn. She missed baby chicks hatching from eggs and the fresh-faced calves as they butted and romped in the pasture surrounding the barn. She and Laura would listen to the sounds of frogs and crickets in the evening and catch water skippers on the pond—

Slap! The sound of flesh smacking against flesh brought her up short. "Bitch! I'll show you I mean business."

"Get out, Pete. Just get the hell out."

"Not until you give me what I came here for."

Again the slap, this time followed by a stream of guttural oaths that turned Kate's stomach.

"I'll show you—"

Mama screamed and Kate crawled back through the window. Something hit the wall and glass shattered. "No! No! No!" Mama cried. "Oh, God, help me."

Heart hammering, Kate opened the door a crack and peeked through. Pete's fist was clenched around Mama's hair and he was dragging her kicking and screaming to her bedroom. Mama's fingers were bloody, her nails ripped as she scratched the plaster walls to try and stop him.

Pete's face sported a red handprint and his eyes were narrowed in anger.

Mama saw Kate and choked out a cry. "No," she whispered, her eyes terrified as they touched Kate's. Her face turned the shade of death. "Don't—" She made a shooing motion, trying to get Kate to slide back into the room, but Pete, as he kicked open the door of Mama's bedroom, didn't notice, just yanked her into the dark interior.

Her insides twisting into painful knots, Kate sneaked out of the room and into the kitchen. She heard slaps and oaths and her mother sobbing. Biting her lip, sweat drizzling down her spine, Kate picked up the telephone receiver and with unsteady fingers dialed the only number she knew by heart besides her own, that of her aunt June.

Scared so bad she was shaking, she stretched the cord as long as she could, crawled into a closet, and shut the door while she waited. Uncle Cliff answered on the fifth ring.

"You've got to come," Kate demanded in a harsh whisper though she was trying with all her might not to let panic strangle her. "Riley's gonna kill Mama, I know he is."

"Is this Katie?"

"Yes, but you've got to come and—"

"Calm down," Uncle Cliff commanded. "Now start over and tell me everything."

"There's no time. He's got her in the bedroom and he's hitting her and she's crying and you've got to come." Hysteria caused her voice to rise to a squeak and she was crying, begging her uncle to come and save Mama. Then, once Uncle Cliff promised to drive across town, Kate held the receiver tight against her chest and prayed, long and hard, that Mama wouldn't be hurt. Only when the horrid screams subsided did she slip out of the closet and hang up the phone. Throat dry with fear, she planned to sneak back to her room when she nearly ran into Pete standing in the doorway.

"Well, well, well," he said, his eyes slitted as he glared at her from his tremendous height, "what have we here? Hmm, Katie girl, what're you doing up?" He plopped himself on a bar stool and lit a cigarette.

"I . . . I was thirsty."

"So you got a drink."

"Yeah."

He frowned and let smoke roll out of his nostrils. Kate had never been so frightened in her life. Wearing only dingy jockey shorts, his hairy torso scratched from being raked by fingernails, he studied her. "So where's your glass?"

"What?"

"The one you used to get a drink. I don't see a glass in the sink."

"I—I—um, just put my head under the faucet, but don't tell Mama, she doesn't like that."

"Oh, these days your mama doesn't like much," he said, and the scent of stale whiskey and smoke filled the room. "Including me. Imagine that—your good old uncle Petey isn't good enough for her anymore."

"You're not my uncle."

He sucked on the cigarette. "That's right. I'm not anything to you, am I? You're a smart girl, Katie, do you know that, real smart. I like a girl with some brains." His eyes moved from her face and inched lower where his gaze rested on her small breasts, just beginning to form. "You ever kissed a boy?"

She shook her head.

"Why not, you're pretty enough, and when you grow

up, I bet you'll be a real looker." He rubbed the under-
side of his chin very slowly. "Yep, a real looker."

"Are you leaving?" she asked suddenly.

"In a little while." His expression darkened with concern. "But I don't want to leave your mother as she is.
She had a little too much to drink and got a little out of
hand." He smiled as if they were best friends. "But she'll
be okay. You want me to leave?"

She nodded. "I can take care of Mama."

"I imagine you can. You're a big girl, aren't you?" He
tossed the butt of his cigarette into the sink and it sizzled as it died. "Why don't you come over here and tell
me why you want me to go? Do I scare you?"

"No," she lied, shivering inside.

"Good. That's real good." He reached forward, his
hand stinking of smoke, to stroke the side of her face.
She ducked. "Oh, Katie, come on. I want to show you
something, something you've never seen before, something you'll learn to like."

He reached for her arm. "I don't want—"

"Leave her alone!" Mama ordered. "Take your filthy
hands off her and get out! *Now!*"

Riley swiveled on the stool. "I think it's time she
learned a few things."

"Touch her again and I'll kill you." Mama's voice was
barely audible, just a low growl.

He laughed and grabbed Kate. In a split second,
Mama reached for the knife rack on the counter, slid
out the butcher knife, and plunged it deep into his
shoulder. Blood bubbled out of his skin.

Bam! Bam! Bam!

"Anna!" Uncle Cliff's voice boomed over the pounding
on the front door. "Anna, are you in there?"

"Oh, thank God!" She ran to the front door and
threw it open. Riley, clad only in his skivvies, yanked the

knife from his shoulder and staggered after her, leaving a trail of blood.

Uncle Cliff's eyes rounded to the size of silver dollars, and Aunt June, who was standing primly behind him, white-faced and worrying her hands, didn't venture inside. "What the devil happened here?" Reverend Cliff demanded.

"The bitch tried to kill me!" Riley said, then realizing he was holding the weapon, flung it onto the floor. Snagging his shirt from the back of the couch, he jabbed it at his wound, trying vainly to staunch the flow of blood. "Call a damned ambulance!"

"Now, just stay calm," Uncle Cliff insisted. "The police have already been called."

"Cops?" Riley repeated. "What the hell for?"

As it was, his question was answered with the arrival of the police, the ambulance, and a social worker. Kate, while trying to save her mother, had unwittingly unleashed the hounds of hell on their little home.

Pete Riley ended up in the hospital, where he was treated and released. Anna Rudisill was tried and acquitted of assault with a deadly weapon, but her children were stripped from her and placed in Uncle Cliff and Aunt June's small parsonage.

Uncle Cliff was a preacher and Aunt June a devout servant of the Lord. No profanities were ever issued, no questions ever asked, they all just did what Uncle Cliff told them. He, the ordained minister, knew what was best, and Aunt June never once raised her voice to him.

Whenever Aunt June spoke of her sister, it was in a pitying voice, and Mama's visits, always painful and filled with tears, stopped abruptly when she took an overdose of sleeping pills and ended her life.

Kate remembered the service with Uncle Cliff sermonizing on the wages of sin and eulogizing Anna Rudisill as a tortured being who was finally at peace with her God and joined in heaven with her loving husband.

Kate, grief-stricken, didn't buy it. She and Laura remembered their idyllic life on the farm, their mother's warm smiles, the kind woman who had tended her garden and children with care.

Kate refused to pity her mother or think of her as tortured. Nor did she accept Uncle Cliff's strict, archaic rules about dating, makeup, and school dances. She rebelled as wildly as she could, and on her eighteenth birthday she moved out of the house and married the boy she'd been sneaking around with for two years, Jim Summers, fresh out of college and ready to take on the world. They moved to Boston and a year later Laura joined them.

Cursed as sinners, Kate and Laura never heard from their uncle or aunt again.

Kate tried to build a new life for herself, her husband, her sister, and eventually her little girl. She hadn't been so happy since those early years on the farm, and even Tyrell's unwanted advances were something she could handle.

Then tragedy had struck, her daughter and husband cut down unthinkably by a hit-and-run driver. She remembered that her last words spoken to her husband were in anger over who would pick up Erin from the babysitter. Darling, precious Erin.

Even now, years later, she felt a deep mind-numbing pain when she thought of her baby. The day of the funeral it had rained, and as she stood over the coffins of those she loved most, she'd sworn that she'd never again let herself get close to anyone, because everyone she'd ever loved, except for her sister, had died.

Then Tyrell Clark had offered her a second chance, another baby. Kate had opened her heart to the tiny, unwanted infant and never regretted it for an instant.

But this—this relationship with Daegan—was different. She closed her eyes and rested her forehead against the window. For the first time in over fifteen years, Kate Summers knew she was about to break the promise she'd made on her husband's grave. "Lord help me," she whispered, but knew it was already too late.

She'd already begun to fall in love.

Chapter 18

"Aren't you worried?" Frank demanded, his stomach grinding. He reached for a bottle of antacids he kept in his desk and washed four pills down with a splash of Kentucky whiskey.

"There's nothing I can do if Uncle Robert wants to locate Bibi's kid." Collin didn't seem the least concerned, just stood at the window squinting past the snow-dusted high-rises of the city to the bay beyond, where white caps played. Leaning against the glass, his hands in the pockets of his suit pants, his jacket pushed back to show off the flat stomach beneath his oxford cloth shirt, he could have passed for one of those damned models in any of the upscale catalogs that Bonnie kept all over the house.

Sometimes he wondered if this fair-haired boy was his. Collin didn't seem to have an ounce of Sullivan gumption—that same fighting spirit that had forced the family to flee from oppression and starvation in Ireland centuries ago, the fire in the belly that had pushed his ancestors to work harder and climb ever upward, stepping on whatever pathetic souls got in their way until late in the nineteenth century when, after decades of hard work, some wise savings, and a few lucky gambles, they'd made enough money to buy a slot in Boston society—a slot that each succeeding generation had made more prestigious until now.

None of that Sullivan drive, that fire, appeared in his washed-out son. Too much of Maureen in the boy.

"I didn't know Bibi had a baby."

"That's just the point. None of us did. Back then Robert had some sense and he found a way to ensure that the kid never showed his face here again, never darkened our doorsteps, never expected to collect a penny of any of what he might consider his inheritance, but all that's changed. Robert seems to think his power will live on if he can find an heir, replace Stuart."

Collin winced a little, but tried to hide it, and Frank experienced that same burning doubt he underwent years ago when Stuart had been alive, when the boys had been close and shared secrets. "If you ask me, Robert's blown a gasket and probably needs to see his shrink again."

Collin rubbed his upper lip, as if some beads of nervous perspiration had collected there. "How old is the boy?"

"Somewhere around fifteen, I think. It happened within the year after Stuart's death—nearly killed Adele, I guess. First she lost her boy and then her daughter turned up unmarried and in a family way."

Collin closed his eyes for a second, as if trying to pull himself together.

"What about the father?"

"Long gone. Someone in the military who never knew he'd sired a bastard."

"Does the man have a name?" Finally, Collin seemed interested.

"If he does, Robert's not saying, doesn't want the guy

to come sniffing around." Another spasm of pain curled a bony fist around his stomach.

"Christ!" Collin whispered. "A kid. Who would've thought?"

"No one. Until now. And that's the way it should stay." As was always the case, Frank had to steer his son into the right way of thinking. "Listen, Collin," he said with all the patience he could scrape together, "if Robert finds his grandson, we may as well kiss the family fortune good-bye."

"You mean kiss off his part; we still have control of the mills and factories."

"But they're not as valuable as they once were. Overseas labor and the unions are working to kill us. We've got mortgages and bills. Robert holds the real wealth."

Collin's lips curved into some grim resemblance of a smile. "I imagine we'll get by."

"For Christ's sake, get some spunk, will you!" Frank's temper reared its ugly head and took control of his tongue. The pain in his belly gripped harder. "You're the poorest excuse for a son I've ever seen."

"So you've said," Collin responded wryly, as if he didn't give a good goddamn. A look passed between them, a dark, secretive look that Frank had come to understand, but he ignored Collin's attempt to derail the conversation.

Frank didn't know how to get through to his first-born, to batter down his wall of indifference, to make the kid see red.

"Maybe you shouldn't have been so hasty with Daegan; maybe deep down he was the kind of son you really wanted," Collin taunted.

"Oh, shut up. He was nothing, nothing but a mistake."

"A mistake? Maybe so but he's got spunk. Shit, he's on spunk overload, if you ask me." Collin's eyes were positively frosty. "Anyone who tries to shoot the balls off Frank Sullivan's got a helluva lot of spunk."

"He could be dead by now."

"You don't even know? God, Dad, that's weak."

"He's out of my life, but now, if Robert has his way, that bastard of Bibi's will be back in the family by Christmas."

"So what do you want me to do? Worry?"

"For starters, yes. Then you might think about having a boy of your own."

"It hasn't worked out."

"Well, it can't, not when you're always out of town, sailing and yachting and—"

"Doing business," Collin said, and Frank was reminded that Collin had boosted sales for the company. Ready-wear was the one area that wasn't slipping into the red.

"You should still have time to make a baby. I thought you married Carrie because you were attracted to her. I expected a grandson the next year."

Collin crossed from the window to the desk. "I married Carrie because you thought she would be the perfect mate for me. It was past time, you said, and I stupidly agreed. If you want to know the truth, Dad, Carrie and I are separated, have been for six months, and we're talking about divorce."

Frank felt as if he'd been hit in the gut. "There is no divorce in our family."

"Bull. Bibi's divorced."

"Bibi's not my daughter, thank God. She's always been a wild card."

"Just don't have any illusions, Dad. You won't get any grandkids from me. Besides, you've got Wade, Alicia's little prince. He should be enough of a grandson for you. The way she goes on, that kid is the smartest, brightest, most athletic kid on earth. Any son I had wouldn't be half as good. Just be thankful you've got another generation in Wade."

Frank felt cold as death. Who was this man he'd raised from a boy?

"Now, if there's nothing else . . ." Collin slipped his arms through a wool coat that probably cost a thousand dollars.

"There will be no divorce," Frank said but the door was already slamming shut behind his son, the boy upon whom he'd pinned all his hopes. He dropped his head into his hands and waited for his heart to stop slamming against his ribs, for his blood pressure to slow, for the fire in his gut to subside.

As he calmed, he reached for his whiskey glass and took a long sip that burned a warm and friendly path down his throat. Frank was sick of apathy. Everywhere he looked, his family didn't seem to give two lousy cents. Maureen, hell, she was frigid from the first time he'd touched her years ago in the backseat of his father's Lincoln. They'd both been in college at the time. She'd kissed him and lain down willingly, giving up her virginity without so much as a struggle. When he'd reached under her sweater to touch her tits, she hadn't stopped him, even when he discovered she was wearing a padded bra and that her breasts were a pathetic size, the nipples small and pale, she'd let him stroke her.

He'd figured the size of her boobs didn't matter; she was the right girl. Rich and sophisticated, she rounded out his rough edges, the same edges he'd honed while rebelling against his father for favoring his brothers over him.

Besides, Maureen had been a challenge. None of the other boys had made it to first base with her and here she was practically begging for it.

So he'd kissed her, fondled her, and pushed her skirt up past her waist. She'd been wearing tights and he'd ripped them as he'd pulled them to her knees, then tore off her panties. Her mound wasn't moist, and inside she was tight and dry. She cried out when he tried to touch her with his finger, and nearly screamed when he leaned down to kiss her between her legs.

"What—what—oh, my God, Frank! No, don't!" she'd whispered, horror written all over her face.

Afraid she'd stop putting out all together and knowing that there was a hundred bucks riding on whether he'd score or not, he decided to go for broke. Unzipping his fly quickly, he didn't bother kicking off his pants but shoved himself deep into the driest piece of pussy he'd ever felt. She screamed as he pressed inward, struggling, but he was too far gone. His weight pinned her and he moved faster and faster, kissing her, nipping at her tiny breasts, rutting in her and never once feeling her juices flow. Damned virgin.

Finally she quit struggling and lay there, wide-eyed, as if it were her duty to accept him. He'd come with a great, triumphant roar, the bull elk mating with the most sought-after cow in the herd.

Afterward, he reached for a cigarette and stuffed her ripped panties into his pocket. His trophy. But as he'd inhaled that first puff, Maureen had come to life again. Expertly, she cleaned her blood from the leather seat and plucked the panties from his pocket. Clucking her tongue, she put the evidence deep into a side pocket of her purse. "You should have bet more, Frank," she said, tilting her head in a way he'd found years later to be annoying. "A hundred dollars. Such a pittance. I was worth a thousand, or maybe five thousand." She picked his cigarette from his fingers and took a long, slow drag.

A tic developed under his eye. "How'd you find out?"

"Doesn't matter. What does is that you're going to marry me." She made the statement in a cloud of smoke.

"What?" He couldn't believe his ears. They'd hardly dated and he wasn't about to be tied down to a woman as cold as a frozen fish fillet. "You're out of your mind."

"I don't think so." She went on to tell him that if he didn't comply, she'd tell her parents that he'd raped her—she had the ripped panties and bloody hankie to prove it. Her uncle was a judge, she reminded him, one who was once considered for the Supreme Court. Then there was that little matter of the bet—how ugly. A bet was reserved for common sluts and girls without any breeding or brains. He couldn't believe it and wondered aloud why she wanted to tie the knot.

Because it was time.

Because it was expected.

Because he was a Sullivan.

Had he ever considered that she might have had her own little bet—one with her girlfriends—about whether or not she could wangle a marriage proposal out of the most confirmed of all the bachelors on fraternity row?

Case closed.

He hadn't had much choice but to marry her. What he hadn't known at the time, what she'd kept from him for nearly five years, was that her family money had been squandered by her parents and that to keep her healthy and cultured way of life intact, she'd been forced to marry. She'd picked Frank as the primary target, probably because Robert had already given up bachelorhood.

All in all, the marriage had worked, he supposed, except that his son had this soft, apathetic side he didn't understand. Alicia was stronger, manipulative like her

mother, but with the Sullivan bearing added in. Bonnie—well, Bonnie just didn't seem to care about anything. She was always losing herself in a book, a movie,
some cause célèbre. If it wasn't saving the whales or the
rain forest, it was freeing some loser on death row. She
sure didn't give a damn where the money came from
that kept her from bouncing checks to whichever lib-
eral issue was her current favorite. Another spineless
Sullivan. How could he have spawned two?

Bonnie still lived at home and had no current
boyfriend, no impetus to move.

Frank supposed Collin was right, he was lucky that
Alicia had Wade, a kid who was a little disturbing because he reminded Frank of Stuart. God, how he'd
hated that smart-aleck brat.

Now, once again, it was up to him. While Robert was
determined to undermine his side of the family, Frank
was determined to save both his fortune and his reputation. He put one foot on his credenza and reached for
his drink. No little bastard of Bibi's was going to mess
things up.

"So how's your love life?" Laura teased when Kate answered the phone.

"As if it's any of your business." Kate sank into a chair.
Tension that had been with her for days drained out of
her muscles at the sound of her sister's voice.

"Come on, tell me," Laura coaxed. "It's that cowboy
next door, isn't it? The one you were so worried about."

Kate laughed, blushed a little, and wished to high
heaven that Laura lived closer, that they could share a
cup of coffee together, the local gossip, swap tales about
children—well, if Laura ever got around to having any.
"Why don't you fly out here for Thanksgiving?" she

sked, suddenly needing to see her sister so much it urt. Aside from Jon, Laura was the only family she still laimed.

"Oh sure! With Jeremy's work schedule? Why don't ou just ask me to fly to the moon and back."

"I'm serious. You could come."

Laura laughed. "Sure I could, and then who would lo your snooping for you?"

"Is that why you called?" Kate said, her throat intantly tight. Maybe Laura had found something out bout Daegan or about Jon's real father or if . . . but hat was too far-fetched, wasn't it? Daegan and Jon—reated? The thought had raced through her head before, ut she'd dismissed it. They didn't look alike and the ond they'd recently formed had nothing to do with geetics. Besides, all Jon's talk about his father had evapoated over the weeks.

"Yep. One down, one to go. One of the Daegan O'Rourkes lives in Carmel, California, with his vife and three kids."

"And the other?" Kate hardly dared breathe.

"Still checking, but so far no prison record."

"And Jon's parents?"

"My friend's still looking into it, but so far nothing. Whoever gave birth to him didn't want him to ever find her. You know it's too bad you can't call Tyrell Clark," Laura mused aloud. "I wish I could too," said Kate, "but e's dead."

"Yes, it's too bad," said Laura. For whatever reason, Tyrell had linked Kate with Jon, and for that she would always be grateful. The new baby had given her a reason o live again, to smile, to think about the future.

She heard the back door open and the thunder of his size tens thudding against the floor as he clattered hrough the back hall. "What's for dinner?" he asked,

rounding the corner with Houndog, fur finally begin
ning to grow back, on his heels.

"Got to run," Kate told her sister. "The bottomless pi
is on the rampage and hungry yet again."

"Very funny," Jon said as he rummaged in the refrig
erator.

"I thought so."

Laura laughed. "Give him my love, will you, and fo
God's sake, Kate, lighten up."

"Think about Thanksgiving."

"No way, but I'll try for Christmas."

"And I'll hold you to it."

She hung up just as Jon found a burrito and heated i
in the microwave. "You were talking about Thanksgiving.

"Yeah," she said, snagging a soda from the refrigera
tor. "I twisted Aunt Laura's arm, but she can't come. She
sends you her love."

He rolled his eyes as the microwave dinged. Refusing
to use an oven mitt, he juggled the burrito that was be
ginning to ooze hot cheese onto his fingers. "Ouch.
He flopped the burrito onto a plate.

"I guess it's just you and me and the turkey this year,
she said.

"How about Daegan?" he asked as if he didn't care
one way or the other. He found a fork in the drawer and
settled into a chair at the kitchen table.

"You mean how about inviting him here for Thanks
giving dinner?"

"Yeah." He lifted a shoulder. "Why not?"

She shouldn't have been surprised. It seemed Jon
after his initial distrust of the man, was completely won
over. She only hoped he wasn't setting himself up for a
fall. *What about you? Aren't you playing the same dangerou*
game with your emotions? She had only to think of the las
times she'd been alone with him, how he'd kissed her
how she'd put up no resistance, how she'd wanted to

nake love to him. Blushing, she felt the tops of her ears
)urn. "He might have plans."

Jon shot her a look that called her a fool. "Like
vhat?"

"I don't know, but . . . people have families."

"Not him, I bet. He's a loner." He sank his fork into
hick crust. "So, is it okay? Can I ask him?"

Knowing she was playing with hot emotional fire,
Kate lifted a shoulder. "Sure," she heard herself saying.
'I guess it doesn't hurt to ask."

But deep down, she wasn't so sure.

Bibi Sullivan Porter was a damned good liar. But so
vas Neils VanHorn and he could feel it when someone
vas straying from the truth. Bibi was straying all over
he globe. And she was anxious as hell.

Watching her nervously light another cigarette and
·ecross those long legs he found so distracting, Neils sat
)n the edge of a gold-and-white-striped couch in the
niddle of her gold-plated condominium.

When all else had failed, he'd called on her despite
1er father's warnings. If Robert wanted to find his
grandson, he'd have to let Neils work all the angles.

Bibi had been undone from the moment he'd stepped
nto her condominium on the fourteenth floor. He'd
:aken in the surroundings: acres of plush mauve carpet
covered here and there by sheepskin rugs, weirdo ab-
stract art, sculptures in black and purple, paintings of
inanimate objects all out of proportion, and tables and
chairs—mostly black and Oriental—clustered around
potted plants in odd little groupings throughout the
·ooms.

She'd tried to mask her anxiety, of course, and had
offered him a drink. She'd even kicked off her shoes
and tucked her legs under her on the couch as they'd

talked and the lights of the city had become visible a
night had fallen.

She'd stuck to her story claiming that a sailor name
Roy Panaker had been her lover. It had been a whirl
wind affair lasting no more than two weeks and she'
never seen his wallet, never snooped to see if he'd give
her a phony name, never once thought that he migh
be lying to her. He'd told her he was originally from
Phoenix, that he'd moved around a lot as a kid, and
that he was just about finished with his hitch in the
navy. She didn't even think that he might have used a
alias, or that he could have had a wife and childrer
tucked away somewhere, or that he could have been
scamming her. She'd been young and naive at the time
and when he'd said good-bye, that he was shipping out
she'd never expected to see him again. She'd found ou
she was pregnant the next month.

It was all too neat and convenient in VanHorn'
opinion, and even though she met his stare, eye to eye
she seemed to be holding back. Beatrice, he surmised
was used to adjusting the truth and living with lies. It al
seemed so easy for her.

But he wasn't buying. She'd kept a cigarette burning
during the entire interview. When she'd squashed one
out, the next minute she was delving into her gold case
for a replacement. It was as if nicotine was helping her
stay the course, calming her nerves, keeping the lies un
tangled as he grilled her.

It didn't matter. She could lie until she was blue in
her pretty little face. He'd figure it out. He'd just star
with her phone records, then her credit card bills, find
out if she was in contact with anyone suspicious. He'c
check her fax machine calls, her e-mail, her credit card re
ceipts. He had people in all phases of the industry
those who were totally legitimate and those who made a
practice of breaking the law.

"Look, VanHorn, if you want to know the truth, I'd just as soon not start all this. I know Dad thinks he needs to find my baby, but I disagree. It wouldn't be fair to the child."

"Nor to you."

"Right."

He spread his hands. "It's just a job to me," he said, matching her lie with one of his. "Your father hired me to find the boy and I intend to do the best that I can." He sipped from the expensive scotch she'd poured for him. "You know, I thought you'd be curious about your son."

She closed her eyes a second. "It's too late."

"But he's your flesh and blood."

"I know and there was a time when I wanted to find him, especially once I had the operation . . . when I knew I couldn't have any other kids. But then my life changed, I went through the divorce and now I've met a man who doesn't want to be reminded that I had a past before I met him."

"Don't you think that's unreasonable?"

She swirled her drink and considered. "I . . . I think it's necessary, if Kyle and I are going to make things work. Look, this really isn't any of your business, is it?"

"No, but I'd hate to think that you were working against me or hiding information."

She laughed brittlely and glared at him over the rim of her glass. "The last time I saw my son was on the day he was born. His father never knew a thing about him."

"Ever?"

"Right. So you're barking up the wrong tree, Mr. Van-Horn, wasting my father's money. Even if you do locate Roy, he'll think you're nuts. He probably doesn't even remember me. It's been a long time."

Neils smiled, his gaze moving over her bare calves. "I doubt that any man could forget you."

"Well, he did a fine disappearing act."

"Isn't that something?" VanHorn said, then drained his drink and set it on the corner of a glass and brass table. "It's almost as if the guy never existed."

"If he didn't exist, then how could I have a son?" she asked, tilting up her pointed chin. She looked older than she was then, her hair, mahogany that shimmered as if it had been professionally colored, her blue eyes enhanced with aqua contacts. She wore a short sarong of sorts, black and gold threads woven into some gauzy fabric that showed off a hint of cleavage as well as revealed shapely, well-muscled legs.

"Maybe you're protecting someone else."

"Someone else?" she repeated with a humorless laugh. "Who would that be?"

"You tell me. A married man, perhaps? One with a family? Or . . . someone unsavory—a thug with a criminal record? A boy underage? Lots of possibilities."

"Well, you keep checking them out, Mr. VanHorn, that's a good idea. My father's a very wealthy man and I don't think you're above stretching out this investigation to get as much of Daddy's money as you can. Go ahead. But as I said, you're wasting his money and my time. Now, if you'll excuse me . . ." She stretched out her legs and rolled her bare feet into black velvet slippers, then ushered him to the door.

As he rode the elevator to the first floor, he wondered exactly what her secrets were. At the time of the baby's conception, she'd been living at home with her folks, and the Sullivans had proved to be a clannish lot. There were lots of family get-togethers and even her brother Stuart and her cousin Collin were best friends when they could have easily been rivals. Bibi hung out with the boys when she could and had few girlfriends, but there was one, Tina Petricelli, who had moved away from Boston a few years back and Bibi's first husband

Arnold Porter, who, though remarried, might provide some insight into Bibi's previous love life. Sooner or later VanHorn would find out what secrets she thought she'd buried long ago.

He made mental notes to call on those close to Bibi, and to check on the events of Stuart Sullivan's death, which had to have happened, according to the chronological order of events, right around the time that the kid was conceived. He'd thought for a second that maybe Stuart had been the boy's father—it would explain so much about the secrecy surrounding the birth and Stuart's untimely murder—but he'd tossed the notion aside. If that was the case and Robert had the slightest inkling about the kid's parentage, he would never have hired Neils—or would he have? The old coot was weird and talked about Stuart as if he were some kind of saint.

The elevator bell chimed softly and he landed on the first floor. A woman draped in red leather and walking two greyhounds entered the car as he turned up the collar of his coat and edged through the revolving door.

Bitter cold ripped into him as he hit the street. Snow was still piled along the curb and the wind tore by in a frigid rush that burned his cheeks. Hands deep in his pockets, he headed for a little Irish pub a few blocks away. He'd have a couple of drinks and meet his silent partner again.

One way or another he'd find the truth about the boy's father, discover where the kid was, and then sell all this vital information to the highest bidder.

"Take the kid and run as far and as fast as you can!" Bibi said, her voice nearly strangled with hysteria. "VanHorn's on to us, I just know it."

Daegan felt his jaw tighten to the point of pain. "He will be if he figures out you called me."

"He won't. I'm in a phone booth and I wasn't followed, now, do you hear me, I don't trust VanHorn. He's a slimy little bastard if there ever was one and he's going to find you and the boy so you'd better pack up and leave right away."

"I'm working on it."

"For a month? Christ, Daegan, it's almost Thanksgiving! How long are you going to draw this out?" Standing in his small, dingy kitchen, he could imagine the lines of strain on her face, the worry in her eye. "He's even talked to Arnold."

"Arnold?"

"My ex! Arnold called me yesterday and read me the riot act about VanHorn showing up on his doorstep, asking all sorts of questions, making him late for his damned squash game. He acted as if it was my fault."

"Bibi, for God's sake, get a grip—"

"A grip? A grip?" she repeated. "Jesus, don't you understand anything, Daegan? VanHorn's going to find you!"

"Not if I can help it."

"Then grab the kid and take off."

As if it were all that simple. "And be up on charges for kidnapping?"

"You're the boy's father!"

"Not legally, Bibi, now just calm down," Daegan insisted, though his own pulse was pounding with dread. It was time for the truth. Kate deserved to know what was happening.

"Oh, for the love of God, Daegan, I can't calm down! I'm freezing my butt off out here! Just do the job you were paid to do and get the hell out of Dodge!"

"Cute, Bibi."

"Not meant to be. It's not just VanHorn, you know.

Daddy's putting the screws to me. VanHorn's convinced him there was no Roy Panaker, so now Daddy's asking questions, not just of me, but of everyone else in the family, even my girlfriends."

"And Arnold."

"Yes, and that's not the worst of it. Collin called to make sure I was going to Frank's house for dinner, said he wanted to talk to me about something. Do you know how long it's been since Collin spoke to me? Years, Daegan, years! He's never started a conversation with me since Stu was killed and you left Boston. It's almost as if he blamed me for all the problems, and now, *now* he wants to chat over roast turkey and damned cranberries!"

"Stop it! You're working yourself into a lather about nothing," he said though his own stomach twisted at the mention of his half brother—Collin the blond, the beautiful, the chosen. Oh, shit. "Just slow down, take a deep breath—"

"Don't patronize me, Daegan. I put up with that all my life from Stuart, Daddy, and Collin. I don't need or expect it from you! Okay?"

He ground his back teeth together and suddenly knew what it would be like to be a wounded animal, cornered with nowhere to run. "I'll handle things on this end."

"You'd better," she said, "because Daegan, if this all blows up in my face, I'll hold you responsible!"

"I'll keep that in mind," he drawled before hanging up and running a hand over his face. Bibi was losing it, but she did have a point. What was the reason he was hanging around? Why not put an end to this insanity?

Because he didn't want to. The damnedest thing had happened. In the weeks since Jon's run-in with Todd Neider, the boy had been coming over, not just for boxing lessons, but to learn to ride a horse, shoot a rifle, shore up the old fence line. Even the dog had started coming

out from under the porch, sleeping on a mat just inside
the door as the nights had grown colder and once in a
great while thumping his mangy tail at the sight of Daegan. No more growls from old Roscoe or suspicious
stares from the kid. Jon seemed to find him fascinating,
and Daegan was hard-pressed to destroy a relationship
so tenuously woven.

In the beginning, because of the boy's gift, he'd expected Jon to divine a lot more about him, but if the
boy had figured out that Daegan had ulterior motives
for moving in next door, he hadn't said a word. In fact,
all that talk about seeing into the future or the past
seemed to have disappeared. Or the kid was just keeping it to himself, as Daegan had.

But Bibi was right. Sooner or later this whole mess
was going to blow sky-high. He had to figure out what
he was going to do. With Roscoe tagging reluctantly behind him, he made his way to the barn, where he spent
the next couple of hours cleaning some of the tack and
machinery, then spreading oats and hay into the
mangers of his two horses. As he used his jack knife to
cut the twine of bales he'd bought from a rancher who
lived fifteen miles up the road, Daegan thought about
his ranch in the Bitterroots and wondered why he didn't
miss the place—the one spot on earth he'd once considered home. He called every week and his foreman
assured him that everything was running as well as could
be expected. They'd lost a pregnant cow to black leg, but
had inoculated the rest of the herd and no other animals had been stricken. He should return, should find
his life again, but he was beginning to think that the rest
of his miserable existence was tied to Kate Summers, her
son, and Hopewell-damned-Oregon.

Bibi's call disturbed him. As long as he was here,
close to Kate and Jon, he was like a campfire on the
prairie, a beacon that would lead VanHorn to Kate's

front door. On the other hand, he was the only chance of protection they had. No telling what VanHorn's plan was. Robert Sullivan's intentions were clear—he'd do anything to get the boy back in the family. He didn't give a damn about Kate or her son's feelings. Then there was the Neider family to consider. Todd wasn't about to stop harassing Jon unless his father stepped in and the old man had made his viewpoint pretty clear.

"Son of a bitch," he growled, kicking a bag of oats in frustration and sending a rat scurrying through a hole in the floorboards. Roscoe barked uneasily and Buck-shot snorted.

Daegan had no choice but to put his cards on the table and tell Kate the truth. She'd be furious and hurt and probably tell him to go straight to hell, a place he'd visited more than once before in his lifetime. But the thought of not seeing her again, being separated from his boy, drove a stake of pain through his heart. He could fight her for custody, he supposed, and conse-quences be damned, but then she'd be sure to hate him with a blinding ferocity that would tear at him for the rest of his days.

Charging out of the barn, he felt the breath of the coming winter, fierce and unforgiving, in the wind at his back. A few flakes of snow swirled in the air, and ice had formed in the mud puddles from the rain they'd had earlier in the week.

He heard Kate's car before he saw it, and dread pounded in his heart. Since that night on the porch when he'd kissed her and made mental love to her, they'd kept their distance, at least physically. She seemed to have been as shaken as he, and the few times they'd run into each other, they'd been polite, even friendly, but hadn't come close to the same intimacy they'd shared in those few minutes of passion. But it had lurked there, just below the surface of their civility to each other, that simmering desire that created a raw ache deep in his soul and kept him awake at night for the feel of her beside him.

Her car ground to a stop and she flew out the door, her hair streaming behind her as her boots crunched furiously on the gravel. "Who do you think you are?" she demanded, her eyes snapping gold fire.

His heart nearly stopped. *She knew. Somehow, some way, she'd figured out why he was here.*

She advanced on him and jabbed a finger at his chest. "You had no right, do you hear me, *no* right to bulldoze your way into my business."

"Hey, whoa—slow down," he said, ready to defend himself. Whether she believed it or not, Jon was his son as much as, probably more than, hers.

"I know you went over to Carl Neider's place!"

That's what this furious tirade was all about? Daegan nearly laughed with relief, but the consternation gripping her beautiful features stopped him short. "Weeks ago."

"Doesn't matter when it happened."

"I figured old man Neider needed to know what his kid was up to."

"And so you took it upon yourself to tell him to keep Todd away from Jon."

"I just suggested he might not want to let his boy keep bullying other, smaller kids."

"But—"

He lifted a dark, curious brow and watched as she snapped her mouth closed then threw her arms in the air and turned away from him, as if staring into his eyes was too distracting. "Jon's my son, not yours," she said finally and he felt a rip in his heart. *Oh, lady, if you only knew.* "I guess this might be all my fault, the way I let him come over here all the time to pester you and—"

"He doesn't pester me. I enjoy having him around."

The honesty in his words caused her shoulders to stiffen.

She let out a long, slow breath, which formed a cloud in the frigid air. "Listen, Daegan, I appreciate all you're doing for Jon. And . . . well, to be honest, I thought it was kind of nice—pushy, but nice—that you watched over the place at night. Jon . . . he needs someone other than me that he can look up to or depend on or whatever you want to call it, but you have no right to go up to Carl Neider or anyone else and threaten him and oh—"

He grabbed her wrist and spun her around, his fingers tightening like a manacle. "Something had to be done, Kate. Sheriff Sit-On-His-Ass wasn't going to lift a finger and we both know it. He was hoping the situation would just fade away, but that's impossible with Neider's kind."

"There hasn't been any more trouble . . ."

"Don't you wonder why?"

"No, I—"

"Because Carl Neider understands that I mean business!"

Kate tried to yank back her hand, but he refused to let go.

"I should have been the one," she said. "Jon's my son and—"

"And you wouldn't have made near the impression I did," he said, feeling a hard smile curve his mouth. "Neider heard me."

"The whole damned town heard you, everyone but me! I heard it from one of my students, Daegan. Try and imagine my surprise and what an idiot I looked like as I didn't know a thing about what was going on!"

"It was between Neider and me."

"And Flo Cartwright—Neider's girlfriend—she apparently overheard you giving Carl the business."

He remembered the blonde lounging behind the screen door of the shabby trailer.

"This is a small town, Daegan. You shouldn't have gone over there in the first place, but once you did, the least you could have done was tell me about it. This does involve my son, you know." Her lips drew together in frustration and he saw a gamut of emotions play across her features. At this moment in time she didn't know whether to hate him or love him, and he was hoping she'd find some middle ground. He supposed if she ended up hating him, which was highly likely, it would be better than if she was foolish enough to consider loving him. Love could only end in disaster. "You threatened him."

"Within an inch of his life," Daegan agreed, pulling her closer and leaning down so that his nose was nearly touching hers. "It's the only thing bullies understand."

"You had no other choice?" she demanded.

"I don't think so, no." God, she smelled good and the sight of snowflakes melting on her cheeks and catching in her hair nearly undid him. Her lips parted slightly and he saw the change in her eyes, a dark awareness that transformed her fury into a hollow yearning.

His response was quick and primal. "Oh, hell," he growled and wrapped his arms around her, capturing her chilled mouth with his own. She seemed to melt against him, her heart a hammering echo of his own, her arms surrounding him as if it were the most natural act in the world.

A vital part of him, one he'd kept locked away for most of his life, struggled to break free. His eyes closed, and as the first snowflakes of fall swirled around them, he opened her mouth with his tongue, tasting and teasing and feeling the velvety warmth of her.

A soft little moan escaped her throat and he wound a

hand through her hair, holding the back of her head while the other reached upward beneath her jacket to feel the weight of her breast. Her mouth opened farther and he rubbed a thumb over the cup of her bra, feeling her nipple harden and strain. Already his blood was on fire, his skin itching to rub against hers, his mind ablaze with images of her satiny body arching to his, joining in splendor, her breasts, ripe and peaked with dark button-tipped disks begging to be suckled. Their joining would be a hot, savage union that would leave them both spent and heaving, sweat dripping from their bodies.

He pulled the shirt from her jeans and his fingers scaled her ribs, touching, feeling, slipping the front clasp open.

"Daegan, oooh," she whispered against his ear and he rubbed in slow, sensuous circles belying the fire running through his veins. "I don't think—"

"Neither do I."

"I mean . . . I should go home. Jon is expecting me . . . Oh, God, please—"

With all the willpower he could scrape together, he released her, letting her blouse and jacket fall back into place. Trying to ease the ache in his loins by shifting his jeans, he saw her take in a long, shaky breath as both her hands raked impatiently through her hair.

"I don't think I'm ready for this," she confessed, and the honesty in her gaze pierced straight to his soul.

Squeezing his eyes shut, he tried to rein in his galloping emotions, attempted to find that clear-thinking common sense that had seen him through the most painful and complicated portions of his life. "I'm not ready either," he admitted.

"I—I don't know if I'll ever be," she said softly, squinting up at him before walking to the old split rail fence separating the barn from the house. Wrapping her arms around a silvered post, she stared through the trees toward her place.

"You still love your husband."

"No. I did for a long time, but Jim's been gone for almost sixteen years. I don't really remember what he looked like, even though I still have pictures. And Erin, my baby, she'd be a junior in high school now, probably have a driver's license, be dating . . ." Kate blinked rapidly and looked away. With a squaring of her shoulders, she slapped the post and faced him again. "No reason to dwell on it, is there? I've still got Jon."

But not for long, he thought with a sick feeling that tore at all his convictions. How could he tell her the truth? How could he take her son from her? How could he not? Every day was one day closer to the truth—either from him or Robert Sullivan, and that meant they were one day closer to a day of reckoning when she would realize why he'd come here and then she would hate him forever.

"Does he look like his father?" Daegan asked suddenly and she tensed.

"Pardon?" she said, her voice nearly a gasp.

"You said you couldn't really remember what Jim looked like. I wondered if Jon resembled his dad."

She bit her lip. "No. Not at all."

Tell her. Now's the time! "But he doesn't look much like you."

"He takes after Jim's side of the family," she lied, her mind racing wildly. Why did he want to know? Why now? How had she been so stupid to bring Jim and Erin into this conversation? "His . . . his brother. My brother-in-law."

Daegan's head jerked up. "Does he live around here?"

"No . . . still back in Iowa, I think, but we've kind of lost touch." Oh, Lord, now she was getting herself into the thick of a mess she couldn't get out of. She remembered her vow to Tyrell Clark, how she and Jon would remain without past ties, and now she was confiding in this man—a stranger to her really, a man who heated her blood, yet of whom she knew so little. "I'd better get back," she said quickly, dusting hands that were cold as the November air. "Jon will be home any minute and I want him to eat something and do his homework before he gets any ideas about coming over here."

"He's always welcome," Daegan drawled, staring at her with those stormy gray eyes that caused her pulse to jump and her heart to pound. She climbed back in her car, switched on the wipers, and drove the short distance to her house. But she kept glancing in the rearview mirror expecting Daegan—or someone—to follow her.

Don't be paranoid, she advised herself. *Just because he asked a few questions, he doesn't have to be sinister or evil.* She slammed on her brakes and studied her reflection in the mirror, this time looking into her eyes and seeing the truth. She wasn't afraid for Jon, not anymore. She was afraid for herself, because like it or not, she was giving her heart to the man living in old Eli McIntyre's house.

"You're comin' to our house for Thanksgiving dinner, aren't you?" Jon asked as he unbuckled the cinch of Loco's saddle.

"Did your mom invite me or is this your idea?" Daegan asked. It had been three days since he'd seen Kate, and the invitation sounded suspiciously as if it had been Jon's plan.

"She says it's okay." Jon stared at him with round Sullivan eyes and Daegan didn't have the heart to turn the boy down.

"Sure, I'll be there, then," he said and felt guilty when he saw a smile stretch along Jon's jaw and a light of anticipation brighten his gaze. What would he say when he found out the truth, when he realized Daegan was not only his father but a liar as well? A man who could ruin his life? "Just let me know what time."

"Four o'clock. We eat around five or five-thirty." Jon slid the blanket off the gelding's back and tossed it over the rail of a stall. Snorting loudly, the gray searched for any leftover oats in the manger.

"Am I supposed to bring anything?"

Jon laughed. "Mom said you'd probably ask and she said just bring your appetite."

Unfortunately Daegan was always hungry around Kate, but it didn't have anything to do with food. Lately he'd been thinking of her, hoping to see her again, plotting excuses to get her alone. Ever since Bibi's phone call, he'd been on the alert, listening to the town gossip about possible newcomers, keeping his gaze trained on the gate to Kate's lane whenever possible. He'd also called a friend of his in Boston who was gathering information on Neils VanHorn. Before the guy showed up, if he showed up, Daegan would be waiting.

And then what?

The truth, damn it. No matter what it cost. He glanced at the boy who was his son. Jon's face in the low wattage was set in concentration as he began to brush Loco's muddy hide. At this moment he looked younger than fifteen, and Daegan felt a protective surge race through his blood. He'd missed Jon's first words, his first uneven steps, the chance to teach him how to cast a fly into a swift mountain stream, the best way to break a tackle in football, and the importance of being your own person, but most of all, Daegan had missed the chance to be a father to his only son after growing up knowing what it felt like to have no father who cared. Could he really give up the rest of Jon's youth as well—the few years the boy had left before becoming an adult? And what about Kate? Could he live the rest of his life knowing that she would rather spit on him than talk to him? How would he be able to rise each morning and know that he'd never see her or his son again?

Jon finished brushing the horse and together they crossed the frigid yard to the house where, as they did every time they were together, they split a Coke. Never mind that it was below freezing outside, together they sat near the old wood stove, sipped from chipped enamel mugs, and Jon told him about his life.

"Neider giving you any more trouble?" Daegan asked him.

"Nope." Jon frowned into his mug and blinked as if something was weighing on his mind. When he glanced up, his blue eyes were troubled. "Mom said you talked to Todd's dad."

"That's right."

Biting his lip, Jon scowled, but didn't say anything.

"What's on your mind?" Daegan prompted. He rested the heel of his boot on the brick pad that supported the blackened stove.

"I hate him."

"I know."

"I mean I really hate him."

Daegan nodded, watching as Jon's brow furrowed and his lips twisted into a knot.

"But Todd's dad beats him."

Daegan didn't move.

Jon looked at the floor, avoiding Daegan's stare. "I don't mean that he gives him a swat, I mean that he hits him over and over again when Todd messes up."

"Jesus." Anger and disgust gnawed a hole in Daegan's gut.

"He came back to school last week and in gym class I saw his legs; they were all bruised. Someone asked Todd what had happened and he said he'd fallen down the back steps and scraped himself."

"But you don't believe him."

"Nah." Jon swirled his Coke and the two cubes of ice clinked together. "I . . . um . . . well, you know that I sometimes can see things—not always, though, and sometimes I'm wrong, but usually if I get a clear vision . . ." His voice trailed off and he worried his lip while still rotating his cup nervously. "Anyway, I've touched Todd and seen into his mind, if that's what you want to call it. He's scared shitless . . . I mean scared to death of his old man after he's had a few beers. Todd locks himself into his bedroom, but his dad comes in and hits him with a belt, over and over again, and Todd, he cries for his mother. She left a long time ago, married someone else, had some other kids and never calls or sees Todd."

"Damn." Daegan's anger was white-hot. "No wonder the kid's a mess. What about social services? If you've seen the bruises, then someone else has to have as well, a doctor or a teacher—what about the gym teacher?"

"He's the football coach." Jon's eyes rose from his cup to meet Daegan's. "He thinks everyone should be able to take a hit now and again. 'Makes boys into men,' he says, but it's all a bunch of crap."

"Does Todd know that you've seen what happens to him?"

"Oh, yeah. That's why he hates me so much. He's afraid I'll tell, and well . . ." Jon shifted in his chair as if he'd like to crawl out of his skin. "Sometimes he makes me so mad I say the first thing that comes to my mind. I know he'll stop picking on me or giving me a bad time if I bring up the fact that his old man beats him."

"And you feel bad about it?"

"Sometimes. It makes the other kids laugh at him, and even though he deserves it—man, does he deserve it—I know what it feels like." He took a long swallow from his drink, as if his throat was suddenly parched.

"So what do you think we should do?" Daegan asked, studying the boy.

"I don't know, but I don't want to get Todd into any more trouble, not now anyway."

"What if he starts picking on you again?"

"Then I'll have to beat him up myself," Jon said with a cocky grin.

"You think that would be the answer?"

Jon offered him a one-sided smile that was so much like his own he could barely breathe. "The best one we've got."

"Gotcha!" Adrenalin coursed through Neils Van-Horn's bloodstream. With a hoot, he slapped the itinerary onto the top of his metal desk and silently praised himself for being one helluva private detective. Sullivan was getting his money's worth.

He took a pull on his beer and leaned back in his chair, balancing the bottle on his flat stomach. Perseverance, perseverance, perseverance! Ha! Take that, Beatrice, you snobby bitch.

Finally, he'd struck pay dirt and he could feel his wallet growing heavier by the second. Glancing again at the copy of Bibi's itinerary, he wondered what she was up to.

Narrowing his eyes, he let the cold beer slide down his throat. Recently, about the time the old man started making noise about finding the kid, Beatrice had taken herself a little trip to San Francisco, where she'd met her doctor boyfriend for a fun-filled weekend. But on the way to the West Coast, she'd stopped in Helena, Montana—just a layover, but a strange one considering that there were plenty of nonstop flights coast to coast.

Oftentimes a person had to stop in Denver, Chicago, Minneapolis, even Dallas, but Helena, Montana? Never. Besides, Bibi had already stopped once in Chicago, where she'd changed planes, and rather than take the continuing service to Seattle, she'd opted for a smaller jet with a destination of Backwater, U.S.A. Two hours later she climbed aboard yet another plane, this one headed for her final destination of San Francisco. There had to be a reason she'd spent a few hours on the ground. Why?

To meet someone?

Who?

He picked up a legal pad with his notes scattered through half the pages and thumbed through the wrinkled sheets. He'd already checked and found that the only person who was remotely associated with Bibi or the Sullivan family who lived within a radius of five hundred miles of the airport was Daegan O'Rourke, Frank Sullivan's bastard, the guy some people thought had killed his half cousin, Stuart.

So why would Bibi want to talk to O'Rourke?

What could they possibly have in common? O'Rourke was a juvenile delinquent turned into a goddamned cowboy, for Christ's sake—a cowboy! From South Boston. If nothing else, O'Rourke had a sense of humor. Bibi was a fading Boston socialite, a rich divorcée intent on marrying an uptight doctor. As far as Neils knew, Bibi and Daegan had nothing to share except they were related to one of the meanest sons of bitches of all time—good old Frank Sullivan.

Born wealthy, Frank had spent his life feeling third in line while William was alive and then second best when his eldest brother had died. Insecure and mean, Frank Sulli-

van reminded Neils of a street tough, rather than a guy
who'd been born with a silver spoon rammed down his
gullet.

Why would Bibi fly halfway across the country to see
O'Rourke?

He wrote Daegan's name on the note pad and circled it over and over again, trying to come up with a
reason. O'Rourke had been a private investigator himself; maybe Bibi had hired him to help her. With what?
To check on her boyfriend? Nah! The timing was too
coincidental and Neils didn't put much stock in coincidence.

So what?

Did they share a secret?

Did he know about the kid?

He stopped drawing and concentrated so hard that
his head began to pound. His other leads had dried up.
He'd tried to locate Tyrell Clark's staff but had come up
empty-handed. Even the women who worked for him,
Rinda DuBois and Kate Summers, were no longer anywhere near Boston. Rinda lived in the Florida Keys somewhere, still working for a lawyer, and she hadn't seen or
heard from either Tyrell or Kate for fifteen years. Kate
Summers, well, he was still looking for that one. Her
name was just too damned common, but he wasn't giving up. She'd left Boston soon after the baby was born,
before Tyrell's death. Perhaps she and Tyrell were lovers,
or maybe she knew about his illegal scams that the IRS
was looking into, or . . . she left with a baby?

"Oh, hell, you're really losing it, VanHorn," he
growled at the empty room, but he doodled around her
name on the yellow paper. She might just know something, but he couldn't find her or her family. Her father
was dead, her alcoholic mother dead as well, an aunt
and uncle in Des Moines acting as if she'd fallen off the
face of the earth because of some vile thing she'd done

as a teenager and her sister—hell, what was her name? Linda? Lori? No, Laura. That was it. Laura Rudisill. Something or other. Neils hadn't tried to get through to her because Kate, who had only worked for Tyrell Clark a little while, seemed like such a longshot to be involved in something of this magnitude. She was barely more than a receptionist. Would Clark have trusted her with the truth about Beatrice Sullivan's baby? Or could she have stumbled upon it innocently—is that why she disappeared so completely when she left Boston? Or had she been, as Neils originally suspected, Clark's girlfriend?

He'd given up on that angle for the time being because he had this interesting development with good ol' Bibi and her infamous bastard cousin. He'd start with Daegan O'Rourke. He had his number somewhere . . . Flipping through the pages of his notebook, he found the scrap of information he needed, then decided against making a phone call. No, a visit would be better—harder for O'Rourke to avoid. Face to face, that's how it was gonna be.

Neils dropped the pad back onto the table and swilled down the rest of his cold beer. He'd have to call his silent partner in all this—see how she took the news. She might even give him a little insight.

And O'Rourke, his story should be interesting.

Licking his lips, Neils glanced at his coffee-stained desk calendar and saw that it was only two days until the holiday. It seemed fitting somehow. "Happy Thanksgiving, O'Rourke!" Grinning, he looked through his window with the crack in one corner. "Get ready to spill your guts."

Chapter 19

When did the falls grow so cold? Robert wondered as he reached for his gloves. Snow hadn't seemed to bother him this much when he was younger; ice and sleet were mere inconveniences, not such deep annoyances, and certainly not so bone chilling. Sighing, he reached for his hat. The driver was already warming the car when the phone rang.

"It's a Mr. VanHorn," his butler, Royce, said with a lift of a questioning brow.

Robert's heart nearly stopped. Maybe there was news. "I'll take it in the den," he said and felt his hands begin to sweat. Each time VanHorn called with a report, Robert's spirits soared and he experienced the same sense of anticipation he used to feel whenever he'd won a particularly challenging or expensive case, or the first time he'd called a new young woman to add to his string of mistresses.

"Yes?"

"Good news." Neils VanHorn's voice was smug, and Robert, still holding the receiver to his ear, sank into his desk chair.

"What?"

"I think I'm close."

Disappointment choked off his premature euphoria. "You think?"

"Let me be more specific. I'm in some podunk town in Montana. And believe me, I'm freezin' my ass off here."

"What's in Montana?" he hardly dared to ask. "My grandson?"

He thought he heard a soft chuckle. "It's not quite that easy, but Daegan O'Rourke owns a spread up in the foothills of the mountains—"

"O'Rourke? What's he got to do with this?"

"That's what I'm trying to find out." Robert listened as VanHorn filled him in on Bibi's recent trip to San Francisco, and with each word he felt a mixture of elation and dread. O'Rourke had always been bad news, never good. If it weren't for Frank's bastard, Stuart would be alive today . . . Oh, Stuart, why, why, why? The old familiar emptiness caused him to hang his head. He felt like a husk of the man he was supposed to become, the man who had stepped into his dead brother's shoes oh so willingly dozens of years before. What would William have done? he wondered as VanHorn prattled on. In these last few weeks, ever since his doctor's prognosis, he'd thought about William more than he should have and realized what a great disservice he'd done to his older brother.

". . . I'm not certain why they're in cahoots, but I'm going to find out."

"Wait a minute. Beatrice and O'Rourke?" he repeated, his wandering attention back on track. "What could they possibly have in common?"

"That's what I intend to find out. I'll call ya as soon as I know anything." With that, the phone clicked and he was gone.

For the first time since he'd decided to find his grandson, Robert sensed a coming doom, a reckoning that he hadn't expected. It caused ice to form in the marrow of his bones, but he slid his arthritic fingers into the smooth leather of his gloves. He'd weathered storms before, personal tragedies that had nearly ripped his heart out. Whatever VanHorn uncovered, he and the family would be able to withstand the shock, but he couldn't help thinking of Pandora unlocking her box and releasing chaos.

"Stand firm," he muttered to himself as he made his way to the garage. "Stay the course." He passed by a crucifix mounted near the back door. Crossing himself with the deft moves of one whose sixty-odd years were blessed by the church, he tasted the bitterness of hypocrisy on his tongue and heard the vague and discordant ring of ruin in his ears.

"Where's Daddy?" Wade's eager eyes, as blue as her own, stared into Alicia's. At eight he was tall for his age, blond, and incredibly bright.

That s a good question, Alicia thought. "He's going to meet us at Grandma and Grandpa's house." Leaning on one knee, she adjusted his bow tie, made sure it was straight under his chin, then eyed his suitcoat, sweater, slacks, and shirt. Perfect. Such a little prince. Starched and pressed, his dress shoes shined to an impossible gloss. God, he was cute. She was thankful for all of Wade's attributes because she never wanted to go through the hell of pregnancy again. It had taken a year of diet, exercise, and appointments with the right plastic surgeons to return her body to its normal size four.

"How come he doesn't live here anymore?"

"He, does, honey, but his work in Washington keeps him there a lot. He'll be here for the whole weekend."

She smiled, pretending not to grit her teeth, pretending that Wade's father was a faithful husband and loving daddy. It didn't matter anyway. Her marriage to Bryan had been a sham from the beginning, and she'd gotten what she wanted out of it, a son. A perfect, brilliant son who was her whole life, a son who would someday be in charge of all the Sullivan holdings. A son far superior to Stuart or Collin or anyone else. So Bryan could screw his brains out with his little secretary and she didn't give a damn.

"Come on, the driver is waiting," she said, smoothing a stubborn cowlick in Wade's hair. "We're going to have a good time and Daddy will be there." If he wasn't, if that son of a bitch disappointed his son again, then she'd just have to get rid of him. He wasn't going to hurt Wade. No one was.

"I don't know what you're talking about," Bibi said as she tossed back the rest of her champagne and left her fluted glass on a wicker table. She was trapped, cornered by Collin, who had torn himself away from his reed-thin and wary wife to confront her in the sunroom of his parents' home.

Dusk crowded into the room, and outside, through a hundred panes of glass, the snow blanketing the flagstone veranda and Maureen's once-lush gardens had melted only to refreeze as the sun set. Patches of grass speared through the white mantle, and icicles, looking like the jagged teeth of a huge crystal beast, hung from the eaves and dripped ever so slowly as the hours ticked by. The first beams of pale moonlight bounced off the ice crystals that had formed over the fountains and bird baths and gave a silver sheen to the darkened room.

Bibi shivered, wishing she could leave, but Collin, her once-precious savior, now stood leaning against the door, barricading it with his slim body. He seemed to have lost weight in the past few weeks, his skin appeared paler than normal, and his eyes had sunken deep into his head, as if he were in the throes of some kind of fever. Bibi had chalked up his declining appearance to the divorce that was whispered about between family members.

Alicia had told Bibi weeks ago that Collin's marriage was on the rocks, that Carrie was demanding a divorce and that Frank was fit to be tied that his son was even considering breaking the union. There was even scuttle-butt about Collin being written out of the will, but Bibi dismissed that bit of news as malicious gossip or misplaced optimism on Alicia's part.

"Don't play dumb with me, Bibi," Collin warned, glaring at her with intense eyes. "It's not your style, and even if it was, I can read you like a book."

"Can you?"

"Christ, yes!" He closed his eyes a second, leaned his head against the aging panels of the door. He seemed tormented, his face a mask of pain as he sighed. "Look, I know what you're trying to do here, and—"

"I'm not *doing* anything," she said, wishing she hadn't left her cigarettes in her purse in the kitchen. God, she needed a smoke.

Muttering a curse under his breath, he stared at the edge of a Persian carpet, then raised his eyes to meet her gaze. "I know about the baby."

"That's hardly earth-shattering news, Collin. Everyone in the family knows now. VanHorn and my father have seen to it."

"Yes," he admitted, his lips curling in on themselves as if he were in deep concentration. "But no one else knows who the father is."

Involuntarily, she started. Collin knew? Oh, God. Fear congealed in her heart.

"Everyone bought your lie, Bibi, until now. Until VanHorn started nosing around and discovered that there was no Roy Panaker. Now the family's guessing— who was Bibi sleeping with?"

His nostrils flared as if he smelled something foul, and the drip of the icicles seemed louder in the ensuing silence.

"Wha—what are you talking about?"

Collin's patience was obviously worn thin. "I know the real reason you don't want the boy found. It isn't just because of Kyle and your intentions of marrying again. Nope." Shaking his head, he pierced her with his cold blue gaze. "This goes deeper, doesn't it?"

Her insides crumbled. How had he known? Oh, God, her world was falling apart and she didn't even have a goddamned cigarette.

"I'm surprised you didn't tell me, you know." Hands flat against the door, hips pressed into the varnished panels, he stared at her in awe. "I—I could have helped."

So here was the old Collin she remembered, the hero of her girlhood, the boy who had gotten his suit pants wet in Grandma's creek and taken a beating for it. "I couldn't tell anyone," she whispered, knowing that even now, she had to protect her secret.

"But it was my responsibility, Bibi. You shouldn't have borne all this shame alone."

"Your what?" Again she felt as if she was missing something—something vital.

"I know when the baby was born and about the time he was conceived. Oh, Christ—" He rolled his eyes skyward.

"This is hard, but I guess it has to be said." Stiffening his spine, he said, "You don't have to pretend, at least not with me. I know the boy is mine."

"Yours?" she whispered, disbelieving. Not only was

he world starting to spin off course but a loud roar
begin to thunder in her ears. "You think he's yours?"

"From the night in the pool house—"

"No!"

"No?" It was his turn to be stunned. "But—" Consternation darkened his features. "Then whose?"

"I've told everyone. Roy—"

"Bullshit, Bibi! I was there."

"Do you remember anything about that night?" she
asked. Did he really believe that he and she had . . . ?

"Yes. Hell, I've lived with it all this time." He shoved
both hands through his hair and finally straightened
away from the door, as if he knew that his words were
strong enough to hold her prisoner now. He no longer
had to resort to physically restraining her. Unnerved,
he sank into a Queen Anne chair near a wicker and
glass table. "God, Bibi, I'm sorry. Stu and I—"

"Were shits, I know." She didn't need to be reminded
of her humiliation at their hands.

"But it's more than that." Dropping his head into his
palms, he sat still, as if he couldn't move, as if life had
ceased to go on. "I would have done anything he asked,
you know, and when he suggested that you and I . . .
well, go at it so that he could watch, I argued with him."

"But still you went along," she said, the old pain
climbing up her throat and threatening to choke her.
She couldn't hide the condemnation in her voice, the
anger that knotted her stomach. "Did you have any idea
that I was in love with you?"

His shoulders slumped farther.

"Did you?"

"Yes," he said in the smallest of whispers, his voice
tortured.

"And still you used me."

"For him. I know it doesn't explain things, but you
don't understand how much I wanted to please him."

"Even if you hurt me?"

Raising his head finally, he stared at her with ago
nized eyes. "Believe me, I never wanted to cause you an
kind of pain. In my own way I did love you, it . . . it jus
wasn't what you wanted it to be. Eventually, I agreed."

"Because Stuart thought it would be a good idea.
Her stomach curdled.

"Stu—he liked to watch." Collin blinked hard.

"So you performed like some trained puppy?" Sh
started backing away, furious with him, with hersel
Her hands coiled into fists, and her fingernails dug int
the heels of her hands. "You spineless bastard, I don'
believe—"

"You don't understand. I loved him, Bibi. And no
the same way I cared about you. I mean I *really* love
him—would have done anything, *anything* he asked."

"That's not love, that's sick," she whispered, hardl
believing what she was hearing, silently praying that h
would stop, but Collin seemed, after over fifteen year
to need her forgiveness. "When he died, a part of me die
with him. I just wanted him to love me back."

"Oh, God." Revulsion spit through her as the full im
pact of what he was saying hit her in the gut. Suddenl
every disjointed piece of her youth, of her friendshi
with Stuart and Collin, fell neatly into place. Her exclu
sion hadn't been just an adolescent macho thing—i
had been sexual as well. Stu and Collin had been lover
and they'd let her think, encouraged her to believe, tha
she could . . . Bile climbed up her throat and she nearl
wretched. Oh, sweet Jesus, no!

"Just like you wanted me to love you," Collin ex
plained.

"Don't. I don't want to hear this," she said, backin
away. She died inside remembering how much she love
him, how she'd always believed deep in her heart that i

hey hadn't been cousins, that there would have been a
hance with him. Why hadn't she known? And with Stu-
rt. How they must have laughed at her naive and simple
ttempts at seducing Collin!

"That was the reason I couldn't perform at first," he
ent on, as if unburdening himself to a priest while she
as still reeling from the magnitude of his secret. "Until
saw Stu standing in the hallway watching us as he
rank—"

"Lurking, you mean," she cried, nearly hysterical. In
er mind's eye she was back in the darkened pool room,
ot and anxious for Collin to love her, knowing some-
hing wasn't right. She relived all the humiliation, all the
ain, all the sick, perverted embarrassment. "Stuart was
urking like a damned voyeur, getting his jollies by
atching his sister try and seduce her cousin—his lover."

"We were never lovers," Collin admitted and tears
tarred his lashes. "He could never take it that far—
ever allow me to touch him. He wanted to, he was
empted just as he was with everything that was outside
f what his father considered acceptable, but he couldn't
ven kiss me." Collin, as if inescapably weary, sagged in
he chair. His voice shook with emotion. "He was, with-
ut a doubt, the love of my life."

"And so, to please him, you agreed to fuck me," she
pit, repelled by the callousness, the pure vile malice, of
heir plan.

He nodded miserably. "I would have done anything."

"Even screw a woman." Wrapping her arms around
er middle, as if to defend herself, she started to cry.

"Not just any woman," he said, "but the only woman I
eally cared about, the one I didn't want to hurt. That
as why he wanted me to do it to you. It wasn't a sense
f nobility on his part, he wasn't setting me up with you
ecause he knew that you loved me." He shook his head

and anger destroyed some of his sadness. "The reason
he wanted me to sleep with you was to confirm my utter
and undying allegiance to him."

"That's sick—"

"Yes."

"Stuart was into power. Control and power." Collin
swallowed hard. His jaw slid to one side and his eyes
narrowed in regret. "He just wasn't into love."

"And so you agreed?" She dashed the damning tear
away.

"Oh, God, yes," he admitted, the words torn from his
throat. "And I drank as much as I could hold and convinced myself that I wouldn't hurt you, that I was doing
what you wanted, what Stuart wanted, and it didn't matter. It was just sex between people who cared for each
other. Oh, hell, I didn't mean for this to happen."

"It didn't," she said, finally understanding and feeling
pity for him instead of rage. He, too, had been a victim.

"Of course it did."

"No, Collin," she insisted, still caring for him enough
not to want him to suffer for a crime he didn't commit.
She walked to his chair, laid a hand on his shoulder, felt
him tense. Though he'd mortified her beyond words, he
hadn't fathered her son.

"Liar."

"You just accused me of being a lousy one, of being
able to see right through me."

Slowly he raised his eyes to her and she kissed his
cheek, tasted the salt from his silent tears.

"Do you remember that night, what happened?"

"Most. What I didn't, Stu filled in later."

"And he told you that you and I . . . we made it."

"Yes." A muscle worked at the side of his jaw.

"Oh, Collin, no." Kneeling at his chair, she cradled
his head against her. "Stuart lied. You couldn't do it. Either you were too drunk, or not turned on enough. I—

ried everything to get you in the mood and then, then I
aw my brother and . . . you fell asleep and Stuart and I
aad the fight of the century. I took off and . . ."

"And I woke up with Stuart's arms around me. He
miled at me, told me I'd done well, and that even
hough you were furious with us both, he'd been
urned on enough to want me. I tried to kiss him then,
ut he climbed out of bed, called me darling, and told
ne we'd be missed at the party. I stupidly thought there
vas still a chance for us. But as usual, he was stringing
ne along, playing with my emotions, oh, shit, he treated
ne the way I treated you and then, within the week . . ."
Again tears tracked from his eyes, shining in the moon
ҫlow. His words were choked. "Within the week he was
lead." He moved a hand, raised it from his knee, only
o let it fall again. "Now, years later, I find out that you
vere pregnant—that you had the baby nine months
after that night. You had to have gotten pregnant—"

"Soon afterward. But you aren't the father." She took
ɔne of his strong hands and squeezed it. "Believe me, I
know."

Relief flooded his handsome features. "Jesus, Bibi,
've been such an ass. I fucked up beyond fucked up."

She didn't argue. There was no point.

"I'm surprised you speak to me."

"You forced me in here, remember."

"But who's the baby's father?"

"No one you know, and besides, it doesn't matter. It's
ny business. All we have to worry about now is to make
sure that the child isn't found. If he is, my life, your life,
and his life would be ruined."

Collin snorted. "I don't care about being the next
crown prince or whatever the hell you want to call it for
he whole damned family. That was Stuart's role. He
should have inherited."

"Just like Uncle William," Bibi said, voicing a thought

that had nagged at her conscience for years. "Don't you think it's strange that the firstborn always seems to die?"

"I wouldn't follow that line of reasoning too closely," Collin warned. "Next in line would be that son you want to keep hidden away."

A vague unease pierced her mind. "Another reason for him to stay where he is."

Collin touched her tenderly, his fingers caressing her face. "You know, Bibi, if I were so inclined, you'd be the only woman for me."

"What about Carrie?"

"My wife?" he asked, saying the word as if it tasted bad. "Frigid."

"But—"

He shook his head. "We each had our reasons for marrying. I did it because my father was getting on my case and I was still young and stupid enough to think I had to please him."

"And her?"

"Her family was going broke. She couldn't reconcile herself to being poor, so we worked a deal. Kind of like my mother and father. Ironic, isn't it?"

"But now, the divorce?"

He laughed without a trace of mirth. "It's damned hard to live a lie, Bibi," he said, "but then you know all about it, don't you?"

"Oh, Lord, do I."

"My guess is you even know where your boy is."

She couldn't trust him; not with a secret this big. "No," she lied and felt a little tenderness for the boy he'd once been, the boy she'd loved so long ago. "I don't. And I pray to God that I never do."

There was a soft rap on the door, and then it opened a shaft of light piercing the gloomy shadows to fall on them huddled together. "Bibi?" Kyle asked, standing in silhouette, a strapping man with thick hair and a voice

hat rarely showed a note of concern. He frowned
lightly as Bibi climbed quickly to her feet and put some
distance between herself and Collin's chair. She felt
guilty as sin and he knew it. His brow furrowed in silent
accusation. "Not that I really want to know, but could
you tell me what the hell's going on in here?"

"So your mom's pretty and can cook, too," Daegan
said, winking at Jon across the table covered with a
turkey carcass, as well as platters of candied sweet pota-
oes, gravy, stuffing, white potatoes, peas, and cranberry
sauce.

"Watch out, Jon, Daegan is piling it up so high we're all
gonna need boots in order to slosh through it."

"Mom!" Jon admonished, but delight registered in
his eyes, as it did every time she stepped out of her con-
rolled,   I'm-the-mother-so-I-do-everything-as-expected
mode.

"Well, okay, I was laying it on a little thick and there
was a problem with the dinner."

"Oh?" She arched an eyebrow high, daring him to
ind fault with her masterpiece of a meal. She'd been
working on it for days though she wouldn't admit it.
Ever since Jon had announced that he'd invited Daegan to dinner, she'd wanted everything to be perfect.
Foolish woman.

"There wasn't enough food."

Jon nearly choked on a bite of stuffing.

"Not enough?" Kate leaned an elbow on the table
and held her chin in her hand to stare at him.

"Well, not if you intend to feed the rest of the town
the leftovers tomorrow."

"Very funny," she said, but felt her eyes sparkle.

Daegan found a toothpick in a little glass holder and
jabbed it into the corner of his mouth. "I thought so."

"Me, too," Jon agreed, anxious to have someone o
his side when he and his mother battled.

"Okay, okay, let's not argue," she said as she pushe
her chair back and realized that this was the first hol
day that she and Jon hadn't spent alone since Laur
had visited one Easter two years ago. Never a grandparen
an aunt, a cousin, or a brother or sister for her boy. Nor
father. Just the two of them. Sometimes it was too muc
for her—other times she was fiercely proud that they'
made it on their own. But today was different. She'd er
joyed having Daegan over and had even spread a
ivory-colored linen cloth over the old dining room tabl
and made a centerpiece of gourds and small pumpkin
in a basket of candles and flowers. For the first time in
long, long while, she felt content. The nagging restles
ness that had been chasing her down was at bay thi
afternoon, and though outside it was bitterly cold wit
swollen dark clouds and snow falling from the leade
sky, she felt warm and safe.

"We can have dessert by the fire," she suggested, noc
ding to the living room. "Jon, help me clear—"

"Awe, Mom, it's a holiday."

"I'll help," Daegan said.

"No way, you're the guest!" Jon was horrified.

"That's right. You don't have to—"

"I'm used to cleaning up after myself. It's no bi
deal." Daegan shoved out his chair and gathered up hi
plate and silverware.

"It's not man's work," Jon argued.

"You know better than that," Kate muttered.

"It is unless you're lucky enough to have a woman d
it for you, and even then, you'd better be careful," Daega
said, "because some women take offense to duties bein
described as theirs, especially when it comes to kitche
duty. Get downright testy about it. Don't say as I blam

them." To Jon's utter horror, Daegan picked up Kate's plate and his as well.

"But—"

"Be smart, Jon," Daegan advised. "This is a holiday for your mother."

"So now you're an expert on family relations?" Kate asked.

Jon eyed him strangely. "Is this what your mom taught you? Or your dad?"

A sadness scurried across Daegan's features, but was instantly replaced by the same hardness Kate had come to recognize—tight jaw, thin lips, furrow between his eyebrows. "My mother," Daegan said so softly that Kate barely heard the words over the clink of the glasses Jon was collecting. "But that was a few years back." He made a sound of disgust in the back of his throat. "My mother doesn't talk to me anymore."

Kate's heart dropped and she felt a sudden ache for this hard-edged man; so there was a softer side to him, a place where he hurt. He just kept that part of him hidden.

"Why not?" Jon asked.

"Because of something I did a long, long time ago," he admitted, frowning.

"What?"

"Jon, it's none of our business—"

"It's all right," Daegan said as he set the dishes in the sink and Kate slid the platter containing the turkey carcass onto the counter. Jon joined them in the kitchen and his gaze was glued to Daegan.

"My father was a jerk of the highest order. Never married my mom. In fact, he was married to someone else but kept coming around, cheating on his wife with my mother and cheating on my mom with his wife." His gaze touched Kate's briefly before he stared out the window and forced his hands into his back pockets. Kate guessed that he wasn't seeing the snow falling in tiny icy pellets from the sky, that he didn't notice how dark the sky had become. No, he was lost in his own private space—trapped in forbidden memories. "I finally took offense and had it out with my old man. And my mother . . ." His jaw clenched even tighter. "My mother stood by him even though he beat her and treated her like scum." He said the last words as if they tasted bad. "You asked me once if I killed anyone." His gaze moved back to her son, and Jon, swallowing hard, nodded.

"Yeah."

"Well, I didn't lie. I never killed anyone in my life, but I tried to kill my bastard of a father once, aimed a gun right at him, but I missed."

"Holy shit!"

Kate didn't even admonish her son. She held on to the edge of the counter for support. Inside she was shaking. "Dear God."

"So you never talk to your mother?" Jon asked, his eyes round as proverbial saucers.

"I tried. It's a one-way street. Let's not talk about it."

"When was the last time you saw her?" Jon asked, unable to let it go.

"The day I moved out. A long time ago."

"But what if she gets sick? What if—"

"I have someone who will let me know," he said, then cleared his throat and wondered what had possessed him to open up to them. Hell, considering that he was here to break apart their little family, he had no right to try and garner any sympathy for his own sorry home life. Kate blinked rapidly, as if fighting tears. Jesus, he was making a mess of things. He'd been lulled into a sense of belonging this afternoon, of being a part of a real family. "Look, I'd better be leaving."

"But dessert—" Kate said, motioning toward two pies

cooling by the window. Apple and pumpkin from the looks of them.

"And you were going to teach me how to play pinochle and poker," Jon reminded him.

"Another time." Daegan's insides churned when he saw the look of utter disappointment on the boy's features. Kate tried to disguise her own sense of loss, but it was there in her eyes, lancing through the thick skin he'd tried so hard to wear as a shield. "Thanks. Thanks for everything." It sounded like an exit line and it was. He was getting too close to Jon and Kate, trapped in all the trimmings that a family meant. Candles and flowers and pumpkins and big meals. Laughter and wine and playing cards. Jokes and flashing smiles and disappointments. His insides churned and for a few fatal seconds he was the boy from South Boston again, the kid with no grandparents, no father and a mother who scraped by on her own delusions. He loved that woman for how fiercely she'd fought for him and cursed her when she'd chosen his father over him.

That old searing pain shot through his soul and he silently cursed the family who had used and abused him.

"Daegan—don't go," Kate said and her voice wrapped around him like a balming mist. "It's Thanksgiving."

"Yeah, stay. Please." Jon's voice. His son. His own flesh and blood. But no one knew it. If he were a true man, a real father—the kind who put his son above himself—he'd walk out now, return to Boston, and tell Robert Sullivan the truth, that he'd sired Jon, that if Robert insisted on tracking the boy down, he would have to go through Daegan and face a scandal so dirty and shame-filled he'd never be able to raise his head among the social elite again. Jon would never know. Kate would be safe.

"I'll see you," Daegan said and walked to the front

door, where his jacket hung on the curved spoke of a wooden hall tree.

"Happy Thanksgiving," Kate said and he turned to look into her worried, whiskey-colored eyes. His heart twisted as he saw the accusations and disillusionment in his son's gaze.

"You, too." He grabbed his coat off the hall tree and shoved his hands through the sleeves.

Jon rushed forward, and as Daegan reached for the door, Jon touched his hand. Bare skin on bare skin. "You're leaving," he accused him.

"Yes."

"But not just for today."

"Eventually I'll have to move on."

"Soon."

"Probably."

Kate made a strangled sound in the back of her throat. Daegan glanced at her over Jon's shoulder and his insides curled in disgust when he recognized the pain he'd caused her.

"Why?" she asked.

"It's time."

"You're a bastard," Jon accused him, backing away from him as Daegan yanked open the door and a cold blast of wind tore through the house.

Daegan turned his collar up around his neck. He stepped out onto the porch and slammed the door behind him. "You got that right, Jon," he said to the bleak, frigid afternoon. "You sure as hell got that right."

Chapter 20

"You little shit!" Todd Neider's voice, a harsh whisper, seemed to resound off the lockers, and Jon, already late for class, froze in his tracks. "Stay away from Jennie."

Gritting his teeth, Jon turned and found Todd striding toward him. The older boy was like an enraged bull, eyes full of fire, nostrils flared as if he smelled something foul, black T-shirt barely covering his gut.

Stand firm. Don't let him push you around. "You can't tell me what to do."

Two juniors stopped halfway up the stairs as if they smelled a fight in the air. They yelled to some other kids, who turned quickly to gather by the freshmen lockers near the gym. The smell of the locker rooms—sweat and disinfectant—was only overridden by the scent of fear—Jon's fear. All he really wanted to do was run as fast as he could, but it was time to make a stand.

The final bell buzzed loudly and a few more kids who would've been tardy for their next class anyway stopped to watch as Todd bore down on Jon.

"She doesn't want anything to do with a freak like you," Todd said. "No one does."

For the first time, Jon didn't believe him. Jennifer Caruso had written him a note—just a friendly note, but a note all the same—and it was now tucked deep in his wallet. She'd asked him to call her, and no one, not even Todd with his I'm-going-to-beat-the-living-crap-out-of-you scowl, could change Jon's mind. All in all, it had been a lousy day because he knew that Daegan was leaving, hadn't heard a word from him for nearly five days, but Jennifer's note had raised his spirits. Neider wasn't going to change that. "I think Jennifer can make her own decisions."

"You're bothering her."

"Nah," Jon said, spying Dennis Morrisey and Joey Flanders hanging out at the water fountain, looking over their shoulders, too cowardly to do anything on their own but loving the fact that Todd intended to play hardball. Well, this time, Todd was in for a surprise. Jon was ready. Not only had he learned a little bit more about the bully the other day when he slammed Jon up against the outside wall of the audiovisual room and Jon had glimpsed into his small mind, but Jon was made of tougher stuff these days. All of Daegan's lessons were about to be put to the test, and even if he lost this round, he'd put up a better fight than Neider with his limited imagination could ever expect. "I'm not bothering Jennifer, but I'm sure as hell bothering you," Jon said.

"Me?"

"Yeah. For some reason you feel inferior to me and you have to—"

"Inferior?" Todd repeated with a laugh as he reached Jon and sized him up. "To you?"

"—show off and try and push me around so that you can feel like a big man when everyone knows you're a mental midget. It's probably 'cause Jennifer and a lot of other girls wouldn't give you the time of day."

Whispers rippled through the semicircle of boys who had gathered. Todd's face burst into color. "You little prick."

"At least I don't jack off looking at pictures of Miss Knowlton!"

Todd's mouth slackened and everyone laughed. Brenda Knowlton was the music teacher—probably somewhere near thirty-five—with flaming red hair, matching scarlet lips, and a figure that wouldn't quit. She also had a voice that rivaled fingernails on a chalkboard and a burly boyfriend who was an officer in the town's police department. "I don't—"

"Sure you do," Jon taunted. "And unless you stop this right now, I'll tell more."

"No way—"

"Like the way you steal *Penthouse* and *Playboy* from Parson's Drugstore. Mrs. Olsen saw you, too."

"The busybody?" Todd asked, suckered in for a second.

"You're goin' down, Neider."

Todd's big fists clenched. His two eyebrows became one. His glower was downright murderous. "I'll kill you," he said so quietly that Jon's blood turned to ice.

"I don't think so."

"Just watch." Rounding, Todd threw a punch, aimed squarely for Jon's jaw. Jon ducked and rolled onto the balls of his feet. His heart was hammering and he watched every muscle in Todd's face as the bigger boy came at him again, both fists swinging wildly.

"Fight! Fight!" some of the boys yelled as Jon feinted right and Todd's fist hit his shoulder in a glancing blow that didn't do much damage.

Jon swung. Two punches to the ribs and he backed away, ready to strike again when Dennis Morrisey shoved him back at Todd and he lost his footing.

Crack! Todd's fist connected with his jaw. Pain jolted,

like a bolt of lightning down his spine. Bam! A hard blow to the stomach. His insides cramped. The floor rushed up at him and he fell, hearing Todd's sick laughter. Jon tasted blood, but didn't stop. As Todd took a step forward, Jon swept his legs in a deadly arc, knocking the bigger boy off his feet.

Todd went down hard, a thud shaking the floor, his head snapping back to smash against the thin carpeting and cement underneath.

In a howl of pain, Todd rolled over and grabbed Jon by the neck. Jon kicked and punched, but Todd was seventy pounds heavier and he just tightened his grip, cutting off Jon's air, hauling him toward the bathroom.

No! No! No! Jon's mind screamed and he writhed like a slick eel, trying to get away, swinging at Todd's bulging tummy, his sneakers dragging along the carpet. He heard the sniggers and whispers as the bathroom door flew open and the smell of urine and running water greeted him. Jon fought and snarled like a hound from hell, but Todd cornered him against one of the urinals, thrust his head in, and began flushing. A rush of cold water sprayed over him. Jon hit his head on the porcelain and coughed and sputtered.

"Bastard!" Todd yelled. "Cocksucker!"

"Cretin!" Jon screamed.

Todd kneed him in the groin and he doubled over, water still spraying everywhere and washing down the back of his neck. In that moment he saw an image in his mind of Todd, coughing and crying, water filling his lungs, drowning. Jon froze. "It's gonna happen to you," he yelled between gasps for air. "You're the one who's gonna drown . . ."

"Shut up, Summers. You don't scare me."

"I'm serious." Jon tried to look at the other boy over his shoulder, to convince him. "Todd, it's gonna happen!"

"Like hell!" Again the rumble and gush of the urinal.

The vision was clearer—Todd was trying and failing to swim. "The lake—or river—or—" Again the flood of water and Jon gave up, the vision leaving as he tried to gasp for breath.

"Stay away from Jennie!" Todd ordered again and suddenly the room changed. Still coughing and barely breathing, Jon felt it. People had cleared out.

"What's going on here?" a hard male voice demanded. Mr. Jones, the algebra teacher and varsity track coach.

Neider's grip on his neck slackened, and Jon, soaked to the skin, slid on the wet floor.

"Come on, you two. I think it's time you took a walk down to the office. The rest of you get to your classes or you'll all be suspended, too." He shepherded them out the door, and Jon, dripping and mortified, started toward the office when he saw her. His heart dropped and he wanted to die.

Jennifer Caruso's choir class was in the hallway by the auditorium, waiting to enter. She was with a group of girls laughing and talking until her gaze landed on Jon and she bit her lip. Conversation stopped as they passed and several girls tittered at the sight of Jon.

"Take a shower?" nerdy Dwight Little muttered as Jon walked by.

"Would ya look at that?" Belinda Cawthorne frowned in disgust, as if he were covered in maggots.

"I guess Jon didn't *see* Neider coming. All those visions and what good are they?" Dwight was enjoying someone else being the brunt of jokes.

"Don't worry, he'll run to his mama and she'll talk to the sheriff," Belinda said in her goody-goody know-it-all voice.

"I heard he took a drink from the urinal."

"Shut up, Little, you're *so* gross!"

But Belinda and several other girls laughed. Jon prayed the earth would open up and swallow him whole. Every shred of pride he'd had, every ounce of self-respect, had been flushed away.

Jennifer didn't say a word, just stared after him, and he refused to meet her eyes. Deep in his heart he knew he'd never find the guts to call her. Not now. Not after Todd Neider had stripped away all of his dignity. A lot of good Daegan's lessons had done him. He scowled more darkly as they rounded the corner to the vice principal's office. He didn't want to think about Daegan. The guy was leaving town—just walking out of Hopewell as if he didn't give a damn. As if Jon and his mother didn't care.

Grinding his back teeth together, he decided the less he thought of O'Rourke the better, but he couldn't help feeling that he'd been betrayed. The same way he felt when old Eli had kicked off, except this was worse. Eli hadn't had a choice when he'd left. O'Rourke had.

Kate hauled her briefcase from the car and tried, as she had for the past five days, not to dwell on the fact that she'd obviously lost her heart to Daegan and that he was leaving soon. Just when she was learning to trust again, just when she'd convinced herself it was time to love again, just after she'd felt the joy and elation of falling in love, he was taking off.

"Pathetic," she muttered and told herself it was probably for the best. Houndog yipped from inside the house and Jon was waiting for her at the door. His eyes were dark and sullen, his face bruised on one side. "Don't tell me," she said, tired from the inside out even though fresh rage was burning through her blood. "Todd Neider."

"Yeah."

"Do I want to know what happened?"

Jon shook his head. "The good news is that I'm not suspended again and I didn't lose any teeth."

"And the bad news?" she asked, bracing herself.

"I got the crap kicked out of me." His discolored jaw tightened. "And I'm never going back to school."

She started to argue with him, but thought better of it. He needed to work this out and so did she. She itched to pick up the phone and call the school, the police, *Daegan,* anyone who would be her son's ally in this ongoing and dangerous battle, but instead she tried to hang on to her rapidly fleeing patience. "Tell me what happened," she encouraged and set her briefcase on the entry hall table calmly when she wanted to scream and rant and rave.

"There's not much to tell," he said, trying to squirm away.

"I need information, Jon."

"Oh, hell," he said, then looked at the floor. "Okay, Neider was mad at me for talking to Jennifer Caruso."

"His girlfriend?"

"In his dreams," Jon said, and Kate, still so furious she felt like she might explode, held her tongue. She'd known that Jon had a crush on someone, but so far had never heard a name. "Anyway, he came at me and we got into it and . . . oh, man . . ." He sighed loudly, crossed his arms over his chest, and reluctantly gave her the blow by blow, his face awash with color.

"I can't believe it," Kate said, sick inside when she realized how mortified her son was.

"Yeah, but even though I was in a fight with him, enough kids stuck up for me and told McPherson the truth—that Todd started it and there was no way I could back down. McPherson didn't really buy that, he's the kind of guy who thinks there's always a way to avoid a fight, but he knows what's gone on in the past.

So he suspended Todd for a week. I think Neider's dad had to come in because he might even be expelled."

"Good." Kate had had it. Even though the Neider boy never caught many breaks in life, it didn't make it right that he was always picking on younger, weaker kids. "I want to swear out a complaint against him. Then I'll tell his father that—"

"No!"

"What, but Jon—"

"What good did it do before? You talked to the sheriff and Daegan, he"—Jon's voice cracked—"he went over to Neider's place. All that did was get Todd a beating and make him madder. At me."

"He's a menace and dangerous and this time is different because you've got witnesses. Kids that will stick up for you and tell the police what happened. It's not speculation. And if as you say, his father's abusing him, then it's only right that Todd be placed in a foster home and—"

"No! Oh, man, he'd kill me! No police." Jon dug his heels in. "Just stay out of it."

"I can't!"

"The school's handling it."

"But next time it could be worse. I can't stand by and let some bully—"

"I mean it, Mom," he said in a voice that was so deadly calm it scared her. "If you go into the school and make a big stink or go see the sheriff again, it'll only be worse. Already the kids think I'm some kind of pansy because of you. So don't. McPherson will call you. You don't have to do any more. Besides—" He hesitated a second and he worried his lip. "I have this feeling . . . that Todd's gonna be in serious trouble."

"With his father?"

"Yeah, but it's more than that . . ."

"What?"

He shook his head. "Just leave it alone. Besides, it doesn't matter. I'm never going back to school anyway."

"Of course you are."

"No, Ma, I'm not," he said with such gritty determination she nearly believed him. "Never again."

"You'll change your mi—"

"I won't. Not after today." Jon was defiant, his eyes narrowing as if he hoped she'd argue with him, as if he still itched for a fight. Whistling to the dog, he strode through the back door, and Houndog, clumps of fur still uneven, darted outside.

Kate's fingers curled over the edge of the counter in a death grip. She wanted to run after her son and have this battle right now, but she knew instinctively that she had to give him a little time and space; they'd talk later, after dinner, when they were both calmer. But she was sick inside, her stomach churning, her anger snapping through her bones. Slowly and surely, Jon, the baby she'd adopted fifteen years before, was slipping through her fingers. It didn't matter that the visions he'd had months ago hadn't come true, that the man he feared hadn't shown up, just as certainly he was being ripped from her by his growing up. And she wasn't ready.

But he was right about one thing: she couldn't keep treating him as if he were seven.

Shoving her hair out of her eyes, she glanced out the window toward the copse of pine trees and the old McIntyre spread beyond. She suddenly felt hollow inside, the same emptiness she'd experienced from the moment Daegan had walked out her front door on Thanksgiving. It was silly, really, she thought as she poured the remainder of this morning's coffee down the sink and dumped the filter of wet grounds into the trash. She'd found herself listening for the sound of his truck or making up silly little excuses to go visit him— which she'd never done, thank God. She'd told Jon to avoid any contact with Daegan. He'd made it all too clear on Thanksgiving that he didn't want to get too close to them, that he planned to move, that in a matter of days or weeks he'd be gone. Whatever it was that had held him here had lost its allure.

Jon, standing under the old apple tree, looked suddenly like a man, much older than his fifteen years. Yes, he'd be leaving soon and she'd be alone. Just as she'd been before Tyrell Clark had changed the course of her life forever.

Houndog spied a ground squirrel in the wood pile and took off at a gallop. Jon's gaze followed the pup then moved farther away to the horizon and old Eli's cabin. Jon, too, was missing Daegan. How had she let that happen, she wondered, how had she let Daegan O'Rourke become so integral in their little family?

"Found him," VanHorn said through chattering teeth. Damn but it was cold and that howling wind—as swift as a freakin' hurricane. He was in a phone booth outside the local watering hole and a few drinks plus the knowledge that he'd finally located the boy elated him. He heard Robert's swift intake of breath.

"Where?"

Neils glanced up and down the main street where only a few pickups and cars pushed the speed limit. "Oregon. The town, if you can call it that, of Hopewell."

"Never heard of it."

"Not too many people have. Believe me it's nowhere. A good place to get lost."

"How is he?" Robert's voice shook with emotion.

"Fine, fine, a great kid," Neils lied, unwilling to pass along the information that the boy seemed to be an odd duck, that people felt sorry for his pretty little mother, that the kid was more than a handful and getting in trouble at school. No reason to upset Sullivan or give him a chance to have second thoughts. To tell the truth, the kid's reputation bothered Neils, and the sooner he was out of this Sullivan mess, the better. All he wanted was his money—truckloads of it. "I'll bring him to you, Mr. Sullivan," Neils promised. "Within the week."

"Good, good, now, what about the mother?"

"She might be a problem."

"I was afraid of that."

"From what everyone says, she's crazy about the kid."

"Then you'll just have to persuade her it would be in her best interests as well as the boy's for him to return to Boston. She wouldn't want to face formal charges of kidnapping, would she? How would her son feel about her then?"

"Good point, but there is one other slight problem," Neils admitted, wondering how much he should divulge. If his gut instincts were right about Jon's parentage, Robert might call him off, but if he held too much back, the old man wouldn't trust him.

"What problem?" Robert asked, sounding bored.

"Daegan O'Rourke."

"What about him?"

"He's here, too."

"What the hell's he doing there?" Robert was suddenly interested again. Good.

"Don't know, but I imagine he's looking for Bibi's son. I think they talked. She spent a couple hours in Montana on a layover of a flight to San Francisco a couple of months back. She must've told him to start searching for the boy."

"But why?"

"Don't know," Neils lied, already having put two and two together. If he wasn't mistaken, O'Rourke was the kid's real father. How about that? Frank's bastard siring one of his own—with his first cousin. Good-time Bibi getting it on with her black sheep of a cousin and having his illegitimate kid. Boy, would that make some of those stuffy old Sullivan ancestors roll over in their graves! Robert would probably have himself a heart attack and not have to worry about the damned prostate cancer. "But I intend to find out everything I can about Kate Summers and O'Rourke, as well as the kid."

Old Eli's cabin creaked in the wind that moaned across the valley. Daegan sipped coffee and knew that he couldn't put off the inevitable. He'd called a travel agent yesterday and his flight was scheduled for six this evening. He'd drive to Bend, take a small plane to Portland, and then hop aboard a red-eye that stopped in Chicago before landing in Boston, where he planned to square off with his uncle. It was time to own up to everything—put his cards on the table, then threaten Robert with a scandal that would ruin the Sullivan name forever if the old man didn't back off.

Still, despite his eagerness to confront Robert, Daegan was leery of leaving Jon unguarded. Daegan's Boston PI, Sandy Kavenaugh, had confirmed that Neils VanHorn had left town, so Daegan had stuck around here wondering if old Neils would show his face. Was he in Hopewell or somewhere else barking up the wrong tree? That was the part that bothered Daegan. He couldn't stay here and protect Kate and square off with Robert at the same time. According to Sandy, VanHorn was a little on the shady side, but he'd never been involved in anything overtly illegal. VanHorn might try to persuade Kate that she had to give up custody, but she would stand firm and he wouldn't force the issue. Or so Daegan hoped. He was counting on Neils's integrity and that worried him.

So Daegan would cut his trip to Boston short. Once

he'd dealt with Robert, he'd be back and this mess would be straightened out. Robert and the rest of the Sullivans would back off, VanHorn would return to Boston, Kate would have full never-to-be-doubted custody of her boy, and Daegan would move to Montana and never see them again.

That was the part that was the most difficult. "Hell," he muttered under his breath. The first order of the day would be the toughest, saying good-bye to Kate and Jon. He couldn't leave them without ending it once and for all. He had no choice but to turn his back on them in order to ensure that they would be safe from the Sullivans forever.

A sour taste filled the back of his mouth, and a deep rendering, a pain like none he'd ever imagined, tore at his soul. Never in his life had he wanted home and hearth—a wife and kid. No, he'd believed himself to be a loner. He had shunned the family who hadn't wanted him in the first place and become a man who needed no one—not even his own mother. Now, after meeting Kate and Jon, he doubted his deepest convictions.

He finished his coffee in one gulp and refused to dwell on everything he found fascinating about Kate— her whiskey-colored eyes, her soft little smile, or the sheen of her hair when the sun's rays set it on fire. He'd make a point of forgetting how beautiful her breasts were, forgetting the soft contented sighs deep in her throat when he kissed her.

Nor would he allow himself to remember how easy his relationship had become with Jon, how natural, how he looked forward to spending hours with the boy teaching him everything from shoeing a horse to shoring up a sagging fence post. "Idiot," he muttered as he kicked back his chair and tossed the remains of his coffee into the stained sink.

Snow piled against the windows, and the lack of insulation was evident in the drafty kitchen. It was amazing old Eli had lasted as long as he had living in these conditions.

Turning his collar against the wind, Daegan dashed through the drifts to his pickup and hoped that he could catch Jon before the boy took off for school. It was best to get this over with. Now or never. He was going to say good-bye to a son who would never know him.

Chapter 21

The images came on so quickly, biting into Jon's consciousness as he worked the bar of soap into a lather in the shower.

Soaping up one arm, he felt an odd tenderness around his wrist, and suddenly both forearms were bruised and raw, encased in unforgiving steel bands.

Handcuffs.

The soap dropped to the shower floor as he held his arms up to the warm spray and studied his skin. Nope, normal. All a trick of his mind, which was the last thing he needed this morning, his first day back at school.

He reached for the shampoo bottle and leaned against the shower wall, trying to relax as hot beads of water pelted his skin. How could his mother think it would be good for him to get back to school? Despite his protests, she and McPherson had cooked up this morning's plan, clueless to the dangers that awaited him there. Maybe the halls were safe for a normal kid, but he was no normal kid. Hard to believe that after all this time, his mom still didn't get it.

His fingers raked through his hair, scraping lather

over his scalp. A glob of foam ran down over one eye. When he quickly swiped it away and opened his eyes, he was staring out through bars—some sort of metallic cage. Staring out through dark glass windows as a blur of landscape raced past the speeding vehicle that propelled him forward against his will.

What the hell . . . ? Panic surged through him as he flattened his palms against one window and banged in desperation. He had to get out! Why couldn't anyone see him, hear his cries? His hands coiled into fists that pounded the glass in desperation.

And just as suddenly, the dark window beneath his hands became the white fiberglass wall of the shower stall. The roar of the vehicle's engine was now the sizzle of the water as it sprayed over him.

It was all in his head. Another freakin' vision.

Quickly, he rinsed himself and cut the shower off. His heart was still pounding as he threw the curtain aside and stepped out into billowing clouds of steam. What the hell did it all mean, handcuffs and a cage inside a car? Was Todd planning some kind of kinky torture for him now?

He toweled off, trying to shake off the weird vision. When he wiped the layer of moisture from the mirror over the sink, he was surprised by his own reflection: the curve of the muscles in his arms and shoulders. Biceps. Working out with Daegan was beginning to pay off. Another few weeks and he'd actually be buff.

If, of course, Daegan was going to stay another few weeks, which he wasn't. Wrapping a towel around his waist, Jon decided he shouldn't let his new pumped-up body go to waste. Sign-ups for track were going on at school, and Jon knew he was a fast runner. He would sign up today, but Mom didn't have to know until after the tryouts. The last thing he needed was her pushing him to get out there and make some friends. Yeah, right.

He pulled on jeans, a T-shirt, and a flannel shirt, then hearing his mother downstairs in the kitchen, crept into her bedroom. The top drawer of her dresser was where she kept loose change, old bills, photographs, and family documents. Somewhere in these stacks of folders and envelopes was his birth certificate, which he'd need to sign up for the track team. Reaching into the drawer, he sifted through papers, thumbing the corner of files marked: BILLS, TAXES, and MEDICAL.

His birth certificate was in a folder on the bottom, its embossed seal from the Commonwealth of Massachusetts catching his eye as he slid it out. Did his mom ever wish she'd stayed in Boston? He wondered about it sometimes, but always figured she'd needed to get away from the memory of his dad.

The crystal paperweight on the dresser glimmered in the dim lamplight as he slid the drawer closed. Mom had always loved this thing, a glass porcupine. He picked it up in one palm and immediately felt seared by the energy encapsulated in the glass.

A name flashed before him: Tyrell Clark.

He wasn't familiar with the name, but it had popped quickly into his mind along with a vision of a dark-haired man in a fancy suit. Tall, dark, handsome, and a little cheesy. Jon didn't know who the man was, but he sensed his mother's strong disdain for him.

And his mom . . . she was so much younger, like a college kid, her brown eyes outlined in makeup.

"I'm offering you a son," Tyrell says as he tosses the glass paperweight into the air and catches it. "No strings attached."

He can feel his mother's shock and fear. *"You—you want me to adopt him?"*

Adoption . . .

Stunned, Jon fell back onto her bed and let the crystal paperweight drop from his hands to the thick comforter. Adoption? It couldn't be true. His father was Jim Summers, the man who was killed when he was . . .

He stared at the birth certificate in his hand, the sharp pain in his gut telling him to put the facts together. It was true. Undeniable. Hadn't he always wondered why he didn't resemble his mother? He was adopted, and she'd been lying to him all along . . . all his life.

Fifteen years old, and so far, his entire life was a lie.

Kate hung up the phone, but the sound of Don McPherson's voice rang in her head. True, he was giving Jon another chance but there had been a hint of doubt in his words. She knew that deep down the vice principal was hoping that Jon would transfer to a different school and become one less problem for Don McPherson.

"Jon," she called up the stairs. "Hurry up. The bus'll be here in less than ten minutes."

"I know," he said and thundered down the stairs, his hair still wet, his expression unforgiving. He blamed her for forcing him to go back to school.

She had his breakfast, toaster waffles and orange juice, on the counter. He ignored the food and snagged his backpack and jacket from pegs mounted near the back door.

"I'll be home late," he said, reaching for the doorknob.

"Late? Why?"

He stared at her and his expression didn't soften. "Group project." It was a lie and they both knew it.

"Can't you do it here?"

"No, Ma, we can't." He opened the door and she reached forward, not wanting him to leave with such bad feelings—hoping to mend fences.

"If you want, I could drive you," she offered, but he just stared at her hand, touching his bare arm, and he swallowed hard. Drawing away from her, he took a step back. "Jesus."

"Jon?"

Running his tongue around his teeth, he shook his head. "No," he whispered, his voice strange and unfamiliar. "I—I don't believe it."

"What?"

"You . . . you've lied to me."

"About what?" she asked, but his eyes, wide and serious, glared at her, and he swallowed as if there wasn't a drop of spit in his mouth.

"Who's Tyrell Clark?"

"Oh, God." Her knees nearly buckled. Somehow he'd broken through and seen her thoughts.

"Who is he?" Jon demanded, his voice rough, his expression still as death.

"A man—he's dead now," she admitted, her throat barely working, her insides trembling. Why hadn't she told him before? Why did she let it go so long so that he had to find out this way?

"You're not my real mother," he accused her, backing away from her as if being in the same room was against everything in which he believed. "Oh, God, you're not my mother!"

"Of course I am."

"But I'm adopted!" he accused her. "Adopted!"

There it was, hanging in the air between them. The lie. The one they'd lived with for fifteen years. "Yes," she admitted, her voice catching. There was no reason to keep up pretenses any longer. All the lies she'd so carefully constructed over the years were falling around her feet in ruin and dust. "I—I adopted you. Soon after Jim and Erin died," she said, her voice empty. "And I wouldn't

have loved you any more if I'd carried you in my body
and—"

"Don't!" he said, nearly frantic, his hands on either
side of his head. "This Tyrell guy—was he my father?"

"No—I don't think so."

"This is so weird," he said, eyes blazing with accusations. "Were you ever going to tell me?"

"Of course."

"When?"

"When the time was right," she said, trying to stay
calm though her heart was thundering and her throat
was tight.

"And when was that going to be?"

*Tell the truth, Kate. Don't back down now. No matter how
much it hurts.* "I don't know. I—I wanted to, but you were
too young to understand, and then, once you were
older, I was afraid."

"Of what?"

"That I'd lose you," she admitted.

"I can't believe this." He looked at her as if she were
the embodiment of evil, as if everything she'd ever
taught him wasn't to be trusted, as if his entire life was a
lie.

"Jon—" She reached forward, but he stepped away, as
if afraid to let her touch him again. "I think we should
talk this out."

"No way! I don't want to talk about it. You lied to me.
Daegan lied to me. Everyone lied to me."

"No! Oh, baby, no."

"Don't call me that ever again. I'm not and never will
be *your* baby." Angrily he shoved his arms into the
sleeves of his jacket.

"If you don't want to go to school, if you want to ask
me any questions—"

"Why? So you can lie to me again?" he said, nearly
tripping over Houndog as he backed to the door, and

for the first time since he'd been in the fight with Todd, he seemed anxious to return to Hopewell High. His fingers scrabbled for the knob.

"We'll talk about this tonight, when you get home. I'll explain everything."

"You bet you will," he said, his lips white with fury.

"Jon, trust me—"

He made a sound of disgust deep in his throat. "I think it's only fair that I know who I really am."

"You're my son," she called after him, but he was already off the porch and running through the blanket of snow, his head ducked against the wind. "You always will be." But her words bounced off the walls of the little house and echoed around her, mocking her—calling her every kind of fool, letting her know that she'd lost her boy forever.

"Damn it," she muttered, fighting tears, her fists curled into balls of frustration. She couldn't lose him! No way. No how. Jon was her son and he was only fifteen, not old enough to make any life-altering decisions. He might be hurt or angry, but he was still her boy and she'd fight tooth and nail to prove it.

She was still trying to pull herself together when she heard the rumble of a truck's engine, and her heart, in eager anticipation, kicked into high gear. Houndog began barking, and through the window she saw Daegan's ugly green pickup and the cowboy himself, stretching out of the cab. Her breath caught somewhere deep in her lungs at the sight of him, tall and lean, his features as rough-hewn as the mountains to the west. A stranger and yet intimate, a man she didn't dare trust but to whom she'd already carelessly given her heart. Before his boots stopped ringing on the steps of the porch, she flung open the door.

"Hi, I—Something's wrong," he guessed, his eyes narrowing on her face. "Jon?"

"He's . . . he's fine, I think," she said, drawing on some inner reserve of strength she didn't know she had. "Or he will be."

"Neider used him for a punching bag?"

"That's part of the problem." How much did she dare tell him? He was leaving soon anyway; what could he possibly care about her or her son? Yet the glint of anger in his eyes convinced her that in his own way he was concerned.

"What's the other part?"

"It's personal."

He waited, kicking the door closed with his foot.

"I don't suppose it matters anymore," she allowed. Now that Jon knew the truth, there was no reason to protect him any longer. "Jon and I got into an argument this morning," she admitted, watching Daegan's reaction. "And . . . and he found out that he's adopted."

A jolt, like a ragged bolt of lightning, passed behind Daegan's eyes. "I thought—"

Waving away his arguments, she said, "I told everyone he was mine, including Jon, and there just never seemed the right moment to explain that he was adopted." Tears burned behind her eyes but she wouldn't give in to them. "It doesn't matter to me that someone else gave him life. I love him as much as if I'd carried him for nine months. Oh, I don't know why I'm telling you all this. Jon will come home after school, we'll hash this out and then, I suppose, if he wants to, I'll help him try to locate his birth parents."

"Who are?" he prodded, an edge to his voice.

"I don't know." How much should she confide? How much could she? She let out a sigh. "But you didn't come here to listen to me go on and on." Her heart tugged as she met his gaze. "I thought you were leaving."

"Tonight."

Oh, God. Her world was crumbling apart. "So soon?"

"I'll be back to move the animals, but I've got some business I've got to take care of and it won't wait."

Her throat was suddenly clogged and her heart beat a desperate, painful rhythm. "Jon will miss you."

"And you?" he asked, stepping closer to her, studying her with an intensity that burned straight to her soul.

"No way," she lied, but her lip quivered, belying her words. His gaze shifted, and slowly he lowered his head, brushing his mouth over hers so gently she thought her heart would surely break.

"Good thing you're so tough," he said, then linked his fingers through hers. "Come on. Grab a jacket."

"Why?"

"I think you need to get out of here."

"But my job—"

He leveled a flinty gaze at her that cut her to the quick. "You deserve a day off."

"You make it sound very appealing, but I'm not the sort of person who blows off work just because . . ." *Because my world is falling apart,* she wanted to say. *Because you're leaving and it's my last chance to be near you, to savor your lips brushing against mine the way they just did.*

"Come on, Kate." His fingers tightened over her hands, seductive and convincing, chasing away any lingering doubts. "It's my last day in Hopewell."

Liar. All these years his mother had been a liar.

Correction . . . the woman he'd *thought* was his mother.

Jon kicked at a stone along the roadside, sending it skittering ahead over the frozen earth into a ditch. She'd lied to him all along, treated him like a baby, an idiot who couldn't handle the truth.

Her deception made Jon feel sick, his emotions raw

and tender at the knowledge that she'd controlled and manipulated his life all these years, hiding the things that were most important. He was in no mood to actually go to school now, but he didn't have much choice. On a frozen autumn day in Hopewell, Oregon, there weren't a lot of recreational options for kids cutting school.

He would get on the bus, keep his head down, eyes on the ground, and push through the day. Basic survival was the only plan for a day like today. His feet scraped the ground, the toe of his sneaker rolling a handful of pebbles down toward a white van on the side of the road. Some guy kneeled beside it—no one Jon recognized. The man was working a jack under the van, just replacing a tire.

Seeing that no traffic was in sight, Jon cut a wide swath around the van, stepping onto the black tar roadway.

"Pretty cold morning," the man called cheerfully. His breath lingered in puffs before his face.

"Yeah." Jon walked past the van as a few snowflakes sank through the air. Snow . . . what else could go wrong? An inch or two of snow and they'd close the school, sending him home to have to deal with her . . . his so-called mother.

"Hey, can you give me a hand?" the man asked, interrupting Jon's thoughts.

Jon turned and saw that the man was now in front of the van, tire iron in one hand. He wore a belted leather coat—one of those long coats that came down to his knees. The guy had to be a city slicker, not from around here.

"I have to catch my bus," Jon said, gesturing down the road. The man's smile was making him uncomfortable.

"I don't think so, Jon," the man said, quickly pushing back his coat and pulling something from his waistband.

A gun . . . pointed right at Jon.

Jon's throat went dry. Shit! "How do you know my name?"

The man nodded toward the back of the van. "Get in. We'll have time to talk inside. Plenty of time."

Quickly, Jon weighed his options. He was a fast runner. If he made a break for it, he could be down the road in seconds, darting off the roadside to hide behind trees or bushes. He was fast . . . but a bullet was faster, and the ditch at the roadside was too steep to cross. He'd be trapped down there, a clear target.

He strained to hear the rumble of an approaching car, the hum of tires on pavement, but there was only silence. A passing car could save him now, but who was going to be heading this way at this time of the morning? Sure, the school bus would pull by the intersection ahead, but that was a good half mile away, out of sight.

His eyes swung back to the gun, the metal pistol aimed at his heart and coming closer as the man approached.

"Got a problem, kid?" the man said, striding toward him. Keeping the gun trained on Jon's chest, he reached down and snapped something over Jon's right wrist. "Hands in front of you," he ordered, and when Jon raised his arms, he watched as the cuff was clipped over his left wrist.

Handcuffs.

The sight sent him reeling back to the vision. Oh, God.

His throat grew tight, knowing the future, knowing that his wrists would become red and raw from trying to writhe out of these things. It would hurt like hell, but

he'd have to try. He had to get away from this man, because everything in his gut told him this guy was the
one chasing him in his nightmares.

The killer.

Oh, God. This was the man . . . the gun . . .

His heart pounded, his pulse thrumming at the realization that this was the man who wanted to end his life.

"That's better," the man said, his tone light, as if they
were talking about the weather. "Things'll go a hell of a
lot better if you follow along, Jon. Now, into the van."
When Jon approached the passenger door, he shook
his head. "Nah, no death seat for you, kid. You're riding
in the back. I told your grandfather I'd take good care
of you. Luxury accommodations all the way."

"My grandfather?" Jon said. "He's been dead a long
time. You got the wrong person, man."

"You Jon Summers?" the man pulled open the back
door of the van. When Jon nodded, he said, "Then
you're mine now, kid. You're all mine."

Glancing into the van, Jon felt fear stab through his
chest at the sight of the bars separating the front seat
from the back.

Here was the metallic cage . . . the dark tinted glass . . .
the horrors of his vision.

His nightmare was unfolding before him.

He had seen his own death in his dreams, and now
his life was collapsing around him.

"Come on, kid," the man said, shoving Jon into the
darkness. "We've got miles to go before we sleep."

I will always remember this day, Kate thought as she
watched Daegan saddle both horses. First Jon learning
that he was adopted, and now Daegan leaving . . . it was
too much to absorb, too much difficult emotion jam-
packed into a short period of time. As soon as Kate had

called the college, they'd driven over to Daegan's place, where he'd filled a thermos with coffee and started saddling the horses, despite the cold temperatures. Inside the old McIntyre barn, away from the wind, it was warmer, but the animals snorted nervously as their hooves pawed the straw in anticipation of the cold outside. Bridles jangled as Daegan snapped them into place.

"If you haven't noticed," she said, eyeing him suspiciously as he packed the thermos into a battle-scarred saddlebag, "it's snowing outside."

He shrugged. "A few little flakes. Nothing to worry about."

"Nearly a blizzard," she protested.

He buckled the saddlebag and extra blanket behind the saddle, then threw her a look over his shoulder. "Not in Montana, it isn't. Come on, let's get you better acquainted with Loco, here."

"I should have my head examined," she muttered under her breath but followed him outside. He rode Buckshot and she settled into the gray's saddle, following the colt through a gate to a longer field that wound up through the foothills.

The wind was chill against her back, but there was an air of exhilaration about riding through the snow-crusted fields and across a small creek that was nearly frozen. Only a trickle of water still gurgled over ice-covered rocks.

Daegan sat tall in the saddle, reining in the nervous colt, keeping to a steady path that curved past a thicket of naked trees far from the house. Twisting upward through a narrow draw, the trail cut through the steep hills to level at a ridge overlooking the valley. Far below she saw her house, snow piling on the roof.

Daegan helped her off, spread a bedroll over the ground, and poured coffee into the metal cup of the thermos. "I discovered this place the second week I was here. Seems like a good spot to unwind."

"And why would you need to 'unwind'?" she asked, the warmth of her cup seeping through her gloves.

"Everyone does. Thought it might help you today."

"And the day is yet young." She laughed without much mirth. "What is it, not quite nine-thirty, and it already seems like a torture that's gone on for hours?"

He grinned that sexy off-center smile that caused her heart to skip a beat, then took a swallow straight from the thermos. "Things can only get better."

Not when I know you're leaving. "Oh yeah, how?"

"You want me to show you?"

She licked her lips. "Show me what?"

"This." His lips were feather-light and laced with coffee as they slid over hers. "And this." He set his thermos in the snow, took the cup from her fingers and wedged it up against the root of a tree, then wrapped his arms around her. Gazing into her eyes, he settled his mouth over hers, and a part of her, a vital, very feminine part, responded. He made no promises, told her no lies, but kissed her so hard she couldn't breathe, couldn't think.

Snowflakes fell from the sky, catching in his hair and on her eyelashes, and yet her skin was warm, her heart a wild drum, the ache deep within her beginning to pulse. "Kate," he mouthed against her skin. "Kate, Kate, Kate."

His voice cracked and she nearly cried. He was leaving and she couldn't bear the thought of never seeing him again, never touching him, never hearing his voice. She kissed him desperately, her hands holding his face, her eyes burning with tears.

Don't leave me, she silently begged, though her pride wouldn't allow her to whisper so much as a tiny plea. He kissed her lips, her cheeks, the shell of her ear, and she quivered inside, wanting more, kissing and touching and tasting him, believing that this crystalline morning was the last time she'd ever feel like a woman, ever have a chance to make love with him.

Gaze still locked with hers, he yanked off his gloves with his teeth and his fingers found the zipper of her jacket. It slid quickly open and Kate didn't protest, but helped him shed the unwanted denim. He trembled as she kissed him back, her tongue finding his, her passion colliding with his, her heart thundering in a shared cadence with his.

Groaning, he lifted her sweater over her head then slid the strap of her bra over her arm to free her breast. Snowflakes collected on her bare skin and he kissed them away before the powdery sprigs of ice could melt.

"Daegan," she cried as cold air blew over her nipple and it puckered. His tongue, hot and slick, rimmed the anxious bud. "Please," she cried, bowing upward, tangling her fingers in his thick hair, wanting so much. She ached inside with yearning, a throb so deep it pulsed in the darkest part of her.

Finally his lips clamped over her nipple and she cried out as he suckled hard and firm, pulling and drawing while his thumb teased her other breast.

The world began to spin as his tongue tickled and teased. *Love me, oh, Daegan, please, just love me!* His fingers skimmed her skin as they moved lower to the waistband of her jeans. With a quick hiss the zipper gave way and he slid his fingers over her skin, shucking off her jeans to delve beneath the elastic of her panties, skimming hot fingers over the nest of curls at the juncture of her legs. Her hips lifted of their own accord and he kissed her there, through the nylon, hot breath against cold skin and moist curls.

"Be patient, darlin'," he drawled through the lacy fabric. "We've got all day."

But Kate was ready. It had been so long, so very long

since she'd made love to a man, and now that she knew this was her one chance, her only chance to love Daegan, she couldn't stop herself.

She shuddered as his fingers grazed her skin and delved. She cried out, feeling hot as warm honey where he touched her, and when he finally stripped her of that last flimsy barrier, she couldn't wait. "That's my girl," he said, his breath whispering deep inside her as he kissed her lovingly in her most intimate of places, his tongue playing with the bud of desire that welcomed him.

He lifted her knees onto his broad shoulders, and slowly, drawing out her exquisite torture, he kissed and touched her. She was swept in a whirlpool of sensation and her heart, drumming so loudly she thought it might burst, was a wild thing. "Let go," he murmured and she did. The world tilted and stars flashed behind her eyes. She bucked and cried out and slowly he released her, stripping himself of shirt, jacket, and jeans, laying his long, sinewy body over hers, kissing her so hard she was sure she would die.

Her fingers explored him, touched him where she never would have dared, thrilled by the textures of hair, bone, and muscle as he came to her, parting her legs, prodding her with his erection, delving deep into her very soul with that first, mesmerizing thrust.

"Love me, Kate," he cried, thrusting hard enough to force her to catch her breath before withdrawing slowly. "Love me."

"I do," she cried, tears falling from her eyes as he buried himself in her again. "Oh, Lord, Daegan, I do." And his tempo increased, faster and faster, harder and harder, hotter and hotter, he moved, gritting his teeth, holding back, denying himself until finally she convulsed. And then with a cry as wild and raw as the storm surrounding them, he poured himself into her and collapsed, sweat sheening his corded muscles as he fell against her.

Kate clung to him, her passion spent, her mind still dizzy with the colors of a kaleidoscope. Why was she fated to love this man who had come a stranger and in the course of a few short weeks become her lover?

He kissed her and she blinked against the wash of tears and the snow still falling from a gunmetal sky. "Better?" he asked.

"Mmm." She stretched languidly and watched as his eyes, so recently glazed with passion, focused on her face.

Silently he toyed with a strand of her hair. "This was probably a mistake."

"There's no probably about it."

He glanced to the heavens, then closed his eyes and rolled off her. "I didn't mean for things to go so far."

Already he regretted making love to her! Disappointment shot through her, and her pride, so battered earlier, came back full force. She didn't lament a single kiss; if he was leaving, she wanted something to remember him by. "Neither did I."

"But I wouldn't change anything."

Relief swept through her and he kissed her softly on the cheek. She shivered and he gathered her into his naked arms, kissing her crown as the breeze teased at her hair. His naked chest, all tough, rigid muscle, pressed hard against her. He held on tight, as if he was afraid of losing her, as if he, too, wanted to deny the horrid truth that he was leaving.

"You're one helluva woman, Kate Summers," he whispered. "I never expected this. Never."

She nearly sobbed as she clung to him, and when his lips found hers once more, she was eager, hungry, anxious to join with him again, to prove deep in her heart that their attraction was more than physical, that theirs was a spiritual and emotional melding as well.

She thrilled to his touch, and this time she touched him everywhere, her fingers brushing across the hard wall of muscles that was his chest, to tease his flat nipples. He groaned and kissed her so breathlessly she could hardly think, then she reached lower, feeling the curve of his spine, his buttocks, his legs... "Sweet Jesus," he whispered, half in prayer, as she slid her fingers around his erection and soon he could stand the torturous pleasure no more. He pulled her on top of him and lifted his hips to pierce her. She folded over him and he cried out in ecstasy, then savagely thrust again, holding her close, his mouth and tongue finding her breasts, licking, kissing, teasing, suckling as he made love to her.

With a cry she felt the earth tremble and she fell forward, feeling him shudder beneath her, his arms opening to catch her and wrap possessively over her, his breathing as torn and shallow as hers.

"Daegan," she whispered and he dragged her jacket over them, kissing her temple and eyes as her heartbeat finally slowed. "Oh, Daegan."

"I love you," he murmured into her ear, and her tears began to flow as he stroked her hair. "No matter what else happens, believe that I love you as I've loved no other woman." His words rang like the knell of doom. A deep wracking sob tore from her throat and he sighed against her hair, then pushed her away from him so that he could stare into her eyes. She saw the shadows of sadness in his gaze, the quiet determination, and her heart shattered.

"You're going to leave me."

"I have to."

"But why?" she cried and he silently cursed himself. He couldn't tell her that he was Jon's father, that it was better for her and Jon if he disappeared from their lives and made sure that they were never bothered by the Sullivan family again. "I would stay if I could," he swore, "but I can't." He stroked her cheek with a finger and felt the moistness of her tears. Damning himself silently, he kissed her again. "Come on, we can go back to the house and spend the rest of the day in bed."

She shook her head. "Not if you're leaving."

He couldn't help cocking an insolent eyebrow. "So now you want to barter?"

"How can you joke about this?" she said, her eyes brimming. "I love you, Daegan O'Rourke. I don't want to, in fact I curse myself every time I think about it, but I can't help it. I love you."

The words seemed to crack in the cold autumn air.

"Jon loves you, too."

His heart, already bruised, suffered another blow.

"How can you disappoint him?"

"I have to," was all he said as he handed her her jeans. Sniffling loudly, she dressed, but she was obviously through begging and pleading and having her self-worth dragged through the mud. He watched as her shoulders stiffened and pride straightened her backbone.

Good. She'd need all the strength she could round up.

They dressed and rode back to the house in silence, leaving their hearts and vows of love on the ridge. Daegan mentally kicked himself over and over again for making love to her—not that he wouldn't do it over again if he had the chance. God, she was beautiful and prideful and loving and more woman than he'd ever met before, but by making love to her, he'd stepped across a line that was too dangerous to even contemplate—emotional commitment which he could never vow.

After taking care of the horses and leaving them with

fresh hay and water in the barn, he offered her more coffee, which she drank slowly in Eli McIntyre's dilapidated little kitchen. Though sadness lingered in her eyes, she managed a half smile. "I can't imagine anyone wanting to give up all this luxury," she teased.

"It's hard."

"But Montana beckons?"

"It was a mistake to think I needed to move away."

Her gaze held his. "There must be another reason." Was it his imagination or did the cup in her fingers tremble slightly?

Time to come up with a lie that will make her hate you so that she never comes looking. "There is."

He counted out the seconds in the pulse at her throat. She didn't move, and quiet despair twisted her features. "Which is?"

"I was running away."

"Do I want to know from what?"

"Probably not."

"Oh, God, you have a wife."

He should have said "yes" and gotten it over with. Instead he said, "Ex-wife."

"And children?" she barely said.

His throat closed in on itself. "A . . . a son. About Jon's age. He, uh, lives with his mother and it's probably better that way. I wasn't much of a father."

Disbelief clouded her eyes. "But you're so good with Jon." Her voice failed her. "You lied to me."

"Yes." *Oh, lady, if you only knew.* "But you lied, too. About Jon."

"You were going to leave and not let me know."

"No, I came by to say good-bye."

"Even though we made love."

He reached across the table and took her hand in his. "Believe me, I'll never regret it."

Her life, already falling apart, seemed to unravel even further. He read the pain in her eyes. "That's it? It's over?" Disbelief warred with disappointment.

It will never be over. Not with you and me. He felt it in his soul. "It has to be."

"You *bastard!* You lying, no-good . . ." Before her anger carried her away, she stopped and stared at him for a heart-splintering second. Standing abruptly, she let out a little sound of protest and dropped her cup, sloshing coffee. "Good-bye, Daegan," she said, snagging her jacket from the arm of the couch and heading out the door.

"Kate—" If only he could tell her the truth, let her know how he felt, who he really was . . .

She was already outside, down the steps, plowing through the snow, striding as if she couldn't get away from him fast enough. Swearing under his breath, he ran to the truck, fired the engine, and took off after her. He caught up with her before she'd reached the end of the lane.

"Get in," he commanded, rolling down the window. Her face was red, her jaw set, snow collecting in her hair.

"Go to hell."

"Kate, please—"

"Just leave, Daegan," she said, reaching the county road and turning into her own lane. "That's what you're going to do anyway."

He couldn't fault her logic. "Get into the truck."

She whirled on him then, fury masking her features. "And you get the hell off my land." Again she strode away from him, her fists knotted in anger, her breath fogging furiously in the air.

She turned again, walking briskly, but he followed her, and when she reached the house, he climbed out of the pickup and barged up the front steps. She tried to bar the door, but he forced his way past her. Knowing he should let her hate him, he stood in the living room of her cozy little house.

"What do you want?" she demanded. "Another romp in the snow?"

The barb stung. "I just want you to know that I didn't lie about anything I said or did up on the ridge."

She made a sound of deprecation and walked into the kitchen. "I don't know why you're here."

"Neither do I." She turned then and he held out his hands. "I should just let it go, Kate. The best thing for both of us is for me to walk out the door, but I don't want to leave until you understand that, despite everything, I love you and I will always love you."

Closing her eyes as if to shield herself, she reached for the telephone answering machine and pushed the PLAY button. "Don't do this, Daegan. Don't tease. Just leave. Now."

"I will. But just know that I care, Kate. I care a helluva lot."

Tears ran down her cheeks and she brushed them quickly away. "Okay, you've made me cry. Is that what you want?"

"No."

"Mrs. Summers," a male voice said and her eyes flew open. "Don McPherson at the school—"

"Oh, no," she whispered, shaking her head. "Not now, not again."

"We're calling all our absentees who don't have pre-arranged excuses or who haven't called into the attendance secretary. We assume you're aware that Jon is on the list."

Neils VanHorn had never slept with his silent partner, though he'd spent more than one night in bed with other women picturing the perfect, aquiline contours of her face. Fantasies of her long legs wrapped around his torso, her bloodred manicured nails digging into his back, were the one thing that kept him on her payroll, despite the dangers of being caught.

Now, as he pumped quarters into the pay phone at a truck stop on some godforsaken stretch of Idaho highway, he had to admit that she frightened him more than a little. Just like the kid locked in the van, working to slide the cuffs off when he thought Neils wasn't looking. The kid had such a hollow look in his eyes, like a goddamned zombie. Neils must have scared the piss out of him when he pulled that gun. Grimacing, Neils shot a look at the van across the parking lot. He had played a part in some half-baked investigations before, but kidnapping was a first for him, and it was all a worry. Maybe he should have insisted that Robert pay him more up front. Maybe he should forget about trying to get the woman into bed and just deliver the kid to the old man.

But then her sultry voice came on the line and Neils's manhood sprung to attention. Just at the sound of her voice. Damn, he had it bad.

"You've got the boy," she said, the excitement in her voice making him go harder.

"That's right."

"Where is he?"

"Safe," Neils replied, enjoying verbally sparring with her. "You know I can't tell you where he is until we strike a deal. But I'm bringing him your way. Robert wants to see him."

"Bad idea. I don't want him here. And I thought we agreed that I'd pay you twice what Robert offered."

"I know, I know," Neils admitted, raking his hair back with one hand. Over the phone he could hear soft music—a symphony or something—playing behind her. Classy lady. "But it depends on what you want me to do."

"A deal is a deal."

"Is it? I don't think so. Otherwise I wouldn't be double-crossing your uncle now."

Although she was thousands of miles away, he could feel her contempt over the phone line. How he'd love to play with her, whip her into an angry frenzy, then wrestle her to the floor, pinning her beneath him.

"If you don't go through with your end of the bargain," she said in measured beats, "I'll go to Robert and tell him you tried to up the ante by dealing with me."

He imagined her in schoolmarm glasses, threatening to whip him with a yard-long pointer. *Yeah, baby. Whip me hard.*

"I don't think so," he said, enjoying the fantasies, loving the fact that he had the upper hand.

"I told you I'd pay double for finding the boy," she growled. "But I'll add a bonus, Neils. I'll pay you twice that if you get rid of him for me."

Neils froze. He didn't like the turn in the conversation. Sure, the kid gave him the creeps, but he didn't want anything really bad to happen to the boy. Hell, that'd be murder. Not his thing. Christ, wasn't kidnapping bad enough?

She sighed. "Ah, Neils, so naive." He couldn't tell if she was amused or mocking him until she went on. "Don't be an idiot. Do you really expect me to pay top dollar for you to let that bastard free? Just do yourself and me a favor and kill him." Her voice oozed with impatience, malice, and blood lust. "Kill him now."

Chapter 22

Kate stared at the clock. Three-thirty and still no word from Jon. She'd called the sheriff, but Swanson wasn't interested. Not until Jon had been missing for twenty-four hours. The police in town were no more anxious to help her. The school hadn't seen him. Daegan had gone out searching for Jon but hadn't found hide nor hair of the boy.

She drummed her fingers on the counter and thought she'd go mad with worry. Outside the snow continued to fall, and as night was approaching, she could only wonder where he was, with whom, doing what? She'd called all his friends once they were home from school, but no one had seen him all day. Daegan had even driven over to the Neider place, but no one was home.

"He'll be all right," Daegan said, standing at the window and staring toward the end of the lane.

Kate had wanted to throw him out, to tell the liar to just leave and let her worry about her boy. But the lines of strain on his face, the way he'd called his travel agent and changed his flight, convinced her that he cared, if only a little. And she liked having him around, damn it,

even if she did feel a little like a weak woman who was
finding her strength from his.

He'd made coffee for her, built a fire, taken Roscoe
and Houndog and searched the places where he'd expected a boy to hole up. And now they waited.

The phone rang and she nearly jumped out of her
skin. Dashing to the kitchen, she picked up the receiver
before the second ring.

"Hello?" she said and met Daegan's dark gaze. Though
he was still in the living room, she could see the worry
in his eyes.

"Kate?" Laura's voice sang over the wires. "Are you
all right? You sound breathless."

"It's Jon. He's missing." She shook her head at Daegan,
silently communicating that there was no news about
her boy. "I—I can't tie up the phone too long in case he
calls." Quickly she told her sister what had been going
on, only holding back on her involvement with Daegan.
To think that while Jon was missing, she was making love
in the snow to Daegan . . .

When she was finished, there was a weighty pause on
the other end of the line. "Maybe this isn't a good time
for me to give you my news," she said.

"What news?"

"About Daegan O'Rourke."

Kate's gaze flew to the living room, where Daegan
was standing glaring out at the dark sky. Her heart
pounded with dread. *Not now, oh, please not now!* "Tell
me," she said, her insides already beginning to shred.

"Okay, but it's not pretty. It turns out that the
Daegan O'Rourke from Montana did grow up in Boston,
the son of Mary Ellen O'Rourke and Frank Sullivan.
Mary Ellen was Frank's mistress and he, being already
married, didn't divorce his wife. Instead he kept
Mary Ellen as his mistress in a small apartment over
some dive of a tavern."

Kate's heart twisted for the little boy Daegan had been, but fear curled in her heart. Who was this man? What did he want? Was he the criminal—Jon's natural father?

"Anyway, Frank Sullivan's a real bad egg, the worst. Treated Daegan like he didn't exist."

"You found all this out through records?" *Oh, God, now what? She loved Daegan, trusted him, believed in him.* A part of her began to wither as quickly as a flower in the desert.

"Nah, I dug around a little bit on my free time. I have a friend who's a PI who used to work for the police department as a detective. She did some snooping and this is what we came up with."

Kate swallowed back her dread and listened.

"Anyway this kid—Daegan O'Rourke—was really messed up and tried to shoot his old man once, but the shot went wild and the Sullivans managed to sweep it all under the rug—nothing in the papers, no charges filed."

"None?"

"That's right. A while later the legitimate Sullivan offspring got together with their bastard cousin and the fireworks really started."

Kate leaned against the cupboard for support. Her palms were sweating, her mind racing with images of Daegan teaching Jon to ride a horse, showing him how to box, lying above her ready to make love in the middle of a snowstorm.

As if sensing something was wrong, Daegan gave up his post and walked to the kitchen. He was reaching for the coffeepot when his hand stopped in midair, and as if by silent communication, he divined the tenor of her conversation.

Laura continued blithely on, unaware that Kate held Daegan's stare and noiseless messages were being passed. "O'Rourke and his cousin Stuart got into a huge fight, though no one apparently knows or remembers why. Knives and a crowbar were involved, and Stuart, the heir apparent to the Sullivan fortune, ended up dying on the docks before the police, whom O'Rourke had called, showed up."

Kate's blood turned to ice water and she hardly was able to look at the man she'd so recently given her body.

"Who is it?" Daegan demanded.

Laura wasn't finished. "Once again O'Rourke got off for lack of evidence or something. Again, no charges filed. Then he disappeared. Left Boston for good."

"How'd you find this out?" Kate asked. "If there was nothing in the papers . . . ?"

"My friend talked to one of the employees in Frank Sullivan's household. Then he looked up O'Rourke's mother, Mary Ellen. She wasn't too happy about it, but admitted that the last time she'd heard from Daegan, he was in some small town in Montana."

"Oh, God."

"The guy's bad news, Kate. I was wrong about him."

"And why is he interested in Jon?" Kate asked, her blood rushing in her ears, her world tipping precariously.

"I don't know. I think you'd better ask him."

"Thanks, Laura, I will," Kate said.

"So call me when you find Jon," Laura said, her voice edged in worry. "And let me know what kind of game O'Rourke's playing."

"As soon as I find out." Kate hung up and tried to contain the rage that gnawed at her gut. Daegan had lied to her, lied to Jon, and used them both. Over and over again. As if their feelings were meaningless.

"What do you want from me?" she asked as she advanced on him and looked into eyes as dark as obsidian. "And what have you done to my son?"

"Nothing."

"Who are you?" she demanded, then let the dam break. Pointing to the phone, she said, "That was my sister, Laura. She told me all about you, how you're related to some Sullivan family, how you ended up here. I just don't know why!"

Daegan's eyes squeezed closed for an instant, and he pinched the bridge of his nose between his thumb and forefinger.

"You lied to me. To Jon!" she accused him, barely able to voice the words.

"I'm sorry."

"Why, Daegan?"

"Because I'm Jon's father."

The room seemed to shrink, his admission bouncing off the ever-closer walls. Kate had trouble catching her breath. She *loved* this man? This liar? This man who had tried to kill his own father and probably did murder his cousin? The stranger who had stalked her and her boy. *Jon's father!*

"You're not, you couldn't be . . ." she whispered but she felt the truth as surely as if he'd driven a stake in her heart.

"I didn't believe it either. But it's true."

"Why would I believe you? First you're single, then you're married and divorced with a son, and now you're Jon's father."

"I'm single, never married, and Jon's my boy." The words ricocheted through the house as if they were bullets from a rifle.

"I can't . . . I don't . . ." She wasn't making any sense, couldn't think straight. Finally the one question that was important formed in her mind. "Where is he?"

"I don't know."

"Where, damn it?" she demanded, nearly hysterical.

"I want to find him as much as you do."

"So you can take him away from me!" Raw emotion tore through her, and she wanted to hit and scream, to wound him. She flung herself at him, ready to do physical damage, but his arms circled her, strong and protective, and she couldn't do anything more than sob wretchedly and strike his shoulder with a weak fist.

"I wouldn't do that," he said, kissing the top of her head.

"Like hell!" Horrified that she'd fallen into his trap again, she pushed away from him and her fears gave way to fury.

His jaw tightened and he tried to touch her, to lay a calming hand on her shoulder, but she backed quickly away, standing on one side of the table, he on the other. "Who are you, you son of a bitch, and what do you want?"

He raked his hands through his hair, then poured two cups of coffee. "Okay, Kate, I suppose you deserve the truth."

"I deserved it from the first time I met you."

He handed her a cup, which she ignored, then walked into the living room to warm the backs of his legs against the fire. As she sat rigidly on the edge of the couch, he explained everything, from the time Bibi had given him the news to yesterday when he'd decided to go back to Boston and have it out with his uncle to protect Kate and Jon.

She wanted to believe him, to think that there was a small streak of nobility in his heart, but she didn't. Even all the attention he lavished on Jon was for his own ulterior motives. Nothing he did was anything but selfish.

The fact that Daegan had conceived a son with his cousin didn't bother her nearly as much as the thought that now Jon had two biological parents, one who wanted him desperately, the other who preferred he never show up.

Her ears were still ringing, her head pounding in pain, as she listened to Daegan and wished she could hate him. It would be so much easier to feel nothing but loathing and abhorrence for this man who had taken her love and abused it. Rage was a much safer emotion than despair.

"So I'm afraid I underestimated this investigator Robert hired—VanHorn. He probably snatched Jon and it's my fault," Daegan admitted. "I must've led him here. I should never have stayed as long as I did, it wasn't part of the plan, but then I met you and . . . Oh, hell, I got caught up in something I had no right to."

Her heart constricted. "So—where is Jon?"

"If Neils has him, and since he hasn't come home that's a real possibility, then he's on his way back to Boston, to Robert."

Kate was off the couch in a second. "Then what are we waiting for? We should call the FBI and go—"

She saw the sheriff's car rolling through the powdered snow covering her drive. Her heart leaped. Maybe Daegan had been wrong. Maybe the police had found Jon . . . But a lone deputy slid from the interior and slogged his way to the front porch.

Kate was already at the door.

"Ms. Summers?"

"Yes."

He was tall and dark skinned with a black moustache and a grim expression. "Deputy Brown," he said in a short introduction.

Her hopes plummeted and she was suddenly scared. More scared than she'd ever been in her life. Had Jon been hurt . . . or worse. "Have you found my son?"

"Not yet, but an anonymous tip came into the office. Someone claims to have seen your son with Daegan O'Rourke. He moved into the—"

"I know who he is," Kate said, stepping away from the

door, allowing the deputy to enter and motioning to Daegan, whose every muscle was tense. His eyes collided with that of the law. "He's here now."

"Someone called in and said they'd seen you with the boy early this morning, Mr. O'Rourke. A little before eight, driving west."

"A lie."

"You were—?"

"At home, feeding the stock. I got over here just after eight, I think, and been here ever since."

"That . . . that's true," Kate added.

The deputy rubbed the back of his neck. "Anyone see what time you left your place?"

"No."

Kate's heart was hammering. The deputy couldn't be serious . . . or could he? Hadn't she, herself, accused Daegan of knowing where Jon was?

"Maybe you'd like to come down and make a statement," Deputy Brown suggested. "Just so we can clear this up."

"I don't think, I mean Daegan's been here with me . . ." she protested, wondering why she was protecting a man who had no heart, no soul. A man who would use her as well as his own son. For all she knew, he could've been sent by Robert Sullivan, and this Neils VanHorn character was just a figment of his imagination.

But she didn't believe it.

Daegan was too passionate, too caring. He loved Jon. He loved her . . . or did he?

"I'm just doin' my job," the deputy reminded her. "You're the one who reported that your boy was missing." He turned his attention back to O'Rourke. "Now, just for the record, you're saying you haven't seen the boy today."

"That's right," Daegan said through tight, flat lips.

"And you've got a ranch in Montana, but originally hailed from Boston, right?"

Daegan hesitated a heartbeat. "Yep."

"And a long time ago you were the primary suspect in an unsolved murder case, the victim being your cousin Stuart Sullivan?"

A tic developed at the corner of Daegan's jaw. "You'd have to ask the Boston police about that."

For the first time Deputy Brown smiled. "We have," he said in a voice that was oily as contaminated water. "I think you'd better come with me . . ."

Jon strained against the metal handcuffs, tears stinging his eyes at the pain caused by the harsh manacles digging into his raw skin. If only he could collapse his fingers a millimeter more, roll his thumb into his palm a bit tighter. Getting out of these cuffs was the first step to surprising the slimy man named VanHorn—Jon had gotten a glimpse of the name on his credit card when he'd pulled it out at a gas pump—and escaping.

"Hey, take it easy," VanHorn called to the back of the van, his beady eyes flashing in the rearview mirror. "Who do you think you are—Houdini?" He snickered, as if he'd just cracked a hysterically funny joke. Asshole.

Jon stopped pulling on the cuffs and gritted his teeth. What a fool he'd been, falling into the smarmy guy's trap. Ever since the man had closed him into the van, Jon had been watching and waiting, poised for escape. But in two days and nights trapped in the van and chained to the bed in a cheap motel room, his chance never came. VanHorn was always careful to lock him up to the metal grating in the back of the van. Even when they stopped to take a piss, the creep stood behind Jon, gun pointed at his back to keep him from bolting. Jon figured the man would slip up soon, as he'd been driving over forty-eight hours without sleep. VanHorn's once-clean shaven jaw was mottled with blond stubble and his eyes were starting to sag.

The man was ripe for a mistake.

And the moment he slipped, Jon would strike.

Somehow, he would escape. He had to get away, because the alternative . . .

He didn't want to think about the man chasing him . . . the killer of his nightmares.

He took a deep breath against the wave of sickness that made him sag against the dark glass of the van's windows. Although he was too exhausted to be terrified at this point, every muscle in his body was cramped and the burger he'd been given from the fast-food drive-through now burned in his gut like a ball of flame. He stared out the passenger window and noted the acres of wire fences and frosted, plowed-over fields that stretched across the flat horizon. From the road signs, he figured he was in Ohio somewhere, though he never was very good at geography, and except for the lack of hills, the miles of farmland out here didn't look much different from the countryside back home.

Home. It was hard to believe he could be so desperate to get back to Oregon, back to the life he hated, but then the instinct to survive was a strong one.

Even when all the odds were against you.

As they seemed to be now with this lowlife private detective "returning" Jon to his legal family. A clan of rich people back East, according to VanHorn. That was about as much information as Jon had gotten out of the man, who'd shut down when Jon had asked him what kind of parents would have their own son kidnapped at gunpoint.

Now, with VanHorn's energy fading, Jon figured it might be a good time to get the guy talking again. "You

know, you could let me go right now and no one would
have to know anything," he said, pressing his face to the
grill of the divider behind VanHorn's head. Jon had
seen some true crime shows on TV that showed victims
who had actually gotten away by talking firmly with
their captors. He figured it was worth a shot. "Drop me
at a train station or a bus depot or something, and no
one would be the wiser. I'll keep my mouth shut. I can
say you kept me blindfolded."

"Sure, kid." VanHorn's grin was almost jovial. "I'll
just drop you off and turn away a bundle of money. Why
don't I just find the nearest airport and you can fly
home, first-class?" he snorted. "Thing is, you'll be flying
first-class once you hook up with your real family. First-
class all the way, with their kind of money. Believe me,
you'll thank me when you get a load of them."

"My real family is back in Oregon," Jon said, thinking
of Kate's dark brown eyes, the way her forehead crin-
kled when she worried about something. The way she
hummed when she baked in the kitchen. He ached to
be back there now, safe at home.

"Not so, kid. Kate Summer's not your mother, remember? That adoption was as phony as a three-dollar
bill. You knew that, right?" VanHorn's eyebrows elevated in mock surprise. "No?"

Jon swallowed hard. "I don't care if it was legal," he
lied.

"Ooh, got to respect the law," VanHorn said. "Because, and here's the thing, if Kate Summers actually
isn't your mother, then she kidnapped you years ago. So
what I'm doing now? It's not kidnapping, per se. I'm
just a Good Samaritan bringing a boy home to his real
family."

"Yeah, right." Jon's voice was flat. "My parents who
decide they need me fifteen years later."

"Don't start getting all warm and fuzzy about your

long-lost parents," VanHorn said. "They're not in the picture anymore."

"Then who's paying you to do this?" Jon asked in disbelief.

"Your fat-cat granddad, for one. He wants you to come and rule the family empire. Of course, there's another bidder in the auction. Your sweet Aunt Alicia. She wants to see you out of the running as heir to the family fortune. Seems your existence screws up her kid's chances of inheriting the family fortune. Too bad you were born a boy."

Jon squinted, shaking his head. "What the hell are you talking about?"

"Elimination. You ever studied history, kid? Do you know how Henry VIII got rid of some of those bothersome wives?"

A thread of panic seeped into Jon's veins at the thought. "He killed two of them." He pretended not to care. "So what . . . ? Are you going to kill me?"

"Nah . . . I'm just delivering you to the highest bidder," VanHorn said casually. "I'll have you know, I never killed a man. But I have done some damage, messed some guys up pretty bad." He wrenched his neck around to glare at Jon face-to-face. "Which is what I'll do to you if you ever cross me, kid."

Jon's throat went dry at the blatant threat, and his mind opened to the image of running from the man.

Running, running . . .

Racing through the dark streets, his sneakers slapping against the wet pavement, his heart pounding in his chest.

Running from a killer . . .

"You're a fucking liar," Jon said, shivering despite the heat blasting from the front seat of the van.

"Do ya think?" VanHorn just lifted his eyes to the rearview mirror, his stare as cold as ice. "Maybe I am, kid. Maybe I am."

* * *

The plane landed with a jolt as the first rays of morning were visible in the eastern sky. Kate's throat caught as she realized she was finally back in Boston, the city where it all started. The flight had been long and nerve-wracking, not because of turbulence or any delays. No, her worries had been focused on her son and the man she'd so recently loved. Jon had been gone over two days and a creeping sense of panic clutched at her throat. She couldn't lose him, not now. Not ever.

She didn't know Robert Sullivan, couldn't imagine what the man had planned for her son, but she was bound and determined that she'd find out. Rather than contact him by phone and let him have the chance to hang up on her or flee, she planned to meet him face to face in his own home, and she wasn't about to leave until she had answers.

Laura was expecting her, and thankfully her sister had done a little more digging, determining that Robert Sullivan usually spent most of his workdays at his office, sometimes stopped off at his club for a drink or dinner or workout, but was always home by nine in the evening.

Tonight he'd have company.

For a second as the decelerating jet screeched down the runway, she thought of Daegan, just as she had all during the flight, but she wouldn't let her wayward mind dwell on him. He'd callously used her and toyed with Jon's emotions. Under the guise of the friendly neighbor, he'd burrowed his way into her home as well as her heart. He'd admitted to flattening her tire, to lying about his need to use her phone that first week, to wanting to get to know her because of Jon.

But he did save Jon from Todd.

He did teach him to ride.

He did laugh so deeply the mountains seemed to ring.

He did touch her as no man, not even Jim, had.

And there was a slight chance that she could be pregnant with his child.

"No," Kate whispered though the thought wasn't unpleasant. She'd always wanted another baby, and she was more than willing to raise that baby on her own.

The plane taxied to the gate, and she unbuckled her seat belt. Through the small window she watched snow fall from a pewter-colored sky while a ground crew scurried under the belly of the plane.

She grabbed her single piece of carry-on luggage and filed with the rest of the passengers into the behemoth that was Logan International Airport. Soon, she'd face the grandfather of her son—the rich self-serving son of a bitch who had done everything he could to get rid of Jon fifteen years ago and now wanted him back.

Her fingers tightened over the handle of her bag, and cold determination steeled her. No one was going to take her son away. Not even Robert damned Sullivan.

There was no disputing the fact that Jon Summers would be killed. In Alicia's mind, the only issue that remained was how best to get the job done.

The question had thrummed in her mind for days, ever since she'd planted the seed in VanHorn's puny brain. She had expected the man to take on the task, baited by the promise of a tumble in the sack, but VanHorn, like most men, had proved disappointing. Alicia Sullivan McGivens let out an exhausted breath and rolled away from her husband, Bryan, who was hogging the sheets again, damn him.

How difficult would it be to kill a person?

Really . . . how hard could it be? Just make sure he was dead and get rid of the body . . . as easy as that. And when the victim was a naive fifteen-year-old, he would certainly be unsuspecting, especially when it came to a woman like Alicia.

Not that Alicia relished the thought of snuffing out a life. She'd always recoiled at having to smash a spider in Wade's room or, God forbid, swat a fly. The crunch of their fat insect bodies sickened her, and the dark stain left behind on the woodwork was so disgusting. How much worse would it be to kill a person?

Not that Bibi's bastard was destined to make any great contribution to humanity. Really. An orphan child growing up in some godforsaken pasture out West? His intelligence was probably on par with the pigs rolling in the muddy pigpen. Didn't VanHorn say the boy had been raised out in the middle of nowhere? A hillbilly misanthrope. Too bad old Robert hadn't left well enough alone. In any case, she had come to think of the bastard boy as not so much a human being who mattered as a nonperson, a family problem, an obstacle to Wade's success.

With the bastard under Robert's wing, the whole chain of inheritance—everything Alicia had worked so hard for—would be ruined. Currently, without a male heir on Robert's side, the fortune would fall to Frank, then to Collin, who would certainly never have children. Which left her beloved Wade next in line for the Sullivan mantle.

My Little Lord Fauntleroy, she thought, clasping her hands under one cheek as an image of her apple-cheeked prince danced in her head.

Well, she wasn't about to let the bastard get in the way of Wade's future. Her son was the crown prince of the Sullivan dynasty, and he was going to rise to power and wealth without this traitor in his kingdom.

Which meant someone would have to get rid of the bastard.

How hard could it be?

She'd spent the last few nights in bed, staring at the crown moldings overhead and fantasizing over the perfect murder as Bryan lay softly snoring beside her. She'd seen enough detective shows to know the pitfalls of murder, the stupid ways people got themselves caught and convicted. Fingerprints, blood and hair samples left behind in cars, witnesses . . . and motive.

Well, it would be hard to tie her to the bastard, especially since she had never seen his face, never been seen with him. And she would keep it that way.

She hated to dirty her hands, but if Neils VanHorn was going to wimp out on her, she would get the job done. Hiring another private investigator or some sordid contract killer would only widen the path of evidence and cost her another chunk of her son's inheritance. No, she didn't need some low-life blabbermouth out there owning a sensitive piece of information about her. It wouldn't be fitting for the mother of a future CEO, governor, perhaps even president.

If she had to, she would do it herself.

Neils could deliver the bastard to the summer house, blindfolded, of course. If the bastard was bound as well, it would be a piece of cake. She could loosen him up by lacing some of her tranquilizers into a nice soothing drink for him. Then, she would take him on a little lake cruise—after dark. The lake would be empty this time of year, and once she got out to the deepest part, it would be so easy to push him over the side. Of course, she'd need to attach some weights. A couple of those minibarbells she'd been training with would work—wiped clean of fingerprints. She wasn't about to slip up and leave prints, and fortunately, this time of year, no one would question her wearing gloves.

That settled it. Tomorrow night when she met with VanHorn, she would tell him to deliver the boy to the lake house and she would take care of the rest. What was that old adage? If you want something done right, do it yourself. She took a deep, relaxing breath and felt soothed by the image of the bastard securely anchored to the bottom of the lake. Safely tucked away.

Contented at the thought of all her problems buried in a watery grave, Alicia McGivens stretched out her legs amid the Egyptian cotton sheets, closed her eyes, and drifted off to sleep.

Boston.

It was not the city Jon had seen in movies, not the place he'd imagined when he'd spoken to his aunt on the phone, but then, he didn't think Laura lived in the rundown neighborhood VanHorn had brought him to when they'd checked into the Ivy Motel. Through the grimy window he'd gotten an occasional view of a dark alley lined with trash cans and the drab shingled building that backed up to the motel. This place was a hellhole, made worse by the fact that he felt like he was sitting here on death row, waiting for VanHorn to sell him off to the "aunt" who wanted him dead.

A sitting duck, that's what he was.

But not for long.

If he'd learned anything from Daegan, it was that he didn't have to cower and take abuse . . . not from anyone. He was going to fight back, escape, go to the police and Aunt Laura. If everything went according to plan, VanHorn would return to his room tonight to find cops waiting for him. That would be sweet.

But first, he had to get the hell out of here.

Reaching under the mattress, his fingers searched for the small bar of soap he'd tucked away when Van-Horn wasn't looking. It was something of a long shot, but with just one hand cuffed to the bed, he planned to

soap his way out of the other manacle. Carefully, he
used his free hand to douse his wrist with water from a
bottle VanHorn let him keep by the bedside. The soap
stung the abrasions on his skin as he worked it into
a lather, but he winced and rubbed the bar over the inside of the cuff, trying to make it as slippery as possible.

Then, it was a matter of collapsing his hand, pulling
and tugging until the cuff tore into his bruised swollen
skin, scraping and pulling despite the excruciating pain.

He tried to block out the pain by reminding himself
of the freedom ahead. Escape from the man who was
ready to sell him off like a slave; VanHorn had told him
as much.

"Well, boy," VanHorn had said, cackling. "You're my
gold mine. I'm going to sell you off to the highest bidder.
And no doubt that'll be your auntie. She's got everything to lose, and I enjoy doing business with her. Thing
is, she's promised me a few perks your old grandfather
can't offer, if you know what I mean."

And as VanHorn had begun to close the handcuff
over Jon's wrist that night, Jon had caught a glimpse
into the man's dark soul.

"You won't be safe in Mexico," Jon had said.

"What?"

"Or Canada, either. You can't sell me off to a killer
and get away with it."

VanHorn's mouth had dropped open a second.
"How did you know . . . ?" And he'd backed away warily,
before he'd had a chance to crank the cuff closed to the
tightest notch.

Which was why Jon might have a chance to escape
now, despite the throbbing pain in his swollen wrist. As
he pulled, it felt like he was going to shave the fingers
right off his hands, but he couldn't stop now, not with
the cuff now squeezing the base of his thumb. Bracing

himself against the dizzying pain, he pulled hard. With an agonized groan, the cuff slipped off.

At last . . . he was free.

With no time to lose, he unlocked the door and fled down the rickety steps covered in rock salt, careful to avoid the icy edges. Not sure which way to run, he squeezed between two parked cars and bolted across the small motel parking lot. On the corner a handful of men gathered around a trash can fire, laughing as someone threw something in and stirred sparks in the night. Now that he was outside, the edginess of the neighborhood was more apparent, with its boarded-up windows, doors covered by wrought-iron gates, walls of graffiti, and cracked, peeling paint.

He had to get out of here—fast.

He hit the sidewalk running and didn't slow when two headlights loomed down the dark street. Just a passing car.

Then why was it screeching to a stop beside him?

The door flew open and Jon gasped as the familiar man emerged, his face red with fury.

VanHorn.

"What the hell are you doing?" VanHorn shouted.

But Jon backed away and raced down the street, his shoes scraping over rock salt, his legs pumping.

Run, run, run!

Adrenaline shot through him as he tore through the dark streets, his sneakers slapping against the wet pavement. His heart pounded so hard he thought it would explode. Piles of dirty slush lined the unfamiliar streets.

This city was so foreign to him . . .

Except that he'd dreamed of it. He knew this cityscape.

He was living out his worst nightmares, but he had to run. Escape from the killer.

Behind him a siren wailed, and he plunged on, toward the lights, the music.

Christmas music.

"God rest ye merry gentlemen, let nothing you dismay . . ."

Here the streets were better lit. Buildings gleamed with shiny glass windows, their doors adorned with wreaths and winking Christmas lights. It was the sort of neighborhood Aunt Laura might live in. The door of a pub opened, and laughter and music drifted out with two patrons. Jon had to lunge to the left to cut around them, though the couple didn't seem to mind.

A man walking his dog looked up and shook his head. "What's your hurry, kid?"

Running, Jon panted, the cold air fire in his lungs.

From my killer.

God, help me.

". . . to save us all from Satan's power when we have gone astray . . ."

Breathless, Jon glanced over his shoulder. No sign of his pursuer. He ducked into the doorway of a shop that was closed, trying to catch his breath and think.

Reality didn't have to mirror his vision. He could control the outcome, escape VanHorn, get himself back home to Oregon. Right now he had to believe that. He was going to get away.

Hearing only the animated conversation of two passing shoppers, he leaned out of the doorway. No sign of VanHorn.

Feeling relieved but cautious, he stepped out and strode down the street behind the two women. I can do this, he thought, easily falling into step behind them. I can lose him and find the nearest police station . . .

"Jon . . ." The voice slammed into his consciousness as a dark figure stepped out of the shadows of a storefront behind him.

Oh, God!

Cold steel pressed into his shoulder blade—the gun.

The cold tip of the weapon stopped Jon in mid-stride as VanHorn's thoughts flashed into his mind.

He wants to kill me. He's seriously considering squeezing the trigger.

Just kill the boy now and be done with this. . .

"That's where you're wrong," Jon said aloud. "If you shoot me now, you'll never be done with this. You'll be paying the rest of your life."

"Just shut up," VanHorn said with a low growl.

Jon felt something clamp on his shoulder—his jacket. VanHorn was using it to hide the gun.

"You left without your jacket, son." VanHorn's voice oozed with paternal concern. Two women in hooded jackets and boots passed by unfazed, unable to smell Jon's panic as they ducked into the door of a boutique strung with tiny white lights. "You can't run around here without a coat," VanHorn reiterated in a cheerful, booming voice. "You'll catch your death of cold."

"It's not a bad way to go," Jon muttered under his breath as the pistol jabbed into his ribcage. Caught. Deflated. And running out of time.

Chapter 23

"What do you think you're doing here?" Kate demanded, spying Daegan in the hallway of her sister's apartment. Laura had answered the door and Daegan had barged in, looking as out of place as spurs on tennis shoes. Wearing a rawhide jacket, jeans, boots, and a faded blue work shirt, he looked the part of a cowboy in the city. His flinty eyes when they connected with hers were just as sexy and throat-catching as ever. God, she was a fool!

"I came to find my son."

"*Your* son," she repeated, disbelieving. "Other than being involved in his conception, you've had nothing to do with him—"

"Because I didn't know about him."

"Your problem. If you're so careless as to . . ." Her words faded as she realized what she was saying. As if he could read her thoughts, his gaze strayed to her flat abdomen, where there could be another life—their child's—beginning to grow.

"Whoa," Laura said, "I think I'd better disappear for a while."

"That's a good idea," Daegan said.

"Stay put. You're the only family I have, the only family Jon has."

"Not true," Daegan asserted, his lips flattening over his teeth and his nostrils flaring, "but we can argue about this later. Right now we're wasting time."

She couldn't argue with his logic, and if the truth were known, she was grateful that he'd be with her when she faced Robert Sullivan. Not that she needed any kind of support or prodding; she'd fight the man tooth and nail all by herself, but it was still fortifying to know that he was there, whatever his motives.

Laura fluttered her fingers nervously. "What do you want me to do?"

"Stay here," Kate said. "If Jon's in Boston and he can get away from VanHorn or whoever it is who's got him, then he might come here. He knows your address even if he's never been to the city before."

"Okay, I can do that," Laura said, nodding, her gaze straying to Daegan again before landing hard on Kate. "Will you be all right?"

Kate understood her sister's silent message and she waved off her fears. No matter what she thought of Daegan, she didn't believe that he would hurt her or her son, at least not physically. Though he'd put them through emotional hell, he wouldn't intentionally let any harm come to them. That much she still believed. Despite his faults, there was still some smidgen of honor in the man. There had to be. "I'll be fine," she said as she grabbed her coat and gloves.

"We'll be at Robert Sullivan's house if the police or the FBI calls."

She stopped dead in her tracks. "What?"

"Believe me, I've never been all that fond of the law, but in this case, it's important that all the state, local, and national agencies are notified." His lips twisted. "I spent the last day being grilled by the authorities, think it's someone else's turn. What if VanHorn didn' hightail it back here? What if he took Jon to Canada? O has him holed up somewhere in the Black Hills? O locked away on a boat in the Pacific Ocean? Unfortu nately, we're going to need all the help we can get. I'v got my own private investigator on it, too. My frienc Sandy Kavenaugh. He's watching the Sullivans and ha his ear to the ground for VanHorn."

Kate shivered. "Do you really believe that he's some where else?"

"No," he said as they waited for the elevator in th hallway outside Laura's apartment. "My gut feeling i that VanHorn brought him here for Robert and tha dear old Uncle Bob has been working at trumping up charges against me and finding flaws in the paperwork surrounding Jon's adoption. According to Bibi Robert's become obsessed with his grandson." The ele vator doors opened and they stepped inside.

"But she isn't?" Kate asked, wanting to hate the woman who gave Jon up when deep inside she wa thankful for the chance to become his mother.

"Bibi still thinks he's better off with you or me or any one but her."

"Oh, Lord," she whispered, dying a little inside. The adoption hadn't been legal. She'd known it for years but assumed that the legality of all the documents would never be questioned. Outside the ground was cov ered in snow, but paths had been cleared on the side walks and streets. The noise of the city hit her full force as Daegan hailed a taxi.

He spouted off an address and the cab took off blending into the uneven flow of traffic. Kate leaned her head against the cool glass of a back window and silently prayed that her son was all right. Christmas lights blazed on buildings, and wreaths with huge bows hung on doors. Pedestrians in wool scarves and hats ducked their heads against the wind and snow while cars, trucks, and buses vied for space on the busy, narrow streets.

She slid a glance in Daegan's direction, noting the stubborn set of his jaw, the determination glinting in his eyes, the tough, obstinate seam of his lips. Silently he seethed and she felt that same bone-chilling aura of danger that she'd sensed when she first met him. His hands gripped his knees, knuckles bleached white, fingers clenched in a death grip.

The cab slid to a stop at an address on Louisburg Square. Daegan paid the driver, then helped Kate out of the car. "Let me handle this," he said.

"No way. He's my son."

"And mine. We've been over this before. Just let me have a first crack at Robert, then you're on." She wanted to argue but the fire in his eyes convinced her to agree. For now.

"I can't promise I'll keep my mouth shut."

"You might not have to." Together they walked up a brick path that had been shoveled clear of snow. The red brick town house rose four stories to a gabled roof. Black shutters guarded tall windows and lamplight fell through the paned glass. A garland of cedar boughs was woven with thick red ribbon and tiny lights, then draped around the door frame. Everywhere there was the spirit of Christmas. Except in Kate's heart.

"I wish this were over," she whispered.

"I wish things were different." His voice was so quiet, she barely heard it.

Daegan lifted the knocker three times. Kate's stomach plummeted to the frozen ground as a butler, tall and thin and pale, opened the door.

"We're here to see Robert."

"May I ask who's cal—"

"Just tell him Daegan wants to see him and won'
take no for an answer," Daegan said and shoved his foo
across the threshold to prevent the door from being
slammed shut. Robert wasn't going to weasel out of this

With a disgruntled frown, the man let them into the
tiled foyer, and it was all Daegan could do to stay calm
His hands were fisted in his pockets, his muscles tigh
and rigid from restraint. He heard the butler's clipped
steps as he retreated, noted the gilded mirrors and
elaborate chandelier with hundreds of lights sparkling
over his head. In the center of the room stood a table
with a cut-crystal bowl full of floating jasmine, and poin
settias spread their red and white splendor up a sweep
ing staircase.

The butler, his face expressionless, returned. "Thi
way," he said. "Mr. Sullivan will see you now."

"No shit," Daegan muttered.

Taking Kate's hand in his, Daegan followed the stiff
spined employee through wide double doors and into
Robert's den. To Daegan's way of thinking, he was strid
ing through the gates of hell.

Although Neils kept telling himself the woman was
poison, that he ought to take his money and run far
away from her, every time he saw her, he weakened. He
tossed back his scotch and let his eyes run down her
body, trying to soak up her slick beauty. Composed and
sophisticated in her own bitter way, she definitely pos
sessed the talons to scratch his itch.

"So the boy is here?" she asked, tapping a manicured
nail on the bare table top of the quiet little bar where
they'd agreed to meet. She wore shaded glasses and a
scarf to protect herself from being recognized, creating
an air of mystery that he found sexy as hell.

"Got him here in Boston," he replied. "I'm just weighing in on final offers." Twin lines of frustration appeared above the bridge of her nose. How he'd love to rip those sunglasses off—along with her cashmere coat and everything underneath. "Your offer tops Robert's," he said. "Both in money and other areas."

"I'll bet."

He watched as she crossed her legs, letting one high heel suspend from her toes, showing off the arch of a delicate foot. Neils's manhood sprang to attention.

"So what's the holdup?" she asked.

"I like your offer," he admitted, shifting against the pistol between his legs, "but I'm not cool with what you want me to do with him. Let's just say it's beyond the range of my specialty."

"Too bad." She lifted a shoulder and her smile turned pouty and damned seductive. "But I still want the bastard. I'll just have to switch to plan B. Which means I'll accept delivery as soon as you can arrange it, out at my family's place on the lake."

He nodded, images of the two of them cozying up by a warm fire at the Sullivans' lake house. "And my money?" he asked, finishing his scotch and signaling for another round. Her glass of wine remained untouched.

"Half on delivery, half a month later, when the dust settles."

Neils ran his tongue around his teeth, thinking of the many things they could do in a month's time. Normally he demanded his money on a more timely basis, but he would enjoy stretching things out with Alicia. And it would be a huge relief to dump the boy off with her, get that bit of walking, talking trouble out of his hands. The kid worried him, with his weird visions. Not to mention the fact that Jon had almost run off yesterday, which would have left Neils royally screwed. All that

work and he would end up with jackshit. Which was why
he'd left the boy with his wrists and ankles cuffed this
time. That would hold him.

He picked up his refreshed drink and, feeling rather
suave, toasted her. "I think we have ourselves a deal."

Daegan didn't believe in pussyfooting around and so
he confronted Robert head-on. "You can't have Jon," he
said, striding into the room and watching the smaller
older man try to get his bearings. Robert's mouth
worked and he glanced several times at Kate as he tried
to push himself out of a tufted leather chair. A cigar
burned in an ashtray at his side. A snifter of brandy had
been placed on the folded pages of the *Wall Street Jour-
nal.* A fire played in the hearth and cast cheery golden
shadows around this ancient, paneled room.

"Who are you to say who will have custody of—"

"He's my son, damn it! *Mine.*" Daegan hooked a pos-
sessive thumb at his chest. "You're not getting him! Not
now. Not ever!"

"You think the courts would give you custody after
you nearly shot Frank and beat Stuart to death?" Robert
demanded, his white face contorting in a fuming, silent
rage as he settled back into his chair. Behind rimless
reading glasses his eyes narrowed in anger.

"I didn't kill anyone."

"Still unable to face the truth."

"The truth, Robert, is that you're going to give up
any custody fight for Jon, and if you don't, I'll personally see that the old Sullivan scandals along with the
new ones come scampering out of their little locked
closets to parade before all the newspapers in town.
Your clients, Frank's business associates, Collin's friends,
Bibi's fiancé, everyone will know. If that isn't enough,
I'll call the police and demand my own investigations

and I'll see to it that you'll never raise your head socially again. All this blue-blooded sophisticated act will be over. It's all bullshit anyway."

He leaned over Robert's chair, his face menacing, his voice the barest of whispers. "Now, let's get down to brass tacks. Where's Jon?"

Robert's Adam's apple worked up and down. "I don't know."

"Bull!"

"I don't!"

"We know VanHorn has him. The police have been informed, so things will be better if you tell us the truth."

"I don't know," he repeated and Kate almost felt sorry for him. So old and ill. And yet so conniving.

"I want my boy, Mr. Sullivan," she said with a quiet calm that she didn't feel. Her muscles ached from tension, her hands were curled into hard fists.

"He's not yours. He never was, Ms. Summers," Robert said, his watery eyes fixed on Kate. "The adoption was not a legal proceeding, as I'm sure you know. So in fact, it is I who should be demanding the boy back from you."

"When hell freezes over." Daegan crossed the room, snagged the receiver from the phone, and began punching in numbers.

"Now wait a minute," Robert groused. "You can't just barge in here and start bullying me and using my things and—"

"Like you did to me?" Kate demanded. "For God's sake, you had your own grandson kidnapped!"

"Correction: Jon was not kidnapped. He's simply being returned to his family."

"No," Kate said, her voice deadly. "You will never be his family. Not really."

"You're deluded," Robert said.

"I took your grandson when no one else would have him," Kate said, over thickness in her throat. "When you

wanted to be rid of him without a trace. I followed
Tyrell's orders, took him far away from here, and raised
Jon as my own son. He *is* my son. I love him, and no
court of law can change that."

"We're at Robert's house," Daegan said into the
mouthpiece. "I'm here with Jon's mother, and you better get over here. It's time we all had a family meeting."

"What?" Robert cried. "Who are you calling? Put
down that phone or I'll have you arrested."

"Go on and try." Daegan slammed the receiver back
into the cradle. "The police are probably already in the
area, the FBI, too. Keeping an eye on you. They're concerned about Jon, and you should be, too."

Raising a shaking finger to his upper lip, Robert
scowled down his patrician nose. He wasn't accustomed
to losing, and his thin lips pursed in frustration.

"Is VanHorn coming here?" Daegan asked.

"No," Robert answered, staring down at the Persian
rug. "He most certainly is not."

"Where is Jon?" Kate asked, sure she would go mad
with worry.

"I don't know." Robert leaned back in the oversized
leather chair. "VanHorn was giving me information
about the boy. However, he hasn't phoned in a few days
and has not had the decency to return my calls. At first
I thought he was holding out for more money, but now
I can only deduce that the scoundrel is double-crossing
me. I suspect he's going to sell Jon to a higher bidder."

"Who would that be?" Kate asked.

Groaning, Daegan pressed his face to one palm. "It
could be any thieving cutthroat in this dysfunctional
family." His head snapped up, his gaze burning at
Robert. "Who is it? My father? Collin?"

Robert didn't move, but Kate noticed a vein pulsing
in his forehead as the phone rang.

With a soft knock on the door, the butler entered.

"What is it, Royce?" Robert barked.

"The telephone, sir," Royce intoned with great pomposity, "is for Mr. O'Rourke."

At last, VanHorn had slipped.

He'd acted so cocky and clever when he'd bought a second pair of handcuffs to secure Jon's legs to the bedpost. "This outta keep you from running," VanHorn had mumbled as he'd closed the links around Jon's ankles, looping the chain around the bedpost.

The cuffs were secure, all right. But VanHorn had forgotten to pocket the keys.

Even before the man left for his "engagement," Jon had eyed the set of shiny keys sitting on the nightstand. Locked to the bed, he wasn't able to grab them with his hands. But as soon as VanHorn's footsteps had faded outside, Jon had gotten to work hauling the bed closer to the night table, stretching his face toward the shiny silver keys.

It wasn't easy. It must have taken a full half hour to close the distance, a quarter of an inch at a time.

But now, at last, he was near enough to press his face close to the tabletop and close his lips over the keys.

Got 'em!

Working quickly but carefully, so as not to drop the keys, Jon worked the shiny silver tab into the hole and sprang the handcuffs open. Gently, he rubbed his tender wrists for a second before bending down to unlock the cuffs at his ankles and free his legs.

Jon faced the door tentatively. This time, he couldn't afford to make any mistakes. If VanHorn returned, he didn't want to meet him in the motel hallway.

He'd go out the window. Quickly, he crossed the

room and unlocked the old rusted paned window, cracked in one corner. It had been painted shut, but he banged on the sash and finally wedged it open.

Just as footsteps shuffled in the hallway.

There was no time to escape now. He'd have to pretend to be locked up, then spring out when VanHorn least expected it. He pulled the window down, leaving it open just an inch, then dove toward the bed.

As VanHorn's key rattled in the lock, Jon sat down on the bed and placed the cuffs loosely around his wrists and ankles, pocketing the key in case they somehow got tightened.

The door burst open and in staggered VanHorn, reeking of stale whiskey and smoke. "Looks like we have a winner," he announced as he toppled onto the bed. Without a glance at Jon, he rubbed his bloodshot eyes. "Christ, I'm tired."

"A winner?" Jon said.

"Yep. Your mother's cousin Alicia is willing to pay top dollar for you. I'm to deliver you to the Sullivans' lake house tomorrow night, and from what I hear, it's pretty swell digs. Moving up in the world, Jonny boy."

But she's the one who wants me dead, Jon thought. *She's the real killer. And you're going to hand me over like a head of cattle, like a horse sold at auction.*

"Don't look at me that way," VanHorn said, though his face was still buried in his hands. "I'm a businessman. This is business, kid."

"She'll kill me," Jon said evenly.

"What the hell would I know about that," VanHorn said, nudging off one scuffed loafer with the toe of his other shoe.

"You know what she's planning, and you'll be tried as an accomplice."

"Nah." VanHorn kicked off his other shoe. "Only if

she gets caught, and that won't happen. She's smart, real smart. A classy lady."

A rich psycho, Jon thought, sweating hard now, his brain on overload. He had to get out, away from these crazies, back to his normal life, the one he hated back in Oregon! He had to get away, but only when VanHorn was off-guard. He had to be patient, he reminded himself as he wiped the perspiration from his brow onto the sleeve of his flannel shirt.

"Yeah," VanHorn said, leaning back on the bed. "She is one hot lady."

"Well, she can burn in jail," Jon said, trying a different tack. "Because my mom won't let her get to me."

VanHorn lifted one brow. "It's a little late for mommy to come to the rescue, isn't it?"

"She'll be here," Jon said firmly. "And so will Daegan," he added, thinking aloud.

"Daegan." VanHorn cackled as an evil smile spread across his face. "You mean O'Rourke?"

Jon froze. How did this guy know Daegan?

"He's the reason I found you, you know. Led me right to your door, though he didn't mean to. Believe me, he's no problem. O'Rourke's an emotional hothead and a loser. He's not ganna save you, Jon. No one is."

"You don't know him," Jon said. He couldn't let this slimeball cut down the only decent man he knew.

"Neither do you, I'll bet." Neils sat on the edge of the bed, the mattress sagging. "For example, I don't suppose he told you he was your father."

Jon's mouth opened and closed. His throat tightened. "Liar," he said, but the word came out as a weak denial.

"Think about it, Jon. I got no reason to lie. But O'Rourke, he had plenty."

His father? His father? Daegan? No. No . . . no!

And yet, on some level, Jon knew VanHorn was telling the truth. His stomach roiled and his mouth filled with spit.

"Isn't that a hoot?" VanHorn taunted, letting out that snide cackle. "And the kicker is, your mother was his first cousin. Sick, isn't it? Bad enough you were a bastard, but throw in the shades of incest and, well, no wonder they put you up for adoption. Just damned lucky you didn't turn out retarded, isn't it?"

Again, he let out the perverse laugh that made Jon's skin crawl as the world seemed to collapse under his feet.

"I didn't think you'd want to wait on this. Not with the boy involved." Sandy's navy down parka cut a wide swath in the night.

"You've got that right," Daegan said, emerging from Robert Sullivan's stuffy townhome. It was good to see his old friend, better to hear the promising news.

Standing at the bottom of the brown stone stairs, Sandy extended a hand toward Kate to prevent her from slipping on the new dusting of snow on the landing.

Quickly, Daegan introduced Kate to his old friend, then got down to business. "Where do you think they are?"

"In a motel on the other side of town. A dive called the Ivy. A friend of mine who tends bar there thought he spotted someone who fit VanHorn's description meeting up with a high-class woman who was obviously slumming. I took it from there. Manager says VanHorn is in Room 203, but insists it's all aboveboard."

"Jon is here? In Boston?" When Daegan nodded, Kate gasped and covered her mouth with one hand. The light in her whiskey brown eyes was so hopeful, so expectant, that Daegan didn't want to think about all the things that could go wrong. He couldn't bear to read more disappointment in those eyes.

They had to save Jon. They would.

"Can you drive us there?" Daegan asked Sandy.

"You got it, and I'll help you muscle down VanHorn. The guy's probably armed, and I doubt he'll be happy to see us."

"No doubt," Daegan said, striding down the street to Sandy's Jeep. No doubt an invasion by the two of them would be the biggest surprise of VanHorn's career.

He was close . . . so close.

Again, Jon measured the distance between himself and the window, calculating how long it would take to spring out and trying to remember the configuration of the fire escape stairs to the ground. He was biding his time, waiting for VanHorn to hit the can or doze off.

VanHorn was stretched out on the bed, rambling on about how he was going to spend his first million bucks, something about Vegas showgirls and tuna fishing in the Caribbean. He was vacillating between a Mercedes and a Porsche when three sharp raps sounded on the door.

VanHorn sat up and slid off the bed.

"Neils VanHorn?" a voice—an unfamiliar male voice.

"Who wants to know?"

"Collin Sullivan."

"Well, what'd'ya know?" He grinned at Jon. "Your uncle. Yep, you got a ton of 'em around here. Maybe Uncle Collie wants to sweeten the pot."

Opening the door, Neils stood aside and a tall man with thinning blond hair and a long coat swept into the room. "This is the boy?" he asked, no smile on his thin features.

"Bibi's kid."

"And Alicia wants you to what? Do away with him?"

Jon's stomach sank.

VanHorn scowled. "She tell you?"

"No, I just know my sister and recognize her faults," was his reply as he unwound his scarf. "Once Robert started hunting for the kid—Jon, is it?" he asked without any warmth in his eyes.

Jon nodded.

"Once Robert started looking for him, I knew Alicia would want it stopped. She doesn't want any competition for Wade, oh, no," he added, seeing the distress in VanHorn's features. "I suppose she promised to pay you."

VanHorn's eyes slitted. "We have an agreement."

"A healthy one, I'd assume. Well, I'm here to cancel it. I'll pay you whatever your time's been worth and buy this boy a ticket back to his home, wherever that is."

Jon felt his spirits lift. Could it be that simple?

"No way." VanHorn wasn't giving up that easily.

"Why not? You get your money," Jon voiced. This was all so crazy, he couldn't believe it.

"How much?" VanHorn wanted to know.

"A fair amount."

"What's 'fair'?"

"I don't know—twenty-five, or thirty thousand dollars should cover it . . ."

Van Horn snorted derisively. "Get out of the peanut gallery and into the ball park, would ya? We're talking millions."

Collin's lips pursed. "No one in the family can give you millions."

"That's not the way I heard it."

"Uncuff the boy."

"Not until I get what's due me." VanHorn's voice had gotten louder.

"You'll be compensated fairly."

"Christ, you expect me to believe that?" He reached under the pillow.

"Watch out, he's got a gun!" Jon shouted as footsteps pounded up the stairs. Another man, a huge beast of a man with gray at his temples and a fierce face, burst into the room.

"What the hell?" VanHorn said, stepping backward, the gun trained on the door.

"Jesus H. Christ, Collin," the beast roared. "What're you doing here?" His eyes landed on Jon with pure hatred and then he saw the gun in VanHorn's hand.

"Isn't this nice? A family reunion," Neils said with a smirk. "Jon, meet your great-uncle—no, is it grandfather?—Frank Sullivan."

Jon had to get out of here now. The big man was out for blood; he could see it in his eyes.

"Let me handle this," the giant commanded.

"No, Dad—"

But the big man pushed his son against the wall. VanHorn was distracted and Jon couldn't stand the tension in the room a minute longer. He flung off the loose handcuffs, sprang across the bed, and flung the window open.

Aware of the loaded gun behind him, he didn't take a minute to look back, but burst through the window and landed with a bone-crunching thud on the fire escape. Propelling himself forward, he rolled down the flight of stairs. Pain exploded in his shoulder.

"What the hell?" VanHorn yelled.

"Hey—wait!"

"That little bastard!"

Jon scrambled wildly, ever downward.

Footsteps. Swearing. The crack of a gunshot. An ear-piercing scream of pain.

"Oh, God, oh, God, oh God!" Fear congealing his

blood, Jon swung from the ladder to land on the icy back alley somewhere in Boston. He didn't think about where he was going, where he could run, he just took off, his shoulder throbbing, his feet slipping, traction nearly impossible as he passed men huddled around fires in trash cans, traffic trying to maneuver in the snow. Run, run, run!

The sound of the gunshot tore through the building.

"No!" Kate cried, her heart in her throat as she bolted up the stairs behind Daegan and Sandy. "No!" They couldn't have killed Jon, they couldn't have! "Please, God, let him be safe!"

"Keep her with you!" Daegan commanded, throwing a don't-cross-me look at the tall, red-haired private detective.

"But you might need back-up."

Ignoring him, Daegan pressed his back against the wall of the corridor, then leaped in through the doorway, assuming a combat stance. For the first time in sixteen years, he was face to face with his father, Frank Sullivan.

"You!" Frank huffed, his lips curled in disgust. Although he was still burly and tall, Frank no longer posed the indomitable threat that had haunted Daegan's childhood. Having aged noticeably, he seemed grayer and softer, a beast who'd lost his bite.

Daegan straightened, holding his ground. "Where is Jon?" he demanded, scanning the room but seeing only Frank, Collin, and some oily creep.

"He went out the window," said the worm of a man who looked like he was going to faint dead away. "Just a minute ago, he popped out."

Daegan scowled. "You must be VanHorn."

Before the weasel of a man could answer, Collin staggered forward, and Daegan noticed the blood staining the front of his shirt and long coat, dripping to the floor.

"Well, look who dropped in," Collin said, then fell back on the bed.

"Call an ambulance," Daegan ordered.

"I'll—I'll be fine," Collin whispered.

"Like hell." He leveled his eyes at VanHorn. "Call a damned ambulance."

Frank, shaken by his tone of voice, stared at his legitimate son as if seeing for the first time that he was injured. "Collin?"

VanHorn reached for the receiver just as Kate and Sandy slid through the open door.

Kate's eyes were round with fear and she glanced desperately around the room. "Where's Jon?"

"Out the window, I think. I'm going after him." Daegan motioned to the other men. "You'd better stay and talk to the police."

"I'm coming with you," Kate insisted.

"No!" Frank thundered. "There will be no police—"

"Just do it," Daegan ordered VanHorn. "Now!"

"I won't stand for it."

"You don't have a choice," Daegan said, rounding on the man who'd spawned him. "When Collin goes to the hospital and he's got a gunshot wound, the hospital will inform the police. It's the law."

"Not if we call my private physician."

"Dad, give it up," Collin said, his voice a rasp, his skin the color of chalk.

Kate moved toward the bed. "Let's see if we can stop the bleeding. I'll get some towels." She leveled her gaze at Daegan. "Wait for me and we'll find Jon!"

VanHorn shouted out the address into the receiver then slammed the phone down. "Okay, the ambulance is on its way. Now, I'm outta here."

"You're all staying," Daegan insisted, then looked at his friend. "Sandy."

"I'm on it." Sandy calmly took a gun from his shoulder holster.

Kate hurried back into the room with clean though dingy towels, which she pressed against Collin's chest. "Hold these," she instructed VanHorn.

Daegan moved to the window and glanced back at Kate. "After the police arrive, meet me at Robert's."

"I said I'm coming with you!"

"For the love of God—"

"Don't argue with me, Daegan. Jon's still my son!"

Daegan frowned but eyed his friend. "She's coming with me. We'll meet you back at Robert's town house."

"Got it," Sandy agreed.

"I'm not going to go down, O'Rourke! Not like this. Not because of you and your bastard!" Frank glared at his son.

Daegan's smile was pure venom. "Doesn't look like you have a choice, now, does it?"

"Give it up, Dad," Collin croaked. "It's over."

"Like hell! I'll go down fighting, like a man!"

"Jesus!" Collin whispered then shuddered violently on the bed.

"Look at this," Frank said, motioning to his legitimate son. "This is all your fault. If you would've left everything alone—"

"It's not Daegan's fault," Collin whispered.

But Frank had a target in his sights as he rounded on his illegitimate son. Hate and loathing seethed between them and the room was suddenly hot with anger. Frank's nostrils flared and fury mottled his face. "You should have kept your nose out of this, O'Rourke! It was none of your goddamned business."

"My son is none of my business? Guess again, Frank. Let's go, Kate!"

"He wasn't your son any more than you're mine."

Daegan bristled. "That's where you're wrong, old man, and where you and I are different, thank God."

"Daegan—" Collin said weakly from the bed.

"Just take it easy there."

"Wait! I'm sorry." Collin was beginning to shake, his teeth chattering.

"Shock," Kate explained. "Hold on. Don't talk."

"No, please, Daegan, you didn't do it," Collin admitted, trying to sit up. Blood trickled from the corner of his mouth.

Frank's head snapped as if he suddenly understood what his son was trying to say. "Shut up, Collin!"

"Let him talk," Daegan said and Frank's eyes narrowed with a rage that he'd carried since the day of Daegan's birth.

"You miserable bastard, your mother should have had the abortion like I told her. Then I never would have had to deal with you." He stepped closer. "You've been a burr up my ass for a long time, O'Rourke, and your ma, always trying to trap me. Thinking I'd leave my own wife for her, the foolish woman. Thinking I'd stay with her and her bastard son." He drew himself up, his chest puffed out proudly over his now prominent belly. "I moved on from Mary Ellen years ago, on to younger fillies."

"Amazing what you can buy with a little Sullivan cash," Daegan said, his guts roiling, rage surging through his blood. Still, he held himself back, knowing that there were more urgent matters to pursue. Jon was missing, running scared. Jon was his first priority.

"Let's get out of here," Kate said as if sensing a fight of horrific proportions.

"We will." With all his willpower, Daegan managed to contain his fury. "You're a pathetic excuse for a man, a father, a son, and a husband, Sullivan. I feel sorry for your kids and wife, the ones who had to see you every day."

"You ungrateful shit, I'll kill you with my bare hands," Frank vowed and lunged, throwing all his weight at Daegan.

But Daegan was ready. He'd been preparing for this all his adult life. Fists curled, he connected hard with Frank's belly, then snapped his father's head back with a sharp left cross to the jaw.

With a thud Frank went down. He staggered to his feet, swung wild, and Daegan threw a combination punch that sent him reeling against a bureau. Wood splintered and Frank slid to the dirty tiles.

A bruise darkened his jaw and blood discolored his lips. Daegan, still standing, hands curled into tight fists, loomed over him. "You want more? Huh? I got more."

"Go to hell."

"Been there. Now it's your turn."

Frank glared up at his bastard son. He tried to stand but his legs wobbled and Daegan towered over him, ready to do more damage.

"I despised you from the day you were born." Blood stained his teeth.

"Believe me, *Dad*," Daegan said with a sarcastic sneer, "the feeling's mutual."

"Daegan," Collin whispered as sirens wailed through the broken window. "Listen please . . ." He coughed and choked, fighting to stay conscious. "You have to listen . . . it was me . . . fifteen years ago, it was me—"

"Don't," Daegan whispered, his right hand aching from the blows he'd landed. He didn't know what kind of deathbed confessional he was about to hear, but suddenly he didn't care—didn't want to know any more family secrets.

Collin was desperate and reached forward, clutching Daegan's sleeve with long white fingers. "Dad and I," he said in a deep, rattling breath. "We . . . we killed Stu."

"Oh, Christ," Frank moaned.

"What?" Daegan couldn't believe his ears.

"It's true, we saw the whole fight, saw you run off to phone the police . . . and then we got to him and I wanted to call an ambulance but Dad . . . Dad kicked him in the head hard enough . . . Oh, dear Jesus, we killed Stu. Forgive me, Stuart. Please, please . . . I . . . Stuart I love . . ." Tears flooded his eyes and he was shaking.

"You let me take the heat for it," Daegan said, turning dead eyes on his father.

"You deserved it."

Daegan's throat worked. The anguish of fifteen years of not knowing, of doubting himself, welled up inside him. "And you're gonna pay, you miserable son of a bitch," he said through lips that barely moved. "You're gonna pay big-time."

Chapter 24

Run . . . run . . .

Feet slipping, Jon sped through narrow alleys and zigzagged across streets that smelled of diesel and seawater. He needed to find a policeman, but would they believe him? VanHorn said the adoption wasn't legal, that the police couldn't help him, and those men were talking about millions of dollars, *millions!* What could they possibly want with him?

Don't you get it? Someone wants you dead!

His breath was burning in his lungs, his shoulder hurt, and his legs ached, but still he ran, sure that someone was following him.

He charged steadily uphill, his lungs ablaze as the tenements gave way to nice houses and shops and wrought-iron fences. Christmas lights flashed by his eyes and an overwhelming sense of déjà vu washed over him. Somewhere not too far away he heard the melodic strains of a Christmas song.

". . . a beautiful sight, we're happy tonight, walkin' in a winter wonderland . . ."

He swallowed back his fear. This was another repeat

of his dream, and the footsteps behind him weren't imagined. Someone very real and evil was chasing him!

Forcing his feet to keep going, his heart pounding furiously, he heard his pursuer and cast a glance behind him. In the thin lamplight and through the shadows, a man was following, running at breakneck speed, catching him.

No! No! No! Don't stop, keep running!

"In the meadow we can build a snowman . . ."

Heavy breathing, thudding footsteps, his name called into the night. "Jon! Stop!"

Jon lunged as a huge hand dropped down and clamped over his shoulder.

"Shh. It's me!" Daegan said.

Jon nearly crumpled in relief. He wasn't going to be shot! Turning, he saw Daegan's face in the watery glow of a streetlamp.

"What're you doing here?"

"I came looking for you."

Daegen . . . my father.

Jon backed up. "You lied to me," he accused him, still walking backward, his breath fogging in the night.

"I thought I had to. I was wrong."

"I don't believe you."

"I know and I can't make you. But I'm your father and—"

"No!" Jon said, anger spewing from him. "My father wouldn't have left me, my father would have stuck around while I was growing up, my father is a great guy who . . . who—"

"Never knew he had a son until a couple of months ago, who couldn't believe it but, once he met you, found out he loves you. He never realized a child could make such a difference in his pathetic life."

The words echoed through the night and resonated in Jon's battered heart. *Daegan was his father! His damned father!* Biting his lip, he silently told himself he wasn't going to cry, even though Daegan might walk out and leave him again.

"And it's not just because you're his son," Daegan was saying with a sad smile curving his lips, "but because he cares about you, likes to be around you, gets a kick just hanging out with you."

"Then why did you leave?" Jon demanded, challenging this man he'd once admired. Daegan looked sincere, but Jon didn't want to trust him. After all, the guy was pretty good at disappearing acts.

"I thought I had to. I thought it would be best if you never knew. I thought your mom and you could go on with your lives and never have to deal with what you're dealing with now."

"The Sullivan family," Jon sneered.

"That's right." Daegan shook his head and frustration etched his features. "Unfortunately we've got to face them, force them to end this, convince your grandfather that he has no claim to you."

"He doesn't."

Daegan's smile slashed white. "Okay, so let's go tell him."

"I don't want to see him."

"You have to, Jon. To end this. Besides, your mother's going out of her mind with worry. She was with me a minute ago and then I sprinted ahead when I saw you . . ."

Jon looked over his shoulder and spied Kate, breathing hard, jogging toward them. Tears were running down her face, and when she reached him, she threw her arms around her son and clung to him.

"Jon, oh, baby, Jon, Jon," she said over and over again.

"Ma—"

"Are you all right?"

"Yeah." He swallowed hard. He was *not* going to cry.

"I mean it, Jon," she said, blinking hard. "Oh, God, I was so scared. I knew you were with that horrible man and then we heard the gunshot and . . . I'm just glad you're not hurt." She buried her face in his neck and sighed with relief.

"I'm really okay," he assured her.

Stepping back from him, his mom swiped at the tears on her cheeks with her gloved hands. "I'm so glad. I was so worried."

"You two . . ." Jon pointed from his mother to Daegan. "You came here together?"

Kate gasped at the sight of his bruised, chafed wrist. "Oh, baby . . . your arms. You need to see a doctor!"

"No!" Jon yanked his hand back. Right now he needed answers. "I'll be fine, Mom. Did you come here together?"

Daegan glanced at Kate, then back to Jon. "Not exactly. But we both came here to find you."

"Because I'm your son," Jon said, squarely facing Daegan.

"I came because I care about you," Daegan said. "But yes, I'm your father."

"Did you know about this?" Jon pressed his mother. "That he's my father?"

She shook her head. "Not until after you disappeared." She pressed one gloved fist to her eye. "I'm so sorry about the way this happened, Jon. I had no idea, no idea anyone would ever come after you."

"How could you?" Jon shrugged, then pointed back down the boulevard, toward the decrepit motel. "But the scary part is those guys aren't the worst of it. I've got this crazy relative, her name is Alicia, and she's ready to pay a million bucks to get me killed. VanHorn will probably go to jail, but that psycho Alicia is still going to be out there, plotting to bump me off."

"Don't worry about Alicia," Daegan said. "Believe me, I know how to handle her. I'll take care of her. I say we settle up with Robert, and then we'll take you home."

"To Oregon?" Jon asked and saw his mother catch her breath.

"If that's where you want to go."

Jon rolled his eyes. "I never thought I'd miss that place," he admitted, his hands buried deep in his pockets as they dashed through the neighborhood. A band of carolers sang at a doorstep.

"God rest ye merry gentlemen, let nothing you dismay . . ."

They reached a busy street with stores aglow in Christmas lights and shoppers wandering beneath the streetlamps. Daegan hailed a cab and soon they were in the warm interior, speeding through the city.

So Daegan was his father. Jon glanced at the man who'd sired him. Decent enough looking as far as cowboys went, he imagined. Jesus, he could barely believe it. He had a father, a real father, and the guy was Daegan damned O'Rourke. Now, Todd Neider couldn't say Jon didn't know his old man. But then he had the feeling that Daegan wasn't sticking around. Not that he could see into his mind, not now at any rate, but because Jon couldn't believe that anything would ever work out.

"Tell me what happened," Daegan said, and Jon, glancing nervously at the cabby, hesitated.

"Believe me, he's heard it all," Daegan added.

So Jon told them. From the moment Todd Neider yelled at him in the hallway and dunked his head in the urinal, until he ended up in the crappy motel room, scared spitless.

"Dear God," his mother said, twisting her fingers. "If I'd known . . . oh, dear God."

By the time the cab slowed, they'd swapped stories and Daegan had frowned when he looked at Jon's wrists and shoulder. The taxi rolled to a stop on a quiet street with houses facing a manicured park.

"This is it," Daegan said as he handed the driver a bill and helped Kate from the car. "Come on, Jon, it's now or never."

This phony with her fancy fingernails, fake red hair, and bloodshot eyes was his mother? No way. Jon stared at Bibi Sullivan Porter as if she were some kind of attraction in a freak show.

"Way to go, Daegan," Bibi said. She was seated in a peach-colored chair in the parlor, smoking a cigarette. "Has anyone ever told you you're a lousy private detective?"

"She hired you?" Kate whispered, eyeing the woman as if she were a Jezebel. "She was going to *pay* you to find Jon, to return him, to ruin our lives?" She turned tortured eyes on him.

Daegan scowled. "Not exactly. I think she wanted me to kidnap him to Canada."

Bibi shrugged, as if it didn't matter.

Jon hated her. She'd abandoned him, given him away, and she was so different from Kate. There was a part of him that wanted to know more about her, about this whole circus of a family, but he didn't dare ask.

Sitting in the chair, legs crossed as if she was bored, she looked like a rich bitch. How could Daegan have ever slept with . . . ? Sick at the thought, he tried to be practical and supposed he should be thankful that she'd given him up and started the first of a long chain of lies; otherwise he would never have known his mother, Kate. Still, it was easier to hate her, better if he didn't try and understand why she'd rejected him, safer if he didn't realize she was only a few years older than he was now when she'd found out she was pregnant with her cousin's child. He ground his back teeth together and swore under his breath that he'd never call her anything the least bit maternal—not birth mother, not natural mother, not biological mother—and he hoped that he'd never have to see her again, never have to deal with emotions he didn't even know existed before he'd laid eyes on her.

"I just wanted to find my boy," Daegan said. "I wasn't running anywhere."

"Well, come over here," Bibi said, motioning to Jon. She was frowning slightly, wrinkles showing near her mouth and over her eyes. "Yep, you look like a Sullivan."

"Indeed he does," the small man standing near the staircase said. "Indeed he does." Judging by the way the old goat acted like he owned the place, Jon guessed that this was his grandfather, Robert Sullivan.

Daegan intervened. "You've heard the news—that the story's gonna be in all the papers, that the police were called, and that Collin's in the hospital, shot by VanHorn?"

"Yes, I know." Robert's voice was clipped, his eyes filled with distrust. "But I'd still like to meet my grandson."

Kate stepped firmly between Jon and the elderly man. "He's not your—"

"Come, come. Let's see you, boy."

Jon didn't like being called a boy by anyone, but he whispered to Kate, "It's all right, Ma. I can handle this." Jaw so tight it ached, he walked up to the old man and stared down at him.

"Big. Strapping. Do you do well in school?"

"Christ," Bibi said, drawing on her cigarette.

"I hate school."

Bibi laughed. "Takes after his father."

Robert wasn't amused. "Oh, no, no, no." He wagged a

finger at Jon's nose. "A boy's lessons are the building blocks of life. They store knowledge and create character."

Jon zoned out and looked at Kate. He couldn't believe this old geezer was for real. Eli McIntyre with his moonshine and whittling knife had been more of a grandfather to him than this guy could ever hope to be.

"Sir?" the butler inquired, softly rapping on the door. "There's a call for Mr. O'Rourke."

Daegan left the room and Jon felt suddenly adrift in a sea of people he despised, people who all had plans for him, one way or the other. Except for Kate. She was standing next to him, looking as nervous as he felt.

The old man started asking him questions—stupid things like whether he played lacrosse, and what were his scores on the SATs. Near as he could tell, he wasn't coming up with the right answers because the guy's smile, so bright when Jon had entered the room, began to fade.

Daegan returned to lean insolently against the corner of a bookcase. "Okay, so let's figure out where we are. I just talked to a detective friend of mine. The important thing is that Jon is leaving with Kate and the adoption papers are going to be reworked so that there are no complications, that the adoption is legal here in Massachusetts and any damned state in the union."

"Wait a minute, the boy might want to stay with us and—"

Jon shook his head. "The 'boy' wants to go home," he said. "I didn't want to come here in the first place and I can't wait to leave."

Daegan seemed satisfied. "That's pretty explicit, I'd say."

"It doesn't matter to me," Bibi said, squashing out her smoke and sighing loudly. "Kyle's already having second thoughts." She stood and walked up to Jon. "I didn't mean to foul up your life, okay? I wanted you to be happy and . . . and I wasn't cut out to be a mother."

A muscle bulged in Jon's jaw and he glared at the woman who bore him, who gave him life, then gave him up. "I didn't ask for an explanation."

"No, you didn't, did you? Hell, I can't get anything right." Tears stood in her blue eyes and she forced a smile at Kate. "You've got yourself a good boy there. Take care of him."

"I will," Kate promised, surprised at the grudging respect she felt for this woman.

"Good." Bibi dusted her hands on the front of her skirt. A tear slid from her eye as she cast one final look at her son. "You be good," she said. "If I hear you're messing up, I'll swoop down on you like a screaming bat from hell. Believe me, that's not a pretty sight."

"Jon," Robert said. "You must reconsider. I could do so much for you."

"Leave him alone," Kate said, placing a supportive hand on Jon's shoulder.

But Jon wasn't afraid to face Robert now. "It's not going to happen," Jon said. "Look, you paid some loser to kidnap me. Like I'm going to give up my life and the people who care about me because you've got money?" Jon shot a look at Bibi Sullivan, and for a moment, he actually felt sorry for her, a grown woman still under her father's thumb, stuck in an unhappy world.

"We're not simply about money," Robert said, his furry eyebrows rising. "We have high standards, a family code."

"Would that involve killing off family heirs?" Jon said. "Because your niece Alicia was making big plans to do me in."

Robert shifted uncomfortably and Bibi's jaw dropped. "That bitch!" she said as her pack of cigarettes fell from her fingers.

"Don't worry about Alicia," Robert said. "She has no power."

"Not after the police get wind of her plans," Daegan said, heading toward the wide double door. "Alicia might be keeping her father company in the big house, which is where Frank is headed. My source told me Frank is at the police station now. It looks like he's going to be charged with Stuart's murder."

"Frank?" Robert's throat worked, his eyes narrowing to slits. "Whatever for? You're the one who killed my boy, O'Rourke. We all knew that."

Silent wrath glinted in Daegan's eyes. "Collin confessed today, in front of a handful of witnesses. Apparently he was there, he saw it all, and the guilt has weighed on him for years. Frank did it, Robert. Your brother murdered your only son."

"I don't believe you!" Robert railed.

Jon was relieved to feel his mother's pressure on his shoulder, guiding him out of the room. They were out in the foyer when Daegan answered, "Fine, old man. Live with your lies." *Just let the old guy sit and rot in his mansion,* Jon thought as the butler swung open the big walnut door for them. It would feel great to say good-bye to these crazies.

And then, he was stepping out into the snow, flanked by Kate and Daegan, his mother and his father. It had been a shitty week, but Jon knew things were going to get better. He'd escaped, he'd found his father, and he was going home. It didn't get much better than that.

Trying to respect Jon's desires not to be babied, Kate was content to let him wash his swollen wrists at Laura's house, then douse them with disinfectant. Only when Jon was asleep in Laura's guest room did Daegan take Kate's hand and lead her outside, down the stairs, and onto the street. The night was alive with lights and traffic and people hurrying down the street. Despite the mood, Kate pulled up the collar of her jacket and tried to get warm. She felt a loneliness burrowing deep in her soul.

"I don't know whether I should curse you or thank you," she said, pulling her hand from his.

"Thank me. That sounds better," he joked, but she couldn't scare up a smile.

"Okay, I will. Thanks for finding Jon and bringing him back to me. I . . . I appreciate it, but I can't forget that you were the reason he was in danger, that you lied to us both, that you used us, that you were going to accept money for—"

"That wouldn't have happened."

"But you didn't tell me why you were in town, you let me believe that you cared about me, about Jon . . ." she said, hating the words that tumbled out of her mouth, wishing she could alter the course of the future.

"I did. I do. I always will."

She touched the side of his face with her chilled fingers and he held them there, against his skin. "I wish I could believe you," she said.

"So it wouldn't matter to you if I told you not only was I sorry, but that I wanted to change things."

The night seemed to grow still. There was a lull in the traffic, and somewhere, not too far away, church bells pealed, resounding through the darkness. "How?" she asked, hardly moving, listening over the sound of her pounding heart.

"I think I'd like to start over. With you. With Jon."

"With a clean slate?"

"For the most part," he said, his gaze drifting to her lips.

She trembled, but not from the cold. Oh, Lord, how

she wanted to believe him, how she needed to trust him. Tears filled her throat, but she refused to cry, refused to be weak. Yes, she loved him, but he, the liar, the man with the secret past and hidden life, could never be trusted. And who could say how long he'd stay? A drifter by nature, a man who had run from his past for fifteen years.

"No family in Montana? No wife and child?" she taunted.

"There never was either." He kissed her fingers.

"And all those brothers up in Canada?"

"Nah, they don't exist." Another kiss.

"What about the cousins in Boston?" she asked, drawing her hand away.

"They're a part of my life long over. The only person I care about here is my mother and she won't see me. Still has her priorities all screwed up and pledges her allegiance to Frank Sullivan, the god of adultery."

"So you're alone?" she asked, her heart squeezing. *Trust him, just once more, for God's sake, Kate, you love him!*

"Yeah."

"Why do I get the feeling that you like it that way?"

" 'Cause I did," he admitted, his words gruff. "Then I met you and it changed everything."

Nervously she licked her lips and his jaw grew hard as granite. "But not enough to tell the truth."

"I couldn't."

She squeezed her eyes shut, blocking out the vision of his rough-hewn face. Staring into his night-shadowed eyes, the lamplight and snow swirling around them, she almost gave in to the wayward wishes of her heart.

"Kate," he whispered roughly as his strong arms circled her, drawing her close. His breath feathered across her hair. "Don't you know that I love you?"

"No, Daegan, don't," she said firmly.

"But I do and I will forever, but I won't ask twice
Marry me, Kate. Say you'll be my wife." His lips found
hers then and she fought the sobs building in her
throat. Warm and solid, his body seemed to shield her
from the elements, and she was lost in a swirl of emo
tions that ripped at her soul and stole all denial from
her mind.

Love him, just love him, her willful heart pleaded
You'll never find a love like this again.

Never trust him again, her mind insisted. *He'll only li
to you and hurt your son.*

"I—I can't do this," she cried, pushing away from
him. "Please, Daegan, understand."

He stood for a second under the blue light of the
streetlamp, and in that instant she witnessed a change in
him, the stiffening of his spine, the squaring of broad
shoulders, the pride in the jut of his chin, the sudden
condemning censure in his gaze, and most of all, the
hardening of his heart.

"Never," he said.

"But Jon—"

"He knows where to find me. It's up to you whether
see him again." A tic moved a muscle in his jaw. He
shoved his hands deep in his pockets and started walk
ing away. Wrapping her arms around her middle to
ward off the emptiness in her soul, she heard his voice
"And if you don't want to see me, I won't bother you
again, Kate," he vowed, not even glancing over his
shoulder as she crumbled inside. "Never again."

"If I ever hear of you going near that boy or sending
anyone else, I'll personally come down here and pay
you back tenfold," Daegan promised, his voice filled
with malice. His eyes were bright with hatred as he
stood on the other side of the threshold, his fist

clenched, his face set in harsh determination. Snow swirled around him, and the fury radiating from him was nearly palpable.

Alicia swallowed hard and thought of Wade, her precious son. She couldn't believe that Daegan would actually hurt him, but then again, what did she know about the bastard? How ruthless was O'Rourke? How much did he care about his own illegitimate son? The man could be a raving maniac, a savage for all she knew.

"I was just . . . just protecting Wade's interests."

"By trying to kill his cousin," Daegan said in a voice of deadly calm. But that serenity was belied by the tic beneath his eye and the cords bulging in his neck. Grudgingly she realized that he was a handsome man, a ruthless man, and a man who should never be crossed. Not that she would lay a finger on Jon Summers now. The idiot didn't want to be a part of the Sullivan dynasty, and Robert had given up playing mentor to the little bastard, what with the detectives swarming around the entire Sullivan family, sniffing out facts on the boy's kidnapping and even digging back to Stuart's death eons ago.

It was all a tangled, sordid mess, one which Alicia had fended off with flat denials. No, she didn't know a Neils VanHorn. No, she'd never had contact with the man. (Thank God she'd met him in anonymous bars!) Did she ever offer him money to kill Jon Summers? Well, that was just laughable! Ludicrous. Preposterous.

"Mommy?" Wade's voice called from the top of the stairs. She glanced over her shoulder and saw his precious face peering through the rails. "Is everything okay?"

"Yes, honey, it's . . . it's fine. You just go on back to your room and I'll be there in a minute."

"Who's he?" Wade asked, his gaze trained on Daegan.

The devil, Alicia thought, *rising straight from the depths of hell!* "He's . . . he just stopped by to give Mommy some advice and wish her a happy holiday."

"Happy holidays," Daegan mocked.

Satisfied, Wade shrugged and headed back to his bedroom.

"You stay away from my boy," she hissed, cold, angry fear burning in her heart.

Daegan's laugh was brutal. "I don't want anything to do with him, but you keep away from Jon, because if anything happens to Jon, *anything,* I swear, Alicia, you'll wish you'd never been born."

He glanced up at the empty hallway. "Wade's got nothing to fear from me, but you do, *sister,* you do. Remember that."

"Oh, don't be so damned dramatic," Alicia said. "The only reason I was interested in Jon Summers was because Robert wanted to make him an heir. Now with that bit of insanity over, I could care less about your precious bastard."

"Then we're on the same page," Daegan said. He turned away, calling over his shoulders, "And Happy New Year."

A breath of cold air danced into the room and Alicia slammed the door shut, blocking out the image of his deadly face, the silent accusations in his eyes. Trembling, she leaned against the door and caught her breath. Didn't anyone understand? Didn't they know that she only did what she did for her darling son?

"Honey," she called, her voice shaking as she mounted the stairs. She was at the landing when she heard the garage door go up.

Daegan! Oh, God, he'd changed his mind and was back. She ran down the stairs, nearly stumbling, kicking off one of her high heels. Sprinting through the kitchen, she grabbed the first weapon she saw, a fillet knife from the rack, and stood poised, ready to do damage when the door opened and Bryan entered.

"Oh," she said, "I didn't know it was you, I—"

Her husband stopped dead in his tracks, keys and briefcase in his hand, the shoulders of his wool coat dusted with snow. "I just got a call from our attorney," Bryan said, licking his lips nervously, "and I didn't understand all of it, but he was very concerned. There was something about you facing charges for conspiracy or kidnapping or something."

"No—nothing's been filed. It's all a big mistake."

"But you called him?"

"What I told him was in confidence."

"I'm your husband, Alicia, or have you forgotten?" Bryan asked, his lips folded in on themselves.

"No, Bry, I think you're the one who forgot." Tears filled her eyes. "A long time ago."

Grumbling under his breath, Jon tossed another log onto the fire and didn't even manage a smile as the flames licked and crackled against the pitch and moss.

Their Christmas tree, a small pine, was decorated, lights shining merrily with frosty bulbs of blue, yellow, red, and green, and several packages with bright ribbons were scattered underneath.

Christmas Eve and they seemed so alone, so apart from the world. If only Laura and Jeremy had decided to visit, Kate thought as she poured Jon and her each an eggnog. Since she had no parents and was estranged from her aunt and uncle and Jon's family . . . well, she hadn't heard from the Sullivans since returning from Boston. Just today, on Christmas Eve, her attorney had called and said the new documents were on their way; it would take time for all the adoption paperwork to be complete, but it looked like smooth sailing.

"Here you go," she said, handing Jon a glass cup of the frothy eggnog.

"Any booze in it?" he asked.

"Oh, right, I added three shots," she teased.

"But I'm almost—"

"Still far away from being legal," she said. He took the cup but she noticed his restlessness, knew something was bothering him, and could guess what it was. Hadn't she felt the same pangs of despair for the last couple of days? It was Daegan or the lack of him that had changed the tenor of her days, even though Kate knew that he was still just a field away, through the trees and across the snowy landscape to Eli's old cabin. Her throat grew thick with a lump she couldn't swallow, and she noticed Jon staring out the window that faced the McIntyre acres.

It's better this way, she told herself though she hadn't seen or heard from her neighbor ever since flying home from Boston. She knew he was there—she had spied his rattletrap of a truck and the horses—but he was probably getting ready to move. The word in town was that the McIntyre place was still for sale and Eli's heirs would be satisfied with another tenant if they couldn't find a buyer.

"Come on, a toast, on Christmas Eve," she said, clicking the rim of her cup to his. "May all your Christmas wishes come true."

He scowled and didn't meet her eyes, just stared into his cup as if reading tea leaves in the thick opaque depths. Eventually, he took a long sip. "Christmas wishes are for little kids."

"Something's bothering you," Kate finally said, deciding that it was time to face whatever was troubling him head-on, even though she inwardly guessed at his answer. Her fingers tightened around her cup as Jon finished his drink and paced from one room to the other. Houndog, his fur less patchy, tagged after him, a tennis ball in his mouth, his tail wagging as if he hoped Jon would finally get some brains and play fetch.

"Just a feeling."

"You had a nightmare last night."

He slid a glance in her direction and frowned. "Yeah."

"About?"

"Todd."

"I thought he was expelled." Kate didn't believe Jon's restlessness had to do with the Neider boy. No, she knew the real reason, the same reason she couldn't sleep at night.

"He was, but he's still in town," Jon said, rubbing the back of his neck in agitation. He set his cup on the mantel and kicked at another tennis ball. Houndog scampered frantically to the other end of the house, finally catching the ball under the dining room table.

"Has Todd been bothering you again?" she asked, since Jon had been on vacation for a couple of days already.

"Nah, not really." Jon flopped onto the couch and picked up an old Christmas catalog. "I was just thinking that maybe we should have Daegan over. It's Christmas and he's all alone; he's just got a bunch of creeps for relatives and . . . well, I don't know." Nervously he bit at the stubs of his fingernails.

She set her cup on a nearby table. "Do you want him to come over because he's your father?" she asked, paralyzed inside. What if Jon decided at some point that he wanted to live with Daegan, to experience having a father, to do some of that all-so-important male bonding? She swallowed hard.

"I just like him. That's all. And I don't see why just because you two had a fight, I can't see him."

"I know but—"

"Isn't Christmas a time of forgiving, of looking out for others, of . . . of loving thy neighbor and all that?"

"Yes," she admitted.

"So?"

"It's more complicated than that," she said, feeling her son's eyes following her every move as she warmed the backs of her legs against the fire in hopes of chasing a deep chill that had settled in her bones.

"It's only as complicated as you make it."

"Look, I don't want to argue about this—"

The phone rang and Kate's heart nearly stopped. She couldn't help thinking it was Daegan, but when Jon answered and his voice lowered so that she couldn't hear, she decided he was talking to Jennifer as he did nearly every night. She smiled to herself and experienced a wave of relief that she didn't have to deal with Daegan O'Rourke.

At fifteen, Jon was suffering the highs and lows of first love. There was even a present from Jennifer under the tree and Jon had spent all his money on a pair of earrings that he'd found in Boston before they'd returned.

She walked to the window and pulled back the curtain. Maybe Jon was right; maybe Christmas was a time for forgiving. Biting down on her lip, she silently argued with herself and thought of her private Christmas wish, an impossible request really, that she and Daegan and Jon could be a family, a loving, decent, normal family.

"Don't be silly," she told herself, her breath fogging on the windowpane. "There's nothing even remotely normal about anyone related to the Sullivans. And Daegan can't be tied down. Be glad it's over."

Kate's hair fanned around her face and her whiskey gold eyes looked up at him with love and laughter. "Again?" she teased, her body naked and rosy in afterglow, her breasts already taut, the nipples dark and inviting.

"I just can't stop." He was apologizing again, as he always

did when he was with her. It was so hard to believe that she was finally his . . .

"*I wouldn't want you to.*"

Her fingers linked with his and she pulled his hand forward to press it against her breastbone so that he could feel her heart beat, hear the steady thud, thud, thud . . .

"Daegan!"

Thud! Thud! Thud!

Daegan's eyes flew open and he blinked.

"Daegan, help me." Kate's voice, anxious and loud, echoed through the old house.

"Coming," he yelled, rolling off the bed and feeling his erection—still stiff as marble with his erotic dream. "Damn it," he grumbled, stepping into boxers and jeans and snapping the fly as he hurried to the front door, and hit one light switch with his elbow.

She stood on the porch, bundled in layers, her face peeking from beneath the hood of a red parka. Her eyes were dark and round and in one gloved hand she held a flashlight, its beam directed at the old floorboards. "It's Jon," she said as he kicked open the screen door and let her inside. Her face was tight with worry.

Fear clawed at his heart. "What about him?"

"He's missing, I thought maybe . . ." She let her voice trail off as she saw the boxes stacked in the corners, the evidence of his moving. "Maybe he would've come over here. He said something about seeing you earlier and I followed tracks leading this way . . ."

"He's not here," Daegan said, grabbing a flannel shirt from the back of his couch. He found socks and boots, then donned his jacket and hat. "We'll find him."

"Oh, God, I hope so."

Without a thought, he grabbed her, held her close, stared down into her worried eyes, and said, "I'll find him, Kate. You can count on it." Then he let her go and was out the back door and whistling for Roscoe.

Footsteps and hoofprints led from the barn. "Damn it all," he growled, staring at the evidence. "He's taken Buckshot."

"But where?"

"We'll find out," Daegan insisted as he snapped on the lights in the barn. Loco, whinnying in protest, blinked under the harsh single bulb. "Have you called the police?"

"No, I thought, I mean I was sure he was over here. I followed the tracks and then your house was dark and—" Her voice failed her.

Desperation stilled her lungs as they hurried back to the house, where Daegan called the sheriff.

"I'll do what I can," Swanson told Kate once Daegan had connected with him and handed her the receiver. "But it's Christmas Eve and we're short a few hands. I'll put out an APB, but I can't promise anything."

Kate hung up. Her entire body shook and her imagination ran in horrifying circles. "They won't do much."

"Don't really need 'em. Come on."

She was still stunned from finding Houndog whining outside her door and investigating to discover Jon missing, his window open, the butt of a fresh cigarette ground into the snow of a gutter. She'd found his tracks and had assumed that he'd decided to visit his father himself, not wait for her approval, just take the bull by the horns and show up on O'Rourke's doorstep. But he hadn't. Instead he'd stolen a horse in the middle of the night. *Why?* she wondered. *Why? Why? Why?*

"We'll take the truck," Daegan said, "for as far as it will make it. After that, it's snowshoes."

"Oh, God." *Where could he be? Where?*

"Here." He tossed her the keys. "Start the pickup and warm it up. I'll get some supplies."

"Supplies?" she whispered.

"Just in case."

She didn't ask in case of what and did as she was told, fighting sheer terror as she saw him toss two pairs of snowshoes, a couple lengths of rope, a pick, an axe, a first aid kit, a tarp, a lantern, blankets, and flares into the back of the truck.

"Better safe than sorry." With a little effort he put the truck into four-wheel drive, slid behind the steering column, and followed the horse's tracks through a field adjoining her house to the government property beyond. An old logging road, that had originally been used during the gold rush days, cut through the sparse jack and lodge pines dotting the hillside. The night scape seemed eerily serene. Much too quiet.

Grateful for the moonlight that aided the beams of the headlights, Kate stared out the windshield and silently prayed that Jon was safe.

"Why would he do this?" Daegan wondered, casting a glance in her direction.

"I wish I knew."

"You two have a fight?"

She fingered the disintegrating upholstery on the door. "Not really . . . but, well, as I said, he wanted you to come over tomorrow for Christmas."

"And you didn't," he guessed, his voice edged with bitterness.

"I don't know what I want," she admitted, biting her lower lip. "Funny, isn't it? A few months ago I could tell anyone who asked exactly what I wanted out of life, what I expected, and then . . . then you came into town, into my life and now . . . now I can't even figure out what it is I need in life." Sighing, she kept her gaze trained on the underbrush looking for something, anything that would help. "Right now all I care about is Jon."

"That makes two of us." The road was narrow and treacherous, winding along the side of a steep cliff, cut-

ting ever downward toward the river. "Look," he said.
"Footsteps joined him."

She saw them, too, the double tracks. Someone was
walking with Jon. Her heart froze in fear. Who? Another
kidnapper? But why had Jon willingly met him? Maybe
he'd decided to meet Jennifer in a secret rendezvous,
but why so far away? It was miles to Jennifer's house in
town.

"Who would he meet?" Daegan asked.

"Just you . . . or his girlfriend."

"Girlfriend?"

"Jennifer Caruso, a girl he's liked for a long time, I
think."

"Does she wear size thirteens?"

"She's small. Petite."

Daegan's jaw was so tight, his bone showed through
his skin. "From the looks of it, Jon hooked up with a
man."

"Oh God," she whispered, clenching her fists and
gnawing at her index finger in frustration.

Rounding a hairpin corner, the truck shimmied a little and Daegan worked the wheel, letting the pickup
slide toward the edge, pumping the brakes. "Hang on," he
ordered, and Kate could do little else. She closed her
eyes as the ravine gaped in front of the nose of the truck.
Her heart hammered and she stood on nonexistent
brakes. "Come on, you overrated piece of scrap metal,
hold, damn you."

With a groan the truck's wheels caught and again it
nosed down the road the right way again. She let out
her breath.

So slowly she was sure she was going out of her mind,
the truck inched down the mountainside then leveled
at the river, where the old bridge had long ago washed
away. The water, black and menacing, rushed swiftly
through the cliffs, cutting a jagged path. "We'll have to

go on foot from here," Daegan said, "though it looks like we're close."

Kate followed his gaze in the darkness. "Buckshot?" Her heart stopped as she recognized Buckshot, riderless, reins wrapped around the lower branch of a tree.

She jumped out of the truck and approached the animal. "But where's Jon?" Back to the wind, one leg cocked, ears flat, the colt stood, only flicking his ears and snorting when Daegan placed a gloved hand on his nose. "Good boy," he said. "Now where's Jon?"

Both sets of footprints headed downstream, and over the rush of the water she heard voices, faint but definite.

Kate dashed forward while Daegan grabbed something from the back of the truck. "Jon!" she yelled.

"Slow down, you don't know what you're going to find," Daegan warned.

She didn't care. She wasn't going to lose her boy again. Slogging through the snow, slipping on rocks near the shore, she ran.

"So much for the element of surprise," Daegan said, catching her and plowing forward as they slipped at a bend in the river and spied their son and his companion. Jon was on the shore, holding a stick, running alongside the river. Someone was in the icy depths, screaming desperately, trying to grab on to Jon's slick, outstretched branch.

"Holy Christ!" Daegan swore.

"Todd," she whispered, sick when she saw his head sink below the rippling surface.

"Hang on, Neider, hang on!" Jon yelled, reaching out a little farther, trying to hold on to the branch of a tree that bent over the river while stretching out farther and farther.

"Wait!" Daegan yelled but it was too late. Todd grabbed hold of the stick. Jon strained under the weight of the heavier boy and the power of the curren[t] snapped the branch like a matchstick. Both boys sli[d] into the icy depths, their heads bobbing along with th[e] current, screams reverberating through the dark gorge[.]

"Jon, no! Hang on!" Kate cried.

Running toward the riverbank, Daegan kicked off hi[s] boots and shucked out of his jacket. Then, still sprint[-] ing, he wrapped the end of the rope around his fingers[.]

"Hurry up!" he screamed at her. "And grab the othe[r] end!"

"No, what're you going to do?"

He dropped the coil of rope, ran around a tree, an[d] then took off into the water, splashing and yelling at Jo[n] to hang on while the rope uncoiled.

She didn't think, just reached the end of the rop[e] and looped it once more around the trunk of the tree[,] tying off the end and digging her heels into the snow[.] Watching in horror, she saw Daegan's head surface an[d] bob, far away from either boy. "Save them," she prayed[,] wondering how she could ever have doubted him[,] knowing that she would never love another man as sh[e] loved him. "Please, please, save them. Jon!" she crie[d] when he disappeared from view.

Neider crashed into a rock and clung on, sobbin[g] loudly over the current's roar. "You hang on, Todd[.] We'll get help." But her eyes searched the darkness o[f] the river's frigid depths and she saw no one.

"Help me!" Todd cried, hysteria evident in his voice[.]

"We will."

"Please, help me!" Dear Lord he was probably half[ ] frozen already, suffering from hypothermia. And Jon[,] where was Jon? She scanned the deadly water, her hear[t] pounding out a cadence of dread, her mind silentl[y] screaming that they had to be safe, they had to be.

"I love you," she whispered into the night. "I love yo[u] both."

Was it possible because of her stupid pride that Daegan would never know how much she cared about him, that he'd never live to hear her say the words that now filled her heart and soul?

"Daegan!" she screamed. "Daegan!" And then she saw him, slogging toward her out of the icy depths of the river, carrying Jon in his arms, breathing hard. She cried out and ran forward, her arms outstretched.

"Stop!" Daegan ordered and she froze. "Stay dry, for Christ's sake. Someone's gonna have to drive the damned truck!" At the shoreline Jon scrambled to the ground and Daegan ordered him to the truck for blankets, then he turned, and shivering, his wet hair plastered to his face, he walked upstream and dove in again.

"No," she whispered, watching as he let the current carry him toward Todd. Her eyes stayed on him as she removed her jacket and tucked it over her son's shoulders. Daegan swam, gasping, crossing the water's swift current. At last he reached the rock. Then, while the huge boy clung to him, he made his way to the shore.

Kate and Jon, teeth chattering crazily, helped by dragging on the tow line, pulling them forward, easing them to the shore. Once Todd landed on the icy bank, Kate and Daegan helped him up to the truck, with Jon wrapping them both in blankets, seating them in the warming cab.

As Daegan closed the door of the truck to keep in the heat, Kate flung herself at him, kissing his cold skin, holding him tight, ignoring his protests that she'd get wet and freeze.

"Oh, God, Daegan, don't ever leave me again," she cried, tears of relief drizzling from her eyes. "I love you, I love you, I love you."

He chuckled and coughed, his skin a sick shade of blue. One strong arm held her close. "About time you realized it," he said, pressing frigid lips to her hair.

"Marry me, Daegan O'Rourke," she insisted and his grin slashed white in the darkness. His arms tightened around her.

"You got yourself a deal, lady," he said, shivering, "but do you mind if I warm up first?"

EPILOGUE

The wind swept low over the Montana hillside and Kate stood on her front porch, eyeing the horizon, waiting for two riders. Snow lay in patches on the ground, but the scent of spring was in the air and a few early buds were visible on the fruit trees.

She and Daegan had moved in January after a quick wedding and a long discussion with the administrators of the college in Bend. It had been time for a new start, Kate thought, and time to leave the little town that knew too much about her and her son—their son. She'd even sold her house.

After Jon had saved Todd Neider's life, Todd had been less than grateful. He'd been running away from his father and blamed Jon and Daegan for making him face the music as well as his old man again. But he'd been moved to foster care, and Carl Neider had promised the social worker he'd change his ways and quit drinking, join AA, and stop beating his son. No one, least of all Todd, believed that was possible.

The Sullivans, according to Sandy, were keeping

quiet. Frank was charged in Stuart's death, Robert refused to speak to his brother, Alicia was getting a divorce, and Collin, recovering slowly, was attempting to reconcile with his wife. But there seemed to be an unwritten law that they would never again bother Daegan or his small family.

Neils VanHorn hadn't fared quite as well. His trial for the kidnapping of Jon Summers was still pending. Legal experts were arguing on the legality of the first adoption and the manner in which Jon was to be "returned" to the Sullivan family. Meanwhile, the Boston media kept citing VanHorn as he insisted that both Alicia Sullivan McGivens and Robert Sullivan had been accomplices in the abduction and kidnapping. Time would tell. His family had given depositions and Daegan had been assured that everything possible would be done to avoid disrupting Jon's new life if they needed him to testify in court.

Kate had been working on reconciling Daegan with his mother, now that Frank was out of the picture, and had talked to Mary Ellen several times on the phone as well as having persuaded Daegan to speak with her on multiple occasions. They had all made plans for Mary Ellen to come out to Montana to visit them so Jon could meet his grandmother, and she and Daegan could see each other.

Since Christmas Eve when he'd awoke seeing a vision of Todd drowning, Jon hadn't had any more visions—or at least none that he talked about. He seemed well adjusted here, catching movies with his friends, spending time after school with his father.

His father. The thought that Daegan was Jon's father warmed her heart.

She spied them riding over the ridge, two tall men on lanky horses. Waving frantically, she heard Jon's whoop and then watched as the two beasts took off at a hard gallop and tore past the barn to slide to a stop just before reaching the fence. It was the regular evening ritual, the race between father and son.

"We'll be there in a second," Daegan called to her and her heart thrilled at the sound of his voice. Her husband, the man she'd eloped with on Christmas Day. Absently she rubbed her abdomen and walked back to the kitchen, where the table was set. In the center of the table was Jon's birthday cake—three glorious layers of chocolate with dark fudge frosting that proudly supported sixteen, as yet unlit, candles.

The coffee had just brewed when she heard their boots on the back porch and the sound of old pipes creaking as they washed their hands. Within seconds, in stocking feet, they walked into the kitchen and warmed their hands by the woodstove.

"Find any strays?" she asked.

"Nope," Daegan replied and his gaze touched hers in a way that made the pulse at her throat leap in anticipation.

"Naw, but we fixed the fence." Jon rolled his eyes as he sat at the table and eyed the chocolate cake. When he thought his mother's back was turned, he scooped a finger full of the icing and plopped it into his mouth.

"I saw that."

"Yeah, because you've got eyes in the back of your head."

Daegan winked at his son and nabbed a smidgen of frosting on his finger. "Like father, like son," she said as she poured two cups of coffee and a glass of milk.

"Don't we have to eat dinner first?" Daegan asked.

She shook her head. "Jon and I have always thought birthday cake should be eaten when you're hungry. We'll have dinner in an hour or so. Okay?" She struck a match and lit all sixteen candles. They blazed brightly in the cozy little kitchen.

"Before you blow them out," she said, "we have a couple of things for you."

Jon grinned. "A new car! A Fiat, or a kickin' truck or a Corvette or—"

"In your dreams," his mother said with a laugh.

"Not quite a Corvette, but transportation." Daegan reached into the inside pocket of his jacket and handed his boy an envelope.

"What's this?" Jon asked, opening the folded white paper and scowling as he read.

"It's Buckshot's papers. He's yours now," Daegan said, and Jon's eyes widened in surprise and delight. "You can sell him if you want and buy a cheap car with the cash—"

"No way!" Jon said, biting his lip and glancing from one parent to the other. "I—I can't believe it. This is great. Really great. Thanks!"

"And there's something else—but it's not from us," Kate said and handed him another envelope, this one perfumed and sealed with wax.

"Jennifer," he said, blushing, his Adam's apple moving. "I'll read this later." He stuffed the letter into his back pocket.

"Okay, so let's get to it." Kate held her husband's hand and smiled at her boy. "Make a wish!"

He hesitated, closed his eyes, then filled his lungs and blew out the candles in a rush of air that could have extinguished an inferno.

Kate handed him the knife.

"Aren't you gonna ask what I wished for?"

She laughed. "And ruin it so it won't come true?"

"Oh, it'll come true all right. I already saw it."

" 'Saw' it?" she asked, her mouth going dry.

"Umhm." He took his mother's free hand and smiled. "You're pregnant, aren't you?"

She swallowed hard. "I, well, yes." She felt color wash

up her neck and Daegan grinned widely as he squeezed her hand. Fortunately, he already knew that they were expecting a baby.

"It'll be born on September 10," Jon said, and when she was about to protest, he held both hands near his head as if in surrender. "I know, I know that's three weeks early, but that's the day it's gonna happen and you'll name him Jason."

"How do you know it'll be a boy?" she asked, but already guessed the truth.

Jon grinned widely. "I know, Mom, trust me. Hey, this cake is great!" He dug into the chocolate, gulped down his glass of milk, and ate a second piece. Then he scooted back his chair and announced that he was going out to check on *his* colt, but Kate suspected that he really wanted to be alone to savor Jennifer's letter. They came regularly and Jon wasn't yet interested in any girls at his new school.

Daegan and Kate cleared the dishes, then Daegan drew her into the circle of his arms and kissed her lightly on the forehead. "You know, Mrs. O'Rourke, you've made me incredibly happy."

She angled her head up at him. "Are you going to show me how happy?"

"Mmm. Later. All night long if you want. But first you should know that Jon's wrong."

"Wrong? About what?"

He laid a hand over her abdomen and closed his eyes. "We're going to have twins, Kate, a boy and a girl, and we're going to name them Jason and Julianne."

She laughed and he opened one eye as if checking her reaction.

"Twins? I don't think so."

Cocking a dark eyebrow, he said, "You doubt me? Doubt my gift?" His gray eye glinted suggestively.

"Me? Never," she said, then blew it by laughing again.

"Just wait and see, woman. You'll be in awe."

"I already am," she whispered and wound her arms around his neck, happier than she'd ever been in her life.

On September 10, Kate's water broke, and at ten minutes to midnight, Jason Patrick O'Rourke entered the world. Twenty-three minutes later on September 11, his sister, Julianne Orchid, joined the family.

An hour after she'd delivered her babies, Kate lay in her hospital bed, a swaddled and sleeping twin in each arm. The hospital was quiet, the lights dimmed, but Daegan, who had spent hours holding his new children, now stood near the bed, as if unable to tear himself away. Tears stood in his eyes and he brushed a kiss across her temple. "Thank you," he said and emotion clogged his throat.

"Geez, you guys aren't gonna get all mushy on me, are ya?" Jon said, but his own voice sounded deeper than usual, and even from his chair near the window, he couldn't take his curious eyes off his new brother and sister.

They, the five of them, were a family, never to be broken. Kate's throat clogged with emotion as she whispered back to her husband, "Thank *you*."

"Really, I can't listen to this," Jon said, but his lips curved into a smile.

Kate laughed, Daegan cleared his throat, Jason gurgled, Julianne whimpered before going back to sleep, and Jon rolled his eyes. Sighing happily, Kate smiled as she realized that sometimes, no matter what the odds, wishes really do come true.

Dear Reader,

Now that you've read RUNNING SCARED, and spent some time with Kate, Daegan, and Jon, I thought I'd let you know what else I've got up my writing sleeve!

WITHOUT MERCY is still on the stands, and if you like high-intensity twisted plots, you'll love the story surrounding Blue Rock Academy, an idyllic-appearing school for troubled teens. The academy, however, has a few dark secrets of its own: One girl has gone missing and a teacher has been dismissed under scandalous circumstances.

Things only get worse when Jules Farentino's younger sister, Shaylee Stillman is ordered to Blue Rock Academy rather than sent to juvenile detention for committing a crime with her loser boyfriend. Jules is worried, but can do nothing to help her wayward younger half-sister.

Upon her arrival at the school, Shaylee swears that nothing is as it appears! The veil of honesty and caring surrounding Blue Rock is all a diabolical, dangerous act. Jules starts to believe her sister just as students at the school begin to die under mysterious circumstances. Worse yet, when Jules arrives at the institution she comes face to face with her own personal hell: she's forced to deal with Cooper Trent, her ex-lover and now a teacher at the institution. Trent, like so many of the instructors at the academy, has a checkered past and as students continue to die, under mysterious circumstances, any one of the teachers and counselors could be the killer. Cut off from the rest of the world by the storm of the century, Jules has to fight her feelings for Trent as well as use her wits to try and flush out a killer.

Before she becomes his next victim!

WITHOUT MERCY is now available in hardcover and will be on the stands in paperback in March 2011, just before my next hardcover, the next installment of the Rick Bentz/Reuben Montoya series, will be in stores in April 2011. This all new Bentz/Montoya novel will be set in New Orleans and a lot of familiar faces will reappear, so check my Web site *www.lisajackson.com* for updates! (By then, I might even have a title for the book!)

Also, don't forget to look for WICKED LIES, the next book in "The Colony" series co-written with my sister/fellow author Nancy Bush. If you've followed the series, you know that WICKED GAME was the first installment. The next two were UNSEEN and BLINDSPOT both already in stores and written by Nancy. WICKED LIES will be available in June 2011! To learn more about it, and all of The Colony Books, please go online to *www.lisajackson.com* and *www.nancybush.net*!

Again, I hope you enjoyed RUNNING SCARED!

Keep Reading

Lisa Jackson